THE LAST BOOMERANG

A NOVEL OF THE COLD WAR

By

John McIntyre

ISBN: 1-4107-9877-1 (e-book)
ISBN: 1-4107-9876-3 (Paperback)
ISBN: 1-4107-9875-5 (Dust Jacket)

Library of Congress Control Number: 2003096962

This book is printed on acid free paper.

Printed in the United States of America
Bloomington, IN

1stBooks - rev. 10/11/03

For Harriet, Chrissy and Dallas

and especially for

Connor

The author wishes to acknowledge
the assistance and support of
Commander E. J. Stetz, USN, (Ret.)
who lived, with the author, through experiences of
the kind described in this story
and whose review of Part II (Flight) was of great value,
and that of
Dr. Fred Milford, whose thoughtful and continuing encouragement
made the whole thing worthwhile.

Table of Contents

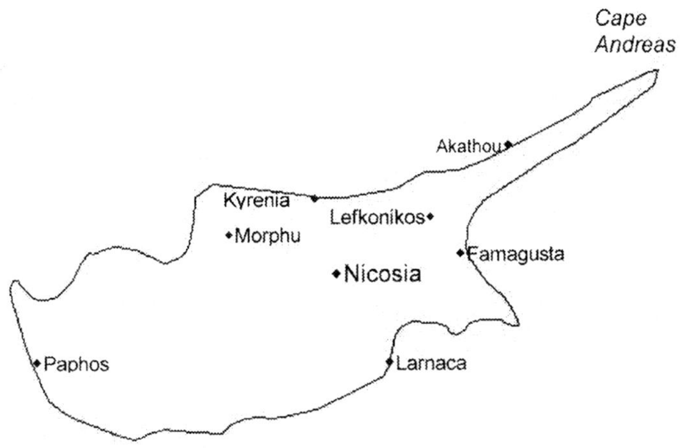
Cape
Andreas
Akathou
Kyrenia
Lefkonikos
Morphu
Famagusta
Nicosia
Paphos
Larnaca

CYPRUS

USSR
London
FRANCE
BLACK SEA
Batumi
TURKEY
SPAIN
Athens
Adana
SYRIA
MEDITERRANEAN SEA
Tunis
TUNISIA
Malta
CYPRUS
ISRAEL
Port Lyautey
MOROCCO
ALGERIA
Alexandria
EGYPT
Cairo
Nile

Enosis—Union with Greece

Cyprus was untouched by World War II apart from a few air raids. In 1947 the governor, in accordance with the British Labour Party's declaration on colonial policy, published proposals for greater self-government. They were rejected in favour of the slogan "enosis and only enosis." In 1955 Lieut. Col. Georgios Grivas (known as Dighenis), a Cypriot who had served as an officer in the Greek Army, began a concerted campaign for enosis. His National Organization of Cypriot Struggle (Ethnikí Orgánosis Kipriakoú Agónos; EOKA) bombed public buildings and attacked and killed opponents of enosis, Greek-Cypriot, Turkish and British. Field Marshal John Harding, chief of the British imperial general staff, was named governor of Cyprus and arrived on the island to assume his post in October 1955. Proposals for self-government were put forward at different times…All were rejected and the attacks continued.

Encyclopedia Britannica

Nicosia, Cyprus
Friday night, December 16, 1955

They make him sit across the narrow street, down the hill just a bit, away from the smoldering ashes and the feeble little one-lung pumper, its stream down to an occasional spray; somebody is fussing over him, in his craziness he can't tell who, isn't aware, doesn't care, just oh my God the stink and the smoke and the smell oh shit oh shit oh shit…

Burned timbers, gasoline and rubber, insulation and garbage, kitchen grease and animal crap, it's on his clothes, his jacket torn at the shoulder, on his hands sticky with…Oh God…her blood…Oh God…and he shakes as they help him up and they have to half-carry him and that hurts too and he starts to cry but he catches it in his throat but not before it hits his eyes and he can't see where they are going with him but he can hear the cackle of the radiotelephone in the jeep and somehow he realizes that the crew is there and shit, this must be a dream, what the hell are they doing here and God it hurts and Oh God! her blood, there it is.

They are gentle with him, getting him in the back of the carryall, Hunley and Kerrigan insisting to the Military Police Sergeant Major that they will be able to care for him back at the hotel, the Sergeant Major distracted by the incessant hubris of the radio. Dazed, totally unaware of the insults to his body from the fire or to his dignity, his trouser leg gone to the hip, he slouches and stares down at a crumpled paper cup by his foot, wondering what it is. He doesn't know, cannot think, cannot orient himself, cannot somehow, mercifully, understand the enormity of what is happening, what has happened, where he is. He watches, stupidly, as the rest of them write things on paper and his last coherent words to himself, the last time his brain had rang up his consciousness with any kind of a message, were repeating and repeating in his head, and he could hear them but not interpret what they had meant.

How in the hell did she ever know about Boomerang?

The British Sapper jeep-driver in his blue beret is skeptical, he's seen blokes in worse shape after drinking through their pay packets home in Leeds on a Friday night, but he realizes that it isn't drink that makes this Yank, he thinks he's a Yank, the others are, look like he's got no bones at all and he wonders what the pack of them, Yanks here in Nick, have been up to with the fire and the explosions and all, but the Sergeant Major shoos him into the drivers seat and the tall white haired Yank guy seems to be in charge and he comes around to the left side and gets in and they get started. There are light poles down and a lorry on fire at the bottom of the slope, nobody around, typical this time of night, wait a minute, it's not all that late, bad night here though, jezus not even midnight, where the hell did them kids come from, never mind, it's a right turn at the corner if he can get through the narrow slit of a street, jezus, there's a friggin' donkey.

In the back seat, newly oxygenated blood, fresh-made adrenalin, endomorphins of assorted shades and sources, liver bile and other bodily fluids under various pressures have hastily negotiated improvised agreements and working together, they are rousing their host over the threshold of consciousness and Lew is beginning to understand where they are and who he is with. Where did the crew go? Oh, just the officers, have the crew got a ride? Where are they headed? Where did you guys come from? You all look awful, and the smell! how did you get here and where are we going Oh to the hotel I heard you tell the Limey kid and…

He feels his heart catch at least it's going he says to himself why did she have to die and Oh God all that we did last night and all the shit we had to put up with has all been for nothing and nothing and nothing Oh God why did she have to die and where the hell are we and Oh yeah I remember it all now and shit, shit, shit.

"Can you walk, Lew" Hunley had asked.

It takes a second for the processing, but the fluids are working hard and the machine is beginning to right itself and grab some kind of rhythm and he tries out his legs and knows he has two, but fifty percent of them hurt like hell but not so bad that he can't wiggle himself out of the carryall and hold on to the door frame and lower himself to the gravel path along the driveway and Oh yeah, it's the Acropole and I'm back and everybody is with me and let's go inside and I guess I'll be OK only…

"You going to be OK?"

"Yeah, Shipmate, thanks a lot. I'm a little fuzzy," he mumbles as they go up the steps into the lobby and there is this guy there. British.

"My name is Roger Wingfield," he begins. "We need to talk."

He's in his bedroom slippers and wears a cardigan sweater over one of those shirts made for detachable collars but there's no collar on it and he has a pad and he has gray hair and he looks friendly enough.

My God, My God, they got her out but she was dead. She can't be dead. My God, My God, and all the stuff in the package. Get the stuff. Get the stuff. The stuff's all burned up. I saw it explode. It's gone. And she's dead.

Now what?

PREFLIGHT

1

Washington
Two Months earlier

Nebraska Avenue in northwest Washington, D.C., is a tree-lined residential diagonal running on a slant off Wisconsin Avenue, and as it meets the open greenery of Massachusetts Avenue to form Ward Circle, so forms the heart of what could be the prettiest part of the nation's capital city.

Across Ward Circle, the American University campus dominates the neighborhood, a wooded setting of academic buildings linked by carefully tended pathways. There, students were doing what students everywhere did on a beautiful October day, dazzled by the Northeast autumn at its peak, watching each maple and elm and elder outperform its neighbor in a jubilant finale of finery before the boorish wind and cold and harshness of November. Even the more conservative oaks, resolutely stodgy in simple Franciscan browns, played their background parts, accenting the temporary triumph of October.

On this side of the circle, at 3801 Nebraska Avenue, a cluster of gracefully aged slope-roofed, stone Tudor buildings, having begun life as a turn-of -the-century manor complex, lounged like a tired dowager at a tea party, admiring the colorful frocks of her junior matrons, possibly the most unofficial looking piece of government property in the Free World. In his second floor office at 3801, once the master bedroom in the "main house", Captain Winslow "Winnie" Barnet, United States Navy, sat and contemplated his calendar, conscious of but purposely ignoring the particularly spectacular golden maple crowding his window as it begged for attention by gloriously filtered the late morning sunlight.

He was not sanguine, despite his surroundings.

The last "calendar" quarter of 1955 had begun on October first - this month - the first quarter of *Fiscal* Year 1956. As the annual round of Congressional hearings and Pentagon horse-trades began anew, and as precious appropriated dollars flowed down to the large, glamorous carriers and super-bombers, Winnie wondered how much longer he could take the pressures of the battle to grab some of the remaining dribbles and drips for the less glamorous, sometimes shabby, purposely obscure "black" programs that meant so much to his embattled Cold Warriors.

He made a noise to himself, a sigh perhaps, had he been a sighing man, more likely a grunt of resolution. He was not a sighing man.

At the larger, more cluttered desk in the adjourning anteroom, he heard the black telephone. He always recognized the outside line when it rang.

Without looking up from her work, the woman immediately registered the characteristic civilian Chesapeake Bell Company ring, selected it from the several others of assorted vintages, colors and complexities, punched a lighted button and connected their arcane world with the greater community at large.

On the outside line she was all business, just this side of hostile.

"Oxford 6-4069," she said, almost a grumble, not at all helpfully. Nobody in the "trade" ever answered an outside line with anything that could remotely be considered enlightening to a prying stranger. If the caller didn't know where the placed call had been answered, tough luck. Shouldn't have called in the first place.

"Hi Jenny, this is Gwen." Sweetly.

Just like Gwen to use an outside line to call back inside. Gwen was a creep.

Communications Technician Second Class Jennifer Howell, United States Navy, in plaid skirt, white turtleneck, penny loafers and frown was not.

She did not quite look the part, but as one of the very few female rated Communications Technicians in the Navy in October 1955, here she was, with talent and skill and guts and plenty of looks to go around - striking Eurasian good looks - but watch the frown.

Born and raised in Japan, the only daughter of an American marine architect and his Radcliff educated Japanese wife, bilingual Jennifer had returned with her tragically widowed father to his Washington roots and a Navy Department office in 1940 just before the outbreak of the war. She was twelve. Convent educated by European nuns at St. Maur's in Yokohama and pampered by her well-to-do Japanese grandparents in the shadow of the Kamakura Buddha, she had been welcomed by her American grandparents whose comfort and love saw her through the worst of times when tragic news from Kamakura so devastated her teen years. Her Japanese grandparents were surviving increasing horrors as war began to touch the homeland islands, only to be senselessly lost in a resentful vandal's holocaust of their cedar wood and shoji paper tatami home in 1944. Lost in the ashes, so many of her childhood memories.

Later, early the following year, through contacts of various flavors and histories, eighteen-year-old Jenny was recruited to the Navy's Japanese Purple Code Project as a bilingual cryptographer, and took to the line of work immediately. She stayed with the Navy, and the Navy had stayed with Jennifer, schooling her in intelligence, electronics, and in her third language at "Moscow West" in Fort Ord. Over the years, she found time, somehow, for GI Bill College, credit by credit, quickly establishing herself as a brilliant "asset" who to this day, could never tell where the time had gone. She loved what she did.

Usually.

Today, her only adornment at work was the business-like beaded silver-colored chain she wore around her neck, a cluster of laminated photo-badges dangling from it, each a pass into a separate fiefdom within the Washington Empire. Her position had no counterpart in the civilian world: technical advisor, personal confidante, doer of deeds -sometimes dirty, sometimes not, always diligently done. Twice she had worked for Winnie Barnet now, and as neither his Deputy nor his Secretary, his "Special Assistant" wondered whether being somewhere in the middle was the best or the worst of all possible worlds. The frown remained.

"Yes, Gwen", she answered, annoyed at the interruption.

Not sweetly at all.

In the middle of working the December "Operationals", she was all business. Much as she should have diplomatically chatted with any Pentagon caller to keep the political peace, she had to forge ahead.

Pentagon politics resembled those of sixteenth century Middle-Europe, and Gwen, the civilian reeve of the Baron of one of the innumerable small Duchies that made up the patchwork Pentagon landscape, was not on her all-time favorites list.

The Operationals were important, this one especially so, and she was orchestrating the details of Clearance and Diplomatic Arrangement. She was couching in the most flagrantly ambiguous terms the monthly mechanics that would "enable" the next of the Navy's planned airspace penetration adventures, so clearly in violation of polite political protocol as to be both delicate and deniable, should anyone ask.

Who us?

But Gwen of the Pentagon wouldn't have known.

Gwen dealt in appointments and directives and budgets and, occasionally, meetings. Gwen was an administrator, and with today's meeting hosted by a government agency with an even more profound constitutional disgust for telephones than the Nebraska Avenue crowd, her office had gotten stuck "administering" the reminders to each of the participants, calling the RSPV list. Scat work.

Jennifer had met Gwen face to face a couple of times, and had no desire to repeat the experience anytime soon.

"Just a reminder, Hon. Tell him the Quarterly's today. If it was the monthlies, sounds like something you and I would get, don't it? Anyway, just in case, make sure he gets there."

Jennifer swore Gwen cackled between sentences.

"You bet, Gwen. Talk to you later."

"No, wait a minute! What's your hurry? What's the story on the Advancement Exam? Jesus, you took it back in September, any word yet?"

"Gwen, 'back in September' was seven weeks ago and no, there's no word yet. It's my first shot at First Class, but I think I did well, so who knows?"

"You guys in the Navy have it so much better than we do. Ours is all politics! When would you put it on if you got it?"

"December 15th, and I'll tell that to some of my buddies out in Lower Slobovia how much better they have it when they eat their fish heads. Talk to you later, Gwen."

"How was your date?"

Whoa.

"Gwen, *what* date?"

"At the Mayflower. Sunday night. I saw you. You looked great, and he seemed nice too. Is it serious?"

As a matter of fact, she had had a spectacular evening Sunday, one she was not at all likely to forget, her third date in as many weeks with a genuinely nice guy. At last. The Mayflower was only the beginning of the evening, and Gwen's big mouth had snared the last of her withheld attention. While she split her feelings between the pleasure of the memory and the absolute disgust of Gwen's ghastly intrusion into it, she carefully controlled her anger. Gwen must have seen them together, at dinner, but godammit, that was none of anybody's business. And, she had to admit, yes, it was getting serious.

"Hey Jenny, you know what you should do?" Oblivious.

"What, Gwen?" really annoyed now.

"You should go on that television show, you know, 'What's My Line' on Sunday nights. They'd never be able to figure out what you do from the way you look!"

"Thanks, Gwen. Talk to you later."

"Don't forget to get the Boss to the Quarterlies!"

You don't even know what I do, she thought. And don't call me "Hon", you goddamn dyke.

Of course he'll get to the Quarterlies. And he'll eat their lunch. And if I make First Class, I'll be eating your lunch. Kiss my ass.

"Who was that, Howie?" He called from the next room. The door was open, unusual, but not remarkable.

"Across the River. Central Casting. 'Quarterly's today'. As if we didn't know!"

* * *

Of course they knew.

Captain Winnie Barnet ran the Naval Security Group.

3801 was his Headquarters.

He had a Deputy who focused on the internal workings of the Headquarters and its staff, a Yeoman who handled the paper, a Driver who did sometimes drive, and Jennifer who helped do everything else.

"Any languages?" he had asked her the first time they had met, inauspiciously, thrown together uncomfortably in a temporary Quonset monitoring station hastily banged together at the Air Force Station in Shemya, as far out in the Aleutians as anybody would want to go. As cold and as gray and as miserable as anybody would want to be, as well.

Both were in civilian work clothes, parkas and boots, she briefed in advance that she would be working with a Senior Officer, he fully aware of her background and enlisted status. Both had endured a wretched flight, neither had slept in a bed for days, and the worst of both their personalities was bubbling under a hair-thin surface.

"Japanese and Russian," she had answered, looking at him squarely.

"We'll see, won't we?" he had growled, not as much at her as in fury and frustration with the joint tri-service agency that had cobbled the awkward operation together. At least he had a Naval Person to deal with.

But "see" they did, dealing with it, both of them, splitting up eleven days later with one off the major intelligence coups of the early Cold War, severe head colds and a professional respect and devotion to one another that would shape the rest of their lives.

The Naval Security Group was a small, distinguished armpit of the Regular Navy, and "everything else" was the generation and safeguarding of its most precious communications and electronic intelligence secrets.

It was usually referred to in the trade, simply, as "Nebraska Avenue."

One small sign near the front entrance of the building marked it, far less noticeable than the placard for a church on which one expected Mass times or the title of the rector's next sermon. Below it, the red-white-and-blue shield-shaped no-trespassing thing, usually seen in post-office parking lots, grudgingly announced that yes, this was government property, not worth a tourist visit, not worth a second glance, a working place in a city of government enterprises, just another church in Rome, another shrine in Kyoto, another pub in London, and be on your way, if you please. Keep the hell away.

Winnie always believed that the beauty and grace of the cluster of buildings housing his offices was, surely, one of the precious secrets to which he had been entrusted, but lately he had been too busy to enjoy the loveliness.

This year had seen the global political battle-lines that had ebbed and flowed informally along Churchill's "Iron Curtain" in Europe and along the edges of Red China now firmly institutionalized. In Europe, the new Warsaw Pact was a reality, antagonizing a NATO that had recently welcomed West Germany into its fold and fanning embers smoldering for a decade. In the Near East, the Baghdad Pact was about to be signed. In Asia, last year's SEATO sputtered along trying to formalize the role of friend and foe, but on the ground, little had changed in his black world.

He worried about that sometimes, but more often the routines and the deceptions and the outright lies with which he dealt daily served to provide a continuity in his life. His only conceit was his comfort in the belief that despite almost a generation of involvement in and with evil, the ordinariness of his appearance and the blandness with which he sometimes presented himself was his disarming grace. He was sure that the crows-feet beginning to track into the corners of his eyes and the encroaching gray in his unremarkable khaki-colored hair were calendar problems, not occupational reprisals, and he could still run a mile in eight minutes. Anytime you wanted to check.

At forty-eight, his job was easy to describe, impossible to imagine in its complexity and often heart-breaking in the skimpiness of what they gave him to do it as it needed to be done. His cryptographers provided secure systems to encode and decode precious Naval messages to and from the forces afloat worldwide. His code-breakers and linguists monitored communications all around the globe.

As the world began to depend more and more on electronic communication, electronic surveillance and electronic weapons, Winnie immersed himself in something being called "electronic warfare," a term that would emerge from the depths of the sinister and black into the open press and into the pages of daily newspapers in his lifetime. He had "assets", as they called one another, in Turkey and Ethiopia and Finland and Pakistan and the Aleutians and in many other even less hospitable locales as Jennifer Howell had been, and would one day be again. He had them on ships and on mountaintops and in submarines and on trawlers.

But his principal "line item" this year, the crown jewels with which he was entrusted, had to be the sums of Navy dollars—staggering when he thought of his other unfilled needs - that had gone into airborne assets, buying equipment and configuring elderly aircraft and training youngsters to fly the perimeter of the Iron Curtain and Red China, snooping, listening, recording, "ferreting" as the currently fashionable term in the community would have it, all in harm's way, all on the sly, all in "areas of Naval interest", always deniable.

Who, us?

Yes, us. The Boomerangs.

This morning, as on the morning of the third Tuesday of the first month of each Quarter, he would be joining his professional colleagues in a meeting intended to keep certain of the principal agents of the separate military services appraised of the activities of one another. Winnie and his counterparts each had their own Service and Agency superiors to whom they reported internally—his was the Chief of Naval Operations, directly - but in the black world, there was a "dotted line" command relationship that transcended Service and Agency loyalties and traditions. The relationship existed to direct the traffic of their endeavors, to minimize collisions, to cut down the duplicate efforts, to alert them to new opportunities, and to insulate them from political embarrassment.

His colleagues were the Commanders and Directors of the various Communications Security Agencies and offices appended to the military services, the Department of Defense and the Central Intelligence Agency, and the focus of this quarterly get-together was electronics. His Naval Security Group, along with the Army Security Agency over at Arlington Hall in Virginia, the new National Security Agency people at Fort Meade up in Maryland and the other "cat and dog" activities working the territory were just beginning to get into the habit of working it together.

It made sense when shared resources could be used to mutual advantage, although Winnie Barnet, for one, found it somewhat difficult to remember that he had to stop thinking of the Army and the Air Force as the enemy and concentrate on more extra-mural threats. During the war they had been comrades in arms, literally, and he remembered his European adventures on the ground fondly, but it was different now. Competition for scarce resources made competitors out of comrades pretty quickly. The "Revolt of the Admirals" over the role of carrier aviation versus long range bombers in the active conduct of the Cold War was technically over, but the scars and wounds from the great "Roles and Missions" shoot-out between the services still smarted. It had been eight years since the Key West agreement between the services had tried to settle things with the National Security Act, but there were still a lot of unexploded bombs and bullets on the battlefield, waiting for a tickle or a jostle to blow up in your face.

The regular participants hosted these "Quarterlies," on a rotational basis. This morning's meeting, scheduled at ten, would be run by the Technical Intelligence Director of the Central Intelligence Agency downtown on the Mall, in one of those dilapidated shanty-town warrens left over from World War I. One of these days, surely within in the next decade, the Mall's "Munitions" complex was coming down, but until new buildings were finished in Crystal City and in Roslyn and out in Langley, everybody made do with what was there.

Winnie's Naval Security Group gray Plymouth Navy sedan was in the shop, and since he didn't like riding around town in a government vehicle anyway and since parking his own car down there was such a bitch, he was looking forward to taking the bus down and back. He felt guilty about taking all that time—time that he didn't have in the first place—but what the hell, he did his best thinking on the bus.

This week he was thinking about Lew Elfers.

Lieutenant Commander Lewis Chambers Elfers, United States Navy, was about to become a protagonist - *the* protagonist, if Winnie's premonitions were correct—in a big gamble.

Winnie never went to a meeting, anywhere, at which the agenda and—to his credit—the outcome might hold any surprises, and he had a pretty good idea how the meat and potatoes they would be putting on his plate this morning would taste. If Winnie's intuition was working as it always did, Lew Elfers and his squadron-mates in their big black son-of-a-bitchin' spook plane were going to get the farm out of hock once and for all, pay for the ride, bring home the bacon, whatever…

And as the pale green and gray DC Transit diesel bus spewed its fumes along the broad avenue on its way downtown, beneath the ambers and reds and golds of autumn, past the Embassies and the Observatory and down 22nd toward the Mall, Winnie played with the concept of the Protagonist in his mind.

Lew was going to be his Protagonist in this one.

He and Lew together. Lew need never know.

* * *

The meeting broke up earlier than expected, the agenda less regularly generating signs of cheerful accord than an inventory of cards held close to the respective vests of people who had been playing the game for years. A zero-sum game, what one player won came out of the assets of the others, and at the end of the day, the plusses and minuses equaled out at zero.

Nevertheless, each of the principals had been in almost daily wire contact with each other, and they all would agree that the face-to-face every so often was a good idea. Winnie enjoyed watching them change with the stresses of their respective jobs—he certainly didn't change—but that was their problem. He had seen most, if not all, of the seamier sides of the business but he still managed to look like a cross between a distinguished brain surgeon and a bank teller worried about his own mortgage. His ambivalent appearance had served him well, through many engagements with many engaging consequences, in all the dark and musty rooms of their "black" world where tellers rarely get to look like brain surgeons and there's always that mortgage.

They all left the building more or less together, splitting out, each commenting on the "beautiful day" or some such crap to one another. The last thing in the world they would ever do would be to talk "shop" outside the "shop" they had just left.

And so he found it unusual that Avery, the deceptively mousy Electronics guy from Fort Meade, had come after him. Avery had McLaughlin, his beer-bellied, florid opposite from the Pentagon, in tow. The three of them were actually good friends and great admirers of one another, not that anyone had ever noticed in their carefully orchestrated false public disdain for the other's endeavors, travails or products.

"Got a minute?" Avery talked the way he looked, but he was always worth listening to.

They walked out of the old building together and turned east down the Mall toward the Washington Monument.

"Shoot," the Captain said. *Oh, oh. Here it comes. Lew, stand by.*

"There's something going on that you ought to know about."

"It's about the Boomerang people," McLaughlin added. He said it in his normally obnoxious, grating voice, not terribly loud, but Winnie winced as if he had bellowed it from the top of the Washington monument down the street.

McLaughlin was Defense Intelligence. The word "Boomerang" was itself classified in any operational context and never used in the open unless somebody actually wanted to talk about Australian aborigine weapons that flew back and conked the originator on the head. There were "nicknames" and there were "Code Words," always capitalized, and as a rule, special clearances were required to deal with, handle, or even discuss genuine Code Word material. Boomerang, still a nickname, had not yet become a special clearance project, nor would it soon, in view of the comparably small cast of characters in the program, but it was certainly special and its specialness was widely respected by anybody who realized what it meant.

"Boomerang is a London project," Winnie said testily, suggesting some annoyance at the use of the word on a Washington, D.C. city-street by a fat guy with a bad complexion. Boomerang was mounted out of the Navy's Grosvenor Square headquarters in London under the operational "auspices" of the Navy's Eastern Atlantic and Mediterranean Command, but everybody involved knew that its scope was National in focus and its "products" were of National Interest. Everybody involved also knew that the Department of Defense was behind the generous funding the program received in addition to what the Navy kicked in, and hence, that the Pentagon pulled its strings.

They also knew that Winnie was "Mr. Boomerang", and it was his program, his brainchild and his headache.

McLaughlin represented the Pentagon, though, and if he wanted to talk in the clear, it was his money and his business. But for Chrissake, not so loud.

"We get to see the good stuff, when they get it," Winnie said innocently, "but they run that show over there. Why? What's up?"

Who, me?

"Yes, but they're your people 'over there.' They may put 'Commander In Chief, Eastern Atlantic and Mediterranean' on their underwear, but the Boomerang guys are your guys, they work for you, and you own them."

If anybody ought to know, McLaughlin knew. He paid most of the bills. He didn't have to get testy about it, Winnie thought, and then realized that it was not like Mac to get testy without worry. Like all of his colleagues, they had worked together in various odd corners of the world and of the bureaucracy all their careers. They were family, beer bellies and all.

"We can't tie it all up on paper yet, Winnie, but there's..." catching Winnie's vibrations, he looked over his shoulder back down the Mall, then went on more quietly into his train of thought. "There's strong suspicion that the operational end is getting leaky. Not the stuff they bring back - that's been good—although there's not much new lately. We've gotten a whiff of what's going on out there from our own stuff, and it may bubble up pretty soon."

"Care to elaborate?" Winnie asked. "We've been through this before, Mac, if you'll remember. Operating quote covert unquote with a big black monster plane that says 'Navy' on the side, that arrives every month in Cyprus when the moon is dark, that's crewed by a bunch of American kids with Navy haircuts, in a town where there's a war almost going on, where the Sovs and the Brits and the Arabs and the Jews all have major presences and the Greeks are beating the crap out of the Brits and the Turks and we wonder about security?

"The plane's a Beast, shit, even the crew call it the 'Beast.' It's a wonder they don't get their asses shot out of the sky every time they fly. We think security is pretty damn good—Ivan never knows we're coming and we get in and out successfully every time. These missions have been going up into the Pond every month for years, almost. If you don't believe it, take a look at the Radar Order of Battle for the Black Sea—it's your own document and where do you think you got the raw material from, Stalin's daughter?"

Was he indignant enough? he wondered.

It hadn't been "years, almost," and the planes were really Navy blue, not black, but things were working. They did call it the Beast. As a pitiful concession to some of his Betters who liked the idea of playing spook and contributed funds, on the margin, to the game pot, he had made it a rule that none of them were to take or wear uniforms on their excursions east, an innocuous order that the crews enjoyed but one which gave some of his purist critics on the diplomatic side of the community a fit.

The Top Secret Radar Order Of Battle document for the Black Sea—the "Pond" to Winnie and his people - was up-to-date. Every early-warning and air-search radar installation had been charted, fingerprinted, checked, and cranked into the National Single Integrated Operational Plan the bombers would use if they ever had to make that run. The Navy did it—if the truth were known—to keep an important finger in a very important pie, and it was simply being smart-ass to equate genuine concern for "areas of Naval interest" with Beat Army, Beat Air Force, that sort of thing. Nothing personal.

But in the course of doing "it," keeping the Radar Order of Battle in the Black Sea, all surface and airborne radar threats had to be included. The folks on the ground in Sinop on the north Turkey coast and the guys in the disguised trawlers kept track of the Soviet surface-navy radar and communication signals—too bad he could never get a submarine into the Black Sea—but it was up to the Boomerangers to track the airborne stuff. And Winnie knew without having his face rubbed in it that actual aircraft-intercept radar intelligence would be crucial if they ever had to blow the whistle and launch the bombers to execute the Single Integrated Operational Plan.

And, of course, Mac was right—they hadn't had any lately.

Lew Elfers again.

Now it was wispy little Avery's turn. On cue, Winnie thought.

"Don't get defensive, Winnie, but think about it. There's an awful lot of interest in the Flashlight, the YAK-25, the double-ender that surfaced at Tushino last summer."

Winnie assumed that "double-ender" was a new cute word for a twin-engine aircraft, but with these guys, you never knew. They lived in their own world. They looked at pictures from the Tushino Air Show and shit in their pants.

Avery went on.

"The people on the ground have it flying three, four hops a week, exercises, all getting more and more slick. Our folks have communications intercepts hinting that the two radars are up and operating. They have a new acquisition job and a new fire control piece, maybe frequency-agile. Your guys have been up there three, four times now, and nothing. What's going on? Are they going in far enough? Are they turning out too soon? Are they even in the right part of the Pond? It may be that London is so in love with their own Radar Order of Battle that they don't send these guys where they should be going."

"Look, we got more to worry about than one single installation. We got the whole rim of the Pond, Batumi to Bulgaria, like a booger on our finger, and we have an excellent success rate—haven't been jumped, no accidents, no sabotage."

"There's another thing you should know, "McLaughlin, again.

"There's the 6905th Air Force Support Group operating out of Wiesbaden, Germany, U.S. Air Force Europe, which you are well aware of. What you may not remember is that they've just taken delivery of the first Air Force versions of your Navy P2V-5F, and they're calling it the RB-69. It hasn't exactly been in all the papers, but this is the same airframe that whipped the ass of your beloved Beast in your own Navy competition. With their Inçirlik base at Adana in southern Turkey opening up next year, unless something materializes quickly, I can see closed-door interest in sending the Air Force into the Pond to eat your lunch."

Now one of those silences while everybody counted aces, then, frantically, kings and queens. He had the Captain's attention, but not in the way McLaughlin had intended.

Winnie, with his own private nightmares, was way ahead of him, had to be. After all, it was Winnie' script being played out on Winnie's stage. He knew damn well the unarmed RB-69 wouldn't cut that mustard but he had to look and act concerned, play the game. If they wanted to threaten him to a turf battle, they should have invited his attention to the work going on out at Rye Canyon in California that his own spies reported to be on the verge of fielding, not just talking about but fielding, goddamit, a super high altitude J-57 powered glider called the U-2 that would eat *everybody's* lunch.

He knew all about the local Cyprus security picture—it was tight, despite the problems he had alluded to earlier—and he made that point to McLaughlin. Tight. But not that tight. He knew it, and he knew why.

"Look, they blend in with the scenery perfectly. The Sixth Fleet is just over the horizon seven days a week, and you know how the Greeks think about the Sixth Fleet. There wouldn't be any Greece if it weren't for Truman and the Sixth Fleet."

The civilian shook his head, lips pursed in annoyance.

"There is also some indication that there is undue familiarity between some of the Navy personnel and people of 'known unreliability' in Nicosia."

McLaughlin looked both ways over his shoulder and went on. He had their attention. Now it was Avery's turn to be annoyed. He hadn't heard a whisper of anything like that. But Winnie Barnet had. He was expecting what was coming, neither relieved, elated or triumphant—under the circumstances with lives at stake he couldn't be—but his back stiffened a bit and his toes curled just a bit as he listened.

"Information has come via intelligence transfer from the British, source code B-two, Source Identifier 'Billposter,' and has been independently substantiated from the Bloc side, of all places, that there is—are - one or more 'interacting' agents on the ground whom their 'Billposter' has under surveillance. See you around, Winnie," and with that he dashed out into the wide boulevard and jumped into a taxi that had just spewed out a family of tourists.

Billposter.

Intelligence data was rated according to a sliding scale that tried to evaluate credibility from A to F and the track record of the source from 1 to 5. F-5 was a joke, generally, but wars had begun on F-5 data in the past. Source code B-2 was pretty good stuff. How the hell the Bloc got into it, nobody knew, just as well, because they were afraid to ask.

But the corners of his mouth turned down into a wry little peeve as he pondered the news that Billposter was getting B-2s. The sonofabitch.

The M-3 bus picked him up on the Mall, and he had more to think about all the way back to 3801 Nebraska Avenue.

It was time for a pre-emptive strike, and although he had enough inside information to know that the threat of using the unarmed RB-69 in the Black Sea was simply that - a threat—he knew exactly how to put the morning's conversation to work for him.

He would like nothing better than to get the Boomerang people out of Cyprus.

It was an absolutely perilous situation, and each time they kicked off the cycle of planning and clearances and negotiations and hassle with the Turks and the Brits, he hated what they had to go through but hoped with all his heart that they would be able to pull it off one more time without a terrible tragedy. He and Howie were working the December one now.

Boomerang. And now "Billposter". The one a bunch of dedicated, hard working American guys laying their asses on the line, the other a sleazy, unkempt son of a bitch he was about to nail, once and for all. And he had a protagonist who was going to do it for him, but he's never going to know it.

Barnet had spent his life on the dark side of security and when he swore to McLaughlin and Avery that security was "damn good," he knew he was whistling in the graveyard, exaggerating. What McLaughlin should have known, had he not had his head so deep up his damn technical ass that he totally ignored the political side of the house, was that the agreement with the Brits on the use of RAF Nicosia expired on January one, and the Navy had already gone to the Joint Chiefs and received the go-ahead to use the new Air Force runway near Adana in 1956. Now, if Mac were serious about "closed door interest," this was the time to pull the fat out of the fire and scotch this damn Air Force thing once and for all. One last super shot.

He would do it. Now. The December Operationals. But there had to be just one Operational in December, not the traditional two. It had to be unambiguous, and he'd have to figure out a way to scrub one of the two usually scheduled flights. Later.

The "interacting agents on the ground" factor was going to play right into his hand.

He had been in the spook business long enough to know how the game was played, that the stakes were rarely the prized "intelligence gems" one heard about. No. The stakes were the funding increases and the technology improvements and the support staff and the infrastructure enhancements that kept each little fiefdom in the empire on its toes. It was time to nail down the Navy's role in the Eastern Mediterranean electronic intelligence picture once and for all, and he knew what he had to do. Get the fox into the coop, finally, get that damn crowd "on the ground" to earn their fee for once, bring home a bag full of nice plump chickens, and we'll all get the hell out of there and buy us a new farm over in Turkey, where we can keep doing it but do it more safely, cheaper, more often, and without all the goddam diplomacy. He hated diplomacy.

That evening he sent a message on one of his many "back channels" summarizing his "concerns." He did not mention Billposter. But it was a very diplomatic message, worthy of Machiavelli.

"Billposter," indeed. St. John—"Sinjin" as he pronounced it - and his greasy hands. He remembered St. John from the old days. He had never trusted the bastard.

Show time for Sinjin.

He'd post some bills himself.

And the following morning, in a perfectly ordinary looking Navy hangar at an isolated—but far from desolate—overseas Naval Air Facility, the Quarterly Planning Sheet was posted on the bulletin board in the Pilots' Ready Room and by the time he got around to checking it, Lew Elfers already knew he would be flying the December Operationals and he nodded with satisfaction.

He'd hand pick the crew.

And Marta would be waiting.

It never occurred to him that his name was up based on a plot finalized on the M-3 bus as it passed the Columbian Embassy.

2

December 15, 1955, Nicosia

Red sky at night, sailor's delight.

You bet.

Ten days before Christmas in the Year of Our Lord 1955 and here I am again in good ole Nicosia, Cyprus, Timmons thought, as he got ready.

Could be worse.

It was sure red enough, the sun a perfect circle floating down through the trees on the yellow, dusty haze thrown up by a thousand cook fires and a thousand goats bobbing along the sandy shoulders of the "highway" out of town. Another day on the pile of a million years of history. He looked out to the west, squinting at the remains of the red ball through the scrawny olive trees, his sunsets a lucky bonus denied the others whose rooms faced north, off toward the twin minaret towers.

Aviation Machinist's Mate First Class Caleb Timmons, United States Navy, liked his trees, a nice touch on the otherwise bleak canvas, a ring of them around the scummy swimming pool by the red tile patio, forcibly kidnapped as shrubs decades ago, he guessed, from the groves on the hills to the north. Trees, few and seldom in the old town, nowhere as florid as they were fancifully drawn on the Sylvan Solace Hotel notepad and matchbook on the end table in the room. But they were trees.

Squinting down at the drawing in the twilight, he squeezed off a crooked grin, the hotel itself drawn on fibrous paper, fancifully exaggerated in every dimension and attribute. Looking up at dusty reality, he caught the high ceilings in the red glow, his craftsman's eye questioning how they were somehow held in place by yellowing plaster walls. Suggestions of lath under-slats were gently highlighted here and there in the oblique light, whalebone corset stays holding the lumpy girth of a fading music hall queen in her skirts.

Sometimes, away from Nicosia, he thought about the gloaming hour just before a "trip", about this time of evening, late afternoon really, wintertime in the Mediterranean, in Cyprus, getting ready to go "out", one more time. Cocktail hour for some, the afternoon whistle at the plant, the kids home from football, put away the tools, hang up the apron. Too old for glamour, too young for cynicism, he wondered what the name was for the excitement he got in his gut and there it was again. Time to go.

He loved what he did, not the way he loved Lureen and the kids, but as much—handling, as best he could, the dilemma of the career sailor who loved to fly and loved his wife, their almost mutual exclusivity a contradiction to be ignored or glossed over. A sailor. A sailor far from the sea. A sailor, if the truth were known, not in the least bit interested in ever seeing the sea. That's why he crewed in airplanes.

As he looked out the casement window, a fleeting care crossed his mind, like one of those wisps of smoke off to the north, there for an instant before hurrying off in pursuit of a passing gust of wind. Why should he be bothered, he wondered. He had flown with Mr. Elfers for years now, and what was bothering him this time? Something he said? Couldn't put his finger on it, but...

Nikki crossed the small courtyard beneath his window, and he watched her as she ducked into her little apartment in the rear of the building. Just before she went through the hanging screen and pushed open the rickety door, she looked up, saw him in the window and waved that jerky back-and-forth of hers, polishing an imaginary window between them, grinning and grimacing as she telegraphed that she was glad to see him and sorry, but she couldn't spend some time visiting right now.

Time for work.

The Sylvan Solace Hotel was wholly British, a traveling man's hotel, wholly middle class, wholly respectable - wholly compromised, too - but what did it matter, everyone knew what was going on. There were sixteen rooms "by the Day, Week or Season" and these days, it was rarely crowded. Before last April, when the troubles started, business was brisk, but in response to Foreign Office Notices and Consular Bulletins, British traveling men now found ways to do their Cyprus business by wire or by mail.

Beneath the lobby, facing back on a lower level because the foundation had been built into a hillside—the lobby was at street level—there were two apartments. Nikki's was the larger of the two apartments downstairs. Off the Lobby and Reception, there was a comfortable "Saloon Bar," in the English style, its hours far more accommodating than the village pubs it tried to imitate and its clientele this week wholly American, unaware of the subtle differences between "bar" and the "saloon.".

Everyone on the crew had once pined for the love of Nikki, each hopelessly persuaded that were it not for the unfathomable differences in their respective cultures and the elusiveness of their separate brief moments alone with her, they would easily win her heart. Nikki had the involuntary knack of provoking such misunderstandings in a broad spectrum of the male population exposed to her almost animal femininity, earlier to her great delight, more recently to her chagrin and distaste. Now, as the Americans had each come to know her and become more reasonably attached to her in a sister-brother way, to a greater or sometimes lesser extent, her exotic Middle Eastern origins still drove everybody nuts, but as the exotic slipped into the more realistic context of their friendship, the immediate danger of broken hearts diminished.

He had rarely actually touched her, remembering the birthday kiss Lucore and he had planted ceremoniously on her cheek last May, she in her mother's traditional Turkish headscarf, pigeon brooch, and triangle necklace, celebrating at the little party they had had for her. He remembered it so well, all of them carrying-on, not this same crew, although Lucore had been along that trip. The ceremoniousness of the event had been partly sincere, partly a ruse to get physically close to her, and when he had, he had had to handle the embarrassment along with the delight. He could feel the warmth of her cheek and the softness of it on his lips, her fragrance foreign to him but hauntingly attractive, the turmoil not unexpected but nonetheless unwelcome. He recalled it, wistfully almost, realizing it was out of place. She was his friend. His buddy.

From behind the bar that night, Dimos, the young Greek with pale, transparent skin and sharply etched features set off by the deep blackness of perpetual five-o'clock shadow, had produced an old Brownie camera. It had a broken flash attachment that they all had tried to fix, first by wetting the contacts on the flash bulb socket with what seemed like quarts of their collective spit, then by Black's professional attack on the contacts with a nail file, scraping away at the metal until bright scratches appeared beneath the tarnish. They had tried it, each grinning absurdly into the tiny lens, gritting their teeth inwardly for the flash that never materialized. It had been Lucore who had finally bent the little contacts just enough, and Dimos had snapped them all with Nikki, but the photos had never turned out, or at least they had never seen them.

What in the world was it about a dozen Americans, in half-assed disguise, no uniforms allowed, each of them street-wise sailors, having it for a young half Palestinian-half Turkish Moslem bookkeeper and loving it. She was as frequently in his thoughts as were Lureen and the kids, to be brushed aside in the handling of details and in the mechanics of the day but always there, grinning at him, ready.

He always grinned back.

He heard the taxi when it came, the black '46 Dodge shined and dusted and shined again. Inside it would smell like cars used to smell, nothing like the new ones did. He stashed the wallet in the drawer, taking only the green ID card, a pound note and a couple of tenners. A last-minute mirror check did nothing to hint that his horrible Personnel Inspection haircut might be growing out, but otherwise, he figured that he looked good enough at thirty-four to catch a pass once in awhile. Ahem, pardon me, Lureen. Crows feet don't count, anyway.

When he came down the staircase slowly, nodding to Dimos behind the Reception now, the unattended bar on the "honour" system, he noted the clock pointing neatly to five o'clock. Timmons checked the bar.

Dimos in turn, mildly curious in his low wattage way, wondered where the "oil-men" - he knew they weren't - went and why they kept such strange hours, but they were Americans and who knew? He just had to keep track of when they left. He never got it, even later on their "work nights" when the window-rattling roar of the big black plane shook the early night sky from a half-dozen miles away.

The Greek kid was more interested in the chance that he might be meeting Dighenis himself tonight. Surely he might at least see him. Not every young Cypriot male longed for the chance to involve himself in the national struggle, to unite with Colonel Grivas in the fight for union with the Motherland and with History, but Dimos ignored anybody who did not agree with his dream. Union with Greece!

Someone had told him that the wealthy were leery of additional taxation by a country far away across the sea, and he could understand that if he thought about it, but he didn't bother very often. Communists wanted outright independence, just to cause trouble, and he couldn't understand that whether he thought about it or not, although he was no stranger to loudness and upset.

To the Turkish minority, or course, union with anything Greek or Christian was an intolerable outrage, although he knew a couple of decent Turkish chaps but that was different and he didn't understand that either. Enosis—Union - was a "state of mind" Grivas had said, a meeting with destiny, and his code name honored the national hero, Dighenis Akritas, who centuries before in Cypriot history, had kept the marauding Saracens at bay with amazing strength. And amazing strength would be needed, Dimos figured, because there was an awful lot of work to do. He would tell the Colonel of his dedication. Tonight. If he met him. Meantime, he would make his call when they left, giving the times each taxi-load departed.

The blatantly unconcerned subjects of his careful surveillance were in the bar off to the right, sticking to single beers, ending their sleepy afternoons, leaving the local Keo brandy for later, up in the room, after it was over.

Lucore wanted to ride out with Timmons and had been waiting for him to show up, so he gave him a sign and they both joined in the foyer and went out into the dust and what was left of the mild December day.

The cab was waiting, Mikos' cab of course. Always. Always Mikos, the bushy hair and the copious moustache and the white handkerchief tied loosely around the neck, an affectation, with winter here. Lucore wondered what Mikos would say if he knew that he got a couple of minutes in every pre-mission briefing they had sat through, and every pilot he had flown with had briefed them all about Mikos as they crouched under the wing for "Last-minutes" on the way out.

They knew perfectly well what Mikos was up to, but he was such a nice guy, so useful in so many ways, so endearing and so…well, American ("call me Mike")…that they quit taking any of that stuff as seriously as they knew they should. But when they called a cab to go to "work", for a ride out to the airport, Mikos would always show up with the black Dodge, its "Fluid Drive" trunk logo glistening in the sun and the briefings validated. Lately, he talked too much. Incessantly.

Tim's mind went back to the glimpse he had had of Nikki, waving at him, pouting to him, saying hi and goodbye and "see you later", as she had picked up from him, hoping he might catch her again for an encore before he punched in for the night. Maybe early in the morning, when they got back, she might be around and they all could relax together, but he thought not. He remembered their last conversation yesterday afternoon as she started out on one of her trips out in the boondocks to see her relatives. He had no idea how she traveled but he was glad to see she was safely back.

One evening, she had held them all spellbound with her story.

'What's your real name?" he had asked whispering, furtively looking over his shoulder, a caricature of a co-conspirator, the others stopping their chatter to listen in. Some stretched over to hear. Nikki's English was perfect but the threads of the prior dozen Mediterranean centuries gave it inflections and tonalities that you had to get used to. There was a decided French bias to it all.

Her given name was Mariam Hamouda, she said, and do you really want to hear she asked, and yes, yes, they had said and everybody had shut up.

She went on.

"My *maman* was raised over in the west", she said, pointing out toward the oleanders and the low houses and the flat expanse of land tabled beneath the northern mountains, toward and beyond the airport, too far in the distance to be seen.

"In Morphu," she murmured, a little dreamily, Timmons thought.

"In those days, the late twenties, there was nothing. Her family was from *Turkye* but not ethnic Turkish, and they lived in a village over by Morphu. When it was time, *Bukuyanne,* my grandmother, wrote to an Islamic agency in Palestine and my mother was betrothed—sight unseen—to my father who was a Moslem Palestinian, and I think, a very distant cousin. That was the way it was done, the only way, really, to enable their daughter and themselves to escape almost certain starvation. It was very bad, very bad, then. There was not what you call an economy, and the land was not hospitable enough to feed the family.

"When *Maman* got to Palestine by boat from Famagusta, she said she was almost dead from the sickness at sea, but my father was there to meet her and the next day they were married. She was sixteen."

She noted Lucore's frown, and looked over at him.

"I know it sounds so bad, now, these things, but by and by they loved each other, and by and by they had a nice house and some land, and they had oranges and they had a steam on the hillside...but I'm sorry, I get very emotional when I speak of it. It is all gone now. My father was an intellectual—he could read, and write, and he had a business.

"I went to school," she continued, almost dreamily, "when almost no other young girls had school, and in the British system in Palestine there was a lot of trouble from my relatives over it, but before I was, oh, nine I guess, I could read both Arabic and Roman—that's the kind of alphabet you have—and I loved to read, loved to read.

"Well, my dear mother stood up for me with Papa's family—some of them were horrified that a *bint* would be in school—and when the war started, I cried and cried about it but I was sent off to Beirut to Papa's very rich aunt and uncle who were not horrified at all that I wanted to learn to speak with my classmates who spoke French. You see, Palestinians in the early forties were, what do you say, 'hybrids' of a sort. There were families who lived with one foot in the sixteenth century and one foot in today. I remember girls in my class in school who wore middies and skirts like everybody else and who put on the *shadoor* to ride their bikes home!"

"Where'd you learn to speak such good English?' one of them wanted to know.

"When everybody you know speaks a different language—two or three, maybe—it is not a hard thing. You Americans don't understand, but where are you from?"

"Indiana," the guy replied.

"Well, how would you be if the people in Illinois spoke Illinoise and the people in Ohio spoke - what Ohioese?" and they laughed and chuckled knowingly, and then she went on.

"Anyway, our little world came to an end. I came back from Beirut in 1946 after the war—I was nineteen—and in 1947 the State of Israel was established and—you don't need to know the details, but with the creation of the State of Israel, we Hamoudas became stateless refugees on our own property in Palestine. We lost everything. I went back to Beirut, and my parents came back here and were, how do you describe it, taken in—assimilated—with the other Palestinian refugees into the Islamic community"

She became more the teacher than the partisan, now, although they sensed the depth of her feeling.

Twenty-year-old Mariam/Nikki had a problem.

She had been schooled in the British tradition in Palestine, to the sharp disapproval of her Palestinian relatives, to whom female education was anathema. In Beirut, she attended the American Girls High School and the American University on scholarship, and when her parents died tragically in 1953, she had visited Cyprus for the first time—and stayed. She spoke English, French, Turkish and Arabic, could make herself understood in Hebrew, although she would rather not, and with three years of college and a year of business school, she soon found an excellent position as a translator with the United Nations' High Commission on Refugees.

Her most significant problem during the early years with the Commission was that she spoke no Greek, and while she was a quick language study, she found that she could get along quite well with the languages she had. The Greek came eventually, casually, simply as a result of "getting along" in culturally divided Cyprus, but she disliked speaking it, disliked everything Greek almost as much as she disliked anything Jewish or Israeli or Hebrew.

"I have lost somewhere my Islamic upbringing in Beirut, and I am a free-thinker now" she had remarked, smiling disingenuously, failing to note her total dedication to the Palestinian cause, wherever it was, whatever its specifications, whatever its justification. There was more, also unnoted. She let it go at that, and there were fresh cool beers passed around and something or other distracted them all and the conversation picked up different threads. Nikki half listened, remembering.

She had not forgotten her childhood.

The longer she lived on Cyprus, the deeper grew her hatred for the Greeks. The seemingly random assassinations of innocent Moslem Turks, the discrimination against her countrymen in all phases of commercial and social life, the deprivation of social services regularly afforded the Greek majority but denied to their Moslem countrymen—these were bones in her throat, exasperations, blinding her with a terrifying fury when her tight emotional control weakened.

On the outside a cheerful, bright accommodating young woman, she became a product of the mixture—her passionate hatred for the enemies of the Arabs, a passionate love for the enemies of the Greeks. There were few genuine friends.

At the Commission, she went on, she met and associated with a diverse group of career civil servants, frustrated would-be diplomats and, Cyprus being Cyprus, "others."

Frits Kreisler, her German superior doted on her, welcomed her into his circle of friends—some of whom seemed so long standing as if they had been formed in a previous incarnation. She met Mr. Hawkins, who had something to do with the British, and through Mr. Hawkins, the Martys, who owned a pleasant hotel and a large, converted luxury home, formerly a British colonial property, now a cabaret restaurant. Soon, then, she was working for them, the owners of the Acropole Hotel and the Chanticleer cabaret, at a significant increase in wages, as their secretary. It was a delightful position, although it encompassed more than secretarial work.

She supervised the accounts and the housekeeping staff at the Acropole, the food and beverage operations at the Chanticleer, and kept things running during their occasional absences. She had thought about moving into one of the host suites at the Acropole, but they had—she felt—preferred that she keep her apartment at the Sylvan, which was cozy and comfortable. When she had broached the subject with them, they had evaded an explicit decision but had increased her salary enough to cover her rent.

And there she had met Timmons, whom she found amusing and avuncular, and had been pleased and flattered at the attention he and his "mates" showered upon her. She was their pet, their buddy and their "fixer" in Nicosia because she knew everybody there was to know.

Everybody.

3

Washington

As the cab waited in front of the Sylvan Solace Hotel in a back eddy of downtown Nicosia, in Washington newly promoted Communications Technician First Class Jennifer Howell could hardly believe it was Thursday already.

And so late in the morning.

Ten thirty Thursday morning and I'm on the bus, in uniform for the first time since, when, fourth of July, and then she smiled because the new First Class insignia neatly sewn on the left arm of her dress blue uniform gave off its own warmth and tingle, and she loved the thought of wearing it. The white eagle—the "crow"—spread over the crossed lightning bolt and quill-pen Communications Technician rating badge now sat on top of three—not two—of the brightest, reddest chevrons she had ever seen.

Never one for preening, well not much of a one, she had purposely sat behind the L-3 bus driver and cribbed peeks at her reflection in the broad mirror over his head. The first glance threw her for a minute, unused to her reflection wearing her practical but unbecoming havelock, the rain hat that always looked like a foreign legion kepi crossed with a nun's coif. One of the Naval Orientation questions on the last rating exam had asked about the word - was it an anchor chain retainer? a confidential equipment security device? a wrestling move? or…and of course she knew the right answer and of course she would bet a bundle that not too many of her male shipmates had ever even heard the word.

But she did look nice. Even in the damn havelock and without much sleep all week.

He should see me, share this with me, and the worry moved over a bit to accommodate the daydream, but then it was back.

She was concerned, worried in a way, over what she had heard last night and distracted by her thoughts, almost missed her stop.

She changed to the green DC Transit bus at the Lincoln Memorial and now she looked out through the gray window at the gray sky and the gray rain on the gray snow and the gray everything that made some kind of a statement about the third week in December in the Nation's Capital. Suddenly, it seemed, they were at the top of the Mass Avenue incline and she quickly got up and strode over to the door, aware of the glances, enjoying them. She stepped down on to Nebraska Avenue and hoped that Winnie had made it too. She had five minutes to spare for the ceremony.

What a week.

Last night she had left the office at eleven forty five, and Winnie had counted on her having today off, but then they remembered that both of them had to show up for the December fifteenth Advancement in Rate ceremony and shit-oh-dear, that was here already.

She thought over the long conversation about the officer crew they had had last night and how it had so filled her head and how she had so wanted to talk it over with someone but couldn't. Mostly she thought about Pluto. God, what a dumb name. The guys in the back of the plane went by "Mickey," so she guessed it made some sense.

She remembered the ride home she had gotten from her buddy Jason who had the six to twelve Desk Watch, and how Jason had been mercifully restrained, and how all she wanted to do was think and get some sleep and now that she was awake and on her way, she really didn't mind coming in late. Even in uniform, which she seldom wore at Headquarters, nor did anyone else.

Navy women were still erroneously called WAVES, once in awhile, but for the last seven years the term was only nostalgic, since the new breed of Regular Navy women Petty Officers were in far more specialties than their World War II Reservist counterparts would have dreamed. They were not at sea yet, but that was coming, and Jennifer figured she'd deal with that when the time came.

Communications Technicians were a covert crowd, only sometimes communicators, rarely technicians, but they were the folks who exercised the arcane craft of electronic intelligence, cryptography and cryptanalysis, foreign broadcast interception, analysis and linguistics. She had cut her teeth in the communications intelligence back rooms; first as a cryptographer, then with subsequent assignments in frequency spectrum research, eavesdropping in Japanese and Russian, and electronics, she emerged from the pack as a well-rounded generalist in a plum assignment.

The December Operationals had burst like bombs early Monday morning. Winnie had persuaded London that the Boomerang guys were going for broke this trip, and the paperwork had gone out to the Brits and the Turks and God-knows-who-else and the guys were actually airborne over the Mediterranean someplace on the way from their African Base when two things happened.

The first almost-crisis was minor, but the Operationals she and Winnie put together rarely had glitches, bumps, burps or, God forbid, anything resembling a real crisis.

When she got in on Monday, Winnie had given her a list of things they both needed to have checked. The last item sounded simple enough.

"Oh, and Howie, find out who's going in the Pluto seat for the trip. Just curious."

They were very close, these two, she, at twenty-eight, an enlisted Intelligence Specialist in an elite job and he, the most seriously qualified snoop in the Navy twenty years her senior. No way to make Admiral—there weren't any snoop admirals yet, but he was at the top of his game, on top of the mountain…shit he had built the damn mountain. He rarely broke protocol to call her by her first name but the sawed-off last name served just as well and she took it with great pride.

But…

Any time Winnie Barnet said he was "just curious' she knew there was a genuine probability that a Problem lurked. In quietly checking everybody's work—a Winnie Barnet specialty - he had discovered that there *was* no Pluto rider formally designated on this trip.

No one.

The directive from London had promised one, the guys in Cyprus were expecting one to show up, but the operations shop of their own Security Group must have fouled up and the crack seemed wide open. A top-quality linguist, specially trained for one of these night-horror missions had to be on board—the "Pluto" seat occupied—for everybody's sake!

"Holy Shit." He was a quiet, restrained seether, and he was seething now, the more he thought of it.

"This is the one time we need a guy on that fucking airplane who can tell them when to turn around and go home and we don't *have* one? Why the hell not, Goddamit?" and when she had gotten to the bottom of things, she wondered how to recount the comedy of errors, from the notes of the morning's hectic calls, without further infuriating him at the offending guilty party down in the bowels of the Operations Department.

Tragedy -not -quite, easily correctable, no harm done, sorry about that, I got it taken care of…

Yes, one had been designated, weeks ago, back in October when we first put the trip together…the day you had the Quarterlies.

And yes, he had been diligently at work out in Suitland, Maryland, with a technical crew and an aircraft electronic package simulator, and a bunch of wire recordings to listen to and yes, he's standing by but nobody has briefed him, patted him on the ass and given him a ticket. The Operations Officer had finally reassured Winnie personally, gave him his name, rank and file number.

"You're right," he said finally, cooled from his seethe, "he's in a crouch to go and he's done his preparations but nobody thought to get him to the fucking gate. Here's his name. Get this guy on his way." And that was then end of it. Not quite.

She took the blue note he handed her and rolled it around her finger without looking at it. She would take care of it from here, now that she had the name.

But…

"Он не будет добираться там вовремя," she said.

He ain't going to make it.

He stared back at her, blankly, and she wasn't sure whether she had offended him, caught him completely off guard or made some horrible grammatical error. Their Russian was good, each of them, but they saved it for playful times, jokes, kidding around. This time she may have misread him badly.

"Did you get what I said?" she asked, meekly, embarrassed.

"Of course," he said, the broad grin beginning at the corner of his eyes, spreading down his face. "You don't think he's going to get there on time."

"Madame, you are correct," he said in his best cryptic manner, playing back. Then, strangely, he winked.

"Let's just cancel them Wednesday and fly him with them Thursday, and if they get lucky, we'll just scrub Friday and bring them home."

"Hey, Big Spender, eh? Think they can pull it off?" What now?

"Jenn, this one's going to be a beaut. I guarantee it", and he winked again. But there weren't any smiles.

Two winks. Her given name. He's either scared, happy, pleased with himself or all three. He caught her eye, finally, and did smile.

Maybe he's just relieved. She certainly was.

But there's something going on. A "beaut"?

And as she stared at the name she had jotted on the blue US Government Inter-Office Memorandum - one of the venerable "Blue Blazers" that fueled the US governmental machine—she could feel color rising in her face as her pulse accelerated and small hairs rose silently in hidden places.

No one could know that she knew the name on the paper.

Sunday evening. Their third date.

She had been first mildly annoyed, then greatly bothered by the deepening intimacy between them. She was used to the long shadow her occupation had regularly cast upon her personal life, but this was different. She had enjoyed herself in the anonymity that she had always maintained in her social life. She never mentioned that she was a Navy Petty Officer, attached to one of the most secretive organizations in Washington. She had dates, met men her own age—and older—and had no problem keeping her social life at arms length. This was beginning to be different and now…

He had said he worked for the Navy, somewhere in Washington, but she hadn't pressed him and feigned complete ignorance of anything related to the military. Impossibly—could it even be remotely possible—he had played the same masquerade as she had, although now she realized that the officer-enlisted rank chasm would inevitably become a factor in whatever she could salvage of their relationship.

So Jennifer spent far more time than she normally would on the phone with their travel people and their immunization people and finally left word with the folks at Suitland to have him packed and ready to go this evening for the Wednesday night operational out of Nicosia. First, though, Winnie had to brief him—personally—and that had to happen this afternoon. She dreaded the encounter that she knew had to happen, sooner or later.

Great while it lasted.

But when Lieutenant Dave Wagoner showed up for his briefing, instead of a dreadful high-voltage, hand-trembling, nervous encounter between two ashamed, unmasked imposters, the split second of recognition-anxiety turned into a pair of momentary silly grins and it was a relief-excitement charge that filled the air. No eavesdropper could have fathomed the true nature of either's feelings during the brief, formal conversation between them during that first encounter in her office, but their expressions said it all. And when she handed him the TWA ticket package before he went in for his session with Winnie, their hands touched and she knew that the masked ball was over for both of them, ended happily, a new beginning.

Later, after she walked with him through the outer office, they lingered a moment or two longer than protocol required in their handshake.

"Спасибо" he said. *Thank you.*

"Возвратитесь благополучно", she replied softly. *Come back safely.*

And then he was gone, and she wondered how bad a "beaut" this one was going to be.

She couldn't shake the feeling that instead of any satisfaction she may have felt in linking Winnie up with his latest Pluto operator, she now felt a little sorry for all three of them.

That was Monday.

The feeling had gotten worse over the next couple of days, and when she looked at her watch as got off the bus and it belched its way up Mass Avenue, she figured that Dave was just about arriving in Nicosia, if he had made his connections, and things were starting to happen out there.

It was show time.

4

Nicosia

Timmons and Lucore climbed in the cab in front of the Sylvan Solace and smiled at one another as Mikos put down his paper, keyed up the not-quite-venerable, never particularly impressive V-6 and began the night's spiel, largely ignored by his passengers. They had heard it all before.

Pardon me while I roll my eyes, Lucore's expression said.

Inside, the Dodge smelled more like gasoline than it usually did, probably just gassed up. Timmons noticed that the sun was only half a ball now over the western rampart as they pulled out of the drive and turned left, hugging the oleander growth by the hotel until they reached the roundabout. He still marveled at the ease with which Mikos navigated the big left-hand-drive Dodge, keeping to the very British left along the narrow path-like streets into downtown Nicosia. Tracked Bren Gun carriers resembling small tanks and Middle East Force lorries passed them going the other way and they both turned to glance after them until they were out of sight passing the hotel.

Aviation Ordnanceman First Class James Vincent Lucore's business was weaponry, and his interest in the side arms and the old water-cooled mounted .50 was a mixture of professional and historical interest. They didn't make them like that anymore. Thankfully. They must be a bitch to keep in shape.

Timmons began to watch their own progress out of the city. They drove slowly through the downtown streets in the twilight, store openings, closings and home-bound laborers claiming much of the available passage-way, pedestrians hopping out of the way of the ubiquitous bicycles, the bikes themselves intimidated by the trucks that served as busses, and the cars. Shop lights, street lights, even the hint here and there of Christmas decorations coming on, sporadically in a town of sporadic Christmas cheer. Mikos seemed to be looking for someone or something. They passed through the Square, Ledra and Onasagoras Streets off to the right, plenty of business at the Victory despite the tension and the time of day. There were people, most of them young men but a few girls too, milling around across the street from the British Institute where a police Land Rover and an Army six-by-six were discharging grim-faced uniforms, each clumping together beside their respective vehicles, the Cypriot cops outnumbered by the commandos. Trouble tonight, probably. The old Presidential Palace was made of wood, he remembered irrelevantly.

They passed the Chanticleer, the nightclub looking different in the twilight, without the accent lights and the small neon sign, a tart not quite out of bed this evening, thinking about getting ready for work. He thought he saw one of the Dutch girls getting out of a taxi. Too early. Must be someone else. She always hung around with her "twin sister". Suppose they were really sisters?

Further along, Greek flags in the windows, "EOKA" banners all over the place, a crusty Tommy sergeant and a cop taking down a Makarios poster from a storefront. It looked funny to see British civilian cops on the street in Nick, but it was probably pretty strange for them too. Lureen's brother was a cop in Baltimore, and he could just imagine him here. Only just. If he craned his neck, he could see the Turkish flag on one of the twin minarets of the mosque in the older part of the city, with its heavy Turkish population. Mornings, at sunrise, he could hear the chant of the muezzin as he called the faithful to prayer, and again in the evening. He suspected they had some kind of a public address system. He would have to ask Nikki.

"Another one today," Mikos said, matter-of-factly, looking at them in the rear view mirror, anticipating—hoping for? - some reaction, one hand gesturing against the firm hold of the other on the lace-jacketed steering wheel. Past the old Tripoli Rampart, finally, to Kinyra and the Paphos Gate check point, then on the highway out to the west.

"We heard," Timmons said, looking over at Lucore with the look he had developed over years of being told stuff he either didn't want to know, didn't want to hear or didn't want to care about.

He hadn't heard and didn't particularly care.

"Kids this time," Mikos went on. "Just kids!"

He only half listened to Mikos's running commentary, losing the train of the one-way conversation thinking about what came next.

Timmons was quiet, and Lucore too occupied in his own thoughts to do more than grunt back, so Mikos shut up and began to pay attention to the road. The security issue bothered all of them, but they had to get used to it. They came out here every month—not each of them, of course, but one of the crews did—and obviously the last thing they wanted was to get jumped when they got up north, over the Pond. As a result, the normal security briefings sailors always had to sit through took on a cogent and very personal meaning to the Beast crews; loose lips sink ships, keep a zip upper lip, all of that stuff.

They made-believe they were oil people, although they knew that was a pretty thin disguise with the airplane sitting out on the ramp all week. What they all tried to avoid, however, was any giveaway as to when they were going flying, where they were going or what they were doing. If bad guys knew they were coming, that would be the end of them all. It was that serious. They had two sets of security concerns. If the Greeks or the Turks or one of their byproduct bad guys did something to step on their collective cranks, then they had to figure that the Russians were up there to the north waiting for them to come around the corner and really be bad guys.

He worried about the night's work.

"You're a friggin' worry wart," Lucore had told him, a dozen times.

And he was, he guessed. Not about the big stuff, he had told Lucore one night over Beer Number Seven, not about getting our ass shot down or anything like that. He worried about the Beast and the guys and getting to the flight line in time and all the stuff Lucore called "the little shit." But this evening, he had another worry, one he couldn't—wouldn't—share with his best buddy. He was worried about Elfers, their Plane Commander, worried that there was something he knew that they shouldn't, something that stacked the deck—he didn't know which way. Shit, they had made this run a dozen times and Timmons never one even considered Lieutenant Commander Elfers in his litany of concerns. The guy was phenomenal, best pilot in the Navy. They'd been together and flown together and sweated out a zillion engineering disasters in the years since Martin in Baltimore...why the worry tonight? Mr. Elfers was different on the way out, nothing you could put your finger on, just different.

He left the thought, incomplete, and went on to other concerns. He'd get back to Mr. Elfers.

But he didn't.

He had an extra quill-shaft in the toolbox. He would rather have had two, but one would have to do.

Soon it would. Sooner than he had hoped.

The coffee and sugar were ordered, and Lucore owed him some for the forward pot. The pre-flight tonight would be a little longer with all the bomb bays to fuel. The leak in the number three bomb bay manifold had been fixed in Malta on the way out. He was thirty-three years old and the war had been over ten years and he was still a first class petty officer because he wanted to be. If he ever made Chief would he still have this much to worry about and would he look ten years older than his age in khakis, because he sure did in civvies...A week of sport shirts!

He knew where the crew was. He had mentally kept tabs on them all day, and all of his people were in the bar when he left. The Mickey gang wasn't his problem, but knowing Mr. Gross, they were certain to be sitting around in a circle in Gross' room doing whatever the hell they did to get ready for whatever the hell they were going to do tonight. They would all arrive together probably, in plenty of time to do their own complicated pre-flight. They flew the back end of the aircraft. They were the snoopers.

Timmons was the Plane Captain, the flight engineer and crew chief.

"You are the Captain of the Plane?" Nikki had asked, when they all first met.

"No, I'm the Plane Captain. The pilot is the 'Captain' of the plane," he had said.

"The Plane Captain is not the Captain of the Plane?"

"Not in the Navy. The Plane Captain is, like, well, the engineer."

"But the engineer drives the train, no?"

"Yes, but this is a plane. I'm the engineer, the pilot drives. OK?"

"You tell the pilot what to do, n'est-ce pas?"

"The hell he does!" Lucore had broken in. They were all enjoying this.

"But you are the chief over all these people," pointing to the enlisted crew gathered around the conversation at the bar that afternoon.

"Yes," Timmons said, and they all agreed to let it go at that.

They hadn't flown last night, as originally planned. The abort had come around noon the day before, unexplained, no elaboration, Mr. Elfers calling through to the hotel, the message getting around quickly.

A pre-flight abort message was unusual but not unheard of. They would feel double pressure later when they got closer to take-off, because this month if anything happened to the plane and they couldn't fly a catch-up flight tomorrow night, they'd have this chance and only this chance to do what they had to do.

Tim had lounged around most of yesterday. Nikki had gone to her uncle's in Morfu at four, and he had said goodbye to her as he was hanging around the lobby. Sleep on a work night had to be during daytime, the Sylvan's shutters ideally suited for it, so he had napped until ten that night and then dressed and gone over to the Chanticleer for something to eat just as the two Dutch girls were beginning "There Goes My Heart". It always came out as "Dere Goes My Hard" and the mixed audience of tourists, Brit officers, and the types the crew called the butter-and-egg merchants from Famagusta loved it. He had seen Mr. Elfers there, applauding the song.

By the time Lucore came in later, Nikki was back, and she came out and joined them at the bar and they visited for a while. When the act ended, she went back to her office while they sat and nursed a last Keo brandy sour and listened to some Brits arguing about what Grivas was really up to. He felt at home in the Sylvan, but the Chanticleer always made him feel out of place. The curfew downtown never seemed to reach out that far and he hadn't had any trouble getting back.

The curfew times varied by day, but as a rule, nightlife shut down at nine and people were off the streets until an hour before sunup the following day. There were allowances for market day, for funeral travel, for medical emergencies, for arriving and departing international travelers, for diplomats and their staffs, including United Nations personnel, and for Her Majesty's Government official business. Allowance documentation was required and repeatedly checked.

There was a constant clatter of bitter dialogue almost everywhere on the island, Greek speakers insisting that the Turks were being allowed to abuse curfew, Turks pointing to the oppressive and arbitrary enforcement by the Cypriot - Greek speaking - police in their towns and villages. British civil servants, business people, teachers, professional men and the families of military personnel complained at the early hour for their dinner parties and the long evenings, with no telly and no cinema. To the credit of the British authorities, the curfew was as strict as it had to be in the areas where it counted, less strict in its least enforceable and least dangerous neighborhoods, but in the main thoroughfares and at the checkpoints in town and out in the countryside, free and unrestrained travel had either to take place beneath the watchful eye of troops rapidly getting used to their duties or be postponed until morning.

At the center of town, in the square and on Ledra Street and in the streets fanning out from the square in which the highest value targets were located, the Royal Army Tommys and the police were hard-nosed about it, more interested in ridding the streets of troublemakers than taking prisoners, writing warrants or making more work for themselves. Consequently, as in the case of many of the curfews in various parts of the globe that year, there was a lot of snarling, a lot of sirens, copious use of whistles, bull horns, rushing motor vehicles full of young soldiers torn between being scared to death and being thrilled out of their skin, numerous petty and some major complaints on the part of the citizenry, and far more boredom than people were used to. When the chips were down, those who wanted to avoid curfew found ways to do it and the law abiders generally ended up at home for the night. Electric power was sometimes spotty, and the whole area north and to the east of Ledra Street tended to be out more than on, as was the far eastern quadrant of the old city. To the west and north, the predominantly British and non-Greek section of the populace was generally permitted to pass about if they had a reasonable excuse, and as on this Thursday night, at both the Chanticleer and the Acropole, there would be some business, at least, with an early cabaret and closing.

Timmons checked his watch, and was surprised that it was five thirty already. All that damn weaving around town. It was only morning in the States. Around ten. He had put his concerns about Lew Elfers out of his head and watched the lights go on as they meandered out of town.

Everybody waved to Mikos. Mikos waved back without missing a beat in his monologue. Mikos knew everybody, too.

Maybe a different "everybody" though.

They sat in silence, comfortable, old friends, each with his thoughts.

Timmons broke the silence.

"Mr. Elfers seem okay to you on the way out?"

"What do you mean, 'okay'?"

"He seem…well, off in the distance?"

"Listen, Sailor, that guys got so much of whatever the hell 'it' is that he can be off in China some place and he's going to be the best friggin' guy I ever flew with."

"Yeah," Timmons said, looking away. "I guess so."

5

As Jennifer looked back on it and the rest of the past few days, Winnie definitely had not been smiling that next day, Tuesday**,** when the message from the Pentagon hit the fan right after lunch. He had gotten it verbally on the red phone that only rang on his desk, the hot-line from the command communications center, and he came out into her office and motioned her in. The hard copy was on its way. She grabbed her three-ring binder and her coffee cup and went in.

"Close the door" he said calmly, and without signal, the two of them sat at his work table in the center of the room.

They were used to one another.

"We have a real one here," he began.

"Remember back in October when I went to the Quarterly meeting down on the Mall? After the meeting, some of our illustrious confreres jumped me about a possible security problem in the Boomerang box. They have their own agenda and it's not always out on the table, and this happens all the time when the money pots get low.

"I tossed it off at the time," he went on, looking out at the gray skyscape, "but here it is today and those same bastards are putting it down on paper now and we're going to have to look it in the eye. The message is on its way. I got a verbal over the red line.

"They're raising the question of crew security integrity on the Operational that's on its way out to Nicosia now. What we're going to have to do—and I want you and I to be the only ones who know about this, understand?…" She nodded, absorbed.

"…what we're going to have to do is build our own profile on every one of those guys on the airplane and go from there."

"They smell a defector or something? Come on, Boss, they're all sailors, there's no way any of them could have been turned or made." She thought of David. No way.

Then a pause.

Then, "Is there?" in a smaller voice.

Then quiet.

"Let's get on it and see what we've got. The six guys in the back end of the aircraft, the 'Mickey' guys, are all ours and we have their paper down below in the basement. The front-end guys, the airplane drivers and fixers and worker-bees, we'll need to look at. Pluto gets a bye—this is his first ride. Got the crew list?"

Her heart slithered up toward her throat when he mentioned David's role in the drama, but it quickly settled back and she hoped Winnie had not noticed her awkward sudden redness. Of course he hadn't, but for a second she had a good preview of a hot flash.

She pulled the Naval Security Group courtesy-copy of their orders from her binder. The aircraft was crewed by regular aviation personnel from a newly commissioned fleet squadron based in Morocco—it had been a nondescript "Unit" for years - and they flew the plane and kept it in the air, the front-end guys. Behind the wing-spar, a specialized crew of intelligence specialists—snoopers—sat in earphoned darkness before sophisticated scopes and collected the beeps and squiggles that certain other nations paid dearly to protect. The snoopers belonged to Winnie, they were his "assets". They just looked like regular sailors.

"Let's see. Front end. Flight crew. Plane Captain is a First Class Aviation Machinists Mate named Caleb Timmons. Huh. Did you ever know anybody, a real person, named Caleb? He and the Ordnanceman, James Vincent Lucore—goes by 'Vinny'—have been with the program since the Martin factory in Baltimore. Radioman is a First Class too, guy by the name of Burdick, a legend in his time they tell me. Curious, a 'White' and a 'Black' as Electrician and Radar Operator, no second mechanic, as is routine on the really bad ones like this, and then there's our six guys in the back end."

"What about the officers?"

"Pilot's the old warhorse - not so old, actually - Lew Elfers, practically invented the program, Squadron Operations Officer. You know him, I believe. Hard to get used to thinking of the Unit as a Squadron now, but so it is."

Winnie had had years of practice keeping the things that he said and the things that he thought and the things that he worried about in separate cerebral bins, high walled, air tight, leak proof. Lew's image flashed between bins for an instant, Winnie's protagonist-elect, but you'd never be able to tell as she went on.

"Co-pilot is Lieutenant Bob Hunley, been there awhile, designated Aircraft Commander but never had a mission of his own. Can't remember anything about him or the Navigator, a new kid named Brian Kerrigan, Lieutenant junior grade, but we have ways, as they say.

"Chief Evaluator—Mickey for this trip—is Lieutenant Commander Mort Gross, you go back a long way, the two of you, and that makes eight up front, six in the back, fourteen souls on board. Fifteen counting Pluto." The blush again. Dammit.

"Where do we start?" she asked, looking up from her book blandly.

"You get what you can on the enlisted crew up front, I'll do the officers. Let the folks downstairs do our enlisted guys, the Mickey guys, can't see that there's any likelihood of a problem there. Let's see, it's Tuesday noonish here, they got into Nicosia seven hours ago—seven hours difference, right? - and they're holed up in those godawful hotels they stay at. We're going to scrub tomorrow night's flight and you'll take care of that through London now, so we have until tomorrow night at the latest to find anything we're going to either find or need. See if you can drop what you've got going and we'll shoot for after working hours tomorrow night—I'm sorry, really, but then you take Thursday off if the bombs haven't started flying. Okay with you?"

"Yes, Sir. You bet."

Neither of them had even thought about the Advancement in Rate Ceremony that each had to participate in on Thursday morning at eleven.

The Naval Security Group is an elite closed community of communications intelligence specialists, officer and enlisted, with "community control" of their assignments and advancements. This means, as Jennifer discovered early in her career, that the guy who you worked with one year in some out-of-the-way listening post or crypto-mill and with whom you became bonded shipmates could—next time—be the guy who assigned you to your new job or who watched after your funding or helped build your advancement exams while he was stationed in a mainstream Navy support job someplace, earmarked to take care of the "community".

It wouldn't do to have these specialists randomly scattered throughout the Navy willy-nilly, treated like so many Bos'uns or Shipfitters. And by midway into a Communications Technician career, as Jennifer was, one knew the ropes and the wiring diagrams and the chains of command and the ins and outs of Getting Things Done with the community. More so, of course, as the Special Assistant to the Group Commander, one of three senior enlisted women in the loop, and as street-wise as they come.

So, with relative ease, she reached the Assistant Head of the Security Group Enlisted Detail Section in the Bureau of Naval Personnel who easily put her with his counterpart in the Group Nine (Aviation) Enlisted Detail Section who was more than happy to ingratiate himself with the very feminine-sounding spook gal and take care of her request. She needed enlisted personnel records on a half dozen guys and she needed to have access to them personally as soon as he could pull the papers. Official, Correspondence, and back channel files, if you please, all three.

By four o'clock Tuesday afternoon, the records had been fished out from the different rating desks—the Aviation Machinists, the Ordnancemen, the "trons" as they called the radar and radio guys, located and bundled for her. Winnie's officer buddies had given him more trouble than he had anticipated, with a Selection Board getting ready to meet, but they would be ready too—and they were all waiting for them now. They rode in the gray Navy sedan and by five they were crossing Memorial Bridge, Christmas lights twinkling on here and there, winter in the air.

Across the river in the Bureau of Naval Personnel at the Navy Annex in Arlington, they were set up graciously in a Jacket Review Room by an all-business civil servant under the watchful eye of a uniformed General Services cop, since it was after hours. Winnie made a phone call and the cop disappeared a few minutes later, beckoned by a faceless uniformed figure who opened the door slightly, and made a couple of gestures. The cop couldn't figure out what the two of them were up to but he didn't show back up, and they worked through the dinner hour.

Jennifer's stack of enlisted record packages was surprisingly hefty. One file for each guy was a duplicate service record, complete with pay entries, leave dates and other trivia, crucial to the day-to-day administration of a large body of habitually nit-picking sailors to whom pay and liberty were sacrosanct and who kept track of these things passionately. The other, bulkier file was the "correspondence file" of items, some general, some pointedly specific, pertaining to the individual from the day he first visited a recruiter. The paper itself -bureautically cheap, yellowing mimeographed "originals", flimsy onion skin carbons, occasional crinkly thermofaxes or greasy photostatic copies of handwritten slices of history—told a story. It was gibberish to the uninitiated, but to the jargon-literate reader painstakingly constructing five careers on a bleak December evening, a gold mine, even if she wasn't sure what she was looking for or what pay dirt, when she found it, would look like. She took lots of notes.

Winnie took his officer records off into the far corner of the surprisingly comfortable room. A miniature Christmas tree on a credenza by the wall smiled out at them. It was one of the specially designated "reading" rooms, where sailors from seamen to admiral came to review their records. During working hours the desk was manned by a monitor who carefully supervised the reader, making sure nothing mysteriously appeared in or disappeared out of the record being reviewed. After hours, no monitor of course, just a long table, comfortable chairs, and desk lamps.

He stretched out, unbuttoned his collar and plowed through the officer equivalent of the records Jennifer was reviewing. Fewer pay, allowance and days-worked details, far more personal details, comments by superiors, stuff marked "Privileged" and "Personal Sensitive" and the details of every Background Investigation ever conducted on the subject in question. Since they were all cleared for Top Secret—and higher, in some cases—there were lots of details.

The Captain took no notes, made no comments, exhibited neither surprise, chagrin, displeasure or enlightenment, and he finished his stack before she did. He sat while she wrapped it up, smoking thoughtfully, looking out into the lowering sky and the reflected lights of the city on the scuddy clouds over the Potomac.

He had unclipped the four-by-five glossy photos from the back cover of each record and laid them out, like a bridge hand, and she came over to him, finally, her stack held against her chest like a schoolgirl with her books, examining them. She stood next to him, then, her skirt brushing his arm as she bent over and picked them up. They both noted the event, another of the shared threads in their lives, each now used to their relationship, neither able to put it in words.

Each picture was a head and shoulders, as prescribed in the Bureau of Personnel Manual, each subject in service dress khakis, hatless to show fresh haircuts, and she noticed that each was dated in early September. These were the "Unit Commissioning" portraits, each taken the same day, right after the ceremony making the squadron a legally accountable organization. They fascinated her.

Lew Elfers stared at the camera, all business, square jawed, huge, brown penetrating eyes, but with a tiny trace of - was in a smirk or a sneer—around the corners of his mouth. She felt she could follow the guy into battle, but she wasn't too sure about the smirk.

Hunley's blue eyes came through the shades of gray the film was able to handle, and the shock of white hair commemorated the fact that he may once have had a short Navy haircut but that was then and this was now. His pleasant smile reminded her of an election poster, and he probably would get her vote.

Kerrigan was all courage and commitment and John Paul Jones, nice looking she thought, probably a good guy to work with, surely not a seasoned salt, about her age, but with fewer miles on the clock. Dry behind the ears. Just.

Mort Gross was a surprise. She did not know why—why had she expected them all to look like they had been carefully cut from a stencil, each a carbon of the other? Faceless names, probably, did that, but Mort's smiling, jovial and - yes round and pudgy - image reminded her of the Hollywood character actors who always played the part of the fawning tradesman, the paunchy banker, the friendly cop. This guy looked like he was in the wrong line of work.

She stacked them back on the table and they exchanged a look that successfully veiled whatever thoughts she might have had, now that she had faces to go with the names of all of them. She knew the Security Group guys, the Mickey crew, if not personally then at least by sight, and she felt that warmth in her cheeks and color in her face as she tried not to think of Dave Wagoner. His papers were not in the stack, she noted. "Their" people were special. But now, at least for Jennifer, all of them were special.

This was the big one, this was the special effort, Winnie had said so, this was different. And Jennifer was puzzled because she felt, well, different, too.

It was almost seven and Winnie made another of his magic phone calls. A Bureau of Naval Personnel Chief Yeoman came up to collect the files, and they headed downstairs. Before they left, though, Jennifer had flipped through each of the enlisted personnel jackets and made what she called "Vital Statistics" notes next to each of the names on the list of "front end" crewmembers. They scrounged a Navy car from the Chief and he arranged for the driver drop her home, while Winnie disappeared into the night, walking, down the hill to the Pentagon a quarter-mile away. They said nothing about the results of the session.

She ate a TV dinner and drank a beer, reviewing her notes until midnight. She guessed Winnie was doing the same thing. Without notes.

When she began to get drowsy, she took a last look at her "Vital Statistic" list, hoping to keep each of them straight in her head. She would probably get to see a lot more of the list in the next couple of days.

Caleb (n) Timmons, 34—Plane Captain
Aviation Machinist Mate First Class
Born 1921 Boise, Idaho Enlisted 1941

James Vincent Lucore, 30 - Ordnanceman
Aviation Ordnanceman First Class
Born 1925 Bronx, N. Y. Enlisted, 1943

Earl (n) White, 25 - Electrician
Aviation Electrician's Mate Second Class
Born 1930 Maynard, Mass Enlisted 1951

Daryl Tubman Black 25 - Radar
Aviation Electronics Technician Second Class
Born 1930 Birmingham, Alabama Enlisted 1951

Lyle (n) Burdick, 40 - Radio
Aviation Radioman First Class
Born 1915 Tulsa, Oklahoma Enlisted 1937

Not much to go on.

6

Nicosia

Every time he gassed the Beast, First Class Aviation Ordnanceman Lucore wondered what the wise-asses in the Instructors' Coffee Mess at the Naval Technical Training Center in Memphis would say, their First Class Authority On Everything humping a fifty-five pound hose assembly sixteen feet up on a mid-wing fueling station, getting ready for the juice to run first into the wing-mains, then the wing-auxiliaries, then the huge hulky bomb bays. The auxiliaries were outboard of the main tanks in the wings, and they fed into the main tanks from which each of the four engines—two piston engines and two jets - drew fuel. Lucore stood on the wing and thought about it for a minute.

First Class Petty Officers do not fuel airplanes.

He looked down at Timmons wrestling with the bomb-bay manifold cap. Maybe back at the ranch they don't, but this was Showtime and he and Timmons were the only folks around that he and Timmons would trust to fuel the Beast on a night with this ahead of them. They had been together a long time, he and Timmons, and they knew each other better than most of their shipmates knew their own wives and kids.

"I wonder what the hell Tim meant with that crack about Mr. Elfers," Lucore asked himself, reviewing the trip out, the stopover in Malta, the post-flight the other evening after they landed. Did he seem like his old self? Sure. Sure he did.

Didn't he?

Timmons, you bastard, why don't you keep your friggin' worries to yourself?

They were totally unlike in appearance, Timmons more wrinkled and flinty than anyone in his early thirties ought to be. When he smiled, the eyes danced in a way that Lureen always hoped their children would inherit. He took good care of himself and tried to avoid his natural inclination to overeat, over drink and over smoke. He generally had control of two out of the three, but never all three at once. After the months of operating off bobbing and pitching seaplane tenders and spending nights riding the hook at anchor or tied to a buoy in seaplanes, Timmons had developed a lot more self control than he had ever imagined possible. Some people liked the "boats," and seaplane duty had its drawbacks, but it made a man out of the Idaho kid.

People called James Vincent Lucore a "juvenile delinquent" in the Bronx in 1943. That was the term. There Was a War On, all over the place, and a smart seventeen year old could find a zillion ways to get out of school, boost whatever came by truck into the Hunts Point market, run with the crowd of otherwise-punks who—absent their elders off to war—kept the home fires burning. He was an inch or two taller than Timmons, darkly handsome with jet-black wavy hair that claimed more of his attention than his peers thought it deserved. People had been known to refer to him as "Greaseball" but never more than once, in his earshot, without extreme prejudice. But the eyes had it for Lucore, Tony Curtis eyes, bedroom eyes, eyes that missed nothing, even when seductively half-lidded or twinkling with some new, minor mischief crossing his mind. On the job he was the consummate professional, on track professionally as a senior petty officer as his thirtieth birthday approached.

He was good at nostalgia.

Just about this time a dozen years ago, "Vinny" Lucore was standing on the corner of 149th Street and Third Avenue under the El, drinking out of his third quart of bag-wrapped Trommers when two of New York's 40th Precinct finest pulled up in their black and green coupe. God, how he remembered the feel of the cold bottle in the brown paper, the moisture on the brown glass melting the cheap paper, the bag giving way here and there, swapping spitty swigs with one another. Yuck.

Anyway, one thing led to another and, before long, the cops were asking embarrassing questions about the .32 automatic they happened to find during their illegal, but very thorough, pat down. After a session in the stationhouse over on 138th and Alexander Avenue, where none of his alibied "facts" checked, he made a disheveled appearance in Magistrate's Court on 161st and Third and wound up in the morning at the new art-deco Bronx County Courthouse on the Concourse.

Damn, what a memory! Even the streets!

By this time, the Sullivan Law gun charge had been obscured and overshadowed by his negative demeanor and his now-accurately-established age. When he, in time, confronted His Honor Patrick J. McGinley of the florid face and the flattish feet, who was simultaneously confronting Vinny's impressively documented litany of misdemeanors, truancies and failed juvenile social experiences, Lucore was ready to deal.

McGinley, shit, remember him?

Nobody could ever say that it was McGinley's idea, but the next week he was at Sampson Naval Training Center upstate with a white Dixie-cup hat, a boot camp haircut and a thirteen button flap instead of a fly, learning to be a sailor. He was not quite eighteen. He hadn't been the same since.

Whatever emotional attraction firearms had held for him in his former incarnation, the Navy wisely baptized and professionalized. Gunnery became his passion. Powder was his perfume, sears and detents and star-gears were his playthings. But guns were his specialty, the big twin .50 turret installations his passion.

Lucore admired Timmons. Then he got to thinking again…

The First Class Aviation Machinists Mate had been a supremely logical choice to be the Plane Captain as the first Beast began to take shape and get ready for flight. He knew the Martin engineering style well and had impressed everyone there with his maturity, common sense and great technical skill. The monstrous R-4360 28 cylinder corncob engines were uncommon in the Navy, jet engines were just beginning to take over, the Beast's technical sophistication was profound and nobody knew what to expect. He was moved off the Martin Mariner seaplane line to the skunk works Hangar at Martin, and he and Lucore had met. As First Class Petty Officers either do or don't—they meshed. Together they shaped the enlisted team that flew the Beast's first all-Navy crewed flight after conversion. And here they were on a chilly evening, in a place they had come to know well, doing something they were good at and liked to do. He wondered how long it would all last.

Back in the present, somewhere in the real world now, he noted that the fuel flow had not started.

He looked down and when he saw Timmons and the driver with their heads together, he lowered the rig on its line and climbed down to the concrete. They both knew Niarchos from innumerable fuelings, and the three of them stood in the glow of the utility light at the rear pump panel. They had taken low-point drain samples from the truck and were shining their flashlights into the mason jars holding the purple liquid. Usually, with the slight trace of condensate water in the average fuel supply, the heavier water will sink out into the drain and the sample will run with a chalky discoloration until the water separates and shows clearly. This sample was absolutely pure in the Mason jar, purple in the light, but Timmons seemed displeased with it.

Lucore looked at it. Something wasn't right. This sample was too good to be true. Timmons went around to the back of the tanker and took an empty jar from the cardboard box inside the utility frame. He crouched under the belly of the truck and let another quart of gas run into it, although Lucore realized that once the first sample had run, any hope of finding a sign of trace contamination had passed. Sure enough, the second sample was flawless also. Their glances communicated exchanged concerns, but their shrugs finally acknowledged that they might just be too picky tonight, and they all went back to the job. Someone probably took drain samples before the truck left the line, clearing the drains. When flow stopped twenty minutes later, the Beast had been topped off and the gas chit signed and the hoses reeled back and stowed against the tanker.

Timmons started the yellow Auxiliary Power Unit, checked the voltages, then plugged the master cable into the receptacle in the nose wheel well. He scampered up into the fuselage and threw the main power switch, and the Beast began to glow red from the inside lighting. The inverters making the 400 cycle Alternating Current power off the Power Unit's Direct Current were humming sweetly, and the rectifiers were buzzing as they changed what needed to be changed back into 28 Volt DC power for the instruments and compasses and what electronic stuff they'd need for preflight.

He noticed a Land Rover drive up on the tarmac, perhaps fifty yards from them, and a pair of figures emerge, one of them almost certainly Mr. Elfers.

He wondered who the other guy was. A stranger.

The two newcomers sat together on one of the Ready benches as the Rover returned to the line.

7

Washington

During the nominal "working hours" at Nebraska Avenue, she had seen nothing of the Captain all day yesterday—Wednesday - until well after six. She had spent most of the day with her "Vital Statistics" list in front of her, checking with sources she knew to be nosy, cashing in chips here and there around the intelligence community, shaking trees and finding a few cherries, all in all, a successful shake. Her list of the enlisted crew working the front end of the aircraft had been vetted, she figured, and when he showed up for the first time at ten after five on a Wednesday afternoon, she was glad to see him, relieved actually, glad that he was in a relatively good mood, even if his presence meant she'd probably have to work late. She had all of her routine stuff to plow through, so she got started and was at it when he came out of his office and beckoned her inside.

They were alone again at the table in the big office.

"Find anything?" he asked her, when they had settled in. She guessed he would not share anything that he had come up with on the officers, unless it was a real show-stopper—in which case, he would leave it to her to grind out the paperwork that would stop the show. The guys in the back end were Security Group guys and she knew that the bell would have rung way before this if anything had developed in that area.

"We've got very good news and then some news that I'm a little concerned about…get to that later. First off, we've have John Paul Jones the first and the second. Going by their records, these two guys are no problem at all.

Caleb (n) Timmons, 34—Plane Captain
Aviation Machinist Mate First Class
Born 1921 Boise, Idaho Enlisted 1941

"Timmons, Caleb no-middle-initial," she began, sliding the four by five black and white photo she had unclipped from the back of Timmons' jacket the previous afternoon. A recent good likeness, like the officer mug shots, also taken when the squadron had been commissioned a couple of months before. She had swiped all the photos from the jackets, and would get them back one of these days if she could figure out how to do it tactfully and without starting a shit-storm.

"Those crows' feet come from hours in seaplanes, squinting through Plexiglas in the old Catalina, then in the Mariner when it came along," Winnie noted.

"How did you know?"

"I was involved up to my ass in putting the Beasts in the air. I rode with them on their first couple of flights out of Martin up in Baltimore when they put the first of them together. Timmons had been handpicked as the first Plane Captain. They call 'em that for some reason, left over from WW One, combination of Flight Engineer, Crew Chief and Big Daddy." He smiled, as she looked up at him. "I remember letting him show me how to put a Mae West on, and how embarrassed he was when he realized who I was. We were all in civvies. We got to pal it up a little on the first couple of flights, and I was impressed. A real pro, that guy."

"Well", she started, looking at her notes. "Aviation Machinist's Mate First Class, born 1921—he's 34 next week—enlisted at 20, December '41. Born and raised in Idaho, orphaned at eleven, bounced through - - looks like a kindly but not overly progressive Foster Care system, cowboying until Pearl Harbor changed his world, opening up that vast unknown expanse beyond the borders of Ada County and the City of Boise. Crewed as an in-flight seaplane-mechanic during the war on 'splash boats' as they called them, working in squadrons off Seaplane Tenders in the Pacific, servicing and fixing and later flying as Plane Captain—there's that term again - in the old PBY Catalina. After the war, stayed in the Navy and as the PBM Mariners replaced the Catalinas, moved up into the newer aircraft and by 1950 he's a Mariner Plane Captain. Looks like he grabbed a chance to take a Shore Duty tour with the Martin Company in Baltimore helping accept and certify newly manufactured Mariners before you got him in the Beast program.

"You did, didn't you?". She averted his eye, and went on, as if to herself, "Why do I think you know more about these birds than I do after soul kissing their records for the last two days?"

No response, reaction or denial from the Captain.

"Anyway" she continued, flipping more notes.

"He was an Aviation Machinist's Mate First Class on flight skins - extra flight pay as you know, on shore duty there in B'more when I guess he and Lucore teamed up in the Beast program. Lucore's the next senior guy, the Ordnanceman. He's next.

"Anyway, Timmons goes on to distinguish himself on every evaluation in his jacket. Lives with his wife and kids in a Quonset hut on the Base there in North Africa. Met her at Martin, she was in Base security, brother's a Baltimore detective, father was a cop. He's recommended for re-enlistment and—this is curious—for advancement to Chief, but he's never taken the Chief's exam. Nothing there, Sir, that I can tell."

Reading again—

James Vincent Lucore, 30 - Ordnanceman
Aviation Ordnanceman First Class
Born 1925 Bronx, New York Enlisted, 1943

"The gun guy, and apparently the Purser and the Cook and the general chief -of the-enlisted -staff, as best I can make out from the commendatory notes people have written about him, is James Vincent Lucore, age 30—no 31, birthday this month too, Aviation Ordnanceman First Class, born 1925, Bronx, New York, Enlisted, 1943. Looks like he may have been dumped on the Navy by the Municipal Court system in New York—some judge signed as his guardian when he joined up—but he's got one of those standout, walk-on-water records too.

"Had a ball turret in a TBM in the big war, 62 carrier sorties under his belt and a snoot full of cordite. Looks like he learned fast, worked hard, took every opportunity to exercise his craft, first as a ship's company in *Oriskany*, then back aboard during two F9 squadron tours off Korea, making First Class Aviation Ordnanceman in July, 1953. He's got a Master Ordnanceman and Armorer Navy Enlisted Classification Code. He had a short shot at training duty at the Technical Training Center in Memphis, as an Instructor in Aircraft Recognition, but somebody must have pulled strings because he got two Changes of Station in one year to get him to Martin for the Beast project."

"Yeah," Winnie Barnet said, "I remember that. I remember him, too."

"Well?" She waited for him to say something, but he just yawned.

"How about some chow, it's supper time."

"Nothing here in the building but the mobile caterer truck—the beloved Roach Coach—comes by around seven down in the back by the gas pumps and we can grab something. If you'd have let me known, I could have had something run in for us."

"It wasn't that kind of a day, believe me," he said, cryptically. "Okay, let's do it," he decided, looking at his watch. "I need some munchies."

They left everything on the table and locked the door.

And so with full knowledge that they had the rest of the crew to get through tonight, they went downstairs to seek out the Mobile Canteen, the corridors that once led between sitting and dining rooms now darkened in the former mansion. It was difficult to ignore the number of pots of midnight oil being burned here and there. Elsewhere in Washington, she knew that other offices in other buildings were also lighted and occupied by bureaucrats adding their share to the paperwork that kept the nation afloat or by insecure underlings, each unwilling to leave while the Boss was still in his office, practicing the age-old sport of competitive late-staying.

At Nebraska Avenue, there were no hours to keep. The job to be done wouldn't keep either.

8

It was actually warm enough to rain in Washington, just barely, although the piles of crystallizing melting snow left here and there by the plows kept the air damp enough and chilly enough to discourage anyone getting a jump on the season. It wasn't even winter yet, the solstice not until next week. It was dark and yucky around the Roach Coach, Jennifer decided, and they both were only too happy to carry the brown sack of hamburgers, cokes and twinkies back up to the office and eat in warmth, if not in style.

"Next?" he asked, chewing.

Lyle (n) Burdick, 40 - Radio
Aviation Radioman First Class
Born 1915 Tulsa, OK Enlisted 1937

"Aviation Radioman First Class Lyle Anthony Burdick, the only one in the lot who comes with a National Agency Check report and a Security Advisory letter written after his Top Secret clearance was updated."

"Trouble?" he asked with a frown, more interested than before, absorbed.

"Not exactly. The clearance is good, the data on the bitch sheet is a record of a conversation the updating agent had with one of the references Burdick had given on his form."

"What's it about?"

"Well, as best I can piece together, here's the story. He was born in 1915 in Tulsa, OK, and that makes him the oldest enlisted guy in the aircraft at 40. He is one of that small group of U.S. military personnel—we all know people like him—who, following World War II, deliberately expatriated themselves. Some Army types did it in Germany, where the cheap Deutchmark and the fantastic bargains persuaded them to jiggle and juggle their career to get consecutive assignments in Bavaria. They eventually retire in-place to live like kings, until the German economy seems to be catching up, forcing them back home to less than regal reality. Some marry overseas and make comfortable second careers in Europe, and to a lesser extent, in Japan and the Philippines.

"The 'source' that this guy quotes must have been one of Burdick's sidekicks, because the writeup is remarkably detailed. Part of this I have to read, so bear with me.

"Burdick had first come to Morocco in 1949 when the American base opened, and he set himself up permanently in a small villa with day-servants eager to work for the embarrassingly low wages even an American enlisted man could pay. His wife worked as a secretary on base, and living was easy and effortless, if you didn't mind a certain amount of political upheaval and the lack of some stateside amenities. When his overseas tour expired, he was able to reenlist on-site for the 'duty of his choice,' which happened to be the permanently assigned Transport Squadron based there.

"In 1953, the Transport tour ended but Lyle Burdick was a politician and, by this time, one of the longest continuous American residents in the region. He played golf with his French landlord, cultivated friendships among the tiny group of Moroccan elites who were shopkeepers and businessmen, and became a pillar of strength to his Navy superiors who could always count on Burdick to 'Get Things Done'...in capitals, by the way, and I'm quoting.

"He persuaded the local Operations Officer, who at that time was gearing up to receive the first Beast, that someone with his unique knowledge of Mediterranean communications could and would be an invaluable asset to the new Unit and he was right. The Navy looked at the deal benignly as a great way to save moving and relocation costs and made it happen. When the first Beast arrived and was assigned to the Air Facility before the Unit was established, Burdick was on hand as the Radioman of choice starting his third tour of duty in the same place. People did it in San Diego and Norfolk and Pensacola, he reasoned, why not in Morocco?

"And it was a good choice. With almost five years of experience handling the crazy-to-hell radio communications common throughout Europe and the Mediterranean, Burdick was a godsend. He was in his late thirties and, as a First Class Aviation Radioman, a dying breed. Radios are modernizing, teletype and radiotelephone are replacing the operator and the Morse code data-rate is simply unsatisfactory for modern warfare. Their specialty is on its last legs and he and the other Aviation Radiomen in the Navy have been told to transition to something else by January 1, 1957 or face permanent pay-grade lock. We all know about that around here—we were in on the decision, remember?

"Burdick apparently resented change - the phonetic alphabet was changing, they were trying to change cycles to hertz, Centigrade was trying to become Celsius and 1957 seemed like a good date, a long way off. He knew that by then he and Dodi would be in an ideal position to come back home with only one four year tour left before 20 year retirement. If he did nothing, he would still be a First Class Aviation Radioman for one more tour—they couldn't fire him—and then he'd be retired for life.

"Well, he began to gather feathers for the nest. The source says it was his love for strong cigarettes that got him started. Monsieur Pierre Aujoulet, his landlord, owned the local racecourse and smoked Gauloises, to which Petty Officer Burdick had taken a fancy. He would swap Luckies for the blue wrapped packs of French coffin nails and before long, other Navy Exchange commodities of interest to Pierre. He would pay $1.25 in Military Payment Certificates for a carton of Luckies—green dollars were forbidden because of the black market—and was soon amazed and delighted at the barter exchange rate possible.

"With a monthly purchase allowance of eight cartons between them, he and Dodi branched out at the request of his local friends who were delighted to have access to brands on demand. Payment was usually in goods, which at first he did not appreciate, but once he saw the resale potential in the camel saddles and inlaid boxes and throw rugs, things changed.

"Soon he began to amass items of aesthetic value and in arrangement with an old retired friend in Norfolk, he was able to barter on order. Meanwhile, once he began to fly with the Transport Squadron throughout Europe supporting the Sixth Fleet, European currencies became the Luckies. By arranging to receive his pay and his now sizable monthly per-diem every two weeks in a US Treasury check—perfectly legal—he could parlay the dollar instrument first into D-marks, then into Lira, and eventually back into Moroccan francs at a thirty percent markup. By the end of 1953, he was the man to contact if you wanted something or needed *flouss*, the Arabic word for money."

"And…go on."

"That's it. The date on the source interview is last year and the statement is submitted by the Security folks to the Commanding Officer, as you know, for the CO is the judge in either extending or canceling his clearance. Happens every five years in the Fleet, again, as you know." She almost blushed.

"Oops, sorry, if I remember correctly, you wrote that directive yourself."

He laughed, good-naturedly. "I did, didn't I. Anyway, this thing seems to have worked the way it was intended. His Commanding Officer knows that he dabbles in the black market, but I guess everyone in Port Lyautey knows that, too. It's a tribute to his professional skill, I guess, that the skipper continued his clearance, so I guess we can assume that he either was told to cut it out or the skipper already knew all about it and let it go.

"Let me think about this one awhile, but I don't think we have a problem with Lyle Burdick."

"Don't tell me you know him, too?"

"Sure I do. He got a camel-saddle for me once, from Morocco. Cheap."

"And?"

"He's an asshole but he's not a leaker. Values his butt too highly."

"Well, that does it for him."

"Now.

Earl (n) White, 25 - Electrician
Aviation Electrician's Mate Second Class
Born 1930 Maynard, MA Enlisted 1951

Daryl Tubman Black 25 - Radar
Aviation Electronics Technician Second Class
Born 1930 Birmingham, AL Enlisted 1951

"Next two are the two Second Class—White and Black, and as you can see by the pictures" - and she slid them to him across the table - "they are appropriately named. Earl no-middle White is 25, born 1930, Maynard, Mass, Aviation Electrician's Mate Second Class. His buddy, roommate and chief competitor for sailor of the century is Daryl Tubman Black, also 25, also born 1930 but not in Massachusetts—Birmingham, Alabama. Grand- maybe-Great-Grand- son of slaves, I would calculate, but he's come a long way.

"White's older by a couple of months, clean cut as you can see, ruddy complexion, reddish brown hair, deep set eyes and a good athlete. His Dad was an electrician in Maynard, Massachusetts, and I guess it was assumed that Earl would simply take over the business one day. When the Korean draft started getting close, Earl enlisted in the Navy and his four-year enlistment is up in July. He's been around electricians from the baby carriage and he aced Aviation Electrician Mate's Class A School after boot camp. He was hand-picked for Beast duty, he's been in Morocco for the whole of his enlistment and he's about ready to get out and go home. He made Second Class on time and he says in his letter request for extension to allow him to take the first class test, that if he doesn't make first he's looking forward to the GI Bill, possibly at MIT.

"Black's enlistment expired this past August, and he has a two-year extension agreement to set him up to take the First Class exam next June. In his letter, he says If he passes it, he'll reenlist for his choice of duty and try to get into the Aviation Fire Control field, which he seems to assume has something to do with the Mickey gang in the back end of the aircraft. It doesn't of course, but if he doesn't pass, he'd probably get out and go back to school too.

"Here, you can leaf through these notes if you want, but there's nothing there and it's probably a waste of time. How about the officers?"

"I spent the day all over town and in the Pentagon shaking trees. I don't think anything we can lay our hands on is going to change the situation on the ground out there one bit. I hate to tell you, but nothing either of us turned up bears on what the fuss is all about. I was slightly interested in the Burdick stuff, not that I didn't know most of it but because I hadn't realized it was on paper."

He looked at his watch and his mood changed.

"Oh, what's the hour? We have a big day tomorrow!"

"I thought I had tomorrow off," she said, puzzled.

"I forgot—and so did you, I guess. Tomorrow's the fifteenth. Ring a bell? Advancement in rate ceremony? First Class Petty Officer? Pay Raise? Eligible for Limited Duty Officer program? Remember?"

Of course she did, now that he brought it up!

They'd both have to be there, she to receive the official paperwork, the ceremonial handshake and the official photograph, he to make the presentation to her and all the other newly rated sailors at Nebraska Avenue. Thank God she had gotten her uniform cleaned and restriped with her new rating badge!

"Well, I can't say you didn't do one hell of a job getting all this stuff together, but let's wrap it and lock up. It's getting pretty late for a work night. Got a way home?" They were cleaning up what little mess they had made, putting papers away, closing blinds and turning off lights.

"Yes, sir, the busses run all night. My buddy, Jason, the guy from the Teletype Repair shop, has the Watch on the desk until 11:45 and he lives out by me so he might be worth a try. I may have to flirt with him, though, and that's a pain."

On the way down the darkened staircase, her mind still on the day's work, she asked him again.

"And the officers?"

"Well," he began, "there's nothing here that is any more valuable than the enlisted stuff you got and the material on our own guys in the back end. Either he or they keep their tracks very well covered, which may be the case, or there's nothing to any of this."

"But who?" she asked. They had reached the outer door.

"You decide," he said, and he started to recap his day's work for her.

She was fascinated, and they stood in the drizzle until it turned icy, and then they went back inside and upstairs, and Winnie used Jennifer as a sounding board.

They were in his outer office, an anteroom where visitors waited before keeping appointments with the Director. The process of winding through to this room was circuitous, determined by the geometry of the old building. To get this far, one had to pass from Jennifer's anteroom through her office, thence closer to the throne under her approving gaze. Entrance to her anteroom was controlled by the Chief Yeoman, the Director's "writer" to use the old Navy term, who held sway at the intersection of the Director's series of connected warrens and the Deputy's arrangement to the other side.

The Chief was a "general service" guy, not a member of the spook community, and everyone wondered how he would get along with the Director's Assistant—two grades junior to him—but Jennifer handled him so well that one would think they were litter mates. They had taken turns one day, the four of them, trying to imagine what purpose each of the interconnected rooms had served in the heyday of the mansion. Jennifer kept meaning to dig up whatever old blueprints were around but they never seemed to get it settled and they lost interest. But the anteroom had easy chairs, a coffee table and a floor lamp that lighted from the wall switch, so they settled in.

Winnie was tired. He was at the top of his game, pulling wires, moving pieces, taking risks, trading information, rumor, scandal and innuendo in what was the biggest gamble of his riverboat career, but he was still bone tired. A serial monogamist bachelor, the Captain had the enormous good fortune of never having given anyone who knew him the slightest reason to believe he had harmed, embarrassed, belittled or offended them. He had, of course, but that was his good fortune.

He had asked to have Jennifer assigned to him when he was appointed Director. The Table of Organization allowed him an officer Special Assistant, but Winnie knew everyone in the community by that time, and could have had Lord Nelson as his Assistant had the old Brit been alive and a member of the "Special Duty" gang.

He had chosen Jennifer, carefully. He had watched her in action ever since Shemya, later in a tricky show in Greece when she had been under his command, and he knew her contacts, knew she had languages, and knew her way with difficult colleagues would make his job easier. One of these days he would tell her that he had quietly but forcefully recommended her for one of the new Limited Duty Officer slots becoming available to the community. That could wait. It might piss off some young hotshots here and there ("a woman for Chrissake!") but she could handle it.

"I'm not concerned about Kerrigan, even though he and Hunley are the two of the four I don't know. With Pluto, that would make five, wouldn't it, but Pluto's not a problem. Even these two aren't, you know, because they're random choices for this trip."

Jennifer wondered for a minute what that had to do with it, then realized he was looking for some thread that tied one of the officer or enlisted men to a series of encounters with persons or things in Nicosia.

"Kerrigan is a young nugget, a newly designated pilot who gets to carry the Navigation bag for a year and a half or so in one of these multi-engine squadrons before they let him into the cockpit on an Operational. He's bright, a new husband, spent a year or so at sea before he went to flight training, and folks like him. Even the white hats, the enlisted men, get along with him well and respect him, no small job. He's straight arrow, although the fleshpots of Nicosia are beginning to be attractive to him and his newlywed eye is beginning to stray."

Jennifer wondered how he knew.

"Hunley is a relatively old timer, something of a politician, not terribly good as a pilot but not bad, either. Working on a Ph.D. in international law—law of the air, actually—now a recalled reservist doing his time. Seems to have died and gone to heaven in this job. He and his wife—no kids—travel a lot and have a grand old time when he's not off in Cyprus. Sticks to himself, drinks more than he should, but not willing, much less able, to exert himself to the extent of getting into any trouble."

Where, she wondered again, did that come from? Nothing like that was in any personnel jacket she had ever seen.

There was more. It was coming. She had to let him get around to it.

9

Nicosia

Aviation Radioman First Class Lyle Burdick usually slept all afternoon in Nicosia if he had a flight that night. He was used to unusual hours, and Dodi had made such a fuss about the damn tapestries that he didn't want to disappoint her. So, since he didn't want to change his schedule even a little, he got up at seven thirty and backing things off from tonight's seven-or-thereabouts briefing, he planned to get his business done and be back in the sack for his afternoon snooze. No changes needed.

This Thursday morning, he had indulged himself with the "Hot English Breakfast (Meat Extra 2 shillings)" at the Sylvan, enjoyed it, and afterward, had sat in the Lounge smoking a Gaulois, a three week old onion-skin air-mail London Times in his lap, crossword up. Finally, hopelessly stumped, he went up to the room, unpacked his cream Palm Beach from the suit bag he always carried on trips - to the amusement and disdain of the rest of the crew - and dressed. From the black and white wingtips to the English scarf cravat looped with studied carelessness at his throat, the image in the lobby full-length mirror pleased him, the sunglasses giving just the right tone of sophistication and mystery.

He checked to make sure that the long strands covered the bald spot. There was a chill in the air but he'd manage without a sweater or a jacket, no sense spoiling the image.

Dimos got him a cab into town and he got out at the Square. He planned to walk up—or was it down—Ledra Street until he found what he was looking for. He did not have an exact address, but with more difficulty than he had anticipated, he had found the shop. It wasn't on Ledra Street at all, but in the side street, one of those half cul-de-sacs that have been around since the twelfth century and are so difficult to find in the old city. He had almost missed it. Ledra Street, the main "downtown" shopping street—the "high street" the Brits called it—was in the throes of the Cypriot Christmas season, if you could call it that.

Burdick was probably the only crewman who had ever really seen Nicosia in the daytime. He had been here in April just after the radio station had been blown up, and during the summer, each of his trips so arranged that they flew nights, slept days, and then went back home. In October, he had been downtown, but only briefly. At night, the officers all went to the Chanticleer and everybody else hung around the Sylvan. Except, of course, when they wanted to see their buddy, Nikki.

It was different now from the way it had been in October.

The Field Marshall—what was his name, Harding, he thought—had just been sent in to run the place and there was a lot of confusion and hassle. The Turks were very upset with the Greeks and the crew had to stay away from downtown. This time, things seemed a lot quieter, although he noticed an abundance of what seemed like British police on the street, and the soldiers he saw in town were armed and in battle gear.

Here, almost smart-looking plate-glass display windows fronted on a street on which every other establishment seemed to be a canvas-covered stall with goods haphazardly heaped on crates and boxes to form rudimentary displays.

A jewelry store with an unlighted neon Rolex logo sat between a shop crammed with sullen Turkish men smoking and sipping thick, sweet coffee and what looked like a real estate office, except that instead of displaying even a semblance of business interest, three small boys chased each other in and out while a middle-aged Greek woman shouted at them. As with everything else on Cyprus, the shops had three distinct constituencies, each living together—"coexisting" came to mind - in the most fragile of balances. There was a charge in the air.

Christmas was coming, and he wondered if it had something to do with Christmas, although he had seen the EOKA banners before and had been told that they were political. The present-giving part was over, he remembered, they had that in early December. At Christmas, the Christian ethnic majority, predominantly Orthodox of the Greek or Cypriot variety, observed their "Christougenna" as a family celebration. As he understood it, the kids went around from door to door singing songs and the families burned incense to keep away the elves who were supposed to prowl around the countryside. The stores carried decorations alluding to the custom, but one had to be in on it to recognize the variations in the storefronts.

He noticed a cross decorated with basil in a number of spots, a certain harbinger of Christmas. For the small minority of Western Europeans, mainly British, the stores imported red and green decorations with abundant nice-try cartoons of Father Christmas and Pere Noel, with even a Santa Claus and a recognizable Saint Nicholas here and there along the street. The large Turkish minority seemed merely to ignore the whole thing and went about their business cursing the Greeks, who went about their business cursing both the Turks and the British.

Peace on Earth, Cyprus style.

This time, it seemed that every day was some kind of a Greek holiday - Greek flags were draped all over the place, every other building seemed to have something Greek to celebrate, light blue and white bunting here and there along the street.

He had gone north from the square, almost missing the sharp right, but when he had made the turn and saw Phaneromeni, he fixed his position sufficiently to realize he was where he should have been. Thank God for the smaller Roman alphabetization beneath the Greek inscription on the street sign. The establishment fit in with the elegant shops up and down Ledra Street, smaller than he had expected but that was OK. No Christmas decorations. Early as it was, it was lighted inside but he when he stopped, he was able to examine and approve of his reflection in the plate glass window.

Instead of Jennifer Howell, Lyle Burdick could have gone on the stateside TV show, "What's My Line" and fooled them all—the last thing he looked like was an American sailor. Then again, he did not look quite the boulevardier he fancied he saw reflected in the shop window, either. The wing-tips.

In recent months, he had branched out into the occasional commercial-volume shipment, and he knew how to manipulate currencies to maximize profits over and above the markup. What he couldn't arrange to have mailed or shipped, his Transport Squadron connections enabled his buddies to carry back to friends and relatives on the East Coast who first benefited from his largess and then became virtual commercial outlets. His ham radio rig, carefully constructed of the finest German components, helped immeasurably and a network of contacts, some of whom he had met, some not, kept him abreast of the both the market and the opportunities.

Perfume and scarves from Morocco first, benefit of the French Moroccan franc. Soon, Turkish jewelry, benefit of the inflated 18-1 dollar-lire exchange rate for US servicemen. Copperware washed in silver and tin from Lebanon, camel saddles from Libya and Morocco, leather handbags, hassocks and pouches from Tangier, women's shoes…all small stuff until his British European Airways connection materialized in the bar at the Continental Hotel in Naples one evening, and the music began in earnest. The shopping trip this morning off Ledra Street was simply a chorus in this latest melody.

The outside appearance of the tiny shop hardly conveyed richness and elegance, but once inside, even the dimmest light could hardly conceal the breathtaking artistry of the wall hangings strewn about inside like so much dirty laundry. The small space smelled of freshly brewed coffee newly purchased from around the corner, sandalwood, henna dye and musk. A small butane heater shaped like a radar antenna sputtered in the center of the tiny room, perched on a packing crate, its red rubber hose snaked through the handle of the crate to its potbellied Butagaz cylinder. The heater brought carbon monoxide to the party, accentuating the odors, and from the reddish glow of its center cone, Burdick could make out the proprietor sitting behind a tiny desk on a stool that might have come from a child's toy set, except for its patina of age and elegance. He was finishing a tiny cup of gooey coffee, washing it down with a tumbler of clear water as he rose to greet the customer.

They had met before, and Burdick was here to do business, but formal reintroductions were in order and Loumides wanted to size the mark up in his own surroundings. Loumides was interested.

The American was dressed expensively, if a bit overly "sharp" for a morning outing on Ledra Street. The black and white wing tips amused rather than dismayed him, but he had dealt with "Mr. Collins" several times—never at the store before today - and found him to be somewhat more multi-dimensional than the Ugly American whose image he resembled. Loumides' had exquisite taste, as might be expected of one who, in a childhood now years past, had spent part of each summer in Monte Carlo and whose parents "holdings" once included homes in Vevey and Beirut. He had not become a bankroll by dealing with Armenians and Turks and Lebanese he couldn't outsmart. He was in his element.

Burdick's ability to put cash, in a variety of flavors and colors, precisely where his mouth was, served him well in their dealings. He inspected several piles of "sample" merchandise, marveling at the workmanship and the beauty of the now-fashionable wall hangings. Two rounds of Cyprus coffee into the morning, with the mandatory glass of cold water, following an extensive lecture on the folly of the Greek, British and Turkish positions in the "Cyprus" question (each side was impeding free trade), they shook hands on a deal.

British European Airways would arrange to have ten dozen meter-square tapestries picked up for three hundred sterling, consigned to Gibraltar. Sterling area transshipments were no problem. Burdick was already committed to provide them to his "holder" in Gibraltar for transshipment, via Navy C-54, to Norfolk, Virginia. His arrangement with the retired Chief Petty Officer, with whom he now dealt in Norfolk, would net him, after the BEA split, just under $62 each, deposited into Dodi's account in the Barnett National Bank in Jacksonville.

For his part, Lyle Burdick was beginning to get cold feet, despite Dodi's assurances that their schemes were foolproof. If this third transaction via his BEA pal came—somehow—to the attention of any of a growing number of possibly interested parties, the consequences would be enormous. Customs inquiries would likely trigger Naval Investigative Service interest and the first thing to go, surely, would be his Top Secret clearance. He had already had his chat with the skipper, but since the skipper was one of his customers, he had discounted its seriousness. Without a clearance, he was, for all intents and purposes, out of a job. Everyone associated with the Beast had to have at least a Secret clearance, and flight crews were cleared further before they even got near the bird. He would have to be so careful from here on out.

In fact, it was probably too late.

A Kodak Special f2.8 camera, an older, reliable machine with a "nice piece of glass up front," which had gone missing from the Hotel Grande Bretagne on Syntagma Square in Athens several years ago might be his undoing. Behind the oversized ornamental tapestry draped over the entryway to the rear of the store, it had just clicked off the eighth exposure on a twelve-shot roll of Agfa 828 film, and its owner was affluent enough to let the remaining four go.

When he left the shop, Petty Officer First Class Burdick did not know that both the handshake with which he had just sealed his deal and the cash he had counted out had been photographed; that people he did not know would shortly report, with some jubilation, a "transaction" with a Beast crewmember; and that the list of "interested parties" was far longer than he had imagined. He knew only enough to appreciate the goods he had just bought, and the value on his side of the ledger.

But so did Loumides.

He penciled in the £300, which would cover a shockingly small number of Imperial gallons of Esso Extra Aviation Grade 115-145, plus the "fee," and placed a call to his wife's nephew at work.

When Niarchos answered, he placed his order for the following week and treated himself, finally, to a cup of the thick, syrupy Turkish coffee he preferred, warming on the hotplate. Cypriot coffee for business, Turk for pleasure. The only thing the Turks were good for was their damn coffee. To celebrate, he poured a gill of Keo into the larger carafe and summoned Lera from the back room.

"Any problem?" he asked.

"No problem," she answered, showing him the roll. She was smiling faintly. He could never figure Lera out, despite the fact that she had worked for him for three years now and every once in awhile gave him what he wanted. One side of her family had some Turkish connections, relatives someplace he thought, but she never spoke of them any more.

Burdick left the store and retraced his steps back down Ledra Street. He window-shopped until the stores closed around twelve-thirty, then he had lunch and a beer at an outside table at the Metropole. Up the street, there was a smattering of activity by the British Institute, and he counted several jeep-loads of Tommys coming and going until he realized that he was counting the same jeep over and over. Must be something up, he thought, but promptly at two, he strolled back the other way and found the entrance he knew was around here someplace.

Inside the Telephone Exchange, he told the operator what he wanted and sat down for the inevitable wait. By the time he was summoned to the booth, perhaps forty-five minutes later, his stomach was churning and he was positive he would never smoke another Gaulois as long as he lived. At two in the afternoon, it was seven in the morning in Norfolk. The thirty-seven second fade-in fade-out conversation, once the relays through Athens, Rome, and New York were fully patched and tagged in, cost five pounds, eleven shillings and eight pence.

The cost of doing business. Well, part of it, anyway.

In the taxi back to the Sylvan, he relaxed and began to think of the flight. Lyle Burdick could switch personas easily, and the transition from rugs to radios was seamless.

His equipment was all "up", fully operable when they landed and should be in good shape for tonight. Air Traffic Control Radio communications throughout the Mediterranean and Southern Europe ware conducted over high-frequency voice circuits, temperamental, weather dependent, tricky to hold on frequency and close to saturation as air travel increased. Single-sideband technology was available, but it would be years before air carriers and traffic control centers made the substantial investment to convert. With nobody yet to talk to, few Navy aircraft had the Collins SSB equipment installed.

Instead, all long range air to ground communication, other than line-of-sight VHF tower and local airways traffic was conducted on one of three or four very crowded voice frequencies. Everyone's favorite was 5551.5 kilocycles, and the radioman's job in the Beast was to make sure that when the co-pilot had a position report to make, the frequency was up and operating. Newly built ground based air traffic control radars in Europe made tracking over-land flights simple, but the long over water stretches and any flights out here required the pilot to tell ATC radio controllers where he thought he was, not the other way around.

The nature of Beastdom, however, was such that half of their flights were conducted off airways, out of civilized radar range, off clearance, off the face of the earth, keeping contact only with military authorities of one kind or another in case of emergency and upon mission completion. For this purpose, Morse keying of continuous wave carrier frequencies (dots and dashes to the layman) was ideal for cutting through the static and the garble and the ionic disturbances to get the message across. Far more effective than the voice microphone in this environment was the hand on the key, and Burdick had a master's hand. It was both a dying art and a dying business, the buggy whip in a gasoline age, but while there was a single buggy around, he would have a job.

Tonight, he would probably be busy, although if all went well, there would be no radio transmission from the aircraft during the entire flight. He would be listening and monitoring all the usual frequencies, but the aircraft would be silent. The thrill of anticipation he always got before an operational mission shoved the apprehension he had experienced earlier to the back of his mind. After he paid off the taxi, he untied the cravat from around his neck, put it in his pocket, and joined the others at the bar, but not before he reclaimed his London Times from the table where he had left it.

He liked most of the crew, although he knew that while they respected him, few were inclined to be buddy-buddy with a guy who had eight or ten years on them.

For their part, when they had their backbiting sessions, age never entered into it. If it wasn't the suit bag, it was always those goddamn black and white wingtips.

That's the way sailors are.

10

When Lucore left the others at the bar to join Timmons, Earl White, Aviation Electrician's Mate Second Class, put down his beer—Lowenbrau, which he could get at the Sylvan only occasionally—looked Aviation Electronics Technician Second Class Daryl Black squarely in the eye and in an unrecognizable but originally ersatz accent, answered "*A quel heure commence le cinema?*"

Then he took a sip, turned back quickly, squinted and said "Portugese"

"*Em que hora o filme começa?* German."

"*Zu welcher zeit beginnt der filme?* Iclandic."

Black thought a minute, and lowered his head. "*Hvenaer…*" he began, then "…I forget," he said, in that little small voice he used when you had him so cold that begged for mercy.

White was triumphant.

He opened his mouth to spout the Icelandic phrase—*he* knew it - for "What time does the movie start?" when he saw Lucore, looking out into the foyer, push his beer aside and get up to go. He turned his wrist over—he always wore his watch on the inside of his wrist—and was surprised that it was as early as it was with the sun going down, and all.

Black decided to ride him. "Why the hell don't you wear your watch like everybody else? You always look like a queer."

If anyone in the world was familiar with Earl White's sexual orientation, it was Daryl, since not only were they best friends, but back in Morocco, they were roommates—along with four other Beasties—in an old farm building just south of town. The rent was cheap, the sofa came out of an old Citroen bus, and the landlord was still hiding from the Germans and figured the Americans were good insurance. It was a "snake ranch" in the parlance of the bachelor sailor, but there hadn't been many "snakes" interested in paying them visits.

White would have none of it.

"You got to take this thing more seriously. I beat you every day!" He turned back to his beer in mock disgust.

Sitting bored in a bar in Rabat one night last week, they had discussed the fact that on long transits out to Nick, neither of them really had a lot to do. Black operated the APS-33 navigational radar in the Beast and as an Aviation Electronics Technician, was technically responsible for the repair and upkeep of anything electronic forward of the wing spar. The Mickey guys in the back broke and fixed their own gear. Other than the radar itself, which Blackie kept in perfect condition, given the limits of the equipment, his charter extended to the radios and radar altimeters as well, but with Lyle Burdick in the crew, nobody dared touch one of his precious radios. And with Mr. Kerrigan on board, who liked to take his own fixes and plot his own bearings off the radar repeater at the Navigation table, there wasn't much operating to do either.

White usually had time on his hands in flight too. The Beast was an exquisitely designed aircraft, decades ahead of its time in every respect. It was powered by two huge reciprocating engines in nacelles on its mid-place wing, and hidden in the nacelles were two great J-33 centrifugal flow jet engines. To start the jet engines in flight, a lot of electrical power had to be available—they were not used for normal cruise—and the Martin engineers had designed a "monitored" system that automatically took electrical loads off the line when the demands were large and monitored the load status continuously throughout each stage of flight. To do this, the typical 28 volt Direct Current aircraft system never would have worked, so the engines had alternators, rather than generators. They made Alternating Current—AC - power out in the nacelles, and the AC then was rectified inside the aircraft into 28 volt DC needed for typical aircraft functions, but there was always AC available for some of the more sophisticated applications inside. Because of this complexity, each operational crew flew with an Aviation Electrician's mate assigned, and White was one of the best.

The bad news was that the alternators took their rotational energy from the main crankshaft of the huge engines via a 45 degree takeoff shaft—the quill shaft—and try as the engineers might, they had never come up with a shaft that would sustain the twisting shear of a backfire on engine startup. For this reason, only the Plane Captains started the engines—pilots weren't welcome in the cockpit until the engines were started—and every Plane Captain carried as many extra quill shafts with him as he could scrounge -*cumshaw* in Navy lingo - outside the Supply System, The Electricians traditionally helped the Ordnanceman when they weren't busy tinkering with instruments and lights and compasses—which was most of the time.

Except when the guns were in. On these operationals, the Electrician manned the forward turret and Lucore had deputized White to enter the World of Ordnance only after hours of indoctrination, check-out, blindfold drills and practice flights out into the Atlantic.

But both Black and White still had time on their hands.

"We should learn a language". Blackie had said, and the two brainy sailors looked at each other with a mixture of skeptical interest, amusement and trepidation, because brainy as they were, they were both constitutionally lazier than they seemed.

"What language?" White asked.

It was obvious to both of them that a working knowledge - or even a smattering—or either French or Arabic would make their current lives far more pleasant, but both of those prospects sounded…well, too much like work.

They thought a minute, then White had an idea.

"Suppose," he began, "just suppose - - that instead of learning one language - - we learned one sentence in as many languages as we could."

When they got done giggling, at first, then belly laughing at the sheer goofiness of the idea, they had thought it over and White had picked up the ball again.

"Let's pick a phrase—how about 'Would you like to shack up with me?'—and we'll learn it in every language there is."

It was a gas, but as with every inspired brainstorm, there was a problem. Eventually, persuaded that "shack up with me" was an uncommon expression not readily translated exactly, particularly in the GI language pamphlets they would be consulting, they had settled on "What time does the movie start?" and so it began.

Neither of them devoted much time to the project, but they did interrogate one another and kept a rudimentary score. White had a leg up, since he had gathered a collection of pocket language guides he refused to share with his buddy. Black knew where he kept them at the ranch and had secretly gone through them and written down what he needed.

Nobody on the crew ever seemed to notice that Black was "colored", although of course they did.

He had to work a little harder, maybe, and watch his manners a little more than the others, but he felt at home in the crew and at home in the Squadron, better off working overseas than back in the States. He wore his hair short, accentuating his pitch-black complexion and his Negroid features, but his French girlfriend Jeanine never seemed to mind. He had entered the Navy unaware of his near genius IQ, a product of Alabama schools and Alabama culture. All his life he had been interested in cars, in vehicles, in tractors and forklifts and steam-rollers and anything that he could drive and feel and manipulate. When the Classifier in boot camp asked him what he thought he might be able to do in the Navy, he had immediately jumped at the chance that someday he might drive a fork-lift. But the Classifier, a first class Personnelman, was older and wiser and, dazzled by his test scores, put him on the fast track for aviation and electronics. There were few enough "colored" Personnelmen like himself, and by God, he was going to make sure that someday there would be more than a handful of "colored" Aviation Electronics Technicians.

Black hated the segregated south where he had grown up, and although he had an extended family in Birmingham, he had his eye on CalTech if he could get in.

This afternoon as they nursed their beers, Burdick was sitting at the far end of the bar in suit jacket, open neck dress shirt and black and white wingtips. He was working a limey crossword puzzle from what looked like a World War II newspaper, and he also looked up when Lucore left.

You couldn't warm up to Burdick, he was so damn superior. He knew everything there was to know about the radios and could get through on the air with anything, whenever they needed it, but he always acted like he was in business for himself and being with you was like taking his time from something else. He was way older than the others, almost forty they guessed. He really brownnosed the officers, Burdick did, and everyone else thought that was pretty silly because except for a couple of scumbag Nuggets who didn't know better, all the officers were square shooters who knew their stuff and gave fair shakes all around.

One Sunday morning, though, must have been a year ago because it was snowing, they had been coming out of Bulgaria where they all knew they had no business being but had to be anyway, when the Greek Air Force jumped them and forced them to land. The hadn't had the star showing on the Beast, and were all blue-black on the outside, so nobody blamed the Greeks, except that it had all been arranged beforehand and never should have happened. Anyway, there they were, way the hell up in the mountains of northern Greece in a frigging snowstorm and old Lyle gets on his key and sends "we been jumped" messages to Washington and London like he did it every day…then he gets on the Internal Communications System—the ICS - and tells the Pilot, "It's OK to land now, I got us taken care of." And he did.

By the time they landed, the message back from Washington to Athens to Larissa, Greece, was that the Royal Hellenic Air Force ought to go back to minding its business, as per prior arrangement. That got things shaken out on the ground and the guys were on their way by nightfall.

Never would have without Lyle.

When Lucore left with Timmons, Black and White finished their beers and had Dimos call them another cab. It was beginning to get dark.

They were relieved when it pulled up, an ancient Morris Minor driven by an elderly Cypriot with one of those funny Turkish knitted caps that they saw around town once in awhile. They each remembered the little lecture Mr. Elfers had given them on the ICS when they had left Malta, particularly about the cab driver what's-his-name who has the black Dodge. They took things like that extremely seriously, and although they had both ridden in the Dodge with Mikos a couple of times, they had no desire to ever see him again after the warning. The driver whined a little when they told him where they wanted to go, pleading roadblocks and checkpoints and congestion, but they offered a pound apiece for the eight-mile ride and he took them up on it.

They rode in silence. Or almost.

About a mile outside Paphos Gate, by a side road leading to a darkened village off to the right, they could see a Bren carrier fitted with floodlights. As they got closer, they saw that the lights were just beginning to cut through the lowering darkness, and a great deal of activity buzzed around the tracked vehicle. Uniformed troops and police were darting in and out of the buildings and on the main road, Tommys in helmets with carbines slung over their shoulders were directing traffic, keeping it moving through the intersection. There were red flares on the roadside. The civilians seemed to be worked up about something, and the two sailors gawked and rubbernecked as they passed by.

"What's that all about?" they asked the driver.

He spat out the window, and smiled a crooked little twisted grin, taking his eyes off the road to look at them both through the rear view mirror over the dash.

"Greek kids! Damn Greeks. Damn Grivas." He was vehement. "Soldiers caught a bunch of them going to blow up town tonight and killed one of them. Now they're going after the mommas and the daddies the guys that give them petrol and they ought to kill them too. Damn Greeks."

"Sounds like Birmingham" Blackie remarked. White chuckled.

But it upset both of them and when they pulled up at the NAAFI and paid the driver, they were glad to be inside and listening to music. They didn't need to be out to the plane for another forty five minutes—plenty of time—so they each had bacon and egg sandwiches on huge slabs of bread and cups of hot tea in horribly stained mugs. It was good, and cost them one and six each.

When they had finished, they walked over to the British Civil Air Ministry line- shack and asked for a ride out to the aircraft. There were two "milk wagons" parked side by side—a newer, light blue number with the RAF bull's-eye painted on each side, the other painted in the bland, faceless faded cream and maroon so common on the civil rolling stock in Nick.

They got into the cream truck and when the Cypriot driver came out, he drove them down the taxiway to the parked Beast. Nobody said a word.

11

Lieutenant (junior grade) Brian Kerrigan got up around four and took a shower, the tepid water dripping quickly rather than slowly showering, but he felt better when he toweled off and sat naked on the side of the bed.

The Acropole Hotel had seen better days, and the plumbing was barely ahead of the cistern-fed wash and flush water supply. It was still the classiest place around—shabby classy—and the officers always made it their home, base and headquarters in Nicosia. The pinkish-tan stucco walls enclosed a compound which had catered to the British and European trade since the first World War, changing little in the process save for the accretion of what Brian always thought of as a coat of British history, brown in color, which scraped off your armchair if you scratched it with a fingernail. When this business first started, conventional wisdom dictated that the officers and crew berth separately in Nick and though he had been invited over to the Sylvan Solace once for a drink, most of the officers agreed that it was preferable to keep their distance.

He kept his Navigation bag in his room, because he had wanted to do some pre-flighting before they flew, but yesterday's cancellation had left him with all his work done. Something must have gone wrong someplace, Brian figured, to have a working flight like this one cancelled.

Maybe it was on account of the Pluto guy.

He knew one had been promised but he hadn't shown up yet—a whole day later—and Mr. Elfers had remarked that they would be flying the cancelled track tonight, instead of the second one they had planned. Just as well, Brian though, because the second one was a "milk run" out to the west and he never could figure why they wasted their gas doing that track every couple of months. Anyway, it left him with the Nav Bag to baby-sit and he opened up the straps to see if he had forgotten anything.

It looked like the brown leather book-bag he hauled to high school every day. Now it held all his charts, the Air Almanac and HO214, the Celestial Almanac (in case he ever got them all so lost that they'd have to rely on celestial navigation to get them home), a set of European and North African En-route Supplements for radio navigation, four packs of the new Winston cigarettes, two sets of navigation instruments in their black pencil-boxes, two E6B plotters, a larger lap-plotter he had never used, a roll of masking tape to secure his charts to the navigation table, a black plastic parallel ruler set, a half dozen grease pencils and a red-lens flashlight. He also kept a divider, and a baby E6B in his flight suit along with an array of grease pencils—every color except red.

He had learned during his first week as a young officer aboard ship that anything you write on Plexiglas with a red grease pencil disappears at night when the red lights come on and everybody gets goosey about their night vision. Once, he had changed all the radio frequencies on the bridge of the jeep carrier he had been on, as he had been ordered, and had recorded the new frequencies in red grease pencil on their tags. When the red lights came on, they may as well have been marked in invisible ink and Kerrigan had paid dearly in prestige. He hadn't done it again. That's how you learn.

Their turn-points for tonight's flight were in his wallet, coded, but he knew them by heart now and would leave the wallet behind in the room and burn the scrap in the ashtray before he left. He lit a Winston, pleased that the new brand tasted as good as his Camels. With the filter, probably better for him—not that he worried about it. He unbuckled the strong leather straps and fished out the chart, checking it once more against his memorized list of points.

He had been careful not to put holes in the paper with the points of his divider when he had laid out the track. The thing would have been dynamite if anybody could have grabbed it with the points drawn in, or even suggested by pinholes. Even their habitually flagrant violation of the minutia in the Manual for Safeguarding Classified Material—operationally necessary when your headquarters is the Acropole Hotel in downtown Nicosia—would not have countenanced such a gross breach of National security, so instead, the points were on the back of a Navy Exchange Laundry chit in his wallet and that was somehow okay. Sure.

This track was a long east-to-west Black Sea transit, parallel to the north Turkish coast. It was less spectacularly provocative than others he had flown, once so far north as to actually glimpse the lights of Sevastopol before their turn-away. But in its early, extremely close approach to the Soviet Batumi area on the eastern shore, it promised to be as hairy as they come, certainly a night to remember.

He bundled the whole thing back up and got dressed, and carrying the bag as if it were a sample case, he walked down the corridor, growing darker now in the stolen light from the vestibule window, and rapped on Elfers' door. He thought he would be early but the guy was already there, a different guy this time, and as Lew introduced him to the Brit, Brian noticed the faint air of deference and respect with which the older man shook his hand. He never did catch his name but it probably wasn't his real name anyway, and Brian would get it again if they ever met. He was as close as faceless as anyone Brian had even encountered, slight and gray, part of the woodwork or the blinds or the tacky curtains, but surely not, Brian imagined, someone's father or lover.

In contrast, he could not help thinking how different Lew was. Just under six feet with closely cropped black hair and a square jaw that spoke volumes about determination and integrity, Lew was not east to forget. His eyes were brown, penetrating without being aggressive, totally focused on the speaker if he was listening, the listener if he was speaking. Lew was forgiving, funny, well-spoken, well read and one hell of a pilot.

He never could understand. This would be his ninth weather briefing in the Acropole Hotel by some RAF weather-guesser attached to what must be a pretty small weather outfit out here, and the same guy had never briefed them twice. Brian thought that the head Brit, whoever he was, would have assigned one guy to the job and the guy would have been read into the program and known want they wanted. Not so.

The Brits called them "Met" people, short for Meteorologists, and each time the Yanks were here, one of them was called into some office someplace, told to knock at a strange hotel door at four fifteen some afternoon and go through an exhaustive weather briefing of this whole part of the world.

Indian Ocean water temperatures and winds aloft over Nairobi, if you please. And oh yes, civilian clothes - "mufti" it would be - and don't tell your wife or we'll have to kill you.

All Brian wanted were winds aloft up to 15 thousand between here and...but he would never ask directly and had to listen sharply to get them when they came mixed up with the winds over Pakistan.

This was his fifth Operational series out here, his ninth flight on the dark side of the moon.

He had joined the squadron in March, while it was still a "cover detachment" of another real but unrelated squadron in the United States.

Ten months go fast.

The Unit had been commissioned as a bona fide Squadron, its mission precise without being even marginally explicit—"Conduct electronic reconnaissance in areas of naval interest." He had progressed quickly in his pilot qualifications and now needed only a few more total hours to be designated as a "second" or qualified co-pilot in the Beast. As was the custom, all newly designated pilots—"nuggets"—spent their first year or so as navigators on operational missions, while they accumulated pilot training qualifications and learned how to handle the Beast.

He was the best navigator in the squadron, the oldest but not the senior nugget, come late to Naval Flight training after two-years shipboard as an Assistant Navigator at sea. As everyone in the outfit quickly learned, things were different here. His first operational mission had been into the Skagerak from Blackbushe, England, but that, however operational it was, wasn't the kind of job people had in mind when they talked about "operationals".

Real operationals began and ended in Nicosia and what they did between wheels-in-the-well and touchdown wasn't anybody's business. They had a casual attitude toward the letter of the law when necessity required that they carry classified stuff inside their shirts or in their wallets, but before and after a real operational, they had a vested interest in keeping their business to themselves. Besides, the Skag missions were boring and flown under

International Civil Aeronautical Organization flight clearances, even though their position reports were always phony and their call signs always spurious. Rumors about the impending installation of radar in the Baltic had everyone wondering what they'd do when someone could actually track their flight path, but for the time, they just filed a standard flight plan out of British airspace to a point in the North Sea and made believe they spent eight hours there hovering about a point, instead of endlessly tracking across the mouth of the straits recording the navigational radar signals from every new or remodeled Soviet heavy that ever left the Baltic.

This was different.

When the weather guy finished and left with a "Cheerio," wishing them both a good flight, he and Elfers exchanged grimaces and got down to business. It was a complicated weather situation. They put heads together over the chart, plotted the winds on an E6B plotter that computed the drift, compass headings and true tracks they planned for the night. With a right crosswind from the east at 9,000 feet entered on the little plastic faceplate, Brian would rotate the bezel until the track he wanted to make over the ground on one scale showed the course they would have to steer to make good that track on the other scale. For example, with a strong easterly component tonight, the first course up there—almost due Northeast—would require that they crab into the wind to make it good, heading well to the east of north on the compasses to compensate for the expected westerly drift, slithering sideways down their track line like a crab.

On the way, they would have four navigational aids, radio beacons they could use their radio direction finders to locate. There would be a beacon at Silifke which would put them over land, then one at Kayseri half way up the track, one at Samsun on the Coast, and one due east at Trabzon to get them a speed check as they passed it abeam to starboard. Lew liked to know the winds along the way at the different altitudes they would be flying to know what to expect, and they were both interested in surface and upper altitude winds in case they had to duck up or down to avoid trouble.

The first order of business was to compute a takeoff time that would put them at their first mandatory check point within the assigned - usually fifteen minute—window. As a rule, they decided on a rough takeoff time for planning purposes based on a "seaman's eye" look at the planning chart and arranged for the crew pre-flight briefing an hour prior. Tonight's briefing was scheduled for eight, local time, based on an assumed nine o'clock takeoff. When they computed it more accurately using the forecast winds, they got 1837Greenwich Mean Time, 8:37PM local.

Earlier than guessed, but close enough.

There was, however, some bad news tonight. A line of severe thunderstorms with well-developed vertical movement—thunderheads—had been brewing along a front running roughly parallel to the Turkish Black Sea coastline. Thunderstorms and squall lines occurred all year round out here, less usual now in December, but there they were. Their inbound—and outbound—tracks took them through, then along the squall line, in the teeth of the worst weather within a thousand miles. The system was expected to break up around three AM local time, about the time they would be heading back to the barn.

From a Safety-of-Flight point of view, this would be a good night to postpone or, failing that, alter the directed track to avoid the worst of it, but they had been cancelled out yesterday and that would never do. There was another factor to consider, however, which brightened things.

For most aeronautical navigation requirements, the idea is to point the airplane in the right direction, know pretty much where you are with regard to where you ought to be as often as possible, and land where intended, hopefully at a pre-computed time. In maritime "patrols," the tracks flown are investigative—the crew has the leeway to go looking for targets of interest instead of following a strict track, but the navigator ought to know where he is when something of interest turns up.

In the operational envelope for which the Beast was designed, however, there was a wrinkle. They were assigned a set of points to reach and directed to fly from the first to the second to the third, in that order, in a given time window. They were assigned to do this in anticipation, not that they would "find something"—as in open ocean patrol—but that *something* would either try to find *them,* or keep looking. And as the attempted illumination of the Beast as a target, as an intruder, as a trespasser, took place, there was furious activity aft of the wing spar. This was the Mickey action.

Again, a wrinkle.

Radar beams, actually electromagnetic impulses, traveling out from the search radars struck the Beast's carefully designed receiver system with each rotation of the searching radar's antenna. The beam, however, had to bounce *off* the Beast and travel *back* to the search antenna for the searcher to be alerted to their presence. If the aircraft remained *within* the envelope in which pulses could reach it from the shore but *outside* the bounce-back envelope, it would be invisible to the searcher but the guys in the back had what they came for.

Back there in Mickey-land, every physical detail of the illumination process was analyzed, recorded, photographed, measured, timed and an immediate bearing taken of the origin from the aircraft. Frequently, several simultaneous illuminations had to be worked, the analysis automatically time-shared in the equipment, and a hand written log of the data meticulously maintained. As the aircraft traveled down it's track, Mickey was generating fingerprint and bearing data on every illuminating radar across the electromagnetic spectrum. A successful night's work might "work" fifty different radar sites, first the big, high-powered long-range Early Warning radars code named "Dumbo", then the progressively shorter range, more discriminating units as the aircraft got closer to the coast and eventually turned away.

The idea was to turn away before entering the bounce-back envelope in which they could be detected and aggressively tracked, with the interceptor network alerted to their presence. The Navigator's job was to know exactly where they were when each bearing line was generated, so that subsequent bearings could be triangulated and the originating site identified by location. If they had to deviate from the planned track, so be it, as long as they knew where they were. Tonight would be a challenge and they both knew it.

This afternoon, as Brian watched Lew's every move, he sensed that something was different, and at first he attributed it to the discouraging weather briefing. As they worked it through, however, Brian saw no sign that the challenging on-track weather had bothered him in the least. Perhaps Lew was preoccupied with some operational aspect. Only the Plane Commander and Mickey ever got the "deep skinny" briefings, or maybe he was dissatisfied with something Brian—or someone—had said or done. Whatever the case, it did disturb Brian's composure.

Brian suggested that they get a bite to eat, but Lew looked at his watch and excused himself. "I have to see a man about a dog," he explained, smiling disarmingly.

The "none of your business" message was tactful and light. That's the way the man was.

Later, in the bar, alone, Brian ate a pub sandwich and had a lemon squash. Out on the patio, now beneath a clear night sky with a beautiful cap of lustrous stars, he heard the music. Horace Lundy worked at the hotel, obviously in some management capacity, and each evening he would play for his own enjoyment—and for those enjoying their cocktail hour. He and his wife—Brian assumed they were married—also had a cabaret act which they did at the Chanticleer, and he had seen them around several times, alone and together. He guessed that the Chanticleer and the Hotel had some commercial tie in—possibly the same owner—but Horace was playing "Blue Star" now and it was beautiful and touching in the dim light. Brian sensed that he would never forget this moment or that song. He wasn't sure why.

He did not exactly worship the ground on which Lieutenant Commander Lewis C. Elfers tread, but it was close. Brian was twenty-seven years old, five years in the Navy, not easily fooled, probably nowhere near as street-wise as he should have been, but he was learning. All he wanted out of life was to sit here in that same crummy room in the Acropole a couple of years from now and have some smart-assed Nugget Navigator think of him with the same awe with which he secretly regarded Lew. When he worked with Lew, he was captivated. Shirley chided him about it back home, almost jealous that her new husband seemed to share his devotion to his bride with some retread who had never gone farther than Operations Officer in a dinky four plane squadron in French

Morocco. Shirley's Dad had retired as a Captain, and she knew! Just ask her. Go ahead.

Shirley.

Oh my God!

His cheeks burned when he thought of Shirley, thought of his encounter with that Dutch girl last night at the Chanticleer, ashamed of what he had done, embarrassed at the outcome and thoroughly disgusted with himself. He should have known better, and as a faithful, moral, new Catholic husband, he should not have done what he did.

Last night, the "twin" sisters had finished singing at the microphone on the tiny stage, and had come back through the cluster of tables to the bar, where the bartender had offered them drinks. They had taken them, then turned to face outward from the bar. Timmons and Lucore and the Lebanese or Turkish girl who must be their shared girl friend were sitting quietly in the corner. Brian had enjoyed the set of songs, a medley of Joni James hits from the States, ending with "Purple Shades," a favorite of his not shared by Shirley.

Somehow, he ended up next to them and he politely mentioned to the cuter one how much he had enjoyed their act. She was about twenty-five up close, although he would have sworn they were both teenagers a minute ago, and he felt almost overwhelmingly attracted to her. He was in love. Then and there, he was in love. Maybe it was the Brandy sours. In absolute, ecstatic, total love. Before long, he and she were, well, he was making, well, an ass of himself and…God it was embarrassing to think about it now.

Why had he…asked her…how had he said it…to come over to the Acropole? He shuddered, thinking of what Shirley would have said if she had seen him how she would have been infuriated and amused and condescending and finally, ready for blood and violence. And then he had to go through it all in his mind, his clumsy pawing, her apparent enthusiasm for the idea, and then…God…"ten pounds for an hour, fifty for the night and you buy me a nice present, OK?"

Like a thunder clap hitting him in an open field, an out-of-body, after-death experience, he saw himself and heard himself and the next thing he remembered he was on his feet, toward the Gents but not going there, toward the door instead, his drinking money still on the bar, his guardian angel to the rescue, out of the building, his face scarlet, his conscience in tatters, his heart in his shoes, his hands shaking like aspen leaves.

But why had he done it in the first place?

Shirley.

12

Out at the aerodrome, Lieutenant Bob Hunley looked at his watch, set on Greenwich Mean Time two hours west, two hours earlier, and figured it was about time to get going if he was going to get any dinner. Well, almost.

He wanted to be at the plane by eight, so why rush. He wasn't one of those Navy fanatics who kept their watches on Greenwich time to show everybody how gung-ho they were. He didn't know what the opposite of gung-ho was but whatever it was, he was. He just wanted to know what time it was back home in Morocco.

It gave him a sense of connectedness to know that it was three where Bonnie was, and it was five here and he was thinking about her.

He didn't mind being by himself and was amused by the late afternoon activity in the Officers' Mess. The RAF and Army regulars now recognized him as an "occasional," and he had made some interesting acquaintances. He was deliberating the metabolic clear-out time of a second Keo brandy sour on top of the one he was cherishing on the gleaming rosewood bar, and was gathering points in the struggle against his conscience. He had never flown drunk, never felt the slightest impairment of his faculties when on duty, but he knew that he had been God-blest with a prodigious capacity for the fruit of the vine and hoped that things continued forever as they were.

He was long and lean, just over six feet, wiry, well coordinated, graceful in his movements and posture, an accomplished dancer. The troops called him "Hairpin".

With a shock, almost a mane, of well tended, longish, prematurely gray-white hair framing a long, aquiline face sparked by remarkably clear blue eyes, Lieutenant Bob Hunley gave the impression that he really didn't want to be with you just now but would be mannerly and listen to what you had to say. This was unfortunate, because he was genuinely interested in most things, with an academic's probing curiosity that sometimes annoyed people who did not know quite what they were talking about. He had the sense of humor designed to be described as "rapier," and he could put you in stitches…or in shreds.

When he finished flight training in September 1945, he was commissioned in the Naval Reserve, almost on the day the surrender was signed, and within the year, he mustered out with a Reserve obligation that he refused to take seriously. He went back to college, married, and worked intermittently between jobs, first on his GI Bill Masters degree, then on his store-bought, self-funded Ph.D. in International Relations. In June 1950, with the Korean War mobilization, he discovered a lot more about his Reserve obligation than he had ever wanted to know, and after a shamefully inadequate, quick cockpit refresher at North Island, he found himself in uniform, in the Philippines, and in a Navy glad to get somebody to fly "administrative missions" (the mail) between Sangley and the Cubi Point Naval Air Station.

As Korea droned on and he paid off his commitment, Bob Hunley discovered the phenomenon of Friends In High Places. Flying around the Western Pacific introduced him to a broad assortment of Senior Naval Officers who were more than happy to chat with their urbane, sensitive, cultured pilot and using these contacts judiciously, he had wrangled himself a set of orders to the Unit.

It was a dream come true—he and Bonnie had no children, they were free to go on a moment's notice anytime, anywhere, and they spent every opportunity they could to grab "space-available" on military aircraft through Europe and the Middle East. They loved being there, loved the travel, spoke fluent French and enjoyed a wide circle of civilian friends. He had voluntarily extended his active duty agreement to take the job and never regretted it.

There was a drawback, of course. He was always in the hole on his leave account, but what was leave for? That wasn't it, exactly, but...well then again, every few months, it was his turn to go operational. He had the hours and the seniority and flew reasonably well, but when they designated him as a Plane Commander, everyone knew that it was an honorary thing and that when the rubber really hit the road, he would be in the right seat. He could fly all the familiarization flights and the milk runs and the training flights to Germany and England, but over the Pond? Well...

It was okay with the Hairpin.

He got to poke around Nicosia, observe the Turkish and Greek constituencies and drink brandy sours in the Officers' Mess as the sun went down on a mild December afternoon.

He rather liked some of the people he associated with in the Unit, although they found it hard to establish where they stood with him. He had watched Lew Elfers carefully, from the moment he had come aboard, and despite his natural tendency to find as much fault with anyone above him as he possibly could, he had nothing but admiration for the Operations Officer. Bob Hunley rarely trafficked in gossip, nor did Bonnie, but both knew—as most people in the Unit knew—that Lew's marriage was terribly unhappy. And on the two or three occasions he had been here with Lew in the past two years, Bob found himself pleased by the justice of the situation when he noticed Lew having a good time socially, usually with Horst and his dark-haired wife. This trip he had found Lew a little preoccupied every once in awhile, but he couldn't blame him with the load he must be carrying.

His favorite sidekick, though, was young Brian Kerrigan, the kid navigating this trip. He had studied to be a Catholic priest before coming in and was one of the better educated of the lot. Also, a damn fine Navigator with the makings of a fine Plane Commander some day, if they every let a Nugget get away with it. A little on the sheltered side, but who wouldn't be with that background?

He was thinking about Brian now. He had a great deal of admiration for the kid, wise beyond his years maybe, but a little bit of wisdom never hurt anybody.

Admiration had come obliquely.

They were on autopilot one dazzling sunny afternoon high above Majorca, seats back, enjoying the incredible blue of the Mediterranean as it washed the tiny Balearic Islands, almost two miles beneath them. Bob was flying, Brian was in the right seat and they were discussing the impending NATO shift from the familiar "Able, Baker," phonetic alphabet to the new "Alfa, Bravo," due next summer, to accommodate the various NATO linguistic quirks. The conversation turned to pronunciation variations, and Brian casually mentioned that while he had actually done his last two years of college in Latin, his "Church" Latin was indecipherable to a classicist.

Latin in the cockpit, thought Bob. Jesus, what next?

Bob had been poking away at a doctoral dissertation on International Aviation Law for years. Interested in the subject initially for a very unworthy reason, Bob was now genuinely absorbed with the idea that the three-mile marine league—the basis for the territorial limit of national sovereignty at sea—needed to be examined historically if it were to be applied in mid-twentieth century to aviation law. In a nutshell, sixteenth century writers figured that since the maximum range of a cannon was about three miles from shore, a nation-state could claim the first three miles of the sea touching their land as their own. Their cannons could defend it and keep other folks away from it if they so wished.

In the forties, that principle was ignored in developing the idea of air sovereignty in favor of the idea - also from the sixteenth century—that land sovereignty extended indefinitely upward. With the advent of high-altitude anti-aircraft guns and the new missiles people were talking about, he felt it was time to compare the two positions analytically. Did Germany own the stratosphere above it? Did India? How about Upper Volta? Bob was casting about for a subject for a doctoral dissertation when the thought struck him that with his background in schoolboy Latin, good French and the knowledge of navigation any pilot possessed, this was the ideal subject. He could slide by the University requirement for three "tools of research" by using Latin, French and Navigation, instead of going through the tedium of learning another research language as a prerequisite for his Doctorate. Navigation would be his "third language".

And so he had chosen the subject and had pitched in, that is, before he learned about Reserve commitments. But he still thought about it a lot, like now, for instance...He'd be back!

All the musty scholarship, all the hours in grubby smoke-filled top-floor library carrels and the feel of those hundreds of ear-marked index note cards popped into his mind that afternoon in the sun-drenched cockpit, and he suddenly felt like pulling someone's chain. Brain was elected.

Recalling his 16th century Latin research and grinning, Bob said "Try this—'*Cujus est terra, ejus est usque ad coelum.*"

He almost added "wise ass!"

It was the key, the seminal statement in his perpetually "in preparation" dissertation, modern international airspace law in one sentence. Latin maybe, but one sentence.

Brain looked over at him with a grin and calmly, conversationally, informed him that whoever owned the ground, owned the skies above it.

Almost stunned, Bob shook his head, and looked out his plexiglass window to the blue Mediterranean nine thousand feet beneath them. They were passing southwest-bound over Palma now, heading home, and he wondered how many people in the whole world could have translated that sentence, let alone this kid sitting next to him jockeying the cowl flaps. Amazing! The whole foundation of modern International Aviation Law.

Disguising his respect and masking his utter surprise, he looked at the kid with a lopsided half-sneer, half-smirk and with a twinkle in his eye had simply said, "You hairball!"

From then on, they were a team.

One day, he would have to ask Brian what he knew of or remembered that arcane bit of sixteenth century legal mumbo jumbo. What the hell else had he learned in that seminary of his?

Cujus est terra, ejus est usque ad coelum.

"Who owns the ground, owns it all the way to heaven".

If you fly over my space, I'll blast your ass.

Tonight, we'll see, Bob Hunley thought. Soberly back to the present. Tonight we'll see.

When the disheveled figure ambled into the lounge, Bob thought he perceived a hush—at least a lull—in the cocktail hour chatter. He turned to look closely at the newcomer. He was short, squat, totally unmilitary in appearance, in a Royal Army tunic with the three Captain's pips, no tie, bloodshot eyes, and a belted but empty holster in his back trouser pocket. The Royal Army's idea of khaki had a green tinge to it, and the shirt under the tunic looked greener and dirtier than it probably was. He slouched over to where Bob sat at the bar and sat on the next stool.

The white-jacketed barman appeared immediately, and greeted "May Jawkins" respectfully, almost in awe. Bob watched the man, fascinated, as he was served a tumbler of Keo. "Jawkins" turned and faced him and Bob was both edified and intrigued when his companion introduced himself.

"May Jawkins" was, in fact, Major Hawkins, Royal Constabulary, MEF, and Major Hawkins, Bob assumed, was newly Major Hawkins, having been too busy to purchase (or however the Brits got) new insignia for what apparently were his work clothes. He was about forty-five, pretty old for Majoring and they sized one another up for a minute. A youngish two pipper appeared and shook Hawkins hand.

"Great show this morning, Major."

"Nothing to it, really. We were expecting them."

"How did it go?"

"Well enough, I'd expect. A bit rum for a minute. Wouldn't tell us where they got the petrol or the lorry. They say I'm obsessed with petrol, but it's the key to this whole thing, you know. They make this jelly-up, trick they got from the Sovs I suspect. Only they found they can't make it happen with the petrol from the corner station, won't work you know, low octane. Rationed anyway, just to cut them down a peg. So they have all this petrol they keep moving around doing other mischief. Cheeky bastard, little devil about fourteen, I guess."

Bob, listening intently but staring away, turned to the pair.

"And?"

"Oh, I shot him. Just like that. In a minute we had the petrol chap's name and the lorry's owner and no more fuss."

"And the kid?"

"Left him there all day, propped up against a rock. Engineer chaps packed him off a little while ago."

The major looked a little wistful. "They nicked one of my lads, you know, with their dammed blunderbusses. I cut one of their fingers off and told them to tell their nannies to get the word out that I'll have no more of that! Cheeky bastards."

Then, after a short dreamy pause, more wistfully, "After that, we counted thirteen different kinds of wildflowers by the side of the road while we had our tea, waiting for G2. In December! Beautiful time of the year out here, you know."

Bob waited a respectful moment before leaving. He was remarkably surprised at his reaction, neither horrified nor amused, just empty.

He thought of what he had to do in a couple of hours and realized that he was neither horrified nor amused about that either. Just empty.

He didn't feel like eating.

13

Lucore loved the Beast as much as Timmons did.

At night, when they powered her up and she came alive and her dark brooding hulk began to glow and murmur, he could feel the power she implied and see the beauty of her lines and appreciate the sophisticated wizardry that had made her what she was. He climbed up through the forward hatch and made his way down and forward through the Navigator's compartment into the nose turret, noting that each chair had a yellow mae-west inflatable life jacket draped over the back. The mount had been fired out over the Atlantic on the test flight last Friday afternoon. New ammunition belts had been threaded and the safeties wired back the way they were supposed to be after the test. He checked each of the power and arming circuits, then activated the master drive and satisfied himself that he had point and train control without activating the Master Arm. He returned the mount to safe-stow, checked the rheostated reticule lights and secured the switches, not before checking each of the red glow-lights that would give White enough vision to strap himself in later on. He put on a headset and clicked through the various Internal Communications Circuits, making sure that the had a head tone on the main, auxiliary and emergency override positions, and then he uncoiled himself from the seat and backed out into the Navigator's station.

The Navigation station had one of the few rheostat controlled white lights in the aircraft, on an adjustable swinging transom, and he turned it on and set it low over the Navigator's table to make sure in the white glow that everything on the backside of the turret-bulkhead was secured, the canvas sound suppression battens fastened and the red extinguisher in place and tagged. He had forgotten to check an extinguisher once on the only flight he had ever needed one, and he had become scrupulous about the item. He had also checked it on the test flight Friday, but crews had been known to cannibalize one another's aircraft over the weekend. Not this time.

The Beast was beautifully designed for the mission, years ahead of its time. The Navigator sat facing out the port (left) side on the main deck of the aircraft, just forward and beneath the raised pilot and co-pilot seats in their Plexiglas bubble. The Navigation table gave him plenty of room, a window to look out, and a universal plotter mounted to the stanchion holding the full-swivel drafting light. Just forward of his swiveled seat, a drift sight was mounted into the deck plate and all he needed to do for a drift sight was to swing around and peer into the thing. It was a downward-looking gridded telescope, and watching the terrain beneath pass through the eyepiece, the Navigator turned the grid control knob to make the ground appear to move down the grid. When he had it moving along the grid line, he read his drift angle directly from the knob setting. Drift angle applied to their compass heading gave him their track over the ground and, if he could talk the cockpit into making a couple of quick course changes while he took drift in three directions—a "wind star" - he could also figure groundspeed.

At eye level over the table to his left, a repeater off the APS-33 radar gave the Navigator an electronic overview of the geography out to about 200 miles, depending on altitude. Above his head, in its own little plastic turret, a fitting accepted the periscopic sextant and provided power to illuminate the reticules, run the averaging clock mechanism and the gyro stabilizer that gave him an artificial horizon for his star sights.

On the other side of the aircraft, a forward mounted seat faced an array of rarely used electronic racks. The crews called this the "Pluto" station—alluding to some relationship with the "Mickey" crowd in the back - but Lucore had only rarely flown with the seat occupied, generally by a stranger, and he had no idea what that was all about. "Mickey" and "Pluto" were nicknames of uncertain origin and vintage, taken for granted, part of the vocabulary.

The Pluto seat normally became the Navigator's storage annex and attic, and the small forward -facing desk usually had the debris from a dozen long flights stuffed into it—dead coffee cups, candy wrappers, an occasional skin magazine and some old worksheets. He noticed that someone had cleaned up the desk and that there were three unfamiliar pieces of electronic gear, regular black boxes, bolted now into the racks. A set of earphones and a microphone hung on the hook beneath the intercom box.

He started aft, ducking under the elevated flight control station underneath the pilot and copilot seats, up on to the flight deck past the radio operator and the radar operator seats, checking life vests. Just forward of the wing beam, the console lights from the Engine Analyzer and the engine instrument cluster illuminated Timmons' Plane Captain station, although in standby with the engines secured, none of them were reading. As the Flight Engineer, as well as the enlisted crew leader and the general expediter of everything, the Plane Captain bore the brunt of responsibility for keeping the thing responsive to the tactical and operational commands of the Pilot Plane Commander. The Pilot ran the show, but not without the Plane Captain, he didn't.

And, as Lucore would be the first to point out, the Ordnanceman's role was crucial as well. Whenever the Beast flew, an Ordnanceman flew aboard. They rarely—as they would tonight—flew with fully loaded and charged turrets, but over time and through custom, the Ordnanceman was also the cook, the logistician, the bookkeeper, the survival equipment specialist, the small-arms custodian and the banker, when collections had to be taken up to pay for in-flight meals and amenities. It was a step beyond the ball turret gunner in the TBM or the red-shirt armorer scurrying around the Oriskany flight deck in the Sea of Japan, but it was his element.

He boosted himself on his belly over the wing spar through the after-station into his "office". You had to be careful doing this in flight if you had a Mae West on. The handgrips had a habit of snagging the CO_2 cartridge lanyard and popping it, and with an inflated life vest on, the crawlspace was impassable. Somebody had to rescue you if it happened when you were only halfway across the spar, and you owed him a case of beer.

The eight-foot section of the fuselage between the wing and the "Mickey" section belonged to the ordnanceman, crammed efficiently with two cook plates, a large twenty-cup coffee urn, a smaller ten-cup percolator and a plug-in soup-cooker that took a can of Campbell's and water. Stowed neatly beneath his workstation, a cardboard carton of canned soups, coffee and sugar filled the Beast's larder. Beside the groceries, he had tucked the brown paper commissary bag Mr. Elfers had given him with an extra flight suit and flight jacket. Welded to the aluminum deck plate, the small arms box was locked with two locks. Before they taxied tonight, the Brits would be delivering provisions for sixteen in-flight meals for them to munch later on and he and Mr. Elfers would unlock the double locked box and hand out the tracer-loaded thirty-eights.

"Mickey" was the euphemistic nickname for the surveillance business. It referred to the work that went on in the last thirty-four feet of the aircraft while it was operational, work done by specialists with whom Lucore had little professional relationship, other than keeping them in coffee and chow, keeping them protected when the guns were manned, and keeping out of their way when they were hard at work in their cramped workplace.

He worked his way aft past the array of classified equipment and boxes and machines—nobody, not even Mr. Elfers probably knew what all that crap did—back to the aft turret where he repeated his checks, and climbed back out on to the concrete.

It was twenty to eight and the rest of the crew had arrived.

14

Washington

"That leaves Mort Gross, our Mickey guy, and Commander Elfers." Jennifer was prodding now, totally absorbed, totally persuaded that Captain Barnet not only knew a lot more that he was telling her, but that maybe she didn't want to know the sources and methods he had used in finding out what he was not telling her.

"Mort and I go way back, way back," he began, on his feet now, pacing up and down with a thousand yard stare, looking out of the building and off into the slushy night as he got warmed to his subject. She could tell it was dear to his heart.

"I'm older—about ten years, I guess, but I have great respect for Mort.

"He's spent his whole career in this line of work, Mort has. He was born and raised in Covington, Kentucky, you know where that is? Right across the river from Cincinnati, where the Grosses had run haberdasheries, dry goods stores and later, a Department Store up on Main Street north of downtown. As a boy, he saved his pennies and bought one of those mail-order cat's-whisker galena 'radio' detectors, complete with earphones, and instead of loosing interest with the thing when he found out how tricky it was to 'bring in stations far and near' as the ad on the back of the Comic Book claimed, Mort was fascinated with finding out why it worked when it did. He progressed from there in both interest and knowledge.

"Once, he told me, he built a transmitter using a Ford Model A induction coil, and transmitted dots and dashes across his basement to his own receiver. He was eleven.

"By the time he was fourteen, he had assembled enough components to put a ham rig together and had strung a wire antenna off neighboring clotheslines. In High School, he started a Radio Club and with the encouragement and guidance of his Physics teacher, a retired Navy Radio Electrician, that's an old Warrant Officer rank, he invented a number of devices to automate the radio communications process.

"He has a remarkable ear, perfect pitch, and a great sense of rhythm, plays the horn, banjo and a great cocktail lounge piano. He entered Rose Polytechnic Institute of Engineering in Terre Haute, Indiana, in around 1938, majoring in electrical engineering, but he was soon dissatisfied. Rose was the finest engineering school in the Midwest at the time, and he was disappointed that there were almost no opportunities for him in electronics, and those that did exist had to be pursued in his free time along with a handful of profs and students who were as frustrated as he was.

"By the time he finished sophomore year, he decided to transfer to Purdue where a new aeronautical program was beginning, but during the summer, working with his High School Physics teacher on a scheme they both had to develop a portable microphone detector—a debugger—Mort decided to join the Navy.

"That summer—1940, I guess it was - Kentucky and Ohio mobilized, then nationalized, their National Guard units and in September of that year, the first peacetime draft was authorized by Congress. Mort's parents had immigrated to the United States from Nurnberg in 1913 just before the start of the First War. They had escaped Europe in time to raise their three sons in America, and while they had to endure the anti-German bias of mid-America during the war and the anti-Jewish bias that continued later, they were welcomed by the small European community in Cincinnati and as industrious shopkeepers, they thrived.

"Having escaped both the devastating Weimar Republic inflation and the early anti-Semitic indignities engineered by the budding National Socialist German Workers Party, Hitler's crowd, they worked hard to bring over as many relatives as possible, and their lives throughout the thirties were comfortable and pleasant. They lived just south of Cincinnati on an embankment overlooking the Ohio River, on the Kentucky side, in a large comfortable home, and commuted easily back and forth. In 1940, they were naturalized American citizens and enthusiastic patriots, but they shed a tear or two when they put him on a train to Newport, Rhode Island, for boot camp. He was twenty-three years old.

"Mort was handsome in a roly-poly way, gregarious, precocious, popular and older than his barracks mates. When he arrived in Newport and found himself in the hands of a Chief Boatswain's Mate Sweeney or Murphy or something like that, his boot camp company 'commander' (as he liked to be called), he discovered that he might have a problem. The Chief—Sweeney I guess it was - was an Irish Catholic from South Boston who had no prejudices, as long as you were Irish Catholic from South Boston. You know the type—we have them here as well."

Jennifer did.

"Well, the boot company of forty souls was an unremarkable ethnic mix except for Mort, a 'hillbilly' as was anyone from Kentucky and incredibly, pudgy and Jewish, at the same time. Mort's a quick study, so he learned to copy Sweeny's Boston-Irish accents and each time they spoke, Mort imitated the Chief with remarkable but respectful precision. By the time boot camp ended and Mort carried the company colors as its honor man, Sweeney was his Sea Daddy, and never figured out what was so different about that fat Jew kid from Kentucky.

"After boot camp, he stayed at Newport for Radioman training and in January, 1941, was interviewed and accepted to join a cadre of enlisted Radiomen assigned by the Navy to the Naval Research Laboratory in Washington, DC. He was a seaman first class when he joined the unit, and he and a young former radio salesman named Howard Lorenson hit it off immediately. When he was sent to Boston that summer to help extend the project to the MIT campus, he kept in touch with Lorenson and in the ensuing ten years, the two of them put together the technology that became electronic intelligence.

"At MIT, he worked hard, kept his mouth shut, and distinguished himself by solving a number of practical problems which reminded him of the job he had getting his clothesline antenna just the right length back in Covington. This time, with the help of others in his Unit and the freedom to take as many classes at the Institute as his schedule could handle, Mort understood the theory behind what he was doing. When he lived in Cambridge in an apartment with two of the MIT sailors, one of the young ladies whom he dated—Millie McGee, who would become Mrs. Gross—began to tease him because she imagined that his name reminded her of the new brokerage house opening in New York. Morton Stanley in her mind became Morgan Stanley. She and her buddies called him Moneybags, a tag that stayed with him until they married, when it got pretty old, particularly most of the time when there wasn't any money.

"When Pearl Harbor came, he stayed on at MIT—now a rated petty officer—and in 1943 he was packed off to Hawaii with a number of his teammates to work on a tactical problem—how to passively locate and identify Japanese combat ships from over the horizon. His laboratory was the Western Pacific.

"We all know this now—at least you and I and the rest of us in this business—but Mort was fascinated by the fingerprints that radar signals - in fact all electromagnetic radiations in the commonly understood electronic regimes - have. Radars transmit on a specific measurable frequency. Their pulses have measurable width and detectable shape. Their antennas rotate at a measurable sweep speed. The transmitting signal is turned on, travels to the target and back, and the radar shuts off to receive it back on a measurable on/off cycle.

"To Mort, this was the most fascinating thing in his life, his religion, I guess you'd call it. If he had a piece of equipment that could collect and correlate all these measurable phenomena, he would have identifiable fingerprints of a specific piece of equipment. If he had a bearing on the signal now, travel some distance and get a second bearing later, and cross these bearing lines, he could roughly fix the position of its source as well. This, as we know, was the world of passive electronic countermeasures. By the time he was twenty-nine, the war had ended, Mort was a Limited Duty (Electronics)

Lieutenant, junior grade, and one of the most experienced Passive Electronics Countermeasures Specialists in the world. He still is.

"When he applied his background to Post-War era problems, Mort worked through the practical electronic installation problems the Navy was experiencing in developing airborne equipment, and at thirty, as a Lieutenant, was a Bureau of Aeronautics project manager on the conversion of a batch of old Army Air Corps B-17 Flying Fortresses to Navy 'ferret' planes. They were horrible looking things, those PB-1Ws as they were called, with huge plastic radar domes mounted above the cockpit giving them the appearance of giant insect mutants from outer space.

"But when the Lockheed Company's P2V Neptune won the competition for the Navy's next Patrol aircraft against its Martin competitor, Mort had enough credibility among his friends in high places to persuade them to champion his dream of converting the beautifully engineered Martin airframes—the losers in the competition - to dedicated mission replacements for the PB-1W. He won. Weight was a factor in the program and the teams were constantly working against a poundage budget, hounded by Mort and his colleagues to bring the thing in at a weight that the massive R4360s and the J33s could handle. From his PB-1W days on, those who didn't know him well enough to call him Mort had to memorialize his battle for flyable weight and settle for 'Max Gross'".

Jennifer couldn't believe the richness of detail Winnie had packed into his word sketch of a guy whom she had never met but really knew only by reputation. He was alive to her now. It was strange.

15

Nicosia

Just as Timmons had guessed, Morton Stanley Gross, Lieutenant Commander, United States Navy, was indeed sitting around in a circle with the rest of the Mickey crew, but it was not in the Acropole or the Sylvan but in the Classified Material Control Cage at Royal Air Force Nicosia Station out west of town.

As the Chief Evaluator on the mission, he was for practical purposes the Mission Commander, although the Navy had no such term or concept in those days. Lew Elfers was the pilot in command and the military superior—by assignment rather than rank - but as a practical matter, Lew's job was to put the plane where Mort wanted it to be. As for Mort, next to the legendary Howard Lorenson, he was probably the world's expert on what they would be up against tonight.

Mort hated to impose on his troops with an extensive pre-flight brief before a flight like this one, but although it was certain to be a long ball-buster, he needed at least these couple of extra hours with the guys to ring them in on the delicate issues he and they would have to face tonight and early tomorrow morning. He estimated an eight-plus-hour time enroute. There was a time when he would have briefed everybody in his room at the Acropole, but the stakes had been raised on this hand and he wanted to be absolutely sure it was played correctly.

This time there were two messages worth of briefing materials. They had received the original Top Secret Boomerang message Friday afternoon around five thirty, soon after close-of-business in London. Anyone who owned a calendar with the moon phases could predict that they would be in the barrel this week and the normal drill went like this. They even had test-flown the Beast that afternoon, anticipating the message. Better a wasted test flight than working on a Saturday before a long trip.

Several weeks before the dark of the moon, the Naval Security Group in Washington—Nebraska Avenue - and the handlers in the Office of the Chief on Naval Operations in the Pentagon would decide on the priority targets for the current operationals.

Nebraska Avenue did not "own" any operational assets, so the handlers drafted and sent a Top Secret "requirements tasking" message to the Theater Commander, Commander in Chief Naval Forces, Eastern Atlantic and Mediterranean in London. The Theater Commander was a four star Admiral, Admiral Jack Cassady, and the only one who could tell him what to do was the

Chief of Naval Operations himself, Admiral Arleigh Burke, so the "handlers" originated the message, preserving the administrative fiction that the CNO himself was actually talking to CINCNELM himself in London. The chances that either Admiral ever saw any of these messages—unless there was a glitch—were remote.

At this point, the Staff Air Operations Officer in London, Commander Stuart Sterling, and the Staff Intelligence Officer, Commander Daniel Arlen took the tasking for action and the London people were brought into the picture. Since the "requirements tasking" message usually came with a suggested flight track, the London Staff had to refine it into a directive suitable to get things moving, and, at the same time, take care of the logistic, diplomatic, and political ramifications.

The British were NATO partners, so the arrangements for the Beast to stage through Malta and into Cyprus were not difficult. Close as the Americans and the Brits were, the sensitivities on both sides were barely understood by the other partner, however.

The British could not understand why the Americans could not stage through the perfectly suitable Halfar Naval Air Station on Malta. Why did they have to use the civilian field—close as it was—at Luqa? The Americans could not understand why the Brits didn't realize that anyone monitoring voice traffic in the Med would immediately know when a Naval aircraft arrived at Nick from Halfar and would put two and two together, while occasional arrivals from Luqa could be anybody, given the variety of imaginative call-signs involved. They sometimes compromised, and came out via Luqa, back via Halfar, but not always.

The Turks had an even larger pill to swallow. Their neighbor to the north was far more testy, far more truculent than their English speaking allies appreciated. The monthly requests for silent overflight and for reserved emergency landing rights in Balakesir, Bandirma and Eskeshir were usually approved, but they took great pains to keep communications as secure as possible. The last thing they needed was an incident.

As a rule, it always seemed to happen that the London Staff would work the problem all during the last available week and sign out the tasking as the last item of business late Friday afternoon just as they were all off to the Columbia Club on Bayswater Road for Happy Hour. The Top Secret message always came around suppertime Friday night in Morocco. Sorry about that.

The message always carried the identifying word "Boomerang". It meant nothing to most people except "here we go again." Mort, however, had been in on the beginning of what had been a new age of electronic intelligence gathering when the Beast had become operational. He remembered someone remarking when the nickname had been assigned that a boomerang always came back. He hoped so.

This time there was a difference in the procedure.

This time, there had been another, highly unusual Friday evening Boomerang message, Eyes Only for the Skipper and Mickey. Base Communications had reached Mort at home just before supper. They were on with the Skipper and his wife as dinner guests, and since the precedence on the message was only "Priority" - everything these days was "Priority" it seemed to Mort—he and his wife went to the Skipper's Quarters first and they all agreed that whatever it was, it would wait an hour or two.

An "Eyes Only" message was an extraordinary event, and the two elders read the message after they had finished their supper at the Quonset Hut Quarters. They had left the wives to talk about commissary shortages, perfume shopping and space-available trips to London, and at the Communications Center, they had been greeted with a mixture of awe and annoyance by the Communications Watch Officer who had had to set the thing up for paper strip decryption by the recipient after it had been machine broken only to reveal the "Eyes Only" designation. He would never let on, of course, but this was the first real EO he had ever handled.

Mort had a decade of experience with EOs in other places, among them the very headquarters that had originated this one, so within a few minutes of fooling with the Rube Goldberg-Captain Midnight device, they had their message. The CO realized that he had been included in the EO as Chain of Command protocol demanded, and he barely read the thing—just enough to realize that he probably did not want to know too much about its contents.

Mort unbuttoned his sport shirt and tucked in the white envelope they gave him, then they both drove back to the Quarters. The Grosses took their leave. When they got home—around the corner—Mort told Millie that he had something to do down at the Squadron. She was used to it, understood it, but in twelve years of marriage, never had been able to dismiss the now-faint resentment she felt every time the Navy took her husband away from her.

He let himself in his office after chatting with the Duty Officer and the Security Watch, who logged his visit with his in and out times. It did not take very long to read it a second time and lock it up in the safe, and went back up the hill and home to bed.

He didn't sleep all that well.

The Naval Air Facility at Port Lyautey, French Morocco, had been built by the Germans originally and now was a bustling US base, the focus of American Naval Aviation activity on Europe's threshold. Military air transportation from the United States to Europe, considering the range of the state of the art aircraft on the North Atlantic run, staged through New Foundland or Bermuda, thence to the Azores, thence generally to North Africa. Each service ran its own logistics chain, Air Force traffic normally originating at McGuire Air Force Base in New Jersey and terminating at Nouasseur in Casablanca. Navy traffic began from Norfolk, Virginia, and landed in Port Lyautey, fifty or so miles north of Casa. Personnel and priority cargo for the Sixth Fleet in the Mediterranean went Navy; Army and Air Force personnel and cargo were Air Force property and crossover was the exception rather than the rule.

The base had to be called a "Facility" since it was not under American ownership—technically the French owned it and they rarely let the Americans forget it. It was heavily transient, temporary home to a deploying Patrol Squadron and "bingo" home to carrier based aircraft in the Western Mediterranean unable to get back aboard on stormy nights or in need of heavier maintenance than could be provided at sea. Its permanent residents were the station personnel who kept things running, the Navy's Mediterranean area Transport Squadron whose mission was to deliver forwarded traffic westward, and the Unit itself whose mission was Don't Ask.

The single landing strip, 8,000 feet long, was oriented northeast by southwest in a vale along the banks of the Oued (pronounced "wadi") Sebou, a small, gently flowing river to the sea, a mile or so downstream. On high ground overlooking the field, a limited number of Quonset quarters were intermingled with permanent and semi-permanent administrative structures, some built by the Germans in '42. There was a chapel, an outdoor movie, a Navy Exchange and both Officer and Enlisted Clubs and bachelor quarters, but the business end of the installation could be found down on the flight line in hangars where the Unit had its offices and maintenance shops.

Each Saturday, the Department Heads generally came down the hill from their quarters or drove in from their in-town places to check the radioteletype traffic and monitor any weekend work in progress. This week was the first time everyone was back in civilian clothes on weekends. Off base travel had loosened up after a couple of weeks of high tension, when the Americans had to wear uniforms to identify themselves on and off base, and were restricted to travel to and from off-base residences.

Sidi Mohammed Ben Yussef had returned to Morocco as King Mohammed V, after an upsetting year of revolutionary activity ending in French acquiescence to the new Kingdom. They could look out their window and see the spot he had landed a couple of weeks ago, returning to a jubilant following that had succeeded in triumphing over French efforts to resist Moroccan attempts to govern themselves. Thoughtful Americans realized that the days of their presence in Morocco, as allies of the governing French, were limited, and that living in a Moroccan Morocco without what amounted to a French occupation would be both different and, for awhile, difficult. Port Lyautey itself had been named by the French for Marshal Lyautey, the pacifier/conqueror of Morocco, and there was a move afoot already to change it to Kenitra, the name of the original pre-French settlement.

Around ten Saturday morning, the Skipper called Lew and Mort together in his office and when he left to go up the hill to start his weekend, he left them there, still at it. The regular mission directive message was in the red Top

Secret clipboard and they had it open on the coffee table in his office when he left. There was no sign of the Eyes Only. Pilot or not, it was not for Lew's eyes—not yet.

The window of Mort's office in Morocco overlooked the flight line. Every time he glanced at a the beautiful grace and elegance of a parked Beast, he felt a father's joy, a mother's concern, a builder's pride, a surge of gratitude and wonderful sense of fulfillment. He never said as much, but they all knew it. He was at the top of his game, the Department Head, the Chief Evaluator, and it looked like he would be going flying.

* * *

Now, six days later, he was on his knees on the floor in a windowless room on Cyprus, the table and chairs pushed back, the Mickey crew bending and squatting as he ticked off their briefing for tonight's extravaganza.

He assigned frequency bands to each of the three passive stations, the lower frequency early warning radars to the lesser-experienced operators, the higher frequency locating radars to the other two stations. They agreed on a time-share protocol and a "request-deny" scheme for the Ampex wire recorders they would be using.

With a "captured" signal on the wire, it could be played back for later analysis, preserving its characteristic audio screeches and whoops to be listened to but more importantly, its electronic fingerprints easily visualized on a standard cathode ray analyzer or oscilloscope. They talked at some length about the capabilities of the newly available recording devices that used a Mylar tape instead of the standard alloy wire. All of them had read about "tape" recorders in the trade magazines but none had ever actually seen one. Mort had even designed a rig that funneled signals from each sensor into a single 16 head recording device; all they needed was someone to perfect a "tape" recorder it could work with.

They all knew about it and joked about the possibility that someday 3M would come up with a 16 channel tape that would record the signals—frequency and fingerprint—from all eight intercept stations while they stayed home and went fishing as the tape recorder did their job for them. Someday, someone said, there might even be a pilotless bird, like a little moon, sitting up there, way out in the stratosphere, recording all these signals. Fat chance.

He took them through the mission from takeoff, through the transit north, out into the area, through the first turn and the reasons for the saw tooth pattern. Each man had a specific set of assignments, by elapsed time, and they were all trained to coordinate their jobs with each other and the time-elapsed clock. He did not discuss the targets he and the Chief would be working. He also avoided, until almost the last minute, placing his finger on the round dot everyone knew was there, as if by touching the airdrome symbol on the map he might ring some extrasensory bell that would reverberate in the barracks and in the line shacks and down the flight line and up in the tower and in the control center of that awesome place, now alive beneath his finger on the chart.

When he was through, he asked for questions, covered a couple of last minute details and stood to signal that they had broken for supper.

"If it makes any of you feel better,' he said, "Pluto will be riding with us tonight".

He looked around for reactions, and getting none, he broke up the gathering. There was desultory chatter for a minute before they all trooped out to the NAAFI for a sandwich and a cup of Nescafe. Mort hung back for a second, and as the last of his crew left the cell-like cubicle, one of the RAF Communications Officers poked his head through the door.

"You have a phone call, sir," he said solemnly. "It's London," the solemnity giving way to absolutely morbid curiosity, ill disguised, polite, but morbidly morbid.

Mort followed the guy into the Communications "shack", through a minor labyrinth of cubicles and cabinets to a genuine office, an orangeish telephone on the desk with its receiver off the hook. He stared at it a second, totally confounded, dumbstruck actually, but fascinated and intrigued by the technical complexity of the project of catching him on the run two hours before flight time.

"You'll need to press the key to transmit, sir. It's a secure line to Whitehall."

Mort was as impressed as he was, but when he took the receiver, he waited with a direct gaze at the door that clearly told the young Brit that Yanks knew about radiotelephones and his presence was an unwelcome intrusion on his privacy—his and London's.

His heart was in his mouth. Was it Millie?

Bad news from home. All he could think of.

Secure high-frequency patches were fuzzy at any time anywhere, particularly around sunset, and Mort was surprised and relieved after the clicks and buzzes to have Winnie Burnet on the line, wire from Washington, God-knows-how from London to Nicosia, luck, genius or divine intervention to catch him on the fly.

"Mort? Winnie. Winnie Barnet."

Relief, then anxiety, a new kind now, hands steady.

"How are you Winnie?"

"Never mind. If you catch any fish tonight, keep them in the boat."

"Got it, Winnie. I got it."

"Good luck." Click. Off.

He stared off at a point a thousand yards ahead of him, as if he could see through the walls out into the car-park, across the taxiway, out to the runway.

The sun had gone down when they got back to the world with windows.

16

Washington

The night before, Jennifer and Winnie had still been at it at eleven when he had lit another cigarette and sat down, obviously burdened.

"Here's the hard part," he began. "Lew is married to Ginny. That's the hardest part of all."

She had no idea what he was getting at.

"Once upon a time, Lew and Ginny married. It was June week at the Academy, immediately after graduation, in 1942. Graduation was souped up under the pressure of wartime, so it was actually the 'Class of 1943' but it was still '42 on the calendar. Off they went to Pensacola. They got to understand marriage during Flight Training, and also got to understand that there was a certain amount of work involved on both their parts to keep the peace between them. Flight Training at Pensacola in wartime was the worst possible time for a new husband and wife to get off to a stable start.

"The husband was out on his own for the first time after three very intense years at the Academy, in a shortened curriculum, spitting them out to accommodate the worldwide need for Naval officers.

"He had a new wife, for the first time; a new status in life as a Naval officer, for the first time; a tremendous, consuming, new challenge in trying to learn how to fly; and the almost certain prospect of going to war, as soon as he did learn, hanging over both their heads. Husbanding might have been the hardest assignment.

"Another first, their son Evan, was born in June 1943 and he was in her arms as Ginny said her tearful goodbye to him the day after he got his wings in January 1944. She learned to cope, learned about life on her own and, along the way, learned that she was her own person with her own dark cravings and weaknesses."

Where is he *getting* this stuff, she wondered.

"Lew's war in the South Pacific ended with the surrender, what, September '45, was in all the papers." Not like him to be a smart-ass. He was looking away, was he wistful? Was that the word?

"When Lew went to Postgraduate School in 1946 to do his Masters in Aeronautical Engineering, Ginny spent more time with her parents in Mendocino than with him in Monterrey. Of course they had Evan to consider by that time, and in the hopes of using 'baby cement' to patch up things between them, Allison had been conceived on one of their weekends together. Two did not work any better than one, although later, when Lew was going through Test Pilot School in Patuxent River, Maryland, things were good enough to give him the peace of mind to finish first in his class.

"So when Lew was sent to Martin to manage the Beast airframe conversion, they both understood that they were walking into a quagmire that too much alcohol and not enough time together—or was it too much time together? - could generate. In a heroic effort to save his marriage, Lew quit drinking altogether, hoping Ginny would see the destructiveness that booze had been causing in their relationship.

"And she did. For a while.

"They moved to Morocco, they had a great circle of friends, the kids did well overseas, they had full time help, everything was great…but there was simply too much controlled drinking going on around her for Ginny to stay on the wagon.

"A 40-ounce Imperial Quart of Beefeater gin costs a dollar over there, did you know that? She was now hovering in that borderland between sobriety and oblivion most of her waking hours. With his exquisite sense of reality and the innate sensibleness that so irritated Ginny, Lew knew that whatever it might have been wasn't any more, it was over, knew that they were destroying each other, and knew it had come to an end. 'Once upon a time never comes again', as the song says. He grieved for the years invested, grieved for the selectively remembered happy times, grieved for the shared experiences of parenthood, but most of all grieved for the person he had been and no longer could be, for the lady that he had loved once who never was. He did this a lot."

He grew quiet.

"You knew them, then." Not a question, but not a statement either.

"I knew them both. The thing is, though, that they don't know me. Our actual paths have only barely crossed. But I knew them. It's sad what's happened. So sad."

And he went back into the same quiet he had just left.

"*What's* happened, Captain?" Jennifer asked almost gently, puzzled now, let down because the story certainly hadn't ended, and what she had heard told her nothing.

He stopped and looked at her a long time, searching her face but not looking at her at the same time, his mind off someplace she couldn't go.

"We'll see," he said. "Come on, it's late. Tomorrow's your big day."

And they got up, wordlessly, each with thoughts they hadn't entered with, each with some new burden neither of them understood. As she turned to leave the anteroom, he unlocked the door to his office on the other side of the room and went in, wordlessly, turning to wave to her with a wry smile as he closed the door behind him.

And then she was alone.

She went to her desk and sat down, and in the darkness she had to realize that she hadn't a clue as to what was going on with her boss…but suddenly, with a flash of woman's intuition cauterized by a decade in the spook business so full of institutionalized deception, it hit her.

Winnie had gone through this exercise all week, had *her* go through this exercise all week, not to find out what a dedicated digger in the paper work jungle could find, not to find out what was there, but to make sure something—what?—was *not* there!

And it had to be something that connected Winnie with the situation on the ground there in Cyprus where it was morning tomorrow, Thursday, December 15th, 1955, right now. D-day for the officers and crew she had gotten to know second-hand in the last couple of days. D-day for David, her own special Pluto, if he ever gets there.

D-day also, she felt certain, for whatever Winnie has up his sleeve.

No paper trail.

So just before midnight when the watch on the desk was being relieved, she went down and made sure that Jason who had the six to midnight would of course drive her home. C'mon Jason, what are friends for?

And that's why on the bus on a Thursday morning, late, she had been so distracted that she almost missed her stop.

* * *

Winnie had spent most of last night in the building, after Jennifer left, but had walked down to his apartment on Massachusetts Avenue around daybreak, and had dozed, shaved and changed into uniform for the Advancement ceremony later in the morning. It had gone well, Jennifer almost late, but between the congratulations and the mandatory but unladylike—she didn't care- passing out of cigars by the newly frocked First Class Petty Officer, she wondered how he had held up so well. There was a bouquet of flowers on her desk, from Jason, and she was arranging them in the office vase when Winnie came through and closed his door.

With the insights she had developed during the night screaming for validation, she was not at all surprised when, a moment later, the "in-use" light on the secure transoceanic telephone line on her desk came on.

She could hear the muffled sound of her Boss punching his way through the airwaves to London—usually she placed the calls and he picked up when the party was on the line. Something special, today—light on, long, long pause, the double-blink of the light when a "cascaded" patch to a third party had been completed, more brief conversation, more pause, then a short burst of two way conversation and a hang-up. Then a ring-back, and she quickly answered, a male British voice announcing that his party in Cyprus was on the line, and he picked it right up.

"Mort? Winnie. Winnie Barnet."

She hung up, quietly. She was right.

Something was up and she was glad she didn't know more about it.

* * *

Later, Winnie and the Deputy and the Chief Yeoman took Jennifer to lunch over on Wisconsin Avenue. A half-dozen of her buddies showed up to join them—they all knew each other—and they bumped tables and chairs together to the delight of the good natured Mandarin waiter who managed to get the chow mein and chop suey orders exactly right. There was some merrymaking, some laughs at her expense, a gag present from the newcomers, some applause at her little speech thanking them, and great deal of good feeling. Winnie found the time and the tongue to announce to the group that he had recommended Jennifer for a commission, and she was stunned—skeptical-stunned, because she knew enough of the procedure to know that she would have to formally apply for it, but still stunned and delighted.

As she left to grab the southbound W-2 bus on Wisconsin to consummate the skimpy remains of her official day off, she motioned him hesitantly over to the checkroom in the little Chinese restaurant.

"You know, I think, how much I appreciate all you've done for me," she began, earnestly, two friends, buddies almost, but with that touch of delighted respect with which one addresses a respected and beloved superior.

"This crow means a lot to me Skipper, and, well, I guess you know that, and a commission…Can't see myself as a lowly ensign, but on payday, it'll be just fine," and she laughed a little thinly and looked away, embarrassed.

"You earn it, Howie, every day, and I think you know how appreciative I am of everything you do—and have done."

She sobered then, looked at her watch, and searched his face for some expression that would indicate he was on the same wavelength she was, at that very minute. He was. He didn't need to look at his watch, but he did instinctively. It was almost one thirty.

Almost eight-thirty in the eastern Mediterranean, far, far away.

"They're almost in the air," she said, and for some reason it was an emotionally charged statement.

"Here goes," he said.

"Here goes," she echoed.

"It's your day off. Go home and get some sleep," and he grinned. "But not too much. I may need you tonight."

"Some day off! *You* get some sleep," she said. "Jason was a perfect gentleman last night, and I slept like a log."

She hadn't, of course, because she was taunted and haunted, by thoughts of double and triple crosses, of Lew and Ginny whom she did not know, of

Mort of whom she had heard, of Pluto who she would soon know better, and of the 'front end" guys she had gotten to know on paper. Captain Barnet was far more deeply involved in this Operational than any of the others. She knew that. And she sensed that this one would turn out differently, so differently from the rest.

And she thought again about Pluto. But this time she called him David.

17

Nicosia

"Technical Airways Enterprises" didn't even sound like an airline, so Lieutenant David Wagoner had absolutely no idea what to expect when he got off the TWA Constellation in Athens. He had been strapped to an airline seat for the better part of twenty-four hours—Washington to Gander, Gander to Rome, Rome to Athens, and now for the last leg. It felt good to walk again. He carried his own bag, a light traveler with a change of shirts, a Dopp kit of toilet articles and a couple of books in an AWOL bag, one of those light canvas always-blue carry-everythings most people associate with gym gear.

Blue blazer, raincoat over the shoulder, gray trousers, blue shirt with a rep tie. Nationality? Thick brown moustache, deep brown eyes, hair longish, sharp features. Italian? Maltese? Maybe.

He was pleasantly surprised to see the TAE counter, a "proper looking" counter as the English would say, obviously recently remodeled and expanded, with smaller logos for Greek Air Transport and Hellenic Airlines as prominently displayed as the TAE symbols. TAE would become Olympic Airlines one of these days, the staff had been told, Mr. Onassis would make it happen, just wait and see, and they were all pleasantly surprised at the progress the shipping tycoon was making buying up the competition.

He showed his ticket and maroon special US passport to a pleasant woman with ample girth at the counter and sat down to wait for the departure of Flight 254 to Nicosia. It was one o'clock here, six in the morning in Washington, and the night guys at Nebraska Avenue had moved his tag to Athens. Gave them something to do on the night shift.

When she sat down next to him, he was pleased and displeased at the same time.

She smelled of promise and excitement, looked great and was about his age but the last thing he wanted to do at the moment was to complicate this already overly complicated, overly planned, overly second-guessed job. Besides, he had spent a dozen hours over the last eight thousand miles first thinking about, then trying not to think about Jennifer Howell and assembling the list of hundreds of things he wanted to talk to her about right at this instant, now, immediately.

The temptress motioned to him for a light and he fished out the Zippo, lit one for himself, although his mouth felt like places of which people do not normally speak. Was that the Greek construction or was it the other way round? He couldn't - wouldn't -ask, certainly not of her!

She spoke to him instead, in Italian, and he replied and she rejoined and he replied and then he felt a twinge of mixed relief and displeasure when he found out she was going to Izmir. So he enjoyed the forty minute wait, less exhausted than he should have been now and when his plane was called away, first in Greek and then, with a nod to him, in Italian, he felt better. The stocky lady with the mustache who had looked at his American passport must have gone to lunch.

He was surprised to see that the DC-3 still bore the Hellenic Airlines paint and logo, but after twenty-four hours on and off a Connie, the first twenty-four minutes in the Dakota were enough to turn him against air travel permanently. It was a clear, warm day for December, with those puffy clouds that look so pretty from the same altitude but which reach out and shake the aircraft as it passes. Turbulence eventually subsided as they drew out over the Mediterranean, and with 600 miles to make in three hours and forty minutes, he closed his eyes and dreamed, now, reenacting his encounter with the perfumed Italian enchantress. Except that she was Jennifer, somehow.

He enjoyed it.

When he woke up, the sun was low in the reddening sky behind them. As they approached the island straight in from the west, he noticed lights on the ground ahead beginning to flicker on. By the time they touched down, the sun had gone as, first the threshold, then the runway lights came up to greet them.

His passport got him through what he assumed was a combination British Customs, Immigration and State Police and he was singled out of the group leaving the roped-off enclosure by a British Tommy in battle dress with a terrible complexion and a Cornwall accent.

"Here, Sir, if you please, Sir," the kid said, ushering him through a frosted glass door into a lighted office off what would be the concourse. The door closed behind and he was alone. He guessed the office belonged to an airport administrator and he snooped around enough to appreciate that security around the complex had been tightened recently. The map of the airport compound had recent grease-penciled notations on its Plexiglas cover with arrows pointing to certain features, mysterious to the casual observer. The office holder smoked Players.

In a minute and a half—he timed it—the door opened again and he felt that beneath the stands the bull had been released, the picadors were grouping up behind him and the crowd was yelling "Ole."

"I'm Lew Elfers," the stranger said. They had been expecting one another.

"David Wagoner," he said. He handed Lew a copy of his orders—vague as they were—and they both heaved a sigh of relief. Passwords exchanged.

"They've cut it close before," Lew said wryly, "but this time I figured the last plane in to Tombstone better have you aboard or we'd all be in deep shit tonight. Turns out you were the only American on the manifest and I guess I guessed right. Lousy way to run a railroad though."

"Stagecoach, actually," Wagoner said, "all the way from Fort Apache," and they both laughed.

They sized each other up, the younger man's brown eyes fixed like nails on Lew's face, Lew pleasant and reassuring, putting him at ease.

"We can talk here but it's probably not a good idea. Feel like walking?"

He felt like sleeping, if the truth were known, in a proper bed please, but his bones and joints screamed their assent and they left the office, walking down the corridor back toward the flight line, then out on the lighted apron. An RAF Land Rover, its driver at the ready inside, sprang to life and they both got in. David began to speak, but Lew shook his head and waved off in the direction they were going. The blue taxiway lights glowed faintly to their right as they drove on the grass, and almost immediately they were back on a hard surface between rows of parked aircraft, each in a floodlit pool of down-shielded white light.

"White lights hurts 'ems eyes" the driver volunteered, pointing at the floods. Yorkshire.

They traversed the line, left the parked planes behind them and about a hundred yards down the tarmac they pulled off and stopped. An Esso refueler was attached to the plane, a hose up on the port wing and another plugged into the belly. They watched for a minute, silently, then they both got out and Lew dismissed the driver. Almost simultaneously, the hoses were reeled back into the truck, a low rumble started as the auxiliary power unit started and red lights appeared through the cockpit hatch as the Beast powered up.

David was overwhelmed.

He had never seen a "real" one, and the manuals and tech notes and briefing sheets he had been made to memorize simply didn't do it justice as it loomed in front of them in the semi-darkness. It was the damdest thing he had ever seen, pitch black in the gloom, the red eye in the co-pilot's position seeming to look his way, a dragon resting, panting, ready for business.

They sat down on a Ready Bench, ignoring the painted "Warning, Do Not Sit" sign. He wondered what the hell the bench was for if you couldn't sit on it.

"Give me a little of your background," Lew began, "so I know where to start."

"Well, as you know, I'm a Special Duty Communications Security guy, 'Cryptology' they call it but that's what it isn't, a Naval Security Groupie out here ten days before Christmas wondering how the hell this is going to work. I've never flown in a Navy plane before, but I've just spent half a lifetime getting here so I guess I can take another hop or so."

He was wry and self-deprecating, neither cocky nor intimidated.

"Not much to tell. Born in the States, mother Italian, father Swedish consul in New York, Grandpa Swedish diplomatic service in St. Petersburg before the Revolution. Mother born there in Leningrad—that's what they call it now - her father the Italian Counsel General, she taught Russian at Columbia. Everybody spoke Italian, Swedish, Russian and English to me until I was six.

"Went back in '31, this time to Moscow, stayed until off to Prep School in Switzerland in '37. Summers in Riga, Latvia, back and forth to Stockholm, left permanently in '40, I was fifteen. Drafted in 43, shoved into the Navy, ended up in the Security Group translating. Out in '45, GI Bill Language and Linguistics at Georgetown, back into the Navy in '49, went Regular Navy, done all kinds of fascinating stuff.

"Never saw one of those things before, though, "he went on, pointing to the Beast behind Lew.

So far, Lew was pleased, as much for his maturity as for anything else, although he felt he could really like the guy. And the background!

"How many languages can you handle," he asked.

"Well, Italian, Swedish and Russian are as good as English." His English was perfect.

"How about Greek?" Lew asked. An idea was beginning to dawn.

"OK, good enough if it's not too fast."

"Good enough to make a radio position report?"

"Sure, if you write it out." Maybe, maybe not, but a good thing to know.

"How are you at listening to aircraft chatter, you know, guys talking to each other in the air, talking to the tower, that kind of stuff?" Lew asked.

"Well, we'll see won't we? I've been listening to recordings ever since this thing came up and I think I can manage."

"Recorders?"

"Just like the ones you have."

"Here's what I need you to do," Lew said, taking a small flashlight out of his pocket and a piece of RAF notepaper on which he had drawn some lines and squiggles.

"Around here" he pointed to a squiggle, "the folks over here" and he pointed to a round circle at the right of the sheet, "the folks over here will be talking to one another. Mickey will have the frequencies patched in and he'll tell you what to listen to. You know about Mickey, don't you?"

"Sure."

"When you hear tower radio traffic - anything at all—we'll want to know about it. The tower is on standby at sunset except for operational sorties and none are scheduled for tonight, unless we stir them up or if they know we're coming. We'll want to know what you hear, and if there is a taxi clearance request, we'll want to know it immediately. From there on, we'll want a running translation. Can you handle that, you think?

"Sure. Where do I sit, what do I wear, what do you call me, when do we eat?"

Wagoner knew the answers to all the questions he asked—except for dinner reservations—but he wanted to hear them again. First hand. And so Lew started to brief him in earnest, reading him into business, baptizing the newest "Pluto" and the next fifteen minutes went by quickly for both of them.

It was seven forty-five when they got up and walked over to the Beast. Bob Hunley and Brian Kerrigan had arrived together, followed immediately by the Mickey crowd and the rest of the flight crew. They were all dressed in civilian clothes, not good clothes, but civilian clothes. Even Lyle Burdick had on boondockers. They wore dog tags and would carry their green ID card in the pocket of their flight suit.

For awhile, there was what appeared to be organized milling around, as each reclaimed his outfit from the extruded-wire-mesh carryall in the bomb bay, then changed, right out on the tarmac in the semi-darkness, some stowing slacks and sport shirts back in the carryall behind the aft tank, others simply suiting over what they had on. The bomb bay had space for four fuel tanks, but only the forward three stations actually held the big, black rubber-coated self-sealing giants swinging from the safety-wired attach points.

On the fourth station, the Unit had rigged a pair of carryalls, one for baggage and clothing, and the other for a Cruise Box containing a collection of spare parts, accumulated and selected based on historical usage. Spare radio power supplies, vacuum tubes, instrument indicators, a dozen spark plugs, spare widgets and gizmos and a collection of larger tools were crammed into a plywood carrier that had often served as their lifeline to help get them back home.

Lew introduced Pluto to Brian Kerrigan and asked Brian to help him change into the spare flight suit and find a place to stow his stuff. By eight, they were standing in a circle waiting for Lew as he climbed out of the aircraft. He was the only one among them in any semblance of military garb. He had on his flight suit, like the others, but he wore a Navy piss-cutter cap with a gold oak leaf on one side and the Navy eagle and anchors on the other.

As usual, they would brief under the wing.

18

Nicosia

Brian had been right.

There was something - actually a couple of things—bothering Lew, and as the day ended and evening rolled ahead, he climbed into his flight suit wondering how much he should share with the crew. He had turned Wagoner over to Brian, and he and Mort had just finished a quiet conversation off in the shadows of the deserted taxiway away from the men.

Mort's bombshell, when it came, added to his sense of - not foreboding, exactly - but vulnerability.

Mort's Eyes Only message had contained a downgrade date and time, a point in time when he would be authorized to share the message with those who had a strict need to know. From seven o'clock on the evening before, when the original flight had been planned, the message was technically no longer "Eyes Only", and Mort had held the only copy next to his skin for so long now that he felt finally liberated to hand it to Lew beneath the wing of the Beast.

Lew's pocket flash was steady as he read again now, and he said nothing when he finished. The presence of Pluto in the mix had almost certainly signaled it.

He had suspected this when he had first plotted the points, before Brian had even seen them. Even then, the target had been unmistakable.

They had tried several times before, tentatively.

No more tentativeness. Here it was in writing. Final. He read the thing again, looking for a loophole, some sign that they were really only kidding, some indication that he would not have to take the Beast so much farther into harm's way than any of them had ever been. It wasn't there, of course, and Lew looked at Mort thoughtfully. They both thought of Winnie, neither saying his name.

Who the hell else.

"Holy shit." Flat, one syllable at a time.

Ho…lee…shit.

The United States Navy for the first half of the twentieth century had the most elaborate long-range communication system in the world. It was built on three pillars, pillars that everyone could understand and everyone could remember in dealing with passing the word to forces at sea—or anywhere else, for that matter. *Reliability*, *Security* and *Speed* drove this complex, intricate machine and the message format the Navy used during these decades of efficient communication reflected the evolved answer to these three demands. The Navy relied on high frequency continuous-wave wireless—Morse code—broadcasts to get the word to the ships at sea, and on Naval ships all over the world, teams of dedicated radiomen sat and copied these broadcasts, insuring the integrity of what would become known, decades later, as Command and Control.

The Navy got into the acronym business around the time Marconi invented the wireless. In maritime wireless communication, particularly on dark and stormy nights when the static flew and the wind and the waves did bad things to flimsy "aerials" mounted atop whipping foremasts or strung between kingposts and jack staffs, brevity was a virtue. Abbreviation was its handmaiden, and early Navy communicators spent a lot of time and effort dreaming up abbreviations their originating radio operators could more easily key into that sea of static and the recipients pluck back from it with their primitive receivers. Shorter words on dark and stormy nights, through the static. "CINCPAC" took seven letters to say seven words - Commander in Chief of the Pacific Fleet.

Speed was a variable. Stock requisitions for basketballs need not be handled with the same urgency as battle reports, so a priority system was developed. The first character in a Naval message gave its priority, with the letter P indicating the highest priority an originator could assign to non-Operational traffic. Following the priority indicator, a date time group indicated the date, the time in Greenwich Mean time and the month and year the message was originated. Addressees were always indicated by acronyms, the beginning of the message by a long "break" signal abbreviated by the Morse letters B and T, and sentences were broken not by periods but by Xs, shorter Morse characters than the period signal. When the letter "X" replaced the longer Morse-code group for the "period" ending a sentence, the acronym was born.

This stylized formatting was ingrained into every Naval Officer, almost from conception it seemed, so Lew had no trouble immediately understanding the flimsy onion skin sheet, blurred here and there by bodily fluids of one sort or another, but nonetheless more readable than one might expect considering its late storage place.

-P-111557ZDEC55

FM: CINCNELM

INFO: CNO…

BT TOP SECRET BOOMERANG X EYES ONLY X FOR CO AND CHIEF EVALUATOR ONLY X CNO FOR OP933YANKEE X THIS

MESSAGE IN ONE PART X PART ONE X DECEMBER TASKING BY SEP MSG X IN CONDUCT OF DECEMBER OPERATION 12-2 ANTICIPATE ACTIVE RESPONSE BY FLASHLIGHT AIRCRAFT LOCATED BATUMI X IMPERATIVE THAT INTERCEPTION OF AIRBORNE FIRECONTROL KILO BAND KITEREST AND FOXTROT BAND FARMFISH BE ATTEMPTED X APPRECIATE HAZARDS INVOLVED WHICH WILL NECESSITATE SUSPENSION OF PARA 5(G) ANNEX CHARLIE MY OPORDER (RULES OF ENGAGEMENT) X WHILE PRUDENT SAFETY OF FLIGHT CONSIDERATIONS ABSOLUTELY NECESSARY CMM AIR TO AIR DATA URGENTLY NEEDED SOONEST X TASKING MSG TO INCLUDE ASSIGNMENT NSG ASSET TO ASSIST IN DETERMINATION OF BREAKOFFPOINT X EYES ONLY RESTRICTION UNTIL 171700ZDEC X GC103
BT

What this thing said in effect was that you were to go find the dragon in his cave, arouse him from sleep, get him mad, make him chase you and bring back a couple of buckets of whatever he spits at you. We'll give you a guy who speaks Dragon-talk who will help you decide when to run from the cave. Do take care, but don't come home without it. Provoke, if you must, but watch your ass.

Whenever an operational mission profile required them to come within the potential defense envelope of Soviet Bloc aircraft, the assignment of a language expert in the Pluto seat had long been acknowledged as an operational requirement. In referring to an "NSG Asset," Pluto's Naval Security Group pedigree was acknowledged, and Lew glanced over at the new arrival twenty feet away as he re-read the phrase.

There had been flights in which the Pluto capability had not been exercised, but there had also been occasions when the Unit had had to request Pluto support and had needed it. The protocol always required the aircraft to turn around and head home the instant Pluto reported that defending aircraft had been heard on either the Ground Control or the Tower frequency, taxiing or lighting off. This was the "break off point" and while it was up to the pilot's discretion and his responsibility as aircraft commander, it was, tactically speaking, a Mickey decision to break-off. A break-off was not an abort, and anytime a break-off had occurred, the voice-track wire-recorders fully supported the decision. It was a defensive action. When either suggested it, in practice, the other concurred. The procedure was set down in the Top Secret Rules of Engagement Annex to their governing Operations Order.

They had been sent many times into the far eastern part of their "area of interest" on a search for the same elusive signals. Each time they had been skunked. They had tippy-toed in, expecting a flurry or reaction—alert messages, long-distance radar paints, and preliminaries to launching the

Flashlights—and nothing whatsoever had happened. This time, though, something had changed. Now the powers-that-be "anticipate active response" and the rules had been changed, the ante upped. The previous luxury of a well-defined break-off event was gone.

They were on their own. No break-off without the bacon.

This was the first time that so provocative an action had been authorized, provocative in the sense that the other guys would be enticed into the air, enticed to light off their fire control radar and then suckered into a run on the Beast. Tonight, break off would have to wait until Mickey had intercepted airborne fire control radar signals from the twin-jet night interceptors - NATO code named "Flashlight" - based at Batumi, just around the corner from the border. This time, the idea was that the mission completion required a wire-record of the chattering whine of acquisition radar in the air, looking for them, followed by fire-control radar, in the air, locked on them.

God only knew how close they'd be to getting their collective asses shot out of the sky, but God also knew that the fix was in. Lew had Marta and Marta was their guardian angel.

"I briefed my guys this afternoon," Mort said. "They're raring to go and eager to please," this with a wry, comical, not-quite-true face.

"After you get over the shock, it's less scary, but 'Holy Shit' just about does it. I gave them the full story." Lew thanked Mort and they both turned back to the aircraft, back lighted now by the glow from the tower and terminal area.

The full story. The hell you did.

As far as he was concerned, Lew imagined that he alone knew the "full" story, and now his self-assurance had to deal with the golf-ball sized lump crawling up throat and windpipe. It screamed for attention as it came careening out of the pit of his stomach, fighting his panicked brain for attention, straining against muscles in a mad, primal struggle to totally vanquish his composure.

His relationship with Marta and his relationship with these dozen sailors and his relationship with his conscience, with his career and with his very life suddenly had become an almost real presence on the tarmac.

This was the reality, shrieking out for attention as he turned into the breeze and felt the scent of moisture in its hint of rain. He had been so successful in keeping this thing caged, glorying, reveling, exulting in the fact that his Marta had faithfully kept them all safe, kept the faceless enemy to the north quiet when they flew, deceived into thinking they were elsewhere and unable ever to respond to threaten them in any way.

Now this reality was bumping into the other reality of his profession, of his life work, of his country, for Chrissake. How far could the tension between the two realities take him? Tonight they would see. It would be quite a ride. Marta would once again save their hides, quiet the Northern Beast, get them back safely and the guilt he would feel on the way home, skunked again, would only briefly bother him because he had bought with it the safety of a dozen good lives.

Brian was in an intense tutorial session with Pluto - what was his name, Wagoner?—showing him how the yellow Mae West life preserver they had given him worked, cautioning him about pulling the lanyard. Of course he pulled it, and of course it immediately inflated, and of course the crew razzed him, but he took it well and they had it deflated and a new cartridge in place in no time. A rite of passage for Pluto, Lew remembered. They did it every time.

Lew held back and climbed up into the aircraft. He disappeared for a minute while mild horseplay continued to dissipate nervousness on the asphalt, then he was back, chart in hand, ready to brief.

He would not have planned this thing this way. It was understandable that if the objective was to get fire control radar on the wire recordings, then one way to do it would be to go where the fire control radar is, get them to turn it on, and then fade back and see how far back they had to go until the signals dissipated and disappeared. That was what they were going to do tonight.

Wouldn't it have been better, he thought, to zigzag in from the far side, approach gingerly, see how close they had to get to get light-off, and then haul-ass out of there? It certainly would have been more prudent, but then he remembered that chilling phrase on the Eyes Only—"imperative interception be attempted." He realized that they wanted it to happen this way. They wanted the lock-on so badly that they were unwilling to gamble that the crew would consider themselves too far into harms way and bug out before they got something of value.

Thank God for Marta.

Ever since the Naval Academy, Lew had realized that he had an innate sensibleness that allowed him immediately to understand objectives, devise actions aimed toward meeting the objectives, and them carry them out as planned. That made him an ideal Operations Officer, to his superiors, but Lew also realized that he had a "bell," a built-in warning device, that every so often disturbed his composure to sound an alarm. This whole operational this week had made his bell ring. It had been ringing all day.

Around noon, he had been lying in bed half-asleep trying to bank rest for the flight when the primitive Acropole phone had sputtered to life. Picking it up, he heard clicks and buzzes, then the unmistakable words "…the petrol, the petrol…" before the phone went dead. He had squeezed down the center post and gotten the desk on the line, but the desk—whoever it had been - had been very sanguine, assuring him that he had not had an incoming phone call, that the system did that on its own from time to time, and that the phone system had been acting up today. It had disturbed Lew. He had a least a dozen of these things under his belt and he had never known the Nick phone system to "act up," but then he had to acknowledge that other than to call the desk for a cab, he hadn't had much experience with the system. Had it been a warning? An omen? A simple wire-crossed inquiry after non-delivered gas someplace? He didn't know, couldn't. Wouldn't.

He tried to rest again after lunch, but the phone call had made him think about tonight's gas load. They would be starting engines with the three installed bomb bay tanks full, more than enough to fly a nine-plus hour flight. He silently did the addition and subtraction and finally fell asleep thinking about Ginny.

At three this afternoon he had gotten up, showered and padded next door to touch base with Mort before Mort turned into Mickey and went out to brief his gang. They both agreed that the mission profile would have made more sense backwards—from far out into close range—but also agreed that their best chance of getting anything was this way.

Mort went off, and Lew walked through the long corridor around to the back of the hotel. Over the kitchen, he hesitated a second on the stairs, inhaling the familiar lamb-cabbage-spice aroma that he would always associate with this particular landing, then continued up to the top of the flight and knocked softly on the door.

After a moment, Marta had opened it.

The Turkish girl who worked at the hotel, Nikki he thought her name was, was with her. The two women exchanged glances before she slipped past Marta and Lew and made her way out the door and down the steps. Had they been weeping? He looked at Marta with a wrenching mixture of sadness and hope and he held her by the elbows and kissed her softy on the side of her mouth.

"Remember, west from Samsun. Toward the Bosphorus."

She nodded, tears now fully dried, no sign of weakness or vulnerability, the way he remembered her. Then he went back down the stairs and around to his own room and waited for the weather guy to come. And he thought about Marta.

He thought about their last time together, before now, before last night, before this trip, before he had acknowledged even the possibility of a problem. He reenacted it, for the millionth time.

They are driving her Opel back from a circular tour that had started in Nicosia and gone east to Lefkoniko, through the Turkish settlements, with their sun dried walled enclosures and the strange animals that looked like American sheep mated with American goats, neither parentage dominant.

At Lefkoniko they stop and walk through the quaint but sullenly quiet Turkish village, shrouded women with dark eyes on them at every turn along the extension of the highway that is the village heart. They turn north through the pretty pass cut in the hills to Akanthou on the coast, and then west along the beach road they had driven before. They speak in the car, then, about relationships, about Horst and St. John and Kriesler and for the first time, Marta opens the door to her own activities ever so slightly.

She is almost coquettish at the end, leading him on, misleading him perhaps, toying with him perhaps, leaving the conversational topic with the cryptic confession that she tells her "circle" everything they do together. It is half-in-jest but perhaps not, Lew decides, perhaps not. What to make of it?

The weather briefing did nothing to ease his state of mind.

19

Nicosia

At the Acropole Hotel, a Notice To Patrons advises that the international cabaret team of Horace Lundy and Marta Mardi will be appearing at the Chanticleer each Wednesday and Friday evening, and patrons are encouraged to "take in this exceptional entertainment, beginning at 10.00 on the above evenings."

The text is repeated in Greek, German and French, and from the looks of it, it has been hanging on the board at the Acropole for a number of months.

The curfew had come and gone, come and gone again in its various incarnations, but when all was said and done, some weeks they appeared, some weeks nobody appeared, not even customers. Had they not performed together so many times, their act would have gotten rusty, but since there really was no "act" to begin with, just the two of them doing music, there were never any complaints.

The two had met shortly after the war in the west had concluded, before the hopeful climate of late '46 and '47 had dissipated against the hardships of the Berlin Blockade and the clear handwriting on every wall announcing that Things Were About to Get Worse. Both in their mid-twenties, they had survived the war separately, coming together as self-styled advanced music students in a Potsdam gymnasia/conservatoire struggling to regain a foothold in the currently non-existent cultural life of Berlin.

She had been born in Bohemia at a time when the language and nationality of that troubled section of Czechoslovakia changed almost annually. Her parents had jumped the border when she was thirteen, moving the few miles south into Austria. There were never any papers, hence never any licit rations, but they survived by their wits.

By the time she was twenty she had survived brutality, starvation, sexual abuse and almost miraculously, a final horror after her seizure by marauding German troops. The rag tail band fleeing the westbound Soviet Army had nothing to lose, and as it prepared for a final gang-bang, it was unceremoniously—reluctantly, really - ambushed and wiped out by a tiny party of American Project 33G nasties who found themselves now stuck with a female.

Operating between American and Russian lines in late April 1945, "33G" military-OSS groups tried to pave the way for the US-Soviet linkup. Multi-service more by accident than by policy or strategy, they were hurriedly organized under civilian auspices in early 1945 and drew from language, communications and dirty-trick specialists from the OSS and both armed services.

Although not in the best of health, she was mobile and fierce. She earned her keep through the May 8th armistice and the leader of the small band saw to it that she was well cared for as they headed back west to the to the covert station at Schierstein on the Rhine. He was a decade or so older than she, clever and resourceful, and during their adventures together that Spring and early summer, they cared for one another, protecting and covering one another through the chaotic nightmare following the surrender. They bonded. At Schierstein they had two months of recovery before he was gone, to the Pacific she guessed, and one day soon after, she appropriated a bicycle and headed back east to Berlin. She felt that she had had her happiness. She never forgot him.

A decade ago, now, when she thought about it.

And when she did, it was a different person thinking, a different body, a different heart. She had made it so, in part so to handle the painful pleasure of their other irregular contacts through the years.

And she had succeeded. She was different now.

Horst had fought through the war in three different uniforms, most recently as a Moldavian, but he was a native German with a short memory for details like that. He was in the process of putting some meat back on his frame, and as he filled out, his open good looks and his boyish charm seemed to come alive, touchingly, day by day, out of some trampled ashes. He had sandy hair and gray eyes so light that they seemed sometimes to be without any iris at all, a startling effect at first, soon ignored in the warmth of what Marta described as a smile that hugged.

She was darker, her straight black hair worn in a pageboy, her bangs framing a squarish face set off by large, almost blue-black eyes. She was dazzlingly feminine, even in those crude times, when the world was crushingly masculine and survival was at stake, but survive she did, elegantly. She was remarkably nonchalant about her appearance, open and seemingly without guile, an easy listener with a ready smile that stopped just short of completely opening her to strangers. Behind the smile there were quiet monsters, sometimes at work even now, almost a decade later.

Potsdam was in the Soviet Zone, but in those early days, getting about the city was easy, and the Berlin version of mass transit in 1947 was a gaggle of bikes. Frau Bemmelmann had been an "important" choreographer and voice coach before the war. In association with Herr Dokteur Francke, a competent piano professor at the University of Leipzig not known in pre-war circles for its piano department, they had cobbled together their little school.

It was an interesting place, the Odeon Practique, its constituency mainly a group of musically talented risk-takers who had found themselves in Berlin for a variety of reasons, many of them quite sinister. There was a lot of musical faking going on, both on the high side and the low side, and nobody probably was what he or she seemed to be. It had been a polyglot group, as well. All of them had acquired excellent American English in their survival journey to 1947. All, also, had interesting moonlight occupations, which helped pay Frau Bemmelmann's tuition and keep body attached to whatever soul was left among them.

Marta Czrodny had a good contralto voice, an aficionado's grasp of several complex operatic contralto roles, and a photographic memory for scores, lyrics and faces. For most other things as well, she soon noticed.

Horst Lümpenboeck was a remarkably talented pianist, initially self-taught, dazzled now by the accelerated learning Herr Dokteur Francke was cramming into his nimble fingers. They became close friends and shared what passed for an apartment in Berlin in those days, furnished with an outrageously inventive inventory of surplus war materiel, reclaimed antiques from the bombed rubble, and bad taste.

Horst was homosexual, a quality Marta came to greatly admire in men after some of her wartime experiences, the memory of the monsters that had populated them and, paradoxically, her single surrender at war's end. Neither did anything to dispel the assumption that they were lovers, and eventually, man and wife.

In mid-1948, the student body at the Odeon numbered an even two dozen—Czechs, Poles, Germans from each of the Zones, two adventurous Frenchmen, two Americans who had more money than either talent or discretion, a Cypriot couple - the Papandreous, brother and sister - and the effectively stateless Horst and Marta. The group was diverse, multi-lingual, wildly idiosyncratic and with the exception of the two Czechs, all were employed in one capacity or another in extra curricular associations with one—frequently two or three—of the intelligence gatherers who roamed pre-Blockade Berlin. It was a great game. As a result of these activities and as a function of their intimate association with one another at the Odeon, they shared the most sensitive gossip with one another and recruited one another shamelessly for the most ideologically diverse masters, living and thriving on the idea that they were sticking it to, in order, each one of the major powers, on a daily basis.

Marta and Horst did odd jobs for the Russians through their contacts in the ramshackle apartment building where they lived. They would meet "Klaus" for *kaffe* - Klaus got real *kaffe* -and trade gossip garnered in their schoolrooms. Horst and he were special friends. He was a sweet, gentle, artistic man, somewhat effete, well educated and self-effacing, in his mid-thirties somewhat older, but established in the system someplace. They never really knew, except that he paid well and helped them set up an account in Zurich. There never was much money in it, but it was to come in handy later.

They would pump Klaus unmercifully, who, like themselves, was of uncertain loyalties. Then they would gather, often immediately afterward, with the Papandreous' and one of their "associates," a rumpled and messy Mr. St. John, who would be delighted to listen to the often valuable and authentic bits of political intelligence they had garnered from their conversations, and which would end up in London before the sun had set.

It was all very commercial, un-ideological, matter-of- fact and profitable.

So, as might be expected, they had inside information about the currency reform in late May 1948. They decided it was time.

On Sunday, June 18 then, Marta, Horst, the Papandreous' and Klaus boarded one of the last un-blocked trains from Berlin, leaving behind their rent bill and all of the awful furniture. The senior Papandreous were indirectly related to the soon-to-be influential Greek political figures of the same name, and were successful innkeepers in post-war Nicosia, due in part from their ownership of a hotel that had been commandeered and refurbished as a Royal Army officers' billet in Nicosia. It had reverted to them, finally, after years of entreaty, and they had called their children back from seeking their bliss - neither had much musical talent - to help run the place.

After a series of administrative adventures with the occupying Four-Power governmental apparatus, helped once by the Cypriots and once by Klaus, they arrived in Zurich on September 30, 1948 with Federal Republic of Germany laissez-passer papers. In Zurich, Marta and Horst claimed their small accounts and parted company with Klaus. The Papandreaous siblings decided that it would be interesting if they became Jewish holocaust survivors, headed for Palestine—a popular and governmentally approved endeavor in Zurich that year—and when they got near Cyprus, bail out and settle down.

Marta and Horst tagged along, and so they had become associated, quite by chance, with the Acropole Hotel and its satellite nightclub, the Chanticleer.

Each Papandreous married, he to a wealthy Maronite from Beirut, she to a Hellenic Airlines pilot, and their separate lives took more and more of their time. When their parents died, they formally engaged Horst and Marti as co-managers of their Cyprus enterprises, and they went separate ways for the greater portion of each year, finally selling the properties to them outright.

The Acropole prospered. It remained the lodging of choice for itinerant and temporary Royal Army officers, as well as for UN types, diplomats, *commercants* and - to be sure—the officer crews of the regular monthly Beast visit beginning late in 1953. Five years had sped by.

Earlier, on a warm March day in 1953, Horst and Marta were having lunch together in the Acropole dining room. They had a large suite of rooms, the host apartments, in the rear of the building where each had a separate bedroom and bath, with a common sitting room and small kitchenette. With business brisk, the oversight of additional holdings throughout Nicosia and the continuing artistic attention they both devoted to the Chanticleer militated against their seeing each other on a social basis except for the occasional lunch. After eight years together, they had a strong, totally compassionate and totally honest relationship with one another.

The British withdrawal from Egypt to Cyprus was in full swing, the economy and the social structure of Nicosia abuzz, newcomers everywhere. A group of Army officers, including a Brigadier, were attending a welcoming luncheon in the private dining room. The Royal Air Force Officers Wives Circle was lunching on the patio. Marta checked the reservation book and, as was their custom, she and Horst went unobtrusively to visit each function, checking on the menu and the service.

In the dining room, the guest of honor, a Mr. Hawkins, was being welcomed to Cyprus by a heady cross-section of the British business, political and social community. They were flattered to receive a private introduction at Mr. Hawkins' request, and since they had known him earlier and elsewhere as Mr. St. John, each wondered what impact the newcomer would have on the placid artistry of their lives.

Coincidently or, perhaps not - they never knew - the United Nations High Commission for Refugees announced it would establish a Finance and Public Liaison office in Nicosia the following month.

At the reception for the U.N. newcomers, also at the Acropole, this time on a lovely evening just before the Easter festivities, the guest list was equally impressive. Each of the arriving staff members and their wives, if present, were formally introduced to Nicosia society, if there were such a thing. With a troubling feeling of déjà vu, Horst and Marta were introduced - reintroduced, actually—to the Assistant Chief Comptroller, Middle East, whom they had known so well in a previous incarnation as their own sweet Klaus.

Taking their cue from him, they expressed great pleasure in making the acquaintance of Mr. Frits Kriesler, late of Stuttgart. They used anglicized stage names, Horst was Horace Lundy and Marta was Marty Mardi in their act—the Monday and Tuesday a "cute" touch in multilingual Nicosia.

Mr. Kriesler, of course, found them charming and they became instant friends. Dear, dear, Klaus.

The first Beast operational mission staged through Nicosia in May 1953. Lieutenant Commander Elfers had arrived in French Morocco to become the Unit Operations Officer the month before, and his family had set up quarters on base in a reconditioned and refurbished Quonset hut. He was the pilot of the first mission, and for the next thirty months or so, he and three other seasoned Beast pilots alternated the missions, but that was later. Lew, as Operations officer, had first refusal, and he generally took the missions offering the most "involvement." The move to Morocco had not pleased Ginny, who was beginning to throw off the hard-won sobriety of the previous ten months.

But on this particular evening, May 19th 1953, Lew was alone in the Acropole, wondering how to spend off-time in a strange, almost hostile, city. It was two years before the troubles, and Nick shared some of the glittering reputation of Beirut as a reasonably sophisticated outpost of civilization in the eastern Mediterranean. The others had gone exploring, off on the tour to Kyrenia everyone took, back when things were quieter.

He struck up a conversation with Horst over a cocktail before dinner, and they had taken to each other immediately. Horst was easy to talk to, a brilliant musician whose playing fascinated Lew. He knew all the songs that had formed the background for his courtship of Ginny—better days that Lew now realized were gone—and after he had played "Don't Blame Me" for the second time at Lew's request, he closed the keyboard and they decided to have dinner together. Lew was drinking again, socially, and he sensed that his sacrifice had been a useless exercise. He liked Horst, although he also sensed that Horst's interest in him had an overtone of intimacy implied in it that Lew found manageable though unwelcome.

But later, when Marta joined them for dinner, he and she had examined each other with that innate sensibleness they shared, and Lew felt he knew, immediately and without the slightest doubt, that they would become lovers.

Perhaps they did. Perhaps they really did.

But not immediately.

They had spent the evening together, the three of them, after-dinner drinks at the Chanticleer, then just the two of them, the whole night talking and enjoying one another as if they had both just been born. They closed the cabaret bar at midnight, then strolled back to her rooms in the Acropole, where they continued their marathon engagement until the dawn lighted the windows and brought sleep to their eyes. They had cuddled, finally, slept together fully clothed, kissed and explored one another's bodies almost as an afterthought to their discoveries, but had not made love. Lew was on an inverted day-night schedule, sleeping in daylight, flying every other night, and their lives took on that rhythm for the few days a month they could share. Marta's nights were always her days.

In the ensuing months, there was an intimacy, no doubt. They communicated wordlessly, either because each was totally enmeshed in the other's thoughts and motives and feelings and yearnings and emotions, as Lew would have it, or because they were both extremely clever people. They were both emotional soldiers, both survivors, both "brave warriors in the struggle" as Thomas Mann had suggested, and the time they were together—brief as it was on a bi- or tri-monthly basis—was all they seemed to need to cement some kind of a bond between them.

Remarkably, perhaps not so remarkably, each had a totally full, totally committed life wholly apart from the other, in which each of them performed the duties and the functions of their separate conditions, neither of them intruding or preempting or co-opting the other in the affections and whims and fantasies and sentiments of their individually taken paths.

Lew never shared details of his operational life with Marta. But she knew, intuitively sometimes, sometimes by gesture or frown or grimace or grin, when they would be heading into the worst of it, when only milk runs were scheduled.

He knew she knew.

For his part, Lew knew about Hawkins/St. John and knew about Klaus/Kriesler, knew that they were both there when he entered her life and let it go at that. He soon knew that data was being passed in both directions, knew that each of the two men had hooks that could tear and rip and totally shred any semblance of fragile happiness the two of them could ever have hoped to have.

They dealt with the facts differently, each of them.

For her part, she had lived with the realities of such relationships since 1944, and she brought to her dealings with this "reality," as she termed it, enormous respect. That had been - and was- the key to her survival. His key, she discovered, was difficult to pinpoint. He was extremely good at everything he did, extremely modest about his own accomplishments and talents, and yet, he had an almost blind faith in correctness, in goodness, in oughtness, in innocence proclaimed.

He had not, she realized, experienced innocence betrayed. She wondered, when she thought about it, how closely he listened to his own conscience, or whether he even had one.

"Are you lovers yet?" Horst had asked her one day.

"Do you want us to be?" she asked him.

"Of course, silly, if you want to be" he had answered, smiling broadly, possibly at the absurdity of the situation, possibly just because he enjoyed asking her tough questions.

She had not pursued the issue and neither had he. They had been in the game together a long time.

In the fall of this year, she makes Lew confront the unspoken. They are driving along the beach road, up north. They have often talked about the things each of them did while they were apart, and the conversation this time has gone on, based on their intimacy, into areas they had never entered together. She sets the tone casually, matter-of-factly, but both of them know they are introducing another dimension into their lives. Horst has a "relationship," through Hawkins whom she always knew as St. John, with the British. Marta has a "relationship" through dear Klaus with people whom Marta described as "not so British." They each have their "friends," as Marta put it, and their bitter enemies.

Marta laughs.

"Poor St. John," she says. "The thorn in his side is a taxi-driver named Mikos. You maybe have seen him, he has black shiny car, American I think. Well, St. John wants to kill him, I believe, but Mikos is too smart for him!"

They all deal in political intelligence, and Marta and Horst read the papers, keep their ears open, cultivate their clientele at the Chanticleer and at the Acropole, and pass on whatever they can. The main focus now is to determine the agenda of Israel and the Arab league with regard to the Cyprus Question, in light of the Salonika bombings and the deterioration of the Greek-Turkish balance on the island. She has utterly no choice, under the circumstances, but to continue with her contacts, recognizing that she and Horst, as a couple, sometimes work both sides against the middle.

Their dear Klaus has given them the priceless Nikki, and they in return, provide him with what he thinks he needs. What *will* the Turks do, we all want to know.

Yes, there is some information that is more, well, tactical than political, particularly the information St. John seems so desperately to need.

Does he give it to Winnie, she often wondered.

Poor Winnie. She would make it up to Winnie. Soon.

Everyone seems to need to know about Makarios and about Grivas and about Harding and the people around him and how the Arabs will deal with the Czech arms and about how Nasser will deal with Jordan and Syria now that their military forces are unified and what will Nasser do about the Canal.

The monthly visit by the Americans has become so routine that it is neither a secret nor a major item of interest to anyone. Marta, of course, sets her calendar by Lew's visits, "as well you know," but all of them—Horst, Klaus and St. John, even Nikki, know of the relationship and have encouraged it.

"Not that I need encouragement," she says coyly, smiling lightly.

"They don't ask me anything about you anymore. Everyone here knows when you go out there to fly—it makes so much noise! - and they go about their business."

"Do you tell them when we are flying?"

"Of course I do, silly," she replies mischievously, "I tell them everything about you!"

And then she knew how she would make things right with 33G.

With Winnie.

FLIGHT

20

Thursday Evening, December 15, 1955

8:02PM

There were, understandably, several threads of concern and uncertainty that Lew would have to brush aside before the briefing began.

As they gathered on the tarmac in a rough semicircle, he looked at Timmons and asked his usual question. He led off every operational briefing this way.

"How's the Beast?"

"Beast's fine, Sir. White re-centered the flux-gate compass you mentioned on the way over."

"What about gas?"

"Gassed to about 4020 and dipped. We checked the gas when we fuelled, but all the samples were fine. I'd never seen such water-free gas. Somebody must have spun it and drained it because it all checked fine"

Lew thought immediately about the clicky phone call he had gotten. Imagination does wonders for your composure, he thought. Cross the gas off the worry list.

"Anybody else got anything we need to know off the bat? Nav?

"Looks like ten hours, Sir," Brian began. "Should taxi by eight fifteen local, like to be in the air at eight thirty three to make the slot time east of Samsun. Northeast out of here to Silifke-abeam, then 428 nautical miles to feet-wet. Back before sunup, if all goes right."

The point on their track when the radio beacon at Silifke, on the southern Turkish coast, was on their wingtip abeam was their traditional navigational start-point, even though it was several dozens of miles after takeoff. Up north, the "feet-wet" point would be the location of their departure from land, the point at which they would be over the Pond, ready for business.

"Radar, you up?"

"Radar's up, Sir," Blackie said. "Mr. Kerrigan and me will be taking a departure fix with the antenna rotating, then silent until we turn around to go feet dry. Shouldn't be no trouble."

"We may reconsider that tonight and stay off line all the way. I'll let you both know. Radios Burdick?"

"Everything's up, but everybody triple check your Internal Communications boxes to make sure your transmit key is down. I know I don't have to remind anybody of this but I will anyway. When the key is up and I have an active radio patched into another key on your box, if you call your buddy on the ICS, you're going to be broadcasting. We won't be using radios the whole time until we get back, but I'm going to have to have them in standby, so watch those keys! I'll have the three High Frequency receivers tuned, one to 55 for monitoring traffic, one to the Nick tower's HF frequency, although they never man it unless you beat them over the head, and after we get a WWV time-check, one to our HF emergency frequency. We can get a good time signal here from WWV in Washington, and I'll just leave that on until we taxi if anybody needs to synch up their clocks and watches. Make sure you set your UHF and VHF radio selector switches on 'receive only' in the cockpit—I know you always do—but just check it for me. Radio Altimeter off, your discretion in the cockpit but before we get too far north. I'll have the Loran on for you, Nav, but out here at night, it's one skywave if you're lucky, and that one is pretty shaky."

"All right, then, listen up. First, this is Mr. Wagoner. He'll be riding Pluto tonight."

He took an acknowledgement, waving his hand to the rest of them.

"Next, I want you to know what we're up to. As you may remember, twice now we've gone up there—Timmons and Lucore were with me last time—you too, Burdick, if I remember—and not gotten anything at all. Our people are in a crack, apparently, for some stuff from the Flashlight, their new night interceptor. The thing was first seen last July at their Tushino Show. You all remember it from Recognition. Right name is the YAK-25. Two engines, long radar nose, looks like Badger bomber, swept back wing, two axial jets under the wing, top speed over 500 something at sea level, but that's an estimate. Looking at it, I'd guess there's a low speed problem, high stall speed with that sweepback, ceiling about 32K. Not a high performer but it can sure give the Beast a run for her money.

"What I don't think it can do, though, is go very low and very slow over the water, so we'll be looking at lighting off the jets when they taxi.

"Pluto that's your job," and as he looked directly at Dave Wagoner, a dozen pairs of eyes zeroed in on the newcomer with a mixture of respect, hope and hero worship.

"We'll be staying on our saw-tooth flight path," he went on, gesturing with his hand. "We begin close this time, instead of farther out. When we hear that they're airborne, we'll give them some target-time at about nine thousand feel then start a high-airspeed slow-rate descent. We'll let them crank up after us, so hold on to your hats and seats, we'll probably go over 325. We'll throttle back on the jets, and when they get about eight miles out and lock on, we'll hit the deck, pop flaps, maybe even drop gear depending on weight, and slow to about 100 knots. If it works, they'll go whizzing past and if we're low enough, the low man will have a real problem. They're said to have a rocket pan with 50 fifty-millimeter rockets—little guys—and we'd like to see them fired, but they do have a twin mount like ours in the nose. If we have to, we'll lay some tracer out, but I don't want to think about that until we come to it. Both turrets will man when we go feet-wet.

"If that doesn't work or if they don't want to play tonight, we'll just continue on our track—which is a long one out to the west—and come home with an updated order of battle for the whole Pond, maybe even as far over as Bulgaria.

"I'm beginning to think that they're not yet ready for business up there and we're premature in thinking that they are. The spooks think that their Control Tower goes on standby at night, so if there is any tower radio traffic tonight, we'll know that they've woken up and we'll get a reasonably good warning. We hope."

He briefed the flight as if they were going to fly to Kansas City, pick up the Captain's dog, and take it on to Dallas. Listen to that guy, Brian thought. He's talked about getting us all killed, killing a couple of their guys maybe, and maybe even starting World War III and he's like ice.

"We'll have coffee as soon as we get airborne" Lucore said. "We've got a Nicosia Gourmet special tonight for in-flight rations—tuna fish, by the looks of it - for around midnight or when you're hungry, and lots of soup if you need it. I'll do what I can with the tuna fish, but don't expect miracles. How about Oxygen, Sir?"

"Good point. The book says Oxygen over five thousand at night. You all know me and I'm a little more casual about that than I should be. We'll be up pretty high and the oxygen will be on, if you need it, you all have masks. In the cockpit, we'll have it on and we'll try to have one of us on it. Remember, you guys, no smoking with that oxygen valve in the ON position!

"Anything else? Mickey, you got anything?"

Mort shook his head, looked around at his boys, and when they all shook their heads he said, "Just remember, guys, this is a big one, maybe the biggest one we've ever done. The whole thing has to go like clockwork—times, altitudes, everything and they have to cooperate. If they do, we'll be way ahead and maybe won't have to do this again for a while. If things go wrong, they can go real bad real quick, and you'll all earn your money the hard way."

"All right, guys, let's go get'em" Lew said, and they broke the circle and started to pre-flight the airplane.

He turned to Bob Hunley, who was following him at his left elbow. "Any problem filing the flight plan?"

"No, Sir, piece of cake. I filed Visual to Silifke-abeam, then 'ten hours operational, Visual Flight Rules.' Radio Silence exercise, Codeword Falcon on the flight plan, safety of flight position reports to operational authority. Brits were pleased, they don't have to do anything. Like always. Biggest problem was getting wheels back here. Something must be going on in town, though, both the milk wagons and the Land Rover were off running around and the young creature in the Line Shack was hopping around like the Hittites were coming over the hill. Everybody was a'talkin about it. I walked out from the tower."

Lew thought a minute, frowning slightly. "What the hell does codeword 'Falcon' mean?"

"Beats me," Bob answered, grinning. "Made it up. They really liked it."

"Good, Bob," Lew said, smiling broadly and shaking his head. "Thanks a lot, that's good. Wonder what the townies are up to tonight."

Bob burped, tasting the curry from dinner and the second Keo sour. It made him think of his new pal "May Jawkins", wondering if the townies and "May Jawkins" were mixing it up again.

8:16 PM

They began as they always did, in the nose wheel well. They checked the tire tread, the extension on the gleaming nose wheel oleo strut, the cleanliness of the wheel well and the battery curtains. The aircraft batteries, two of them, were in their frames on either side of the nose wheel well and they wiggled the connectors to make sure they were tight. Under the starboard nacelle, they looked up into the reciprocating exhaust stacks, and then on back aft, looking into the Jet engine rotor from behind to see what they could see. Wing surfaces clean, tank drains secured, wing tip lights on and working, back around to the fuselage and the tail skag, and so it went. A thousand pre-flights, all the same. It was getting late. Time to start. Only Plane Captains started the Beast's engines, so tricky were they on backfires…and a backfire always cost a quill shaft and if you didn't have a quill shaft, you were dead in the water.

8:21 PM

White had the fire extinguisher at the ready, Timmons in the cockpit ready to start, Lew and Bob standing in front on the Port side, watching. A little late, but not much. Thumbs up to Port. Starter activated, props turned, sixteen blades, gas on, priming, switch on, more rotation then a low moaning coughing as the twenty-eight cylinders, each the size of a skinny dog, fired in synchronization and started to power the massive four bladed prop as it rotated through its full eighteen foot arc.

Fire bottle around to the starboard side. Thumbs up outside. Sixteen blades. Gas on…priming…rotation…they had seen it from this position dozens of time. Bang! Backfire! Flames through the outboard stack of the engine, White up at the stack with the bottle, flames out as quickly as they had come, starter off, switch off, oh shit!

Timmons clambered out of the cockpit, anger, disappointment, embarrassment, hatred, possibly, in his face and eyes and brow. He had never done this before, never, not ever, in years as a Beast Plane Captain. The Port engine had been cut immediately after the backfire, and now they were working against the clock. He had ascertained immediately that the backfire had indeed sheared the quill shaft. He had the electrical system drawing from the starboard inverter and the white lollyplop indicator had immediately plopped, indicating that the starboard engine was not providing any electricity to the system.

Making his way quickly through the fuselage, he crouched at his toolbox on the deck just forward of the wing spar, drawing out the boxed replacement shaft. He unwrapped it and clambered forward, then down the hatch on to the pavement. He would have preferred to be greeted with a hail of bullets or arrows, but the quiet, trained efficiency of a crackerjack crew is as evident in times of routine momentary mini-disaster as it is in times of great emergency. White had already gone for a work stand. Black had an emergency lamp rigged off the auxiliary power unit and was unbuttoning the dzeus fittings leading up under the nacelle to provide best access to the alternator takeoff.

Lew felt his stomach churn; used to it, he controlled it and kept the assured calm that had characterized his entire evening. Brian, flashlight in his mouth, kneeling on the concrete, was re-computing required airspeeds needed to make the groundspeed required to fly the 429 nautical miles to Samsun, now interested in making the closing minute of their window at feet-wet rather than the comfortable earliest minute he had been dealing with a minute or so ago.

The window was imposed by the terms of the Turkish clearance. They all knew that there was no Turkish radar available in this part of the world that could or would monitor their time over Samsun. The three pilots—Lew, Bob and Brian—also knew that the whole structure of air safety depended on being where one was supposed to be at one's estimated time of arrival, and making their time was a matter far more precious than simple professional pride.

Timmons had the cowling off and the work stand in place. He had unbolted the alternator a hundred times before, but tonight his fingers had to search for each bolt, the socket balked and backed when he had seated it over the nuts, and his knees shook as he crouched in the awkward position required for him to see his work-piece. White held the light steady, and he gripped the tool firmly, ordering himself to calm down and do the job just as he had done it so many times before.

8:46 PM

The new shaft was in place. He and White together lifted the heavy alternator back into its frame and began to tighten the assembly, finally torqueing the last of the twelve set-bolts and their nuts in their seats. He jumped down and when White finished securing the cowling, the two of them dragged the work stand out of the way. As Timmons passed Lew on his way back into the cockpit, their eyes met, passing a wordless message between them that could only be translated using the dictionary of years that they had, together, worked and sweated and worried and helped each other do a job nobody else ever seemed to understand. His hands shook as he prepared for the new start, and with the fire bottle once again in place and the thumbs up from White, both of the engines were started smoothly with a cloud of smoke from some unburned fuel in the carburetor throat. They all climbed aboard and strapped in, while White unchocked the wheels, pulled the pins from the landing gear, held them up and illuminated them with his flashlight so Lew could see from his left seat in the cockpit, and they were ready to roll.

Timmons opened his hatch in the overhead above the wing spar and boosted himself up into the seat, his torso out in the cool night air, the Aldis signaling lamp in his hand. He checked aft and to either side for taxi clearance, used the white Aldis beam to give a final check to the wing surfaces, then clicked it off and inserted the green lens he would use to flash the tower.

In the cockpit, they were running through the pre-taxi check lists, each of them reading, as required by regulation, although they had done it hundreds of times before and knew the list by heart. It was always better to read it, however, and Bob Hunley knew only too well that a memorized checklist is worse than no checklist when the chips were down. Forward and beneath the cockpit, Brian had settled into his "office". Burdick had patched one of the Naval Observatory Radio Station frequencies into the High Frequency position on his Internal Communications ICS panel, and now he flipped up the switch and reset the boxed chronometer to the WWV time signal. This would be crucial if and when he might ever be inclined to shoot a celestial fix. He hoped it wouldn't come to that but he wanted to be prepared. He spread out his charts and fired off his radio direction finder "birddog" repeater, synchronized his clock with the chronometer and his flux-gate compass with Bob's in the cockpit, and was hurriedly rechecking his figures.

The birddog would give him a completely passive way to take a bearing to any low-frequency radio station in range. Its needle would point to the location of anything he could find on the dial, and by crossing bearings, he could get a reasonable idea of where he was. Birddogs worked well in built up areas with plenty of radio stations, but in Northern Turkey on a dark night, you had to settle for what you could get. He rechecked his time again. Assuming that they got in the air by 2103 Local, there would be thirty minutes to make up to get to the feet-wet point just east of Samsun on time.

Next to Brian on the other side of the tiny aisle, Dave Wagoner was all business. He seemed to have a perfect understanding of the equipment he was dealing with: three self-contained, open channel radio receivers; a fancy headset that he had apparently brought with him, unlike anything Brian had even seen;

and a pair of very sophisticated wire recorders, glowing amber lights probably indicating their standby status. He remembered seeing one like this pair in the after-station on one of his infrequent forays into the Mickey station. Brian watched with great interest as Wagoner drew a fresh wire reel from a storage compartment on the outboard side of the black equipment casing, and carefully threaded it into the recording device.

The reel was a little larger than a large typewriter ribbon reel, the wire the thickness of a needle, but flexible and pliant. Despite the fact that Brian had flown a couple of hundred hours in the Navigation station, he had only seen the Pluto station occupied on those relatively few occasions when they visited the kinds of places on their call-list tonight. He had never really paid much attention to the mechanics of the Pluto operation, but now that he was becoming more and more familiar with the Beast's nooks and crannies, he realized he had never noticed the wire recording reels before and was embarrassed that he did not realize that the recorders held their own supply of spares. There would be at least three recorders working tonight, then, and he presumed Mickey would be recording whatever they were able to detect audibly—the actual sounds of radar pulses, he guessed—and Pluto would be recording radio transmissions.

Back in the cockpit, as Lew and Bob completed the last checklist item, they each stepped on their foot pedals to check their brakes, reported "Brakes Checked" to each other, and Lew picked up his mike. He checked to make sure that all the buttons were in the correct position—he didn't want any inadvertent radio transmission from the aircraft. They were listening to both the tower and the ground control frequencies on each other's Very High Frequency (VHF) radios, both keys up in the "Listen" position. Hunley resisted the impulse, out of long habit, to call the tower and request taxi instructions, remembering Timmons in the hatch aft.

"Plane Captain, Pilot" Lew said, calmly.

"Plane Captain, Aye" Timmons replied.

"Ready for taxi, Tim?" Lew asked.

"Crew ready for taxi, Sir" Tim replied.

Brian chimed in "Nav and Pluto ready for taxi, Sir," immediately followed by Mort's report from the Mickey-world back aft.

"Give them the flashing green."

Timmons aimed the green-lensed Aldis lamp at the tower and began to flash a blinking signal. The arrangement called for the tower to return the signal with a steady green light when they were cleared to taxi. There was no traffic on Ground Control and both pilots fixed their eyes on the tower, waiting for the signal. Nothing.

8:58 PM

After about two minutes, tension in the cockpit rising, the clock ticking off another minute-late every sixty seconds, Lew looked at Bob and said, "Let's just go." He released the parking brake and took the throttles in his gloved hand, flipped up the switch for the taxi light in the nose-wheel well and pulled out on the taxi-way. They had gone about a hundred yards when the tower finally noticed what was happening, and hastily returned their green signal.

The runway orientation was slightly off east-west, Runway 10 in use now with a reported wind on the listen-only ground control frequency from the south at ten knots. At the approach end of 10, Lew's taxi heading as he held short of the runway was due south into the wind, and they locked the brakes and started through the run up. The two huge R4360 reciprocating engines each produced 3,500 horsepower, but as some critics had pointed out, they did the unsupercharged hard way. The newer, smaller turbocharged R3350 had powered the Beast's competitor into the mass-market, but to a Beastie, twenty eight cylinders arranged in four rows were a way of life. It was, however, a challenge to get an acceptable magneto check on the engine. With twenty eight jugs to be heard from, Tim's Engine Analyzer was routinely used to trace each pair of spark plug electrodes, and it took time. The clock seemed to be running faster this evening.

"Standby to start jets" Lew announced, finally, the last stage of the detailed and complex pre-takeoff routine. All stations warned, Bob pressed the starter button on Number 1, bringing the throttle up to the start detent. Lew called "door open" as the intake door dropped, and he watched the tachometer.

"Rotation," he called as the RPM indicator moved off zero. At nine percent, Bob moved the throttle to the next detent.

"Ignition," next, as the tail-pipe temperature needle flew off the peg in the gauge and peaked as the fuel in the plenum chambers ignited. As Bob came "around the horn" to place the throttle in its idle position, they could hear the scream of the Port jet settling down at 33% of peak RPM. They repeated the procedure for the Starboard engine, and Bob reported "Normal start, both engines". It had become noisier now in the cockpit, and both pilots adjusted their headsets so that both ears were covered.

"Nav ready to go," Brian reported.

"Not so fast," Lew came back with a chuckle. "We've got Timmons sitting on the roof out in the cold. Tim, go ahead and give them the signal"

The time was, shockingly, 2115, and over Lew's shoulder, the tower was signaling red.

"There's the problem," Bob Hunley announced dryly, pointing out his right side window toward the west, where a pair of landing lights had just been switched on in an aircraft perhaps three miles out on final approach.

"Patience," Lew sighed, as they waited for the Dakota in Greek Air Transport paint to land and clear the runway. "I thought they were bought up by Hellenic" Lew remarked as it flashed by them at the end of the runway.

"They were both bought by Onassis, I heard, and it's going to be called…"

"Green light from the tower," Timmons reported.

"Crew, Pilot. Standby for takeoff. Tim report when you're ready."

"Pilot, Plane Captain. Hatch secured, flight deck ready for takeoff"

"Pilot, Mickey, ready back here Lew."

"Pilot, Nav. Nav and Pluto ready."

9:20—10:28 PM

Lew taxied the Beast into position and set his brakes. It was an easy aircraft to taxi, even without nose-wheel steering, a feature he had unsuccessfully lobbied for at Martin when they were putting the airframe package together, what…years ago?

"Jets up," he ordered, and Bob smoothly advanced the jet throttles until both tachometers hovered at 100 per cent and the tailpipe temperatures stabilized at 780 degrees. It was 2123. He advanced both main engine throttles and released the brakes, and the great blue-black beast began to charge, angrily it seemed, galloping down the runway, accelerating beautifully, before leaping into the air, nose high, gear snatched from the concrete, attitude set for a 2000 foot per minute climb, incredible, majestic, unbelievable. Lew had done it hundreds of times. Each time it got better.

"Plane Captain, Pilot. Wing surface and fumes check, please." Hunley was running through the post-takeoff list, reporting it complete as Timmons reported his check complete.

"Crew, Pilot. Normal Operation. Smoking lamp is lit throughout the aircraft. Anybody smell fumes, let me know right away. We've got three in the bomb-bay, remember. What's the bad news, Nav?"

Brian was figuring. They were ten minutes short of an hour late. They could burn jets all the way at about 88 per cent and make up the groundspeed to hit the window, or they could cruise with high main engine power and ninety six percent on the jets, aim for the midway point on their preflighted time, and take it at normal cruise for the last hour, arriving just inside the window at 2300 Local. Lew elected to make up the time early, so for the first hour, they climbed up to ten thousand five hundred and cruised at an indicated airspeed of 300 knots, jets roaring, the wind whistling around outside the unpressurized aircraft. Their fuel flow, jets and reciprocating engines at maximum cruise, was 1600 gallons per hour. They kept that power on for one hour and eight minutes, then returned to normal cruise, secured the jets and indicated 188.

With fifty-five minutes to go before feet-wet, things were quiet. The red interior lights were too dim to read by, so Burdick and Blackie each had their dim white spots on and were reading. Burdick's headset covered one ear, and he monitored three frequencies simultaneously. The Mickey crew was at full operation, picking up signal after signal as the range to the coast lessened, Dumbo air surveillance radars, their positions and fingerprints already known and plotted. Pluto was practicing with his machines, satisfied that he had the right settings and the right switches in position.

Brian was having a problem, however, refiguring their ground speed required, arriving at 267 knots required to cover the 428 miles in the hour and twenty-four minutes they had. He unbuckled and went back to stand between Lew and Bob, and the three of them cut a radio bearing from Kayseri to give them a ground speed. They were late. Lew thought it over and increased the main engine power setting until they were indicating 235 knots. He did not start the jets. That would do. Brian concurred, embarrassed.

Lew was engrossed in the details of the flight, peering out ahead in the darkness for any sign of the dirty weather they had been briefed to expect. Shortly after leaving Kayseri behind, the stars in the northern sky began to disappear and shortly, flashes of lightning darted here and there on the horizon ahead. They had secured the running lights and the rotating Grimes beacon light—darkened ship—right after they passed Silifke, so there would be no lights to distract them when they went into the clouds on instruments—which, obviously would be very shortly. Hunley interrupted his train of thought.

"I had an interesting encounter this afternoon," he began. Lew was half glad for the diversion, half sorry for the interruption in his worry process.

"I was hanging around the Officers' Mess" he didn't say where, "when this really rumpled, awful looking Army guy came in and we started to talk. Seems had just gotten back from some kind of an ambush someplace, and he tells me first of all, that he had to shoot one of the kids he caught, then he tells me he cut off a couple of fingers, and then, and this is the strange part, he gets this dreamy expression on his face and tells me that he sat down and counted thirty four different kinds of wildflowers. Gave me the creeps."

"Did he tell you his name?"

"They called him Major Hawkins, but he had Captain's pips on, so I guess either he just got promoted or he was wearing somebody else's shirt."

Lew said nothing.

Marta had long ago told him everything he needed to know about Major/Captain Hawkins/Mr. St. John and he was not surprised. He was glad he was on our side. He could not help wondering what Hunley would say if he knew what Lew knew about "Major" Hawkins.

Meanwhile, Brian was preparing for the worst. He had picked Regulus, which would be over in the eastern sky later on, and Aldeboran in Orion, which would be slightly west, to cross with a latitude by Polaris, if it came to that, to give him a three-star fix if he needed it. With the radio beacon at Samsun and the other at Kayseri, however, he felt confident that once their feet were dry on the way home, he could get them back to Nick. If not, celestial navigation would be his last fallback and he would only have a few minutes to get it right.

He was working out his numbers from the almanac when he thought of the magical night last winter when they had met. He had shown Orion to Shirley, shown her "their special star"—Aldeboran in Orion, told her that it was an orange beauty and that they should always keep it as a memory of this night. Shirley had insisted it was blue. That's the way Shirley was, but he couldn't keep his hands off her when he was around her, or keep her out of his mind when he wasn't. So…so he had ignored his parents' subtle warnings, ignored the back-of-his-head-this-isn't-right premonition—the same one he had had for years in the seminary—and had married her after a courtship of thirty-seven days. Maybe it will work out. Maybe it will. Maybe.

10:48 PM

Twelve minutes before the expiration of their window, they entered the squall line. The airspeed adjustment had worked. Brian estimated feet-wet on the hour and with about forty miles to go, he turned his attention to the eastbound leg to which they would turn, once over water. The window arrival time was close enough for government work, and besides, they had other problems. In the cockpit, Bob Hunley and Lew were discussing a problem that Timmons had been worrying about for the last hour. They had at least seven hours of flight time left. They had 2,700 gallons of gas left, bomb bays dry. Three eighty gallons an hour. No problem. Fuel consumption in fast cruise was 250 per hour. Without jets.

Each jet burned 600 gallons per hour in normal cruise at 92%, lots more at military rated power (101%). So. At normal cruise, without jets, they could be in the landing pattern with plenty to spare. If they burned the jets however, they had better remember that they would have 42 minutes of max jet time *only* if they wanted to make it back, unless they did some imaginative bookkeeping. Of course, fuel consumption decreased as the fuel burned down and the weight decreased, but Lew knew, as every good pilot knows, that fuel remaining computations that end in a "dry tank" solution need either to be carefully recomputed or better, ignored.

Suddenly, he realized that the immediate problem needed attention. They were in a squall line, preparing for their eastward turn, without the slightest feel for the depth of the line from south to north. Should they keep their northerly course and punch through the line, or turn on the pre-computed spot and head east? Lightning flashes, intermittent in the distance a few minutes ago, were now closer and more persistently frequent. The rain had begun suddenly and intensely, and was now pelting the aircraft. Occasional sheets of hail struck the Plexiglas cockpit enclosure, and as the lightning flashed close abeam to starboard, they both ducked instinctively. Slight traces of St. Elmo's fire, static electric discharges off the propeller tips, brightened then dimmed to the right and left, but they had their hands full in the cockpit and left the display to the others.

The autopilot was holding heading, but up- then down- drafts were pitching the Beast like a cork, and the pressure altimeter was fluctuating as much as three hundred feet as they bobbed through it, first up against their seat belts, then down, pressed into their seat-cushions. He made up his mind to continue straight ahead until they were out of the line of storms, and counted the minutes past the time to turn that Brian had requested. Brian had already figured out what was happening and was watching the clock for the actual turn time. In the cockpit, Lew noted that the heading indicator was beginning to fluctuate, sometimes as much as five degrees either side of course, but there wasn't much he could do about it unless he disengaged the autopilot and hand- tooled the thing. He had just dismissed the idea of flying it manually, "white-knuckling" it, when the rain began to slacken and within a few minutes, the lightning had subsided and the clouds thinned, with patches of starlit sky above.

"That's the worst of it, gang" he announced on the ICS.

"Amen," someone sighed sincerely.

Lew lit a cigarette, Hunley lit a cigarette, and Brian lit a cigarette. Thank God for Winstons.

"Can I have that turn now, please Sir?" Brian asked.

"Sure. You want 082," he noted, checking the pre-compute he had given them.

"I would if I knew where we are, but DR-ing us through that mess, I put us about twenty five miles north of track. Lets make it 090 and we'll intercept." Dead Reckoning, "DR-ing" in the trade, the Navigator's fallback when everything else fails. You plot the track you think you've made good, along the heading you think you were on at the speed you think you made good and hope for the best. Brian's Navigation Instructor was always pointing out the fact that it had gotten Columbus to America. Maybe.

Lew disengaged the autopilot and zeroed up the auto-trim toggles, then turned the aircraft due east and reengaged.

"Mickey, Pilot, coming right to 090"

"Mickey, aye. Everybody's sick back here but we'll try clean everything up and get on with it."

"Are you really sick, Mickey? Anybody else sick?"

They laughed it off, of course, they always did, but Lew knew it was no laughing matter and hoped that had been the end of it. It was 2315, and he knew that they were something like 45 miles north of track.

"Crew from Pilot. Man the turrets. Lucore, let me know when we're all hooked up and ready." White and Lucore made their way to the opposite end of the fuselage, climbing over boxes and bodies, and manned the turrets.

11:30 PM—12:10 AM

"Pilot, Mickey. I'll need you to hold it steady now, Sir. Pluto, stand by please." That was the signal they had been waiting for in the cockpit. They were on to something in the back end, and the night was going to be a success. They needed one.

In the red glow, the six sets of boxes with their dials and traces and glowing status lights were surreal. The six operators—including Mort, in the first seat—faced the starboard side of the aircraft, their chairs installed on tracks slightly to the left of the centerline of the aircraft as one faced forward. Mort controlled the presentations on each screen, acting as the clearing-house to triage the incoming signals and decide which ones were of interest. They had had their hands full for the past twenty minutes, beginning just before they had turned to the east. The profusion of early warning Dumbo signals had gradually given way to the higher frequency, shorter-range air surveillance radars which, alerted by the early warning net, were searching for the intruder the Dumbos had detected. As with all radars, the intruder was in a position to "see" them long before they "saw" him, because the signal had to travel from the surveillance antenna out to the intruding Beast and, reflected back, return to the point of origin. The Beast was still invisible to their now insistent probing, but soon would be detected and tracked. When they were being tracked, the pulses were concentrated on them as the ground radar "painted" their blip, and in the almost impossible case that the operators missed the event, alarms were triggered at each station when tracking or lock-on occurred.

As they punched their way eastward, Mort figured that they had more than 100 miles of sea-room before they ran into real trouble—penetration—to the east. With an indicated airspeed of 188 knots now at nine thousand five hundred feet, he guessed the groundspeed at about 200 and watched his clock carefully. He calculated that this leg would run about 130 miles, and their turn should occur around midnight. Mort liked to second-guess the Navigator, and every Navigator in the Unit knew Mort could do just fine on his own.

"Nav, Mickey," he called, his ICS on Select so he would not "disturb" the rest of the crew. It was a privacy device, connecting the speaker only to the selected listener, and he had insisted on its design when they build the system. Tonight he was glad he had.

"Nav, aye," Brian answered.

"What time you going to turn us?" he asked.

"I'm looking at on-the-hour, best I can tell, although I really don't know how far north we are right now. I was just getting ready for a latitude by

Polaris when you called." Mort signed off, disgusted that the APS-33 radar installed had not yet been modified for a partial sweep feature that would have allowed Blackie to look south selectively and grab a quick fix without rotating the antenna fully. He consoled himself by remembering that any signal at all in a situation like this was risky, given the total uncertainty of the electronic countermeasures capability to the North.

At 2348, David Wagoner heard a crackle in his right earphone, and as he switched to binaural to get the full signal, his stomach tightened and his mouth went dry and he was ashamed—he didn't know why—that his hand shook slightly. If ever the shakes were appropriate, he told himself, this was the time.

"Mickey, Pluto" he said quietly into his microphone, also on Select. He had written down the unfamiliar numbers he had heard, and was translating them.

"Go ahead Pluto."

"How about 'altimeter 1010 millibars, wind south force 1, south runway expedite.'"

"Yes!" then a click as he switched to Pilot and Pluto Select. "Pilot, Mickey, they're taxiing."

Lew rogered the message and told Hunley.

"Want the jets?" the copilot asked.

Yes, he wanted those two big J33s, wanted them badly, wanted to feel that power in his hands as he grabbed all four throttles, wanted them as he had when he was in fighters, but he did a quick fuel calculation before he shook his head.

"Not yet."

Wagoner flipped back to split his phones, and gazed intently at a spot a thousand yards in front of him, a spot which became his mother's studio in New York, where his grandfather and his mother had argued and kidded and sang and told tall tales to each other in the Russian he was hearing now in both phones, each reception a different voice, one providing taxi instructions to a pair of Flashlight radar interceptors, the other speaking into what should have been a secure radio-telephone landline as he sought advice and counsel from a superior, far, far away. He was fascinated, intrigued, flabbergasted actually, listening in on a conversation taking place seventy, eighty miles away—line of sight distance from nine thousand feet—and they were talking about him! It was a lengthy conversation and as he followed it, he realized that they had not been expecting this penetration this evening, and if he understood what he was hearing, they had been specifically told *not* to expect an intrusion tonight! Told by whom, he wondered. In the chatter back and forth, he heard the far away station insist that if they were sure it was not an American penetration, authorization would be given to investigate and take appropriate action. Thank God for the wire recorder!

"Mickey, Pluto."

"Go, Pluto"

"They have a launch order with authority Three, whatever that is."

"Do you know?"

"Not a clue."

"Okay. Pilot, Mickey"

"Go ahead, Mort"

"They have launch clearance and…possibly, now, only possibly…splash." Authorization to attack. It was raining like hell in Batumi, and they wanted to get off the ground and "on-top" as soon after they had taxied as possible.

"Roger, Mickey." He flipped his key. "Crew, Pilot, standby to start jets." Discretion got the better part of valor, and as the jets started and spooled up to idle RPM, Hunley breathed easier.

It was 2353. Seven minutes to midnight.

Through the aircraft, each station understood that the sophisticated electrical monitoring system in the aircraft would selectively turn off items in order of descending importance until the system could provide the required power to the starters and igniters, then return the items to their operators when the load had stabilized. Brian had just finished his Polaris shot, and he flipped off the gyro and the timer in the periscopic sextant before the monitor did it for him. Sometimes when the system monitored, gyros were hard to get to run again for several minutes. As he calculated the corrections to the observed altitude of Polaris, a process that would give him his latitude at the time of the shot, he heard the jets wind up and stabilize in idle at 33%. His shot put them fifty-five miles north of the coast, further than he had expected but he could handle it. They would turn on the hour, since he had no reason to believe he was farther east or west of his dead reckoning position.

On the hour, Lew flipped off the autopilot and turned north to parallel the eastern coast off, now, to their right side. The weather had again deteriorated, and Bob Hunley strained to see anything that would indicate a landfall to starboard. He could see nothing but dark clouds and more lightning. They were in it almost instantly, and Lew held on manually, keeping it as steady as he could, heading 349 degrees, north by north northwest.

"Mickey, Pluto, they're airborne on the hour, going to search for an in-flight frequency."

Two Soviet Air Defense Force night interceptors had launched from Batumi, and in the Beast, a complex trial and error process began at two of the aft stations and at the Pluto station to discover the airborne coordination frequency that the two pilots would be using. The other three stations were concentrating on the suspected radar frequency bands of the Farmfish and Kiterest radars, one suspected to be the airborne acquisition radar and the other, the fire control radar in the Flashlight.

Mickey Station three reported "Cherries" at 0007, after seven tense minutes, three sets of fingers dialed in the new-found frequency 137.24 megacycles, and their phones were filled with chatter only Wagoner could appreciate. Mort got the other two operators back on the radar frequencies and Pluto listened, frozen now with apprehension, as the two Soviet pilots chatted about the beastly weather.

The minutes crept by, eyes and ears straining for something anything. Tense.

This was the worst part. Always.

Suddenly, three things happened almost simultaneously.

In the pursuing Flashlights, one of the pilots shouted excitedly that he "had something," and Wagoner relayed it to both the cockpit and to Mickey.

In the after station, both operators announced "Cherries" again as their receiver picked up the searching beams of the two chasers. Their directional blooms indicated that they were approaching from the land side, from the right, on an intercepting course. At his station, Mort was feverishly switching from unit to unit, photographing the blooms, listening in fascination, congratulating their good luck and nursing the priceless seconds of recordings that were spinning through the reels. First the chirps, then the chirps became buzzes, then the buzzing become a whine and a howl before diminishing as the directional sweeps in the Flashlights swept by their position. They had been "acquired" in the lingo, they were in the sights of the bad guys guns. The interceptors were apparently able to acquire and, at the same time, develop a fire control solution. This piece of momentous intelligence exhilarated Mort, and he listened in his own split phones with the fascination of discovery, the Holy Grail, until he could stand it no longer. "Pilot, Mickey, Let's go home!" he announced, as quietly as he could. He had what he wanted, enough to keep, and money had been made. It was break off time.

It was the third thing that happened that none of them would ever forget.

Lew was off autopilot, hand driving now, in and out of heavy rain. He knew that "home" was anyplace in a compass sector to the south and west and he began a turn to the left. The strike was spectacular. A flash more brilliant than the sun, a cracking report louder than anything any of them had ever heard, simultaneously blinding and deafening them all. It was the simultaneity that was harrowing. The sudden smell of burning fabric, the flicker of the red lights as the overstressed electrical system tried to figure out what had happened and correct for it, the disorienting relative quiet in the wake of the strike, the reassuring recognition that the engines were still turning and burning, the hum of the ICS system returning to normal. Nothing remained normal long.

"We're hit!" someone yelled.

"Lightning everybody!" Lew choked, trying to keep the aircraft on some semblance of an even track. "Report any problems right away, C'mon, let's hear from everybody!"

The litany of responses was broken almost immediately by a voice on Override.

"Pilot, Mickey, they're locked, let's go, let's go." Lew pushed over and Bob pushed the mixtures and the props full forward, advancing the main throttles to fifty inches of manifold pressure. Lew grabbed both jet throttles and advanced them quickly to 100 percent. "Hang on everybody!" Lew shouted, as the Beast shuddered and screamed as the airspeed began to build, faster and faster, passing 300, passing 325.

In the aft turret, Lucore had been monitoring the action in his earphones. He had armed and cocked his weapons, trained them level and peered forward through the Mickey compartment where he caught Mort's attention. Mort pointed to his right, to the Port side of the aircraft, and Lucore trained port at the ready.

In the forward turret, White had also been monitoring the action, and he paused now to switch to the gunnery loop and he and Lucore filled one another in on the status of their switches.

In the cockpit, Bob Hunley was watching the red line on the air speed indicator, and as the needle approached 400 knots, he eased back gently to keep the needle at the limit. Lew had both hands on the yoke, riding it hard, his eyes fixed on the unwinding pressure altimeter. He relaxed his grip for a minute, and flicked on the radio altimeter, setting it to low range with the bezel pointed at 300 feet. As the pressure altimeter swept through three thousand feet, he would have given his heart and lungs to know the height above sea level of the body of water coming up to meet them. Surely it was far above sea level, but how far? His eyes went to the radar altimeter and he recalled that the antenna was under his seat just aft of the nose wheel, hoping against hope that it had avoided the ravages of the lightning strike.

In the end, it was Lucore who called it. Good old Lucore, with his Bronx accent and his attitude, always the professional.

"Pilot, Tail"

"Go ahead, Tail"

They were at 1100 feet screaming down, just inside the radar altimeter's range of usefulness, slowing, power back, ready to drop the gear and flaps into what they called the Power Approach configuration, PA, at Test Pilot School.

"Mr. Elfers, I heard all the stuff Pluto said a while ago and if it was raining where they left from and they had been sitting out on the line and not in a barn, they would have had to go inside to arm and load any ordnance. If they had been in a barn, they would have had to spend some time loading and locking between the time they called taxi and the time they got airborne. I don't know whether they are guns or rockets or what but in this weather, you don't just get in, go and shoot. How about it?"

Lew thought about it, and had to agree that it sounded right. He was wondering if he wanted to bet sixteen lives on it, when Lucore called again, this time agitated.

Three hundred feet now on the radar altimeter. Limit light on.

"Pilot, Tail, here one comes, I can see him way off against a cloud heading for us."

There, high and to his right, in and out of the towering thunderheads, Lucore could make out a pair of running lights. They had their lights on, for Chrissake!

"No fire, no fire!" Lew yelled into the microphone.

"No fire, aye!" Lucore responded. Lew was betting.

It happened so fast, that it was over almost before it happened.

Hunley worked the flaps down as the airspeed passed through 195 and by 145, full flaps had been lowered and he pulled the gear handle and the huge tires dropped out of the well with their characteristic thud, the hydraulic pump screaming on the flight deck as it built pressure back up to 3000 pounds. Lew had her riding nose high at 118 knots when they both saw the thing slam by them, the cherry glow from the underwing engine exhausts bright against the coal black sea and the whitecaps, now clearly visible 300 feet beneath them. He had pulled underneath them and then straight up in front of them, twisting as he climbed, his red cockpit lights visible for an instant that neither pilot would ever forget. Two pair of eyes were fixed on the maneuver as Lew fought the plane's bumps and rolls as it twisted and squirmed in the landing configuration almost in the spindrift from the sea beneath them. He could picture the other pilot, looking over his shoulder for something dark against the sea, as he tried to climb his way almost straight up, his attention behind him. And as they watched him climb, their awe changed to horror as they saw him hang, almost vertical now, then with a violent shake to the left, fall off, straight down in full aerodynamic stall, into the sea a half-mile ahead of them. Momentarily paralyzed with shock, Hunley kept his eyes on the spot ahead, dimly visible in the gloom, and as they passed over it, steaming wreckage had begun to sink beneath the surface. It was 0027, twenty minutes from their first airborne reception, twenty seven minutes from the Batumi takeoff.

"Crew from Pilot, we're heading home now. Enough for one night."

Lew looked straight ahead as he added power and came up with the jets, raised the gear, then the flaps and climbed up to five thousand feet, where he leveled off and turned south. The hell with the other one!

Brian's heart was in his mouth. "Try 200, Sir, until I get this figured out." Southwest toward home.

12:30 AM

Everything had happened so fast. From the Navigation table, Brian had noticed the heading swinging as the plane S-turned in the descent, and the speed had varied over a seven or eight minute period from over 300 knots down to 118. Keeping a Dead Reckoning track would have been impossible, even if he had either the stomach or the inclination to do it, but now he had to confront the consequences of his absorption with the tactical situation.

The Navigator did not know, exactly, where they were.

There was land to the south, there had to be, but where their jinking had taken them and what they would meet when the approached the land, he could not say. He tuned the Samsun beacon frequency on his birddog. Nothing. He flipped up the listen key and realized that their troubles were not over.

"Pilot, Nav. I don't have any birddog."

Burdick came on the line. "Nav, Radio, that's right, sir. The lightning got both birddogs, the UHF, the VHF and all our High Frequency radios. I can fix them, it's power supplies we need, but not in the air. We've got the parts in the cruise box."

Lew, overhearing the ICS dialogue, looked at Hunley intently. They both flicked up their birddog keys, checked their tuning—one was on Kayseri, the other on Trabizon. Nothing. The UHF antenna was a spade just above their heads, slightly aft where the Plexiglas canopy joined the fuselage. The strike must have been focused there, because looking back over their shoulders, they could see and smell the scorched canvass padding beneath the antenna attach-point. The VHF antenna was a larger blade antenna, just forward of the cockpit, and the lightning must have jumped the gap. Lew had an idea.

"Mickey, Pilot." Lew had an idea.

"Go ahead, Lew."

"We've lost all our birddogs. Can you tune one of your receivers low enough to pick up one of the navigational beacons—or even a commercial radio station—and get us a cut on it. We're hurting for a fix."

"Sorry, Lew. We're out of the Directional Finder Antenna business back here. No DF capability at all. The rotating DF dipole just twists dead in the wind—must have sheared the shaft and the cabling when it got hit. In fact, we have no reception on anything!"

"Pilot, Pluto," Wagoner came in then. "I've lost everything except one VHF receiver, but I can't tune it and when we're out of range on it, that's it. There's no power to the wire recorders, either." Then Mickey.

"All ours are gone too, Lew"

In the Nav compartment immediately beneath the VHF antenna, Brian considered setting up another star sight. A latitude by Polaris would help, but as he thought about it, he decided not to take the time needed to compute and shoot a two-minute observation. The stars were out now, and they'd be over land sooner or later. As soon as they went feet-dry, he'd know how far north they were because the coastline ran almost due east and west.

In the cockpit, Lew—uncertain where they were - realized that electromagnetic silence, at this point in the game, might not be the most prudent course of action. He was tempted to have Blackie fire up the radar, but there surely would be search and rescue efforts of some kind back where the Flashlight splashed. Pluto was keeping all of them informed of the running radio drama unfolding between the surviving Flashlight and Batumi on the one receiver channel working, but the range was increasing with each minute. While the fact of the presence of an intruder was established, there had been no mention of the intruder's description or identity by the time they were out of VHF range and the transmissions ceased.

But…

My God, he thought, do you suppose they think we shot him down!

If that were even a remote possibility, lighting off the radar—even if it had not been damaged by the lightning strike—would put their signature on the event! The unmistakable fingerprints of an American Air Search APS-33 radar in the area at this time would establish a undeniable link to their presence. Much as he needed to know where they were, he would have to trust Brian to come up with a fix soon—without the radar!

But a more immediate problem had to be handled at once. If they could find land ahead to the south, it would be a minimum of 428 miles north of where they wanted to be. Two hours and twenty minutes. They'd better secure the jets right now, if they didn't want to run out of gas on top of a neat Turkish mountain ahead.

They pulled the throttles back around the horn and turned the starting sequence switches to off. Nothing happened. The jets continued to run in idle.

"Plane Captain, Pilot, you want to come up here a minute, Tim?"

Lew's stomach twisted again as his instrument scan took in the jet fuel flow gauges, steady in idle at about 325 gallons each per hour. He did a quick fuel inventory off the gauges and holding as tightly to his composure as he could, he pulled back the left ear padding on Bob Hunley's headset and said, in normal conversational tones off ICS, "Look at this."

Hunley looked at the figures Lew had written on his knee-pad in his careful engineering drafting hand. A while back, at 13 minutes after midnight he had taken a fuel inventory, then forgotten about it in the heat of whatever that just was. They had had 1200 gallons of fuel remaining and both jets were stuck in idle. Assuming best-case distance from Nick at 500 miles, assuming that the reciprocating engines at best-economy cruise could generate 188 knots true air speed, and assuming that at 9,000 feet the airspeed would equate to a 200 knot ground speed, they would need two and a half hours to get back. At 300 gallons per hour each, stuck in idle, the jets would run them out of gas somewhere in the middle of a Turkish mountain range at night. But wait. You think that's bad? Now, twenty-three minutes later, they *still* had 1200 gallons of gas remaining. And the jets were still running.

Timmons made his way forward and stood between the pilot and co-pilot seats, his arm resting on the control pedestal. He moved the jet selector switches through each stage—doors open, rotation, ignition—and back to the off position. He looked up at Lew when he was done, and Lew was actually a little perturbed that he was not more excited about his than he seemed to be.

"Can't we pull the breakers and cut electrical to the igniters or to the fuel pumps and shut them off?"

"They're all on the Jet-Start—JS—bus. The lightning got to the main circuit breaker board. White has it open now, and he's found the main JS bus on the monitored circuits, and there's a physical break between where the signal goes into the bus board from your rotary switch and where it goes back out to the engine. The circuit breakers are upstream of the break, so they won't work either. The jets haven't gotten the word that you want them off. What he's doing, is taking the copper bus from the circuit that lights off all the aircraft heaters and he's disconnecting it. Then he's going to replace the jet monitor bus bar with the heater bus bar, and he thinks it's going to put us back normal. You'll be able to start them again if you want, if this works. If it doesn't, we'll have to figure out a way to close the main jet fuel valves—which are on the circuit he's fixing—and flame them out. If we do that, we're down to the two mains. The jets won't start without juice."

"How long?" Hunley asked. It was getting late.

"As soon as we get it, we'll give it a try." Timmons turned back aft to catch White's eye and as he did, Hunley caught sight of a thin white streak through the now-broken undercast beneath them. He leaned away from Timmons and stared down into the darkness. It was a surf line, at last.

"Nav, Copilot. Land Ho," he said, and the relief throughout the flight and navigation stations was palpable.

Brian heaved the cardinal-archbishop of all sighs of relief and marked the time, 0047 in the log.

The terrain stretched south as a coastal plain for about sixty miles, then began to rise gradually until peaks between eleven and fifteen thousand feet erupted from the scrabbled wasteland. As he pre-computed the data for a star shot, he could still hear the jets idling in the nacelles and he hoped that the two pilots had a handle on their fuel consumption. He had forgotten to worry about the fuel in his preoccupation. Allowing ten minutes from start to finish, at three miles a minute, he had just short of thirty miles to get a three star fix before they ran out of coastal plain, and he jumped to the job. The periscopic sextant was in the mount, protruding into the aircraft about nine inches. The eyepiece was too high for him to look though without standing on something. He and Wagoner had rigged a stool using the navigation satchel and a parachute taken from the rack on the forward bulkhead, but the experiences of the last hour greatly diminished Brian's enthusiasm for using a perfectly good parachute in an endeavor that might render it unusable any time soon. So he took off his leather flight jacket and rolled it into a ball, a cushion actually, and stood on it to get his eye on the eyepiece. It would work.

The time honored procedure, used by mariners, explorers, surveyors and pilots throughout history, was relatively simple, once you understood the way the sky worked at night. Each star in the sky was at a specific height above the horizon at any given time on any given night, so a "shot" would produce an angle and the shooter knew that he would have to be someplace on a "line of position" on the globe where, at that time, that star was at that "altitude" or height above the horizon. The celestial "altitude" had nothing to do with the altitude of the aircraft.

The Navigator interested in finding out where he was would pick three stars reasonably easy to find. For best results, they needed to be separated by about one hundred twenty degrees in azimuth—the direction from the observer. One hundred twenty degrees gave the observer a third of a circle, and if the lines crossed well, he would end up with a three star fix determined by the triangle at which the lines of position from the star crossed. One could, alternately, use the North Star and cross it with two stars a third of a circle off North, and this is what Brian was doing that night. If all went well, the North Star shot would give him his latitude.

The star sight was based on a simple game. You took an assumed position, somewhere around where you thought you were. Using your almanac and a Hydrographic Office book designed for this purpose, you computed the expected "altitude" above the horizon for the stars you picked and the time you intended to shoot each one. Then you "shot" the stars, observing their altitude above the horizon at a specific time, and compared the actual altitude that you observed with the altitude for the position you assumed. In the final step, you compared the two lines of position and moved them according to a simple formula, and where the lines of position crossed, you had a "fix," generally—hopefully - a triangle, in which you had to be.

There were tricks of course. The stars had to be computed accurately for a specific time, and observed carefully at that exact time. This was hard enough on a pitching deck at sea, and very difficult in any kind of weather in the air. At sea, the only time of the night in which both the stars and the horizon were visible were morning and evening twilight, so sailors shot stars at sea at dawn and dusk. In the air, it was usually impossible to see the horizon, much less measure a star altitude above it, so the periscopic sextant provided an artificial horizon through a series of bubbles and a gyroscopic leveling device, with a two-minute timer to average out the bumps. Celestial Navigation was an arcane art in Naval Aviation by the time Brian climbed up on his rolled-up flight jacket, rarely needed because of the increasing coverage provided by low frequency radio beacons and, in the United States and increasingly in Europe, the VOR Omni directional beacons. In Northern Turkey on this dark night with no radio receivers, the stars were the best and the only navigation aids available.

He checked his chronometer and decided on a shot time sequence. He would shoot Aldeboran in the west for a shot-time of 0056, Polaris on the hour, and Regulus to the east at 0104. To get the shot-time he needed, then, he would start the shot one minute before shot-time. He would keep the crosshair on the star while the sextant timed two minutes, automatically averaging the ups and downs he would have to be making to compensate for aircraft motion and the awkward positioning on the flight jacket during the observation. At 0057, the little window would darken telling him the first shot had been averaged, and he would swing around to the North to get Polaris for the second sighting. Same thing when he had Polaris, two minutes to line Regulus up for the third shot. After each window drop, he would read the averaged observed star height above the artificial horizon in the window at the base of the mount. The horizon was "manufactured" by the spinning gyro. If all went well, he would take the three observed star heights, do a mathematical comparison with the published heights in the almanac, and by filling in the compensation blanks and performing a few other feats of juju, he would get three lines of position, lines of possible places they might be based on the sighting of each celestial body. Then he would advance the early shot and retard the late shot to have them coincide with the middle one, and if the gods had any sense when they looked at a guy who needed a stroke of luck, the lines would cross in a cute little triangle and he would be somewhere in that triangle. If the center shot was any good, he would also know his latitude because that was what they paid old Polaris for.

"Pilot, Nav, would you hold it steady, I'm going to take some stars".

"Good man!" Hunley returned enthusiastically.

And so it happened that on a night filled with interesting mix of pleasant, unpleasant and very unpleasant happenings, Lieutenant (junior grade) Brian J. Kerrigan, U.S. Navy, beat the odds and shot himself a series of three stars that—when computed, compensated, advanced, retarded and plotted—put them reasonably near where they should have been in Central Turkey on their way home from work. As he picked up to key the mike and report his good fortune, he heard the jets wind down as White's jury-rigged monitor bus did its job. The time was 0117.

"Nav, Co-pilot. Sorry to interrupt but did you hear that?" Hunley sounded happy.

"Did I ever, "Brian responded, "and I would like you to know that I am now the only one in this Beast who knows exactly - well almost exactly—where the hell we are. I would like you to come slightly left to a heading of 196, and I estimate feet wet over the Mediterranean at Silifke at 0320, unless you cheat and coast down." Everything was fine. They had 1,200 gallons of fuel left and two hours to get home.

But Lew Elfers knew exactly what they had.

They had a set of four fuel gauges which, when cycled through with the manual knob on the instrument panel, read 300 gallons exactly in each of the four tanks and a pair of J-33s that had been running at various power settings for almost an hour and a half.

When power is removed from Direct Current—DC - powered instruments, the needles go to zero. When Alternating Current—AC - instruments loose power, the needles generally stay where they were at the instant the power supply is cut or lost. The AC powered fuel gauge was a single needle that read fuel quantity in each of the four internal—not the bomb bay—tanks as the switch was cycled through the four positions. The gauge was dead, the needle stuck at 300 gallons, the quantity reading for one—which one?—of the tanks when the power was lost.

They had no idea how much fuel they had left.

1:17-2:00 AM

There was as much reflection, meditation, thanksgiving, prayerful contrition for past sins and meditative contemplation of future pleasures in that aircraft during the next forty five minutes as had occurred in a Government owned structure of any kind during the past year. The release from pressure, after a session with terror and apprehension, is often the most memorable and most commemorating of human emotions.

In the Mickey compartment, the soup was warm and fragrant, served—passed down the line, actually - in steaming "hot-'n'cold" cardboard cups made in the USA and doled out for Operationals while they lasted. The team of one officer, one chief petty officer, three first-class and one second-class petty officers had become the first Americans known to have intercepted, analyzed, recorded and located the signals from the two newest potential air threats their countrymen could be expected to encounter in the coming years. Because of their professionalism, defenses could be planned, tactics developed, technology improved and countermeasures devised that could be expected to pay off in lives saved. They had done it in the cramped, pitching rear-end of a storm buffeted airplane punching through a line of thunderstorms in the middle of the night, thousands of miles from home over a Sea whose name they never spoke and over whose waters they were not welcome. They each had their thoughts that night, and each of them felt that they had been in capable hands through the most memorable experience of their lives.

Just forward of the Mickey compartment, Lucore was officiating—as only he could—over the hot soup assembly line, orchestrating a process that would defy the most imaginative Human Factors Engineer. For some reason, tonight the Mess had given them small cans of tinned tuna, and he had patiently opened enough cans to make up a batch of sandwiches to go with the soup. The RAF Catering Corps' tinned tuna fish and the local bread they supplied with it could have been cardboard and cup grease, but Lucore's sandwiches tasted like the finest gourmet dinner money could buy. The space was cramped, the work surface non-existent, the ride bumpy as they traversed the mountains and the problem of getting hot soup over the wing spar to the flight crew formidable, but he did it with a spirit, a grin and a wisecrack. Thank God he had remembered the rain and the arming sequences, but Thank God more, that he had been right. Like most professional arms specialists, the thought of actually using his carefully maintained weapons in anger—or worse, absent anger or palpable threat—dismayed him.

Earl White's dad was the best electrician that ever lived. He had heard that so often from the old man's cronies that he grinned when he thought about it. "Make it right, make it tight," his Dad's key to the meaning of life, should have been engraved on Earl senior's tombstone after he tangled with a 440 volt feed into a new construction site in Acton that was neither right nor tight. The son had wished the father could have guided him tonight, as he opened up the main breaker panel and looked at the damage the lightning bolt had wreaked as it slashed through—selectively it seemed—the electrical heart of the Beast. The damage was actually minimal, he had decided, and for the thousandth time, he marveled at the engineering expertise that had developed a panel that could be opened, isolated, worked on in flight and worked around the way he was doing tonight. He wished Blackie could have helped him, but Blackie was fully occupied with Burdick as they were breaking each of the High Frequency radios out of their racks, isolating power supplies, making a list of tubes and capacitors they would need to cannibalize or replace.

White had accomplished the difficult job quickly with the circuit breaker panel powered, but he had no choice. The board was thirty inches wide and four feet high and held 188 circuit breakers grouped on monitorable busses. He had opened the Electrical System Manual, spread out the wiring diagrams on the deck and located the bus that must have been affected by the lightning strike. He wanted to isolate and disconnect the circuits from that bus and replace the bus itself with the disabled Cabin Heater System bus. It meant working in the blind, however, his arm twisted uncomfortably and awkwardly backward as he reached behind the scorched JS bus and disconnected the terminals, each now-dead wire deprived of a power source, and he welcomed the chance to straighten up and check the foldout diagram.

He worked carefully at first, then with an increasing sense of urgency and discomfort, exchanging the bus, hooking the circuits back that had isolated the jet engine control system. He was impatient. The memorized jet circuits were in place and the six other leads—nothing to do with the jets, but he had forgotten what they did do and didn't care—were lightly slid into a gang nut and bundled on to the last terminal. Jury-rigged, improvised, woefully deficient as a permanent fix but "good enough for now," control of the two jet engines was assured. There were a couple of circuits that he was not able to accommodate on the new, shorter copper bar bus, and he taped these circuits, tagging them out for future reinstallation. He was done. Timmons was standing over him as he closed the panel, tightened the wing nuts, and punched in the popped breakers. They held. It was done. He gave Timmons a thumbs up and massaged his aching arm.

Neither would admit it openly, but in the midst of the excitement an hour ago, each had drawn strength from the knowledge that the other was sharing the experience.

Now, White was being called to the cockpit again. A few minutes ago, he had stood between the pilots as they brought back the throttles to the cut-off detent, and with a feeling of relief he would never be able to describe, he watched—almost as if in slow motion—as the two tachometers had unwound, the tail pipe temperature bled down rapidly, and the small speed boost the idle jets had provided ended. The jets were secured and the autopilot compensated with a slight nose-down to keep the airspeed. Problems solved. At last.

Not yet. Now what?

Lew pointed to the fuel gauge, and cycled through the four-position rotary switch. Another casualty of the lightning strike. White was back on adrenalin.

As White ducked back on to the flight deck and broke out his wiring diagrams again, Brian—unaware of the latest crisis - relaxed for the first time in several hours. He was thinking of Shirley. What had he been thinking of last night?

He had studied for the priesthood for five years. All through the college years when his contemporaries were out drinking beer and getting laid, Brian had been saying his prayers and meditating and giving his vocation his total attention. At the end of his fourth year, he had to face the fact that despite an enviable record of scholarship and a ringing endorsement by his Spiritual Director, he just wasn't happy with the idea of total celibacy for the rest of his life. He figured that if God wanted to tell him something, this would be the way He would do it. Burning bushes from which God appeared had gone out of style by 1951. So Brian left the seminary in his fifth year, joined the Navy before the Draft Board got him, made it through Officer Candidate School easily and had spent a year and a half at sea before deciding to be a pilot. At Pensacola, almost at the end of his training, he had met Shirley—the first woman he had ever taken seriously, and now he was married for life.

He was thinking of her, remembering last night in the Chanticleer, remembering the pass he had made at that Dutch girl. He detested admitting it, dreaded it, but was he having the same feeling about Shirley now as he had about the seminary after four years—this wasn't right for him, a bad decision, but irreversible. There was no way out. He had married in the Church, married for life. He was going to make it work. You bet!

He glanced down at his neatly kept log on the table before him, each course change and sped change—as best as he could follow them—logged in his clear, clean printing. He looked over his shoulder and saw the hatch between his station and the cockpit above and aft of him open, and Lew enter his cubbyhole. Lew stood behind him and leaned over, peering at the log.

"Problem?" Brian asked.

"Problem. Fuel Consumption. Big problem," Lew answered, concentrating on the numbers. "Did you log 'jets on' and 'jets off' by any chance?"

"Sure I did. Why?"

"Fuel gauge is out."

Brian quickly showed Lew the entries in the "remarks" column of his log where he had tried to keep track of the jet starts and their run times. Mickey liked "jet-start" entries in the finished logs the Navigators submitted because when the jets started, momentary power fluctuations from the monitored bus system affected the interpretation of the signals they were receiving at any given moment. The two cross correlations were needed to identify the differences between valid signal fluctuations and the jet starts.

Lew picked up the sheet and began to estimate the total jet run time at idle power.

He took the sheet with him as he turned to go back up to the cockpit, and as he opened the hatch, Dave Wagoner got up also and followed him aft through the hatch. Lew paused and turned to Wagoner, "I guess you know how much our lives depended on you tonight. You did a fantastic job and everyone of us owes you."

"Thanks," Wagoner said, "but there's something I need advice about."

"Shoot," Lew said, stifling his impatience. He desperately wanted to reconstruct their fuel consumption using Brian's jet-start log.

"The dialogue that I monitored between the base and the command authority—Sdelano was their call-sign, means 'Enterprise' or 'Business", something like that - clearly indicated that they had 'been informed positively' that there would be no intrusion tonight. They had apparently also been tipped off before, at other times before this from their conversation, when we were coming on flights like this in the past, and had purposely not reacted. I got the impression that when we come out here, they know about it, and try to keep quiet. Tonight, they were sure it was not us, and reacted."

Lew took a minute to process the idea, pushing the fuel problem aside a moment.

"What you're saying is that when they know we're coming they keep quiet, and here all these years we've had it backwards? 'Don't tip them off because if we do, they'll try to shoot us down.'"

"Right," Wagoner said, "they don't want to hurt us, they just want to keep us from getting what we're coming after."

"Let me work on that one, "Lew said, frowning in deep thought as he climbed back into the left seat.

Jesus Christ, what a crazy idea that is, Lew thought.

Marta.

"Lew," she had said one gray day as they were walking along the rocky beach a few miles east of Kyrenia, a great lunch only a memory except for the taste of garlic in their mouths, "what is 'boomerang'?"

They had stopped and parked on the shoulder, a few yards from the sea, and walked down and were skirting the incoming tide.

"A boomerang?" he asked, innocently, he stomach suddenly churning to put the garlic on top, and the basil and the lemon chicken chasing one another. "Now where did you hear that word?"

"Boomerang? I always knew the word but I never knew what it was, really. What does it mean?" Her eyes were wide and her lips were petulantly pursed as she stopped and turned him around, holding his little finger with hers as they faced one another.

"Do you really want to know?" he asked intently.

"Yes," she said. "Shouldn't I? Is it a nasty word?"

"No," he said carefully. "A boomerang is something that Australian natives have and you throw it as hard as you can and it comes back and lands at your feet."

"It is something that always comes back?" she asked.

"Yes," he said. "It always comes back. Where in the world did you come across that?"

She turned from him and looked out at the pewter colored sea under the lowering clouds of a early winter afternoon. The wind was from seaward, blowing in their faces as they paused and looked off to the north. She was silent a long time.

"I can't remember," she said finally, cheerfully, smiling and trotted off in pursuit of a patch of receding foam as it hurried back down the sloping narrow beach toward Turkey.

They never mentioned it again, but from that moment, he knew and she knew—because this was her way of telling him. Instead of parting them, of setting up a curtain or a barrier or a wall between them, an unspoken menace in their presence, he found himself inexplicably more drawn to her, more entwined, a new intimacy to be shared. He had cherished that moment, a moment of his giving, of his entrusting her with more of his life than he had ever shared before.

Marta.

2:00-3:00 AM

They were experiencing considerable turbulence at 9,500 feet.

Lew had a World Aeronautical Chart of the region on his clipboard, and checking the maximum mountain tops in a twenty five mile radius of their track, he decided that he would be more comfortable at 12,500, so he informed Brian that they would drift up slowly and up-trimmed the autopilot to give them a couple of hundred feet a minute climb. He would compensate for the airspeed and ground speed loss by a cruise descent once they were clear of the mountains. He picked up his oxygen mask from its resting place between the instrument panel and the side window and put it on, switching his valve to 100% oxygen, feeling the rush of colder oxygen against his face. He took several deep breaths, noticing that the red lights became brighter with each inhalation and after awhile, he put the mask back and put the switch back to the normal position.

"Try it, you'll like it," he said.

Hunley held Brian's log on his lap and was working the figures, his red flashlight in his mouth as he juggled the log and his kneeboard, entering figures in a neat column against Brian's times. He would have needed two more hands to try it now, but he made a mental note to grab some when he was done.

The figures weren't adding up, anyway, but he knew they had more gas than they figured. Of course. He was tired.

"You okay?" Lew asked a few minutes later, when he noticed Bob's head on his chest and the pencil on the deck beneath the seat. Bob didn't answer immediately.

"Bob!" he yelled this time, "Bob!"

Hunley awoke, drowsily looking around with hooded eyes, and his head dropped back on his chest.

"Timmons, come up here please!" Lew called calmly, into the ICS.

When Timmons poked his head up into the cockpit, Lew nodded and pointed to Bob's mask on the right side of the instrument panel lodged between the panel-hood and the window. Tim grabbed the mask, reached across the now comatose co-pilot, and switched to 100% Oxygen on the regulator. Between them, they forced the mask on his face, but in the process, Lew's arm hit the autopilot disconnect button and the nose began to drop slightly, the Beast flying now on the trim setting given it before the climb. Lew sensed it, grabbed the yoke and held it steady, reengaging the autopilot. Hunley was coming around, looking dopey at first, then perturbed and embarrassed as he took the mask from Timmons and held it on his own face as the oxygen revived him.

"Sorry, Lew," he said sheepishly, when he was feeling better. "I knew better."

Lew, smiling, didn't say anything. Jesus, one more thing!

"What did you figure on the gas?" They were an hour out now, at 0220.

Bob composed himself, and back at the figures, he noticed where he had made his previous mistake and feverishly recalculated. With an hour left, he figured that they should have between 350 and 500 gallons in each main tank, dry auxiliaries and dry bomb bays. Lew had also done his calculations and his conclusion was in the same ballpark, that they had at least 1,000 gallons, more than enough for several more hours of flight. Their whole flight tonight would be six hours or so and it was unheard of that a full-tanked Beast would have a fuel problem on a six-hour flight. Of course, that was without figuring almost three hours of jet time, at a cumulative cost of about 2200 gallons.

If God is in the details, Lew thought, the devil is in the "abouts." It would be close, very close, but he kept his thoughts to himself. It this were anywhere else in the civilized world, other than eastern Turkey, he would be looking for a nice, safe alternate field around now, but he had looked that devil in the eye countless times over the last couple of years and the devil always gave him the same finger back.

Nothing doing.

He tried to concentrate, picturing to himself the wiring diagram for the fuel quantity sensing circuit; he had known it by heart when he was at Martin. He had to trust White, but what he feared was that in changing the copper bus bars, they had disconnected the fuel sensing circuit from a power supply and they would not be able to fix it—a relatively simple fix, actually—until they were on the deck. On the flight deck, White arrived at the same conclusion. The fuel quantity sensing system was attached to the same JS bus that he had just replaced. It was one of the three pairs of leads he had connected to the bus just before he buttoned things up. If it didn't work now, the lightning had gotten to the circuit further down the line, probably in a trunk someplace.

Nothing to be done about it now.

Lew then tackled the fuel computation problem again, mentally adding the cumulative minutes of jet run times against his recollection, trying to assure himself that the whole flight duration had been covered in his computations. Did he forget a jet cycle?

He relived the entire climb and descent with the Flashlight on their tail, vividly recalling the shock felt when the thing went in the water - what, a half mile or so ahead of them? Must have been a half mile, 30 seconds of flight time maybe—but they were doing about 120 knots—make it a mile ahead of them. How could they have seen a mile in the dark? It wasn't all that dark, sky was patchy, good horizon to the north and west, they were heading—what—West? North? Concentration again.

All he could really think of was Marta, so he gave up for a minute and remembered the way he had kissed her, only a few hours - a lifetime - ago. He thought of Wagoner's comments a few minutes ago with apprehension rising in his heart, thought about Kriesler and Hawkins and all the intrigue and deception he had undertaken in the last—what—twenty months, keeping his love first a secret from Marta, then from his family and then, when he recognized how deeply committed he was, from himself. He regretted none of it, remembering the total consolation of her warmth as she slept in his arms, as she covertly clutched at his hand in stolen moments of intimacy, and as they had greeted and parted so many, many times. Did he have a conscience problem as he reviewed his pattern of calculated deception?

The conscience problem he had, he told himself, was that he acted like a man who had no conscience, period.

He had betrayed his wife, but not before his wife had ceased to be his wife in all but name and paycheck. He had been an integral part of a double deception, deceiving three people whom he genuinely liked and to whom he felt close, but "close" only counted in hand grenades, horseshoes and dancing. Finally, he guessed that he had deceived his country, and he had, strictly speaking, but if he hadn't, they would be coming back tonight skunked again. Right now, he hoped they'd be coming back.

Hunley broke in on his thoughts.

"With the electrical system gone to lunch like it has, what say we check the landing lights and get our running lights on so they know we're in the pattern when we get there. We won't be able to talk to them I guess, but they're not expecting us to talk to them anyway. Only thing is they're not expecting to see us for another four hours."

"Ouch," Lew said, wincing. "Runway lights may be a problem, if they're not expecting us."

"Runway lights will be a giant problem if we don't have any landing lights."

Hunley was right. They both could land the Beast easily without landing lights if the 8000' runway and threshold lights were illuminated, and he had landed it without runway lights one dark night in Morocco when the Base had gone dark during the troubles, but he had to think hard to figure out how he would do it with neither runway lights nor landing lights. He thought hard, and came up with—as Hunley said—a "giant problem".

"White, this is the Pilot," he said into his mike. "Come up here a minute, I need some professional help"

White popped up between them after a minute or so. He had been studying the wiring diagram and was prepared to give a dissertation on the fuel gauge problem. Yes it could be fixed easily, no he couldn't do it in flight. He was ready.

"Do I have Landing Lights?" Lew asked him.

White's heart sank. The Landing Lights were on the same bus that the jets were on. He remembered that they had tagged out some connections when they had replaced the bus bar, but he had no idea what they were for.

"I don't know, Sir."

Lew gave him a long stare, then looked back out the window ahead of them.

He was heading home, with a bona fide intelligence gold mine in the airplane. All he had to do was get on the deck, rouse the RAF Communications Watch Officer to have him encrypt a Top Secret Priority message—he would live with that at four AM—and the job for the night would be done. He would get them to lock up the wire recordings and the charts and the intercept logs and he could rest easy.

Except.

Except he had only a suspicion about his landing fuel state, he had no radios, no confidence in anything in the airplane that wasn't working now—did he have landing gear? They had raised normally, probably on accumulator pressure. Would they drop and lock? How about flaps? He might have to land the thing on a darkened runway with no landing lights. Suppose he had to take it around? He would absolutely have to have the jets in idle, ready to get him out of the dark hole he could get into without being able to see the runway.

Hell, as far as he knew, the thing would flame out of gas any minute out here in the damn mountains and…

Ginny, the pop psychologist, called it his "process concept," the way he had of figuring out what he wanted to do and how to do it and then mustering the courage and—sometimes—the cleverness to get it done.

He would do it.

*   *   *

Aft of the wing-spar, in the red-lighted tube of the fuselage where the Mickey people lived, it was finally quiet, heads on folded elbows, seats back, some thousand-yard stares, lots of cigarette smoke, lots of cotton mouths from lots of cigarette smoke, all in all a pretty somber lot. Somber-happy, but somber.

Mort looked at his watch, almost three local, eight the night before in Washington, and thought of Winnie. Winnie's last words, on the scratchy phone, reverberated in his ears, overlaid upon the screeches and howls of the audio signatures of the airborne radars that had sung in their ears a couple of hours ago.

"Keep the fish in the boat," Winnie had insisted. Insisted strongly enough to risk a trans-Atlantic, trans-Mediterranean phone call on the outside chance of completing the connection. Winnie knew the routine, he knew where Mort would be, and Winnie had called the shot. Mort could only guess what had prompted it, but he knew that Lew was at the heart of Winnie's concerns, and what little he knew of St. John-Billposter-Hawkins whatever-the-hell-his-name-was told him that he had a serious job to do in the next couple of hours.

He turned in his seat and looked forward in the aircraft, through the after-station hatch to the wing spar, noting every detail of the tiny compartment Lucore used as his kitchen and office. He missed nothing, not the cans in the larder held in place with bungee cords, not the tiny table, not the coffee urn, not the sleeves of cardboard cups and packs of brown paper towels they used to wipe the soup off their lips pretending they were napkins.

He knew what he had to do.

3:00 AM

"Pilot, Nav, we should be going feet-wet again in about twenty minutes. Nothing big on the chart, you might want to start down anytime."

"Roger, Nav. Crew from Pilot. We'll be starting down now. Let's get everything picked up and make sure there's nothing adrift in the aircraft. We may have an exciting time of it trying to get in tonight. The smoking lamp is out until we get on deck." That was part of the pre-landing checklist but Lew never could figure out why they put the smoking lamp out twenty minutes before landing.

"Crew from Pilot, belay my last. Smoking Lamp is lit until we drop the gear."

Hunley thought that one over a minute, hoping that Lew wasn't thinking that the condemned should all have their last cigarette before execution. He was going to make a crack about getting them all blindfolded, but for once, the mordant wit was held in check.

Lew pushed over, hand driving, and they started down, feeling the night air temperature change as they descended. No moon, of course, but in the brilliant starlight he thought he caught a glimpse of the Mediterranean ahead and breathed a small sigh of relief. He gave himself time to chuckle over Kerrigan, pulling that three-star fix out of his ass like that and making it work. The kid was good.

Off in the distance he could see the lights of Adana, and he planned to skirt it to the west just to be safe. The civilian field at Adana was almost always quiet, and he wasn't worried about traffic, but he knew the sound of their engines might attract some Turkish attention. A few miles from Adana, American engineers were putting the finishing touches on a US Air Force strip at Inçirlik and he saw the handwriting on the wall. It made excellent logistic, intelligence, financial, security and safety sense for them to stage from Inçirlik instead of Nick. One day, maybe this time next year, they would be working out of a secure US Air Force installation. No more Acropole, no more Sylvan

Solace, no more Mikos the taxi-driver and Kriesler and Hawkins to contend with, watching over his shoulder, living a double, sometimes triple life.

No more Marta.

The thought of it left him desolate. Through a life of discipline, hard-headed dedication to the mission, iron will and an exquisite sense of duty, Lew had arrived at this point, ending another night filled with peril for which there never would or could be any recognition, other than the recognition of a job well done in his own estimation. But he could not imagine a life without Marta, without the few hours every other month when the world stopped for both of them, and in the stopping, gave them the strength and the courage and the will to keep at it.

He thought about those few hours every other month. Was that really all they had together? Was that a relationship? For him it was. But for her?

The limiting speed for lowering the landing lights was 145 knots. They were in a cruise descent, mixtures in rich, throttles back to about 22 inches, indicating almost 200 knots as the Turkish coast defined itself up ahead and then as they passed over the peninsula—it looked like Silifke but without a birddog, they all looked the same—they should be seeing Cyprus ahead. He decided that for his own peace of mind, he would check out the landing lights before committing himself to landing but he would have to slow down to do it. With the uncertain fuel load and the absolute necessity that he have both jets in idle before commencing any kind of an approach, however, decided peace of mind was too much of a luxury.

First things first. He did not want to have to slow down yet. Let's just get there.

He leveled at twenty five hundred feet, throttling back and slowing. The field elevation was 480 feet above sea level, and he set up for a long entry into a left hand approach to the runway they had used on departure, planning to descend to fifteen hundred feet when he got closer. They had not touched the pressure altimeters since takeoff and with the weather the way it was, there wasn't much reason to doubt that the altimeter setting was the same as it was when they took off.

Finally, when he could stand the suspense no longer, he slowed to 145 knots and activated the twin landing light switches. The switch had a halfway "extend" position and a full throw "illuminate" position. He gave it full throw. Nothing happened. He was surprised to see White peering up at him and as White ducked back toward the main circuit breaker panel, Lew's attention was diverted by the clear outline of the island rising in the mid-distance.

There were more lights on the ground than Lew thought there should have been. As he approached from the north, he could make out the coast with Kyrenia off to the right and Cape Apostolos Andreas passing below them. He and Marta had spent an afternoon there at Golden Beach last summer, free of their worries and cares, lovers at the seaside, and he allowed himself a second of two of wistfulness. They had driven early one morning up past Pentadactylos, the five fingers, westward to Kyrenia. Lew had showed Marta where he had been "imprisoned" in the castle during his Escape and Evasion training exercise the year before. They had reversed their route then, and driven along the north shore as far as they could go, then down through Rizocarpazo south to the other side of the Karpas peninsula and out to the point. This was a bizarre time to be recalling that afternoon, sand on their bellies, salt in their hair, wonder in their eyes and hearts. He couldn't get the image out of his head.

He reviewed in his mind each step he would go through in making a night landing without either landing lights or runway lights, fearing the worst. The thought was discouraging, so he would make a drag pass by the tower with the jets in idle if the runway lights were not on when they got there. He would set up for a normal, left hand downwind, make a normal approach and allow enough straightaway for him the get a good feel for the sink rate. He'd have Bob handle the jet throttles and use some jet on the straightaway, and once over the threshold, he's set up his attitude, come back to idle on the jets and squeak in. Maybe.

White interrupted his thought. "Try them now," he said.

Lew checked to make sure he hadn't accelerated beyond 145—he had, so he had to take off some power and slow again, but this time two brilliant, sweeping arcs of beautiful white light popped out of the wings shining down ahead of him and as they swung up into position, they converged out ahead in a band of dazzle. He left them in the extended position and killed the filament power, so they were off and available when he needed them.

"What did you do?" he asked the electrician.

"Circuit Breaker popped. It's back in and holding"

Lew felt giddy with relief.

Lew could see the lights of Nicosia up ahead out of his window. Something was going on. At three in the morning, Nick looked like Times Square on Saturday night. As they got closer, he could see dots of orange light here and there out in the countryside, then in the city, lots more of the same kind of lights. Hunley leaned up in his seat as he started the jets and looked over and out to port.

"Fires," he said. "Look at the fires. Hot time in the ole town tonight."

He was right. It looked like there was a house fire on every street in downtown Nicosia, and as they descended past the city to approach the airfield six miles out to the west, they could clearly make out a frenzy of activity as headlights and red rotators darted into and out of columns of smoke that had risen to about their altitude.

Just beyond the city, they could make out the airport and to Lew's consummate surprise and delight, the runway lights were on, the blue taxiway lights were shining and the thresholds gave him all the visual references he would ever need.

A routine night landing.

Something routine, after all this.

"Plane Captain, Pilot, position the crew for landing, smoking is lamp out"

"Pilot, Plane Captain, crew in position for landing."

Hunley started the landing checklist with the city abeam to port. The jets had started normally, and he goosed them to check the acceleration and reported "Ready for the gear, Lew."

"Gear down," Lew said.

The gear dropped with the thud they had expected, the gauges showed "Down" and Lew pressed his feet against the top of the runner pedals to stop the wheel spin and check his brakes.

Then he saw it.

The vibration caused by the falling gear and the difference in aerodynamic forces on the airframe caused by the hefty drag of the massive landing gear had jarred the fragile connections that White had quickly and almost carelessly attached behind the JE bus on the breaker panel. The amateur electrician's nostrum "jiggle it first" had proven itself. The "jiggle" had done it. The two fuel quantity indicator system wires had, remarkably, seated to their power source and the quantity gauge beneath and to the right of the two jet engine tachometers now came back to life.

With a vengeance.

Lew noticed it immediately. He could not have helped noticing it. The red Low Fuel Warning light—the light nobody ever wanted to see except on a pre-flight light-check—was glowing bright, illuminating the entire lower bank of instruments. Not blinking. Glowing.

The selected port main tank gauge read sixty gallons and as Lew cycled to the starboard tank position, it read slightly less.

The auxes read empty.

With his hands steady, his head steady and his heart somewhere just beneath his voice box, he took one last look at the glowing indicator light and then twisted the dimming bezel to the minimum brightness position. He glanced over at Hunley, transfixed but powerless to do anything but look on with a mixture of horror and fright.

They were at the 180-degree position now, the runway a wing-tip distance to the left, and Lew started the turn. Every nerve in his body was jingling, screaming in a wild cacophony, but his mind made his hands and feet work in exactly the same way they had worked on dozens of night landings in the past. There could be no mistakes. There could be no wave-off or go-around if the line-up was not comfortable or the sink rate too severe. Most of all, there could be no conflicting traffic in the slot! An emergency landing took priority over all traffic, but only if it were declared and everybody knew what was going on. They were outlaws, no clearance to land, no permission to be in the Control Zone, no trace of their identity, even.

At the 90-degree position, halfway into this turn, he could see up the slot out Hunley's window, but he didn't want to be distracted and he was petrified at what might be out there.

"Traffic check," he called inanely, fully aware that a traffic warning at the moment was the last thing he could possibly tolerate. Through the dimming bezel, the red light on the fuel gauge was accusing him, laughing at him, sticking it to him, an up-stretched finger announcing to all the world that the machine had beaten the man and the jig was up.

Hunley did not answer him.

He turned on to final with three quarters of a mile between him and the threshold.

"Crew, Copilot, standby for landing," Hunley said. Sounded good.

"Full Flaps."

"Full Flaps. Check list complete. Not cleared to land, but let's do it."

Lew wondered if that would be the last thing he would ever hear. He purposely had held to a slightly higher pattern than he was used to, and at 250 feet on the radio altimeter, 730 feet on the pressure altimeter, he heard both jets start to unwind, yellow caution lights blinking over their tachometers.

At 175 feet, the port main engine coughed, then started again with a throb. He lowered the nose, ruddered out the momentary yaw, held the airspeed at 115, and traded altitude for airspeed as the starboard engine simply stopped. No time to feather either one. Let them windmill. Keep it straight. At 90 feet, they crossed the threshold, now a thirty five ton blob obeying the commands of the Law of Gravity, but with enough forward momentum to generate the lift required to allow the elevators to raise the nose to the landing attitude an instant before the backs of the giant tires met the concrete runway at 92 knots. As forward momentum dissipated under the runway friction on the tires, the Beast slowed, gracefully, solemnly, nose wheel now on the concrete, whatever hydraulic pressure left in the accumulator working in the brakes as Lew tapped first one, then the other, then both to keep them on the runway as the rudder ran out of airflow. With a great deal of dignity, it coasted to a profound and silent stop at the 5,400 foot marker on the runway.

It was over and they were stopped. Everything running was running on the battery and Lew hit the switch and everything went dark. 0325 Local.

"Gas off, Switch off, Battery off," he said, out of habit.

Overhead, a pair of engines at maximum go-around power climbed above them as the aircraft on approach with the authentic and valid clearance to land took a wave-off.

Lew sat in the seat, overwhelmed but visibly unshaken. He looked at Hunley with a new sense of admiration and feeling.

"I asked you for a traffic check." he said in mock sternness, watching the wave-off go by.

"You really didn't want a traffic check, now, did you?"

They shook hands. It was a dippy thing to do but it seemed right at the time.

Beneath them, out on the concrete, a jeep with three armed Tommys had arrived just ahead of the "Follow Me" pickup that usually taxied them in. Timmons was out on the pavement, and the Tommys, satisfied themselves as to their identity, had driven off. Lew marveled at their restraint, because the slightest middle-of-the-night excitement usually kept the runway Tommys busy for hours. Must be something else going on, he dimly noted. The Aerodrome Officer, an RAF Squadron Leader, arrived in a Rover, and after a huddle, Lew, Wagoner and Mort took off their .38s, handed them back to Lucore, as the crew somberly milled around. Lew gathered them together and he looked at them soberly, each one feeling that he was looking in one direction only—theirs.

"Tonight goes down in the books, guys. There's no other way I can say it, and there's no way in the *world* they can thank each one of you for doing the job they pay us for in a perfectly outstanding manner. We got what we came for, we almost didn't make it back, but we did and we're here and we all owe each other. In a minute or so, Mr. Gross and I are going over to send our message, and we'll be strongly recommending that since we'll need to do some work on the bird, we'll scrub tomorrow's deal and we'll pack up and go home. Christmas is next week and you've all got better things to do than hang around this place where something's in the air and it ain't Peace on Earth."

They grinned, nodding in assent and agreement.

"Tim, everybody needs some good old fashioned crew rest so let's set takeoff time on Saturday around noon. I know you'll want to check out the engines but they'll probably be OK. White, I'll need you to get the electrical system up to 'Ferry' standards at least. I'll want jets and all the instruments. If you think that jury-rigged bus will hold for the trip back, don't try to fool with it. Burdick, I'll need all the radios I can get—UHF and VHF and at least one HF for the Overwater."

"No sweat, Mr. Elfers. I've already checked for the power supplies against my cheat list, and if we can get the bomb bay doors open, we can do it OK."

"Okay then, Blackie check out the radar. It was secured when we got hit so I don't think it should be down, but check it against a dummy load—that's the best you can do on the deck here. Nav, run up a course to Malta and you and Bob and I will take turns driving home. Again guys, many thanks!"

Everybody went back to milling around until they noticed the Squadron Leader was getting impatient so Mort and Wagoner climbed back into the after station and beckoned to Lucore. Lucore got back in the aircraft and the three of them had a discussion. Lucore was glad to oblige their request, producing a four-inch thick roll of pressure sensitive Ordnance Tape. Decades later, the stuff would be called "Duct Tape" and everybody would know all about it but tonight, it was a relatively exotic commodity and Mort put it to good use. Moments later, they dropped back to the concrete and the three of them—Lew, Mort and Wagoner drove off in the Rover back to Operations, leaving the Beast in Bob and Brian's good hands.

Brian noticed that Mort carried a two inch thick taped manila envelope. The fruit of our labors, Brian thought. It must be the wire spools and there must be three of them, each about the size of a can of shoe polish.

The Cypriot "Follow-Me" driver had a radiotelephone handset mounted on the dash set on the ground control frequency, and after some negotiation about tow bars and weights, he had summoned a tractor with a tow bar. They could hear the other incoming aircraft—the rightfully cleared aircraft—impatiently orbiting in the pattern waiting for a clear deck, and they finally got hooked up and ready for the tow.

Hunley and Timmons went back up into the cockpit to ride brakes—the battery would have to power the emergency hydraulic system - and they opened the bomb bay easily.

Lucore collected everybody else's .38 and locked them away in the box, clicking the lock shut. Mr. Elfers had kept his padlock in his pocket when they opened the box earlier, and he'd have to remember to get it from him.

Brian packed up his Navigation bag, folding his log and chart neatly in his flight suit pocket.

White and Black got under each wingtip and walked the wings during the tow, while the Mickey crew, Burdick, Lucore and Brian walked back following the tractor. They would get her parked and then they would change clothes. Remarkably, nobody said much, each absorbed with thoughts they were unlikely to share until they had them sorted out.

Brian did notice Aldeboran and Regulus, further west now than they had been earlier, and breathed a silent prayer.

"Deo gratias," he said.

Hunley sat in the left seat in the cockpit. Timmons sat beside him in the co-pilot's seat, speaking of what needed to be done to get the Beast ready for the long flight back to Morocco—when—that would be tomorrow. Timmons was thinking out loud about the engines—no sudden stopping, but they'd have to be checked for dead plugs and other damage with all that windmilling. Burdick had enough junk in the carryall to get one HF transmitter and the VHF working, that's all they'd need. White needed to check that circuit panel again, on the ground, and maybe the Brits had something that could work on the bus bar. He'd let them know at the Acropole tonight if they had any problems they couldn't solve.

Timmons realized, after a minute, that Mr. Hunley wasn't listening.

He had hardly been listening to himself, talking out of sense of duty about what he should have been thinking and worrying about. All he could think about was having somebody waiting for him, ready to rub his neck and take the worry and the tension and the memory of another awful night away. Of course, there was no one. Not here. Besides, he had no idea how they were all going to get into town at four in the morning, particularly with trouble and the curfew on top of it. The thought so depressed him that he could feel the lump in his throat threaten to come up higher and turn into a tear. That would never do. They both were silent, then, in the battery-powered glow of the single red cockpit overhead lamp as they rolled silently along behind the chugging tractor.

Hunley was remembering that beautiful October day, not too long ago, when he and Brian had bored holes in the sky on that useless navigational training thing they had to do every Quarter. It was over Palma, and they had gone on about the ancient Law of the Sea, his dissertation subject, and the derivation of the three-mile limit. It all seemed so dry and academic and—well, unreal then.

Three miles, the range of a shore based canon, decided the Limit of Sovereignty. What was the range of a Flashlight at night in a thunderstorm?

And how anxious were any of them to argue sovereignty?

In ten minutes, the tow ended at the hardstand they had occupied seven hours before.

Meanwhile the Middle East Airlines Cargo deHaviland they had forced to wave-off landed, finally, and its Pilot and First Officer were appropriately furious. Briefed on the no-fuel, no-radio emergency that had necessitated their go-around, however, they had desperately wanted to go talk to the poor chaps who had been involved ("Good show, that!"). Dissuaded by the Deputy Aerodrome Officer and their Cargo Forwarder, who reminded them of their pressing schedule, they had offloaded and then departed, on time, for Beirut.

It was 0400, exactly. The Beast sat empty on the hardstand. Brian and the crew had changed and were waiting patiently under the starboard wing.

They were just beginning to talk things over.

POSTFLIGHT

21

NATO TOP SECRET

FROM: HQ MEAF RAF NICOSIA

TO: CINCNELM, LONDON, UK

INFO: ELECTRONIC COUNTERMEASURES SQUADRON TWO
PORT LYAUTEY, MOROCCO

OPERATIONAL IMMEDIATE

BT

NATO TOP SECRET X THIS MSG IN ONE PART X PART ONE X 2J99 SENDS X DECEMBER OPERATION 12-1 COMPLETED AS SKED ALL OPERATIONAL OBJECTIVES YOUR 111557DEC MET X BELIEVE ONE FLASHLIGHT LOST AS RESULT COLLISION WITH WATER FOLLOWING INTERCEPTION X ACFT DOWN MECHANICAL AT LEAST THIRTYSIX HOURS X UNODIR PLAN CNX 12-2 RETURN HOMEPLATE 17 DEC X UNABLE PROVIDE EXTENSIVE DEBRIEF THIS MSG DUE DETERIORATING LOCAL SECURITY SITUATION X WILL ADVISE SOONEST X BT

"You think that will do it? Lew asked.

Mort read it again. "It's pretty damn skimpy."

Dave Wagoner looked over their shoulders. They had gathered enough second and third hand information during the Land Rover ride from the runway to persuade them that this place was a beehive right now and their needs and wants were not likely to cut much ice tonight. Their problem was immediate, however, since without radios in the aircraft, there had not been a way to communicate to the military side of the house that they had flown and had landed safely. That normally would have been done with a simple one-word "Plan" message sent from the aircraft on arrival, giving their military call sign "2J99". The time of transmission would suffice as an arrival time, tidy and neat.

There was an additional wrinkle with this flight, though, since there was important operational information that they had better tell their masters about, and there was no doubt that the telling of it had to be as highly classified as facilities would permit. "Top Secret" was the highest classification possible, but the origination of a Top Secret message at four in the morning was certain to cause heartburn and discontent in the hearts and minds of the people who had to process, encrypt and send the damn thing out.

"Shorten it up," Mort suggested. "That 'Part One' stuff is for the crypto guys to put in, it's none of our business how they bisect it or chop it for transmission". Mort was right. He did it out of habit back home, but there was no need for it here. Highly classified messages were always cut in half someplace within the message and encrypted with the last part first. The message had to contain some directions telling the receiving cryptographer how to paste it back up, and the "part" instructions were added to make sure they got it all.

They hadn't talked much about tomorrow night, but all things considered, including the uncertain mechanical condition of the Beast, they agreed that the make-up flight which ordinarily would have made up for the Wednesday cancellation flight was now overtaken by events, and they had so briefed the crew. There was no way they could top what they had done, anyway. They were planning a noon departure for home on Saturday.

"UNODIR" in the message was shorthand for "unless otherwise directed" and Mort insisted that London would be so pleased with the results tonight that they could call their own shots. Besides, this way London would be spared the hassle of coordinating a formal cancellation with Nebraska Avenue and re-alerting the Turks. Mort correctly guessed that Winnie had put all his money on this one and was way ahead of them. Lew agreed, and although he had misgivings with the "local security conditions" part—he never thought the Brits would let that pass—the three of them initialed the draft form.

They were at the far end of the second floor corridor of the military Base Operations building, seedier and dirtier than the "Operations Centre" across the parking lot that served as the civilian passenger terminal. At the moment, it was hard to say which building contained more stress, because the civilian side of the house appeared to be anticipating a far busier departures day than usual. The freight forwarding area was to the rear, hastily expanded by the looks of it, with several newly installed "caravans" - house trailers to the Americans—serving the expanded military logistics requirements of the past three months.

The Communications Centre was not much more than an expanded office, walls removed to make space for a windowless cubicle constructed around a largish safe, and two other windowless rooms carved out of the second floor of the Base Operations building. The next "suite," as the sign on the wooden door announced, was the Classified Material Control Cage, not a "cage" as much as a secure room, the sanctuary in which Mort had briefed the Mickey crew less than twelve hours before. Both "suites" had a heavy outer lock and a doorbell that could be answered from inside by a buzzer-release on the lock.

The regulars entered by keying in a four-digit combination on a number keypad beneath the doorbell. They changed the code every day. Usually.

As one approached the "Radio Shack," as such Centres were called, the high pitched dits and dahs of rapid Morse Code—"speed-keyed", to those whose ears could recognize the high-volume radio-traffic device - blended in with the clatter of teletype and the occasional muffled voices of local air traffic as radio technicians patched and re-patched receivers into speakers, back and forth. The emergency frequency 121.5 megacycles was always "hot" on a speaker. There were five "positions"—stations the Brits called them—where five earphoned radiomen once copied broadcasted Morse traffic from the high frequency airwaves day and night round the clock. The manned circuits were down to two these days, as teletype communications—exponentially faster and more reliable—had supplanted most of the Morse circuits, so at three of the positions, the machines were left to clatter away, spewing yellow paper line by line as supply requisitions and high priority political traffic rubbed elbows on the crowded airwaves. At four in the morning, it smelled like cigarette smoke, hot insulation, dry paper and sweat, but then again, that was what it smelled like all day. An electric hot-ring kept a teakettle warm. Never hot, though. That had to be seen to.

Inside the cubicle, sharing space with the safe, a goose-necked lamp cast a small envelope of light over a code machine, its "baskets" of rotors in a frame above an old fashioned keyboard, but nobody ever got to see that part of the operation unless they were Officer Watch standers. You could hear the thing bang out its coded secrets, however, letter by letter, each sounding like the stroke of a toy cash register ke-ching, ke-ching. It always sounded so easy, but rotor settings changed each minute, higher classifications required double encryption and great care was required to cut and paste up the single-line tape-outputs as they spewed out of the machine.

Tonight, it was pandemonium.

Behind the counter, protected by a barred bank-teller window, the Communications Watch Officer—an RAF Flight Lieutenant in Flight Jacket and fatigues, wearing a sidearm that looked like a US Colt .45 automatic—was visibly annoyed that they were taking as long as they were. He had had a constant stream of senior officers in and out of the Shack all evening, and at midnight, Field Marshall Harding himself had paid a quick, agitated visit with his aide-de-camp, looking for a message that still had not arrived. The young RAF Duty Officer, whose name was Griffin according to the grease- penciled notation on the status board behind him, was trying to keep all his constituencies satisfied in a stressful situation for which he and his Watch Section were only marginally prepared.

All hell had broken loose downtown tonight—last night, by now—and all heaven and earth, it seemed, had to be informed.

The Communications Center was an RAF show, of course, but having the Communications Guard—responsibility, that is—for an Army Field Marshall-grade command sent some normal priorities askew. Griffin's immediate superior was the Communications Officer, who reported through the Headquarters, Middle East Air Force chain to the Air Commodore. Naturally, having an Army FM as a tenant commander meant that you had an elephant in your nice, tidy living room, but since his arrival in October, they had gotten used to it and it was working. They had a number of other constituencies, all separate commands—the Intelligence types had been the most bother tonight, until now. Hawkins and his crowd always wanted miracles, but Griffin was awed by Hawkins and thrived on giving the bloke what he wanted.

But these Yank chaps were a pain in the arse! They had waltzed in, out of any recognizable uniform, grubby and unkempt (Griffin insisted on military decorum at all times) and had asked for a Top Secret message draft blank.

Top Secret! My God, what next?

Sending a Top Secret message from the Center was not the problem it had been before the Field Marshall had arrived in October, Griffin had to admit, because with the FM's arrival, his Staff had lugged in new Crypto gear which was now up and operating. But what in Nelly's noggin could these blokes be up to now?

Lew handed Griffin the penciled draft and Griffin read it carefully. He had no idea what it meant and was horrified to see his precious crypto gear and air time being used to report the loss of a friggin' flashlight. To his credit, Griffin had heard of code words and was used to circumlocutions so in his most professional manner, he asked each of the Yanks for their identification again, jotted down their names and numbers, and gave them the innocuous tear-off receipt from the bottom of the blank. Then, looking up at the twenty-four hour Greenwich Mean Time clock beneath the lithograph of Her Royal Highness on the near wall, he assigned a date/time group to the message.

The message would, forevermore, be referred to by this label—the day of the month, the twenty-four hour clock time in "Zebra" or Greenwich time, the month and year.

And so Headquarters Middle East Force message 160258Z December 1955 was christened, saw the light of day for the first time, and began an illustrious, long and historic life far more momentous than anything Griffin could have imagined at the time.

In the days ahead, *sixteen-oh-two-fifty-eight-zee* would take on a brief white-hot life of its own before being plunged like a poker into a trough of muddy water, passing from the horizon of man's consciousness in a cloud of stale cigarette smoke, tepid tea and perspiration. As for the Flight Lieutenant himself, he was comfortable with the "deteriorating local security situation" because he had been handling Army traffic on the other circuits all night and he knew that more explicit and more alarmist phrases had passed over "his" circuits within the last few hours.

This was relatively mild, as good a way as any to describe things.

Deteriorating.

"Would you have the kindness to stow some things for us in your safe?" Lew asked politely after the message had changed hands. They had availed themselves of the stowage capabilities of the Centre every time they had flown, and were so used to the routine that they had the dialogue down pat.

"What is it, please?" Griffin asked.

"It's stuff we need to have locked up," Lew answered, looking him square in the eye with a gaze that meant a good deal of business, Mister, and I'm tired of your shit.

"Is it classified?" Griffin asked.

The three Americans looked at each other, bemused.

Lew shrugged his shoulders and gestured, clearly indicating that the question was foolish.

"It will have to be marked with a classification and I'll need to make a Control slip" Griffin said, following regulations and custom and good sense and oh wouldn't these people just go away.

"Suppose we just asked you to keep it for us, and dispense with the formalities, say until tomorrow some time. We've always done it that way in the past."

This was strictly against all rules, Griffin knew. He also knew full well that when the Yanks came through, they were operating at a much higher level of security than anything he and his chaps were used to dealing with. The lock-box had indeed been assigned to transient crews in the past, and it would certainly do this morning. Besides, he was far too busy to inventory whatever they had in their packet, assign control numbers to each document or whatever it was they had, type out hand-to-hand receipts and take the whole lot up into their Control system. It might be contraband or worse, a bomb—he doubted that seriously - but he didn't want to fool with it now so he pointed to bin marked "Hawkins" and showed the three where he could accommodate it for them if they did not want to formally introduce it into his system. He didn't blame them, really. It was an enormous paperwork burden, and he would be inventorying their receipt when he returned it to them for the next two years.

This was simpler. It was a largish pass-through box, something like a post office box in the States. The Watch Officer could put messages and small parcels in it from his side of the counter, but to access the box from the outside, one needed to open the padlocked drawer and remove the contents.

"This is Major Hawkins' hold bin," Griffin said. "I'll mark this 'Save for Americans' and tell him that I've put it here, so it will be safe. Nobody except Major Hawkins and I have the key, and I'll write it up in my Pass-Down that it's in there. Major Hawkins surely won't mind—he cleaned the box out earlier - and he's one of you people anyway, isn't he now?"

This was not following the script. This offer had never been made before. Normally, the guy just took it and held on to it.

Lew let the remark pass, not certain whether the characterization should be challenged, ignored, overlooked or even noted, under the circumstances. The fact of the matter was that this was probably the most secure stowage in the most secure room in the most secure building in Cyprus, other than the consulate, but at four in the morning, as with prior flights, he was loath to tackle the consulate. This might do, but now he wanted to get his own lock box.

Lew felt into his flight suit pocket and brought out the lock that he normally used to double lock the .38 pistol locker in the Beast. They had handed their weapons to Lucore when they came in to Operations, but Lew still had his lock. He had meant to go back and use it to double-lock the gun box, but another idea surfaced.

"Have you a spare, unused bin, like…like that one, over there?" He pointed. Griffin walked over to it and checked around it. It was empty, unmarked, and about half the size of Hawkins', below and to the left.

Lew showed him the lock with the key in it.

"You *could* use this one, in the event," Griffin said grudgingly, hoping to be done with it.

Lew thanked him, watched the package change hands as Mort handed it to the young officer, watched Griffin put it in the bin through the leather flap, and then he opened the front, checked that it was indeed in the box, and locked the box securely from the outside with his padlock.

He drew his dog tags from underneath his tee shirt and put the key on his dog tag chain.

He was so tired. They still needed to promote a ride to town.

* * *

By the time Flight Lieutenant Griffin in Nicosia had processed the message with the date-time group 160258Z through his log-in system and farmed it over to one of the Communications Watch Officers cleared to handle Top Secret traffic, fifteen minutes had gone by. That officer spent an unusual amount of time verifying that the crypto system already set up in the clicking and clacking machine would be appropriate for the addressee—whoever Electronic Countermeasures Squadron Two was—and this required delving into the NATO Communications Guide in his desk.

Eventually, he began typing the text of the message into the machine, beginning with the middle of the text, and when he got to the end he inserted the word "bisect" and began typing the front end of the message. With each stroke of the keyboard, a letter was punched on a long, gummed, paper tape, and groups of five letters separated by a space emerged. When the job was done, he pasted the tape on a sheet of plain paper and handed it to the other young officer—this one a Royal Signals Sub-altern. It looked like gibberish, groups of five letters, no clue of any significance, substance, language or meaning. Just letters. The Signals officer then set the rotors according to a different "key list" and repeated the procedure on the other crypto machine, this time pasting the long tape output to an outgoing message blank. It was still gibberish but the double-encoded Top Secret message was ready for transmission.

The time was 5:30 AM in Cyprus, 3:30 in London and Morocco, and it was on the air.

The Flag Watch officer in London was awakened when the message was received in the Grosvenor Square Headquarters. He had been expecting traffic and he had dozed with his clothes on in the bunkroom, but he had to wait for the Communication Watch Officer to decrypt it. But even before the young Ensign on watch had decrypted the message, she had, according to standing instructions, readdressed it in its encrypted form and it had miraculously found its way through arcane routing channels and untraceable land lines to the basement of 3801 Nebraska Avenue.

By the time it had been deciphered in Washington, typed on a Top Secret message form and routed to the Naval Security Group Duty Officer, sixteen-oh-two-fifty-eight-zee was beginning to take on a life all its own. It would be readdressed several times before daybreak and see the light of day in high places undreamt of by Flight Lieutenant Griffin.

Around eleven on Thursday evening, just as the WRC television news was beginning in Washington, Winnie Barnet's phone rang.

He had been expecting it.

"We have a message you'll need to see, Captain."

"I'll be right over," he said to the Duty Officer.

And as he hurried down to the street and fetched his car from the parking garage, he thought of Marta and St. John and Horst and Kriesler and Mikos, and he hoped the message said that he had gotten his money's worth.

But until he could actually read it, all he could do was hope that he had played the hand correctly.

It should be quite a pot.

22

"Who have you got with you, Kevin?"

From inside the "milk" wagon, Timmons could hear the brogue, thick, slow with fatigue, and through the door on the left—the driver sat on a little pedestal on the right—they could see the sten poking through but they were not terribly concerned. The damn stockless guns looked so flimsy. The driver hit the switch and the bare, unshielded bulb about the size of a flashlight bulb—a little bigger—lit them up.

There were ten of them, side by side, five on each side bench, knees amidships, faces looking forward in the milk wagon now, like kids on a school bus on the first day of school or more properly, like tired subway riders sleepily checking to see if this was their station. On the deck of the wagon, a twenty-gallon thermos of hot tea and a cardboard box of sandwiches comprised the primary load—the rows of passengers an afterthought.

"It's the Yanks, is it?" he said, looking back at them. Timmons nodded, and they all followed his lead. Nobody said anything.

"We got the call," the Checkpoint Irishman said to the driver, "so if you pull to the side we'll sort it all out, and"—looking back to the Yanks - "you lads can climb out now, but watch the tea (he pronounced it 'tae') for we're just after running out in the shack."

They piled out at the Paphos Gate checkpoint, the road flood-lighted and saw-horsed, pinching the open area of the three lane highway to a narrow passageway guarded by Toms in their battle-stuff and side-arms. These tonight were paratroopers, red berets, higher boots, chute patches on their sleeves. Off to one side on the radiotelephone, their Sergeant-Major—obviously the Force To Be Reckoned With—carefully smoothed away any disarrangement of his beautifully waxed mustache caused by the black hand-held transceiver and gave them the full bore of his jaundiced—and very tired - gaze. But the radiotelephone transmission Lew had managed to arrange had arrived at exactly the appropriate moment, and the Sergeant Major cradled the phone and walked over to them.

Timmons noticed the smoke first, before he was aware of anything else. The air was thick with a new smoke smell, not the usual Nick background of cooking and kerosene and exhaust and wood smoke but a city dump smell, the smell of heavy burning. Rubber and gasoline, he thought.

He had his ID out. As the Plane Captain, he assumed the responsibility for the group. Technically, Chief Flynn, the Number Two Mickey man was the military senior, but Tim was used to the role and he didn't know Chief Flynn very well. It was just as well, because all Flynn and his crew wanted was to get back to the Sylvan and get to sleep.

It was almost five in the morning.

The Sergeant Major looked at it, recognizing the green US Armed Forces card, but had no interest in or understanding of "E-6/PO1" notation in the Rank box on the face of the Card. He was just a little older than Tim—not very much—and seemed content to deal with Tim on that basis.

"I've got nine plus myself here, Sergeant, and we've just come from the field. We're trying to get to the Sylvan Solace and get some sleep—we've been up all night. What's the situation here?"

"Well," he began, "this has been quite a night. We've been here the week only, now, and this has been a bloody hell, it has. They burned down the Institute, them Greeks, and they've been running after some of their Turkish mates, they have, and our lads have been trying to keep them apart and keep from getting bollixed in the middle. The curfew has slowed 'em a little but it's given us a piece of work. It would be easier soldierin' it would, if we could lock the place down solid after dark, but every jackleg has some chit or pass and some neighborhoods don't even seem to count. Funny thing, it is, they don't seem to be as eager to take us on, but we're ready for them, them bastards. We were here in '53, up in Kyrenia, waiting to go after Mossadegh, and things were a lot more pleasant.

"It's quiet now, but the curfew ends at six, you know, market day, every Friday, Turk Sunday it is, have to get the greengrocer and the chicken man taken care of. Six o'clock works in the summer, but it won't be light for another hour and that's the time we need to watch. There'll be a transport pool over there by the floodlight, more now than we had a couple of hours ago, and if you go over and see the bloke with the pipe and the blue beret standing there—see'em do you by the petrol lorry?—he'll see what he can do. Tell him what you need."

"Thanks, Sergeant, "Timmons said.

"It's 'Sergeant Major'," he said, with a stern edge to his grin.

At five-twenty that morning, with about an hour or so of darkness remaining before sunup and with the heavy smell of burning in the air, two Rovers made their way in convoy through the Paphos Gate and turned right along the rampart on Kostaki Pantelion, past the square, past dozens of Tommys milling around, mounted Bren carriers, a half-track, and the rubble of a night of violence. Trash was everywhere, smoking bonfires adding to the more serious smoldering from fire-ravaged buildings.

As they passed the Chanticleer on their way to Theodoru, Timmons could hardly contain himself. It was standing, intact at first glance, in complete darkness, but then he noticed that the ornate plate glass facade beside the entrance was broken through, plate shards littering the entire sidewalk.

He hoped Nikki was all right.

"What happened there?" he asked the driver, hoping that his panic was concealed.

"All the electric is out on this block, they got the power transformer off one of the poles, and they've been running around bustin' things. There's lots of 'em like that, they are, and we'll be fixin' 'em in the morning. I'm a Sapper and we do that, run the Motor-pool at night, make them Greeks fix the lines by day. Great job. I wish!"

Right on Theodouru, an overturned Morris Minor looked like the taxi the others had taken to the field that afternoon, but lots of them did. Nobody in sight here, no vehicles, just the smell. Through the roundabout, all in darkness. Into the driveway, past the olive trees, a dim light in the foyer, the front door wide open. They were exhausted. It was just beginning to hint at morning.

Nikki was sitting in the lobby, smoking.

23

When Nikki saw them pull up, she got up quickly, hesitated a moment, then rushed upstairs. Lucore and Timmons looked at one another with question-mark frowns, then went up after her. Just atop the landing, she stopped at Lucore's door and when they got there and opened it, she pushed inside, sobbing. They each put their arms around her, the three locked in an awkward embrace, the men puzzled, the young woman shaking quietly.

It was the closest they had ever been, physically. She smelled of musk and wood smoke and burned rubber.

"What's going on? It's late, very late," Tim said gently, when she stopped. She was completely still.

He helped her over to the leather armchair, the only chair in the room, and he and Lucore sat on the bed. Her tan skirt was crumpled and stained, her legs bare, her hair a mess, puffy redness around her dark brown eyes. They looked at one another and at Nikki, pleading with her wordlessly to let them into her tears. They had never seen her like this, always flippant, always cocky, always in total control, always just a little bit of a wiseass. That's what they liked about her.

Not now.

To their credit, from wherever it was mustered, their combined gentleness and deep concern began to work.

"I went to Morfu," she began, her voice unsteady. "Yesterday, or whatever day it was. Wednesday. What day is today? Friday? OK. I went to Morfu and saw my uncle and my three cousins and my aunt and we had a nice visit and I came home and everything was fine. Last night…" She stopped, and fought for control.

"In the afternoon, Thursday, Greeks came and they went to my uncle's house and they shot him in the face and they killed my aunt and they killed each of my three cousins. Like dogs! They even let the dogs stay alive!"

She looked up at them from the armchair, biting her lower lip, fighting back the sob.

"Why, Nikki?" gently.

"Because they were my people!" she almost hissed it out, bitterness now billowing from her every pore and muscle." "'For the petrol!,' they said! What 'petrol'? It was because of me!"

"They shot them? Why? For gas? Was it a robbery, what?" Lucore knew about robbery. Not about this.

"No. No robbery. Hate. They hate me! They hate us!"

"Why would they hate you, Nikki" Timmons asked, genuinely shocked, at a loss for an explanation.

"They do not like what I do. I hate them, they know that. But they do not hurt me! They hurt my cousins, my uncle…" Bitterness, grief, anger.

"What have the police done? Do they know who did it?"

"You two, you don't understand!," she almost hissed, emphasizing the last word. "This is Cyprus! Who are the Police? The Greeks? Maybe. Only the British can help, and they have their hands full here in the city! Everybody, everything here is hate! The Greeks hate the British and the Turks, because all they want is to take over our lands and burn our mosques and kill the imams and the women and children who are not Greek.

"Why do you think I work there with those people, always snooping on everybody, Russians, British, Arabs, Jews. Even you Americans! Why do you think I have to live here, not in the Acropole? Because you come here! 'When do they fly, when do they come back, how many are there, who are they this month, is the Jew man with them, is the Lew fellow there?'…All these questions I have to answer when you come.

"Then I see that bastard" and she really did hiss this time "…that bastard Mikos with his black taxi and you tell him everything and he tells the Russians and they take what I tell them and what he tells them and they give us both marks, just like we are in school! Just so they know how good I am with the really big things! And then Hawkins comes to the Acropole and Kriesler, he come too, and they all eat with Marta and Horace and have a good time and they split the money they get from what we tell them and…Oh! I hate so much!"

Her English deteriorated as she lost her composure in a rush of fatigue and grief and despair.

Lucore tried to soothe her but…

Wait a minute, here, their expressions said, wait a minute!

Did we get that right?

Timmons, dumbfounded, still trying to process what he had just heard, felt he had to say something, so he asked, "How did you find out?" remembering her wave to him in the window last evening before they had left.

"My oldest cousin, Mahmoud, was in the groves. They have oranges. When he come back to the house, he found everything. Then he went to the British and they let him go and he came here. It's almost 40 kilometers and he rode his bicycle, in the dark."

"Where is he now?"

"He is asleep, in my room. On the floor."

"What does the 'petrol' thing mean? Gasoline?" Lucore asked.

"I don't know. I think it is because Thursday morning, the British caught a gang of Greek thugs who had been collecting and keeping petrol to make bombs, but now the bombs weren't working and they are after another kind of petrol, I don't know, it's all so awful. They caught them but they wouldn't tell them where it was, so they shot one of them and they cut a finger off one who had shot back at them. Then they found some of the regular petrol, but they think a lot of the other kind is still out there. They are worried because it is not the kind you put in the car but the other kind, the kind that you use in the airplane."

"How did you find that out?" Lucore asked, far more attuned to possible intrigue than Timmons, who was now trying to imagine a 25 mile bike ride in the dark, although his heart skipped a beat when she mentioned the plane.

Nikki withdrew into herself and looked away for a minute, chewing her knuckle, debating whether to take the two almost-strangers into any kind of confidence. She had, of course, already opened the door, let herself go when they first had comforted her. She turned around and faced them, eyes downcast at first, then she looked up. She wished desperately that she could go to Marta, have Marta hold her, stroke her hair, kiss her in the secret places that only she and Marta knew, but she would have to wait. Later.

"Major Hawkins told me."

"That's the 'Hawkins' you just told us about?"

"Yes. He is the one who killed the Greek."

"You know him, do you?" Lucore prompted.

"Yes," she sighed, fed up and disgusted and bone weary and tired of the whole thing, just wanting to put it all away for a few hours, appreciative of the shoulders she had been crying on, now recovered and ready to get on with it.

"Sometimes I do things for him." She got up to go. "I go now, thank you for hearing me, you are my good friends, but you should forget what I said and get out of Cyprus as soon as you can. Forget everything I said." and with that, she came over and held Timmons' head and kissed him on the top of the head. Lucore got up and hugged her and she was gone. They were silent a minute, and Timmons got up and took a bottle of Keo brandy out of the top drawer of his bureau, checking to make sure that his wallet and the few Maltese pounds, Moroccan francs and Military Payment Certificates were there. There were two paper cups on the windowsill, and Timmons poured them each two fingers of the local brandy.

"What the hell do you make of that?" Lucore asked his buddy.

"I think we better tell Mr. Elfers and the rest of the crew and make the clock run fast until we can get the hell home. I got to fix the Beast and get some sleep—sleep first—and we have to fuel her up and check the engines, probably later this afternoon, get her back 'up'. That's my main concern right now and I just don't know what in the hell we're supposed to make of that stuff Nikki just said."

But Lucore was into it now, into it more deeply than Timmons, who was still having a problem putting what he had just heard into some kind of framework.

It just would not fit. The devil you know is better than the devil you don't know, so Timmons tried to go back to worrying about the Beast. But Lucore wouldn't let up. Dealing with an overwrought female was not their specialty.

"About her cousins and uncle?"

"That too, but mostly about the Acropole and Mikos and Mr. Elfers and the lady that he pals around with and all that. What's that supposed to mean?" They finished their drinks and sat very quietly, both at a complete loss for words. Everything was so far over their heads that after a couple of false conversational starts that went nowhere, they grunted good night, Timmons going next door to his room. After a minute he came back, opened the unlocked door and stuck his head in. Lucore had just taken his pants off.

"What time you going to get up?" Timmons began. "I think we should drop by the Acropole and let them know about this. Let's talk to Hunley and Kerrigan. Hunley has always been straight up and the kid Kerrigan seem to be pretty squared away too. Then we can go out to the field and play with the Beast." He looked at his watch.

"It's six now, want to call for me at noon?" Timmons knew Lucore long enough to understand his Bronx expressions and he smiled and said, "Okay, I'll call for you at noon."

And so to bed.

Finally.

He would not want to have to write down the stuff he dreamt about when sleep came as the daylight began to creep through the shutters.

* * *

When Winnie Barnet read the message in the basement Communications Center at 3801 Nebraska Avenue just before midnight on December 15, 1955, he allowed himself a brief flash of self-congratulation, almost of glee, so unusual a feeling that he had to glance down at the floor for a moment to recover his composure.

The triumph of "all operational objectives…met" was enough—the feeling he felt as a six-year-old after an enormously successful visit from Santa Claus. But the prospect of the wider involvement of agencies and governments—particularly his own—implicit in the fate of the unfortunate Flashlight was stunning.

As an officer with "direct reporting" status to the Chief of Naval Operations, he knew exactly what to do. On the red phone in the Communications Center, he dialed the number.

The Chief of Naval Operations, Admiral Arleigh "Thirty-One Knot" Burke was a Destroyer sailor and he was used to turning in with the full expectation that his rest would be disturbed by operational signals, urgent messages or signs of hostile forces at any time of the day or night. Just before bedtime, in his Quarters at the Naval Observatory on Thursday, December 15, 1955, Admiral Burke, was informed by the Director of the Naval Security Group that one of his Boomerang aircraft may have, in the successful completion of a sensitive intelligence mission authorized by the President of the United States, witnessed an accident involving a Soviet aircraft in the Black Sea. No further details would be available until the following day. Admiral Cassady in London was the operational commander.

The Chief of Naval Operations thanked Captain Barnet and offered his thanks for a job well done.

Characteristically, he was able to get a good night's sleep, but he wondered if the shit would hit the fan before he had to get up in the morning.

It didn't. Quite.

24

At the airport, earlier, the wheel-chocks were in place, and now the Beast sat alone on the blacktop.

Timmons had long since locked up the Beast and joined the crew as they headed over to the Operations Centre to promote a ride downtown. Lew had sent word back to the plane with one of the runway Tommys that a milk wagon was making a chow run downtown at 4:45 and that he had asked the driver to wait for as many of the crew as could fit in his truck.

Brian Kerrigan and Bob Hunley wanted to make sure that the crew had rides, so they had gone with them to round up the milk wagon driver. It looked like a ten-man maximum load, so Brian and Bob had dispatched the crew and looked for another way into town.

Now, at 5:00 AM, when they saw Mikos coming toward them from beyond the yellow circle of the street lamp back by the NAAFI dock where the milk-wagon had loaded, both of them were pleasantly surprised.

"You ever sleep?" Hunley asked him.

"Big night, big night," he said, shooing them over to the curb by the "Arrivals" sign where they made out the shiny black Dodge. They were in luck.

"What are you doing out here at five in the morning?" Kerrigan asked him when the settled into the car. Mikos turned around and gave them his biggest, most artificial smile.

"Waiting for you!" he said, and they were off, down the darkened approach way to the turn off at the end, out past the hangars and the cargo ramp and the market sheds where, in better days, delicacies and luxury articles were sometimes off-loaded from flight-line fork lifts. Not tonight. The war materiel of an occupying Army fighting a logistics battle as much as a guerilla war was piled against the chain link fence, an endless display of copper tubing, lorry tires, shovels and picks, brand new jerry cans, bunk beds and canvas tents, even, Brian pointed out to Hunley with a grin, several new kitchen sinks.

"What about the curfew?" Kerrigan asked.

"Curfew pass" and he pointed to the paper held to the sun visor by a thick rubber band. "Lets the taxis through if we have 'arriving or departing passengers with passports and tickets"' and he parroted it in a sing song, make-fun-of voice, full of contempt.

"You mean you can drive anywhere you want in town after curfew? All you need is that pass?"

"No," he said bitterly. "They all know me and they look for me and try to give me trouble. You're going to the Acropole, right? Not far beyond the first checkpoint, not into downtown, we'll be all right. Beside, Friday, market day, curfew ends at six, pretty soon" looking at his watch.

When they turned right on to the highway back into town, Brian asked him "What's going on in town tonight, Mike? Everything seems to be…"

"Trouble, trouble, I'll tell you guys, trouble to beat the band.' Mike was so…American.

"First, around supper time, there was trouble on the way back. People were in the street by the Institute and they came and made them move and they didn't, then they came back and there was a big fight, and somebody got killed. Then later on, they came back again and were really angry and they burned it down! That's what they did."

"Who did?" Hunley asked.

"We did," Mikos answered. "It's our country and we want it back."

"Who's we?" Kerrigan asked, glancing sideways at Hunley as he spoke.

Mikos pulled the car over to the shoulder and turned around to face them. "Look," he said, "you want to know? Do you? Do you?" looking squarely at each of them in turn.

"I show you who *we* are, no fare, won't cost you nothing, I show you now!"

With that, they were off again, and not more than a quarter of a mile later they were slowing and Mikos was turning into a rutted dirt road leading north toward the hills. It was very dark, but there were occasional fires burning ahead and some activity around a section of the road that suddenly became smoother and wider, almost as if it had been paved. To their right they could hear the dull clink of bells and animal sounds.

They had the window open and could smell the flock. They were the scrawny sheep so common in the eastern Mediterranean, the ones Hunley always considered were crosses between sheep and goats, "geep" he called them.

"This is a village," he announced, driving slowly, s-turning so the headlights could take in the desolate emptiness and the wretched dirtiness of it. Along the side of the road was a cistern, concrete, rectangular, two figures sitting on its edge, one embracing the other.

'Look at them!" he hissed, "they are comforting each other. Five o'clock in the morning, still can't get over it. This is where it happened"

Kerrigan was intimidated by Mikos' vehemence, and he again glanced sideways at Hunley who was taking in everything he could see, peering into the darkened emptiness of it all.

"Where what happened?"

"The goddam English come in here this afternoon and chased some of the kids, they caught one kid and they cut off his finger and then they shot another kid. For nothing. Just like that," and he made a chopping gesture with the flat of his hand.

They had stopped the car and Mikos had turned off the headlights, but he reached up and switched on the dome light over the back seat. He turned to face them, with his arm on the back of the seat. Hunley's eyes narrowed, clearly recalling now his earlier encounter with "May Jawkins" some time in the middle of the last eternity.

He leaned forward in the back seat, elbows on his knees.

"Look," Mikos began. "I was born in Cyprus. My grandfather owned a hotel in Famagusta south of here, and olive groves up north, just on the other side of these hills "pointing now, "up by Kyrenia. My mother and father got married in a village just like this in the twenties! They took me to Athens when I was little and then they went to the States, and we lived in Erie, Pennsylvania. My father and his brother and my mother all cooked and worked hard and they had a restaurant and when the war came, I was drafted and went into the Army. Just like you guys!"

"I was in Palermo, Sicily when the war ended and I was going to go back to Erie and my grandfather died and he left me and my brother the hotel. Well. My brother got killed in Okinawa, so my father said why don't you go over there and see what it is like now and we will all come and retire there. Ha! So I got out of the Army in Italy and came here and you know what I found? The goddam English cheated me out of the hotel and they took away the olive groves and I had nothing. Nothing!"

"What did they do with the olive groves?" Hunley asked, intent now, wholly absorbed. So was Brian.

"They passed some half-assed property redistribution law and they railroaded me out of it because I had not lived or worked the land. They sold the groves and some rich Turk bought them and I find out later that they had been so neglected that they weren't worth anything anyway. The hotel just isn't there any more and the British have a motor pool on the land.

"Well I stay here anyway, get involved in this and that, and I tell you, I am going to get back at the British! We have EOKA—you know what that is?—that's like your patriots in the Boston Tea Party and we are going to have enosis—union with Greece—when this is all done. We have Grivas, our leader, and we started last spring to harm the British whenever we can. Anybody against the British, we take - but no Communists, no Communists! The Brits kill *kids* to get back at us!"

Hunley recalled Hawkins' story and decided to keep his mouth shut. There was a brief pause while Mikos lighted a cigarette. Brian noticed that it was a Winston.

"These are good," Mikos said, irrelevantly. "New from America."

"Where do you get them in Cyprus?" Brian asked, innocently. Mikos looked at him with a sly, conspirational leer, and said nothing.

Instead, he reached up and switched off the dome light, then started up and drove the full length of the "village" before U-turning in a clear patch of stubble and heading back toward the airport road. He went about a hundred yards when the stopped again and turned off the headlights, leaving the engine running. He checked his watch. Two figures approached the car, and Mikos got out then, obviously pleased to see them.

From inside, Hunley and Kerrigan heard only a prolonged, detailed and very complicated discussion in rapid Greek but when Bob turned around to look out the rear window, Mikos motioned him to turn and face the front. He noticed one of the men had on greasy overalls with the Esso logo on his breast pocket. Next, Mikos reached in and turned off the ignition, pulled the keys and walking around back, opened the trunk. In a minute, the smell of gasoline filled the car, and as the three of them loaded the trunk, it was obvious that the almost overpowering scent came from the cargo in back.

After more heated dialogue—that's the trouble with Greek, Hunley thought, you never know whether they're fighting or making love—Mikos got back in the car. When the two figures had disappeared into the night, he started back up, this time headed back toward the paved road from the airport.

"What was that all about?" Hunley asked.

"That was business. I got three hundred pounds today to buy petrol, and I was gassing up. Taxi's have to run on something."

"Mikos, are you a spy? A terrorist, maybe?" Brian asked, looking at him intently.

Hunley wished he had had the innocence or the balls or the stupidity to ask the same question, but he remembered Lew's briefing about avoiding giving Mikos the slightest bit of information he didn't need to drive the taxi, and he wondered what was behind it.

Mikos didn't dignify that one with an answer.

"Look," he said again, this time calmer and friendlier. "This is Cyprus and we are right in the middle of very bad things. The Arabs and the Jews, the Americans and the NATOs and the Russians and all them, the Turks and the Greeks and the goddam British—everyone is a spy! You stay there at the Acropole - that is almost Spy Palace around here. The UN downtown, that is the *real* Spy Palace. Everybody spies for everybody, like Major Hawkins and…"

"Wait a minute, Mikos," Hunley broke in. "Go back a little. What about the Acropole?"

"The Acropole? What a joke! You know who own the Acropole? The piano player and his wife!" Brian thought that might be the case, but was not sure.

"You know who owns the piano player? Hawkins, the goddam British Intelligence poobah! You know who owns Hawkins? The UN fellow from Germany, Kriesler! You know who owns him? Mr. B. and K. from Russia, that's who!" It was coming too fast for either of them to acknowledge, much less accept. They both looked at Mikos and then grinned at the absolute, bold face hyperbole of it all. B. and K. were Bulganin and Khrushchev, to the tabloids that year, and it all was so…well, absurd.

"Nobody owns Mikos, I guess" Hunley suggested, respectfully rather than sarcastically. He meant is as a probing question, but was prepared for another diatribe.

"I work for them all," Mikos said, proudly, then laughed heartily. "But only when they need a taxi!" He stopped talking then, and withdrew into himself a minute, probably wondering what to say next.

"Why do I tell you these things? You must understand that the Greek cause here is a just one, and the British are evil. But don't make too much of this 'spy' business. You ask me if I am a 'spy'. Yes and no. Everybody here is a 'spy', one kind of another. Look at your pilot!"

The air suddenly became charged and in the embarrassed silence, Hunley was certain that Brian could hear his heart beating.

"What pilot?" he asked.

"The one you went with tonight, the one who hangs around with the other one, the Jew fellow. I don't know about the Jew fellow but the pilot one, him. You know who owns him?"

Again, a silence, so pregnant this time that the clink of the geep bells in the meadow and the faint aroma of burning tires and wood smoke seemed overwhelming.

"Who owns him?" Brian asked.

Mikos coasted to a stop, well short of the turnoff to the highway up ahead, but the road was completely deserted in all directions. Brian was beginning to feel uneasy. Neither of the Americans had the vaguest idea what was coming next.

"Look," Mikos said for the dozenth time tonight, turning to face them both. The air was heavy with cigarette smoke and tension.

Black eyes glowing, he stared deeply at them, first at Brian and then directly at Bob. "He sleeps with that woman for the past two years. He spends every minute he can with her. Her husband is a spy. Her husband sleeps with the UN guy, who works for Russia, who is a spy. Her best friends are spies. Her hotel is a Spy Palace and you ask who owns him?"

Hunley was horrified, for once without a comeback or a rejoinder. He spouted out the first thing that came to mind. "Tell me about Hawkins.," he said, as if changing the subject could make everything go away. "Major Hawkins? Is that who you mean?"

"Major Hawkins my foot!" Mikos said. "Look, there's a new Limey regiment here, got here about ten days ago. Some kind of Highlanders, something like that, see them all over the place with their plaid hats with the little ribbons in the back. All of a sudden, Hawkins is one of them, goes out with them and uses them to protect him from us! They think he's a Major or something, but he don't even have a uniform, that one. He's the Gestapo, he is, that's what he is, just like the Nazis.

"You know what I got in the back of the car?" he was getting carried away now.

"You can smell it! I got them 'cocktail' things, named after some Russian. The kids in that village get gas from the airport and put some stuff in it and fill up the bottles. When you throw the bottles, the stuff sticks to what you throw it at and poof! Anybody get caught with them, get shot. That's Hawkins."

"Why don't you just buy gas at the gas station? Why steal it from the base?"

"You know why? Lots of reasons. This is not just plain gasoline, this is the good stuff you use in the airplane. Ha! I make a joke! We put fertilizer in it sometimes, sometimes other stuff and it makes a big boom! But the big reason is that Hawkins tries to keep track of every drop of gas on Cyprus. Even from the north. Turk stuff.

"We tried to move it in drums, we got caught.

"We tried water bags on donkeys, we got caught.

"We even fill up one car, then go siphon it out and fill up again, we get caught.

"You think Hawkins should be catching spies and guerillas up in the hills, no, he's always out snuffing petrol! You see them roadblocks? You think they just check papers? They watch for gas!"

Brian thought for a minute, than glanced sideways at Hunley.

"Is that why you were waiting for us at the airport, Mike? Are we camouflage or something for you? Because if that's the case, let's get the hell out of here and take us to the Acropole so we can get to bed."

Mikos, disgusted, started the car and they drove back into town, wordlessly. Brian wondered what they would do if they were stopped, but about a quarter mile before the got to the Paphos check point Mikos turned down a side alley they had never noticed before, no more than a path, really, a car-width but barely, they were almost instantly at the back door of the Acropole.

They both got out of the car.

"You said it was a free ride. How do you know we won't call up Hawkins and tell him all about this?" Hunley pointed toward the trunk. "We know damn well that all you wanted to do with us was get an excuse to go into that village and gas up."

"You Americans don't want to get involved. It would be bad for you, with your pilot and all. You want to see something?"

He then did a very curious thing, probably the most uncharacteristic, most chilling, most unexpected, yet most convincing thing he could have done, just as the sun began to peek over the eastern horizon. He opened the driver's side door and twisted the gray, fabric covered armrest. It turned, and the side panel of the door folded down. The first rays of morning twilight, far from bright, were enough to let him make his point.

In the crevice between the door and the folded-down side panel they could clearly see a pistol, a Walther P38 Hunley thought. They could also see a small, perhaps 5 by 7 inch envelope, which Mikos drew out of the hiding place and opened. In the envelope, there were five black and white photographs, obviously enlargements. He turned on the dome light again, so they could see in the dim dawn twilight.

In the first shot, Lew and Marta were standing on the patio at the Acropole, not far from the spot where Brian stood and listened to "Blue Star" last night. They seemed to be kissing, or on the verge. It was daylight.

The second photo was a darker but quite clear interior available-light shot. Lyle Burdick was counting out money and handing it into the outstretched hand of a stranger.

"That's Grivas' banker, his Finance Minister," Mikos said simply. "You know the other guy."

The third shot was a beautiful picture of the Beast, parked on the ramp in bright sunlight, a clearly marked Esso truck beneath the wing. Its relevance escaped them at the moment, and Mikos did not elaborate.

In the fourth photograph, Hunley recognized several of the enlisted crew members he and Kerrigan flew with routinely, although he couldn't remember all their names. There were about seven of them, and in the center, Timmons and Lucore were playfully kissing an Arab or Turkish girl in traditional headdress. He thought he recognized her, possibly from the Acropole or the Chanticleer.

"She's the principal whatd'yacall-it, coordinator, of all the Turkish and Arab anti-Greek activity on Cyprus," Mikos said flatly.

The fifth was the most professional, apparently a posed party souvenir. In the center, Hunley recognized "Major" Hawkins. He was standing arm in arm with Horace and Marta. On one side of the trio was a dignified, older looking man and on the other side, Lew again. "The white haired guy is the big shot in Soviet intelligence here. He and Hawkins work together. You know the guy on the end."

Mikos put them back in the envelope, looked at them with a long thoughtful glance, and got back in the Dodge. He rolled the driver's side window back down and Brian thought he detected a trace of a sneer in his voice.

"Look, "he said, for the last time, "You tell whoever you want." Then he started the car and drove off, and they watched until he was out of sight up the alley and they both noticed that he never did turn on his lights.

"What do we do now, Coach?" Brian asked Hunley, searching his face, really needing some kind of an answer from the older man.

"Beat's the shit out of me, Shipmate," was the best he could muster. "All I know is that you and me have just been used. By a pro. Damn!"

They passed the doors to the bar on their way to the stairs, and were each a little relieved to see Lew and Mort deep in conversation. They were not noticed and they both went off to bed.

It was a little after six and they were finally home from work.

25

It looked and felt and rode like an American jeep and it was probably old enough to have been in the Battle of the Bulge, but the young Gordon Highlander in the plaid cap drove it as if he had personally reconditioned it and plated it in gold. Lew and Mort sat cramped in the back, knees high, as jeep passengers throughout history have been accommodated, Wagoner in front. When they reached the main paved road to town and turned out of the airport enclosure through the checkpoint, the kid had taken the cap off and tucked it in between the bottom of the windscreen and the dash. He was apparently used to using the niche as a stowage place for the cap, and as he picked up speed they could see why. The windshield was up, keeping some of the cool early morning air off their faces—"a touch of dampness, now, December y'know" - but not enough to temporarily wake them from any fatigue they may have felt. There were no complaints, to the contrary, fortunate as they had been to catch the ride through the good graces of the Operations Duty Officer.

They had just missed Kerrigan and Hunley, now in the midst of their own transportation adventure in the black Dodge, and they passed the turnoff to the village without a clue as to what was going on in the darkness off to their left.

When the jeep went through the first checkpoint, the kid reached up on the dash and put his overseas cap on for the two red-berets who challenged them, and once through, they peeled off the main road before going all the way in to the Paphos Gate. He dropped them at the top of the little hill by the Acropole sign, where the road turned south and east into the old center part of town within the walls. Mort and Lew were fully alert and awake now, but Wagoner looked and felt as ready to flame out as the two J33s had been over the end of the runway.

The front door opened on the first try—there was a trick to getting in without a key or a buzzer, and it worked. There was a green-shaded banker's style desk lamp burning over the reception desk, no one in sight. They had returned at this hour so many times that they knew the drill perfectly. A dim light behind the teak regimental bar in the next room cast deep shadows into the main lobby where they stood for a moment, remembering that Wagoner had gone directly to the plane after he arrived and was not registered in the Hotel. Mort had twin beds in his room and he gave Wagoner the key and showed him where the corridor took a down-step then and an up-step before the "200" series of rooms began.

"Leave the door unlocked," Mort said. "I'll be along in a minute. Take whichever bed you want, they changed the sheets this morning."

Wagoner looked less out of place in his blazer and slacks than the other two, as he strolled around the lobby looking it over, and Mort and Lew walked over to the bar and sat down. Wagoner paid his respects and disappeared.

After a minute or so of the kind of silence that might have been broken by small talk directed at the Cyprus Question or the "troubles" in town or the horrific experience they had just been through, had they not known each other so well, Mort walked around behind the bar, picked up a pair of glasses and a Keo brandy bottle and brought them around to where Lew was sitting. Then Lew got up, duplicated Mort's excursion, and came back a second later with a bottle of Beefeaters. They knew where the tiniest refrigerator either of them had ever seen was nestled beneath the bar, and with the advantage of prior reconnaissance, they retrieved one of its three pee-wee ice trays and each poured the other a drink from one of the liberated bottles into tumblers of ice.

His first taste was enough to convince Lew that he had just sipped the most magnificent substance in the universe. He began to grin as the pressure started to dissolve in the 95 proof gin. He felt good. He looked at Mort with a deep sense of affection and respect, and put his hand on Mort's shoulder.

"You know, Cowboy," he began, "tonight was the culmination of everything you and I have worked for ever since the days at Martin-Baltimore." He was grinning.

"We made more money tonight than the whole heartbreaking Project cost, and you know, Mort, this is the first time you and I have ever been able to sit alone and talk about it."

It was true. Whenever the various milestones in the Project had been completed, their technical colleagues were their audiences. Tonight, they had played to each other and Lew was proud of the performance.

Mort fell silent, thinking, momentarily, of Winnie Barnet and his cryptic phone call before concentrating again on Lew.

"You're awfully quiet," Lew said.

"I need to talk to you about something and I don't know how to do it."

"What 'something?"'

"Something, well, pretty bad."

Lew looked away, out through the plate glass window into the courtyard, beyond the oleander and the olive trees, across the rooftops barely visible in the darkness, beyond them, off to the East where the sun would be rising soon.

"What is it, Mort? We've been together too long to have something between us."

"It's Marta, Lew."

Christ, Lew thought, he knows too.

"What about Marta?"

Mort's eyes locked on Lew's face, pain evident in the lines around the corners of his eyes, his lips tight as he returned Mort's gaze.

"I think you know what I mean, Lew," Mort said quietly. He really wanted to talk about it, have it out, hear both sides of the story, or however many sides there were.

Lew turned around and looked once more off to the east. He sat almost a full minute before he got up, wordlessly, and with his head slightly bowed but with determination and purpose in his step, he started out of the bar toward the front door. He stopped, briefly, and came back to Mort, their eyes now locked. Lew put his hand on Mort's shoulder and said, "Thanks, Shipmate. Just thanks. Wait for me."

Then he was into the shadows and out the front door, his steps echoing for a few seconds on the gravel. Mort followed him until he saw him stop and light a cigarette, and suspecting that he might need a few minutes alone, he went back in and sat alone at the bar.

Lew walked into the night, down the little hill beyond the trees, the smell of burning rubber and wood smoke and gasoline in the air, colder than he had remembered it on the drive in from the field. He stopped and looked off to the right, down the path that led to the alley that led to the street and beyond. He had made the short walk to the Chanticleer at this time of the night—morning, really - many times, each with a sense of anticipation, joy and exhilaration, the sailor home from the sea, the expectation of affection after a night of tension, the sun peeping up during the summer months, the sky now - in December - still coal black, dotted with stars.

Spica was going down in the southeast and the winter circle around Orion was just about to splash into the Mediterranean. He thought about Kerrigan, pulling that three-star fix out of his ass, appreciating how difficult the sights must have been and how cool the kid had been under that kind of a Navigational challenge.

He had been good at Celestial, he reminisced dreamily, enjoyed it, but always carried the greatest respect for anybody who could actually do it in "real life". Once on a midshipman cruise, a bunch of them had to take morning stars at sea, and they had all stood on the signal bridge of this carrier they were on and shot a round of stars, bringing the star down to the horizon, as you had to do with a marine sextant. He remembered, there were eight midshipmen, and he could still remember all their names. When they got below, they sat at a table in the wardroom and tried to work out their position. His triangle was something like forty miles on a side, and although it was the best of the lot, it wasn't even close enough for government work. He had vowed from that time on that he would learn to do whatever it was he had to do to the best of his ability.

Marta and her process concept.

Marta.

For Chrisake, why was he avoiding thinking about it?

He thought about Ginny and the kids, remembering how he would long to see the children at the end of a workday, hoping against all hope that their mother would be someplace else—anyplace else—when he got home, but always disappointed. He thought about the mechanical problems Tim would probably find in the Beast tomorrow—today - and with a great rush of mixed emotions, found himself longing to bring the wire recordings up to London and slam them on Admiral Cassady's desk and then longing for another day or a week or a month here in Nick with Marta.

Marta.

He had to confront it. Now. Immediately. Now, dammit!

He tried to find a beginning point, where did it all start, was it a colossal blunder, where are we, what's to happen…the thoughts, bottled up all evening, cascaded furiously down the rocky slope of his consciousness. Methodically, characteristically, he made them stop, made them get in line, made them come in order, and finally they burst in his brain coherently and they began.

Yes, he had maintained an "injudicious" relationship with Marta, violating his conscience routinely, something he had never done before. Before what? Before Marta, of course. He loved her. So what? Marta knew every time they flew, know where they were going, knew why they were there, and he had never had the slightest reason to believe that she had betrayed him by passing the information to anyone, anyone! They had never been jumped, never been interfered with, never had the slightest reason to believe that their missions had been compromised in any way. They had gone like clockwork, in-up-and-down-out, and there had never even been a glitch in the pattern. Their relationship certainly had never, not once, interfered with what he came to do and how he had done it. Horst—Horace - might have known, hell, even Klaus probably knew, but there had never been the slightest indication that any of them had had any impact whatsoever on the routine performance of the missions.

Until this one.

What did happen tonight?

They had been expected.

Someone had told someone else that they were coming, someone made it happen that two Flashlights had scrambled in a rainstorm and come after them. The whole thing had tragic results for the jumpers in the end, and he was a little sorry that it had ended that way, but it was far better than the alternative—that they would have been in the water now, or dead, or worse! Who knew?

But they <u>hadn't</u> been expected. That was the point! Wagoner had it on the wire! They <u>did not</u> expect traffic tonight!

Marta knew only two things—that he was worried about the flight, and that he wanted her to draw them off, tell them they were going west, not east, get them out of the game. Instead, they had reacted, violently, as if they were expecting him, but in the long run, to our great advantage. We got what we came after! His head spun, unwilling to peek at the dark card sitting there before him. Start over.

It echoed again…

But they hadn't been expected. That was the point! Wagoner had it on the wire! They did not expect traffic tonight! That is fucking impossible!

He needed another drink.

He came back into the bar, noticing the fresh drink and the new ice cubes in the glass, and he sat down and laid his hand on Mort's shoulder again. He shook his head, then sipped his drink, folded his hands in front of him and began to speak. He was unburdening himself of a backbreaking load, of a bitter sweet soreness, and as the first faint fingers of a new day began to hint about climbing out of the countryside over to the east, Lew Elfers began his confession.

It was just after six on the morning of Friday, December 16th.

If you turn around slightly and look over past the piano, he began, *you'll see a table for four at the window. The first night any of us came to Nick, I sat over there at the piano and listened to Horst play all my old songs. I was having all kinds of trouble with Ginny, then, and I thought it never could get any worse, so I sat and thought about the happy past, but that just made things worse. Horst took a liking to me - Horst is queer, you know—and I said, what the hell, I can handle him, and we sat over at that table and had a drink before dinner.*

About ten minutes after we sat down, he said here's someone I want you to meet and she walked in and we looked at each other and I almost lost it right there. This is my wife he said and he could have been introducing me to the Pope for all I knew because I didn't care who she was but I knew who she was going to be. I don't remember all the details of that night, and she kids me about it but we were together. We didn't make out, just were together, and together and together.

I suppose it was my need—she certainly didn't need me in her life—but I thought she liked me and after awhile I thought she needed me and after a still longer while, I thought that we had become addicted to one another. I know I couldn't live without seeing her, but it would go sometimes one sometimes two or three months and we wouldn't be together or talk or even write. One time I was in Naples with Number 3 and I had some time to kill and I went to the telephone exchange there that the USO has for the sailors off the ships around the corner from the Londres Hotel and I told the lady I wanted to call Nicosia, Cyprus and she helped me get the number. It rang here in the hotel and she answered and all I could do was hang up, because I was so overcome I was speechless. I never did that again.

I got to come here more than anybody else, as you'll remember, because I would come out every couple of months with the operational crew to keep and eye on things and she and I would pack off and go up the coast to the beach or over to Kyrenia. We were together about four months I mean it was on our fourth time together actually about eight months after we met when we got stuck up in Kyrenia one night and it got real late and her car had something wrong with the ignition and I finally got it working but it was late so we found a hotel room up there. We had had a wonderful day together and when we got in the hotel room we slept together in the same bed without any clothes on but we still did not make love. I have a difficult time trying to explain this to myself, and I have never tried to explain it to anybody in person—always just to me in my thoughts and at night when I'm trying to sleep or on long flights.

I have always tried to be the one who did things the best, not because I was competitive—I'm not—or not because I want to win a prize or get the glory but just because that's the way I was raised and my Mom and Dad always taught me to do everything the way it was supposed to be done and to do it correctly particularly when nobody was looking. I don't know what kind of an image of me you have but that's the way I have always tried to be.

"You are the finest Naval Officer I know and the best aviator I have ever flown with. That's all I can say.

"Go on."

He poured a large one over the last of the ice, and continued.

Thanks, Shipmate. When I got to know Marta and understand the terrible things that had been done to her just before the end of the war, I developed such a devotion and admiration and I guess you could call it captivation with and for her that any resemblance to any relationship I had ever had with anyone else just didn't matter and had no meaning. We told each other everything and she actually gave me the strength and courage to hang in there with Ginny and tolerate the kind of life I have at home. Here she was, married to a homosexual and I came to understand and appreciate that setup and respect them both for the kindness and dignity they both seem to, well, bestow I guess on each other. When we finally made love to one another, it was the extension of our affair if you want to call what we have an affair but it wasn't the beginning of anything or even something we did for its own sake but it was just broadening the experience we had of one another. We sleep together whenever we can now and sometimes we make love but the important thing is that we <u>are</u> together whenever we can be.

I began to realize almost immediately that Marta and Horst had relationships with people here in town that required them both to provide "data" and to have social contacts for the purpose of gathering "data" and to go places and see and be seen and do a lot of things that were specifically intended for them to get information. We didn't talk about that a lot, but it did come up and it became quite clear to me that they were a wealthy couple, that they worked together sometimes and when they could get away with it with their clients, they worked on opposite sides of the same issue, feeding the client bits and pieces from their family supply. I asked her once how she felt about that and her answer told me that she had absolutely no investment in the ideology or the politics or the belief in any thing but it was a business arrangement that she and Horst had been involved in since they lived in Berlin in 1946.

There is a British guy here named Hawkins, that's the guy who had the bin over at the Communications Shack and who is the head Greek-hunter here on the island. His right name is St. John, I think. His job, as I understand it, is to keep tabs on this EOKA thing you see all over the place and he sometimes goes around as a Major in the Army when new units deploy out here. He enjoys getting out in the field and apparently he's been a contact of theirs for a decade or so. They knew him in the war and he helped set them up in Berlin.

Then there's a German guy named Kriesler but they call him Klaus and he is apparently has Soviet connections here on Nick, and his job seems to be pretty much the same as Hawkins', because he's supposed to help the Arab cause any way he can and that means harassing the Greeks too. Anyway, he and Hawkins have known each other for years and they work together all the time but their bosses don't worry about it and it's all mixed up. Klaus and Horst have been lovers for years and they seemed to have the same kind of relationship Marta and I had. And then there's the damn taxi driver, Mikos, the one with the black Dodge, and he's mixed up with both of them someway and I don't know where he fits in but he must be snooping for the Russians too. I told everybody to stay away from him but he's too smart.

So here I am, Shipmate, deeply involved with a woman who is married to a homo who is sleeping with the head Soviet Guy who is best friends with the head Brit Guy and where the hell do I fit in? The book solution was simple. Either never come here again or apply immediately to Washington for a transfer the hell out of this business and take Ginny and the kids and get the hell to Norfolk or San Diego and quit playing like I wasn't ever going to get caught. But, I always figured, Marta was in contact with the folks who would like to get us dead every month so why don't she and I work something out to keep our crews from getting wet in the middle of the Pond. So I never said a word to her about things. I would always make sure she knew when we flew and it would always work. She would always fool them somehow to not expect us, to not be alert to our coming and going, to lull them into a false sense of security so that when we did come, we would never be harassed or jumped or harmed. And it worked. For two fucking years it has worked and worked and worked and tonight for some reason it didn't work and I don't know what the hell happened and I told her goddam it I told here before we left that we were going west fucklng west to the Bosphorus and the bastards the bastards the bastards and he almost sobbed *did what they did.*

He stopped for a minute, searching his tired brain one more time.

The only thing I can think of is that she couldn't get the word out in time. Wagoner talked to me about hearing some stuff in Russian about not expecting us but that makes no sense whatever and when the spooks translate that wire they'll get it right.

So here I am…I said that already, didn't I…half in the bag, saying things I never thought I would ever say. You and I go back a long way. I have always wanted to do things correctly. My life has been an endless search for the correct thing, the correct answer to the problem, the correct solution to the crossword, the correct power setting, the correct airspeed to flare the Beast to get the correct sink rate to get the squeakiest landing.

I never worried about what was right or wrong, Mort, just what was correct, because I always thought that my mother or my father or my teacher or the pastor or the Navy or the government or whoever the hell was in charge would figure out what was right and put the word out so that all I had to do was be correct - what was in the instruction, what was on the memo, what was on the slide rule, what the measurement turned out to be—as long as it was correct. I never realized that at some point I was in charge and it was my job to figure out what was right before I tried to be correct, and that maybe the correct thing wouldn't be the right thing. I came to believe that the right thing for me to do was to keep on doing what I was doing, the hell with the book, and to tell you the truth, it made me feel great. Was I going after the end because I was addicted to the means? I guess.

I wonder all the time about Marta and me. All I ever wanted to do was whatever was right for her and was right for the operation. To keep from getting wet up in the Pond. I didn't care about being correct, just right. At the same time, I wanted whatever she wanted, I needed whatever she needed. Is that what love is? We've never even said that word, never, although sometimes my heart and my head will be busting up because I want to hold her in the night and tell her that I love her but what can she say back? What could she ever say back? That she wanted what I wanted, that she needed what I needed? Or maybe, that all she wanted to do was to keep an eye on me so she could tell her buddies? No, it was me! I was the one that had the need! I finally figured out that what I needed in my life was not to be needed but to join in need and need the same thing somebody else needed! I needed to, what…love I guess…so I did and that's why I have to face the fact that I am so screwed up with 'correct' and 'right' and 'ought' and 'want' all confused that I've made a fool of myself with this woman, that I need to grow out of it, give it up, do what is right and correct for me, right now, here, tonight…what, it's morning already?…and I have to walk away once and for all.

Silence. Quiet.

"Let me ask you a question, Lew. Maybe you've asked yourself this, maybe you haven't. It's not important that you tell me what the answer is, because I don't need or even want the answer. But I think you do." Mort felt that it might be the most important question he had ever asked.

"Who *is* your 'Marta', Lew? Have you invented her?"

And then Lew's body was shaking, just a bit, and the awful thought that he dared not openly address was right there on the bar, staring at him, between the pack of butts and the ashtray, wondering where he had been all these months.

After a moment, he was calmer and he raised his head and it seemed to Mort that he had made a superhuman recovery from a visit to the dark side of wherever he had been.

"It's getting day out there, Cowboy. How about some bed?" Lew drew up, back now erect on the bar stool, totally in control, his speech no longer slurred.

"Go on, Mort, I'll be fine. I just want to sit here a minute. I can hear the kitchen crew tuning up in there and I'll go up in a minute. Thanks for listening, and I'm sorry I put you through what you've probably been through worrying about me, but I feel better. Go on."

So Mort got up and laid his hand on Lew's shoulder one more time, and Lew reached up and laid his hand over Mort's, and they stayed like that for an instant as some kind of energy seemed to pass between them, and then the instant was over and Mort turned and went up to his room.

Wagoner was dead to the world in the other bed and Mort spent more time than he would have anticipated reviewing the events of the past hour. He was bemused by the fact, suddenly realized, that the beauty of the major operational triumph of his whole career had been almost forgotten, obliterated by an early-dawn soliloquy at a bar with a half-drunk emotional cripple.

He had to admit that he was reassured now, willing to take the chance that Lew would indeed remember his parting words worried whether he had done the right thing. He hoped that his confidence in Lew's good sense was well placed.

He had, he felt, successfully fulfilled the tasking.

Reluctantly, without evidence - other than the remembrance of past behavior – he cautiously peered into the recess of his memory where the stored image of Winnie Barnet reposed, businesslike, omniscient, manipulative, waiting for an obscure opportunity to arise and be seized in furtherance of his convoluted agenda.

He was still reliving the events of the night and still not wholly satisfied that a corner of some kind had been turned when the black velvet bag of deep sleep mercifully fell on the second occupant of Room 204 in the Acropole Hotel at 6:49 AM as the sun officially rose on Friday, December 16, 1955.

It was almost midnight at 3801 Nebraska Avenue.

Winnie Barnet had made the only courtesy call he would make that night.

The Chief of Naval Operations knew enough to stay out of the way of this one. He trusted Nebraska Avenue to make the right moves—this wasn't the first time something like this had happened, and as far as he was concerned, it was a Soviet problem. No press, please. No pictures, Boys!

So Winnie went back home to bed and Jennifer got another good night's sleep.

26

Neither Timmons nor Lucore slept very well.

The shutters at the Sylvan were almost ideally designed to darken each room, but in spite of the semi-darkness and the relatively cool morning breeze—a far cry from July when daytime sleeping was impossible—the noises of a busy city on a market day in the midst of a serious civil insurrection, are not conducive to rest. Sirens were everywhere this morning, speeding here and there, not the American kind that began low and went up the frequency scale, then back down, but the wah-wah-wah European kind, as police of various provenances and nationalities, fire teams scrambling after the latest insult to British or Turkish property, and ambulances of every size and shape went about their self-righteous business.

Some were more truly ambulances than others, as various components of EOKA developed ways to travel and transport through the busy streets beneath the watchful eyes of the constabulary. Inside the buff and maroon Chevrolet panel truck that had begin life as a lend-lease token, its red-on-white ΦΟΡΕΙΟ| AMBULANS sign prominent atop the cab and now decorated with both the Red Cross and the Red Crescent of the Turkish charitable organization, two bearded youths drove slowly—for an ambulance—past the Chanticleer, thence out the main highway toward the airfield.

When they approached the road Mikos had used to present his lecture to Hunley and Kerrigan a few hours earlier, they turned abruptly and after negotiating the flock of geep strategically placed as a roadblock to unwelcome visitors, it pulled behind an unobtrusive shed and stopped. The grizzled "patient" in his collarless shirt buttoned at the throat raised up off his stretcher to get a look and have a smoke, and the two caught him just in time and took the matches away from him. They made him get out of the van, then they loaded the four brand-new 20-liter jerry cans on the floorboards, and after they shoved the stretcher back over the cans, they shoved its occupant in as well. Then they sprayed the inside with ether, which changed the odor somewhat, but seemed a more credible ambulance aroma than aviation gasoline.

Phil Nikolaides, the assistant dishwasher at the Chanticleer, sighed philosophically, resigned himself to another hot stuffy ride and they closed the door. Anything for five packs of Winstons and he did not have to be at work until later. Between the trace scent of ether, the gasoline, and the lack of ventilation, Phil soon passed out, and in the symphony of sirens and horns and whistles playing out on the stage of one of the world's oldest cities as they approached it that morning, one more siren did not make a difference, certainly not to Phil, inside for the ride.

At the Paphos checkpoint, the siren was still on and the two Tommys had them pull around the sawhorses and stop. One of them asked for papers from the two now white-coated gentlemen up front, and the other opened the back door. As the driver explained, their unconscious patient had inexplicably passed out at home several miles from here and they were hurrying him to hospital and couldn't they please get on with it because they had no idea what was wrong with him and he was the uncle of one of…thank you, very much Captain, and we're off then to hospital.

They finally got him to wake up in an alley behind the narrowest street in the Greek part of Old Town. He was still puking in the dirt when they covered the ambulance with a tarpaulin stolen from Her Majesty's Quartermasters, drove it into a shed behind the Opel garage, and gave him his five packs of Winstons.

When he got to work, he would trade the five for a carton of Players, but first they walked him through his next appearance in the drama.

It would be several hours yet.

* * *

Hunley and Kerrigan had sleeping problems also.

Unlike the Sylvan, the Acropole was never a great place to sleep after sunup. Most of the rooms faced the courtyard in the back, which, while it was an ideal place to hear Horst play "Blue Star" as Venus was appearing for cocktails, it was also the thoroughfare by which vendors and deliverymen and waiters and busboys and chambermaids made their way into and out of the building, each with an excited story to share this morning. Farther out from the center of the old town than the Sylvan, the Acropole had an balcony seat for the siren symphony, and after innumerable tosses and uncountable turns, Kerrigan was not surprised, when he went foraging for something resembling a breakfast, to find Hunley similarly engaged.

They joined forces in the small library off the lobby and by eleven o'clock, they were sharing a pot of Nescafe and the Cypriot version of the sticky bun, perhaps the only single item in a contentious world having the approval of both the large Greek Cypriot majority in Nicosia and the begrudging but coherent Turkish minority. Brian reminded Bob that they had last eaten a cup of soup from a paper cup several hundred miles north of here, several disconcerting hours ago, and they got down to business discussing their next move. They each had had only five hours sleep.

Kerrigan opened. "If Mikos is right about any of that stuff he told us, then we ought not to be staying here, much less coming to Nick."

"I had a long think about that," Hunley said, "and this is where I come down. I don't believe everything he told us. But when I try to sort it all out, it all is so…connected…that it's hard to see what you can throw out and still believe the other stuff. First of all, did you get the impression that he was saying the Lew is mixed up with all the information exchanging between, what, the Greeks and the Turks and the Brits and the Soviets and the Arabs? I'm sorry, but I fly with the guy and I just don't buy that, at all."

"My problem goes way beyond that. Who are the good guys and who are the bad guys?"

"Well, in the first place, we have to get used to the idea that this isn't Kansas, Toto, and our natural impulse to sort things out that way isn't particularly helpful."

"That's right," Kerrigan said, "this International Relations stuff is your subject, isn't it?"

"You got that right. I am the smartest man in the whole world on all this crap and if you believe that, I've got a bridge in New York that you can have cheap. But seriously folks," he said in a different tone and Bryan knew that he actually was going to get serious, "here's what I think."

"To get to the bottom of this thing, it seems to me that we have to figure out what the interests of the players are and then try to see which of those interests are being 'maximized'—how's that for a Ph.D. word, Sailor? Let's begin with the guy Mikos said was a UN guy who was on the Russian team. The Soviets just signed all the kids on their block up into something called the Warsaw Pact. That was, when, last May, right? Now in this neighborhood, the big boss is Nasser down in Egypt, and while we always make the mistake of thinking all of the 'troubles' in the Middle East are Nasser's doing, that's baloney. He is certainly the catalyst right now, but the troubles were here before he got out of kindergarten. What he's done is get his neighborhood guys—the Arab league - together, and the locals, Egypt, Syria and Jordan, if I remember correctly, unified their military forces in October to get ready for the next go at the Jews. Now we good guys can't afford to let the power equation got out of balance, so we signed up all the other kids around here into something called the Baghdad Pact, that was just last month.

"So now we have a reasonably balanced system. And the principal short-term goal of each of the players—at this moment—seems to be balance.

"Don't get me wrong. The broader stakes are pretty high—the Suez Canal, for example, what happens if Nasser tries to take it over? The British and probably the French might try to take it back, but I'll bet the US would resist anything that would jeopardize the Canal itself in the name of keeping things balanced, particularly when you look at the possibility of Soviet involvement or even when you think about Middle East oil. Nobody ever talks about oil but one of these days, oil will be a big ingredient in the strategic mix around here. And don't ever forget that both the US and British have a stake in the State of Israel as well, and the Oil versus Israel competition for attention is not going to be pretty. Sorry about the lecture. Where was I?"

He licked some sticky bun goo off his finger and went on.

"So if we put all this in the context of superpower relations, the 'Cold War' coexistence thing as it plays out on the ground here in Good Ole Nick, we have the Russian player who backs the 'confrontation' states—that's Nasser and his buddies Jordan and Syria—so we say that he's pro-Islamic, pro-Arab and around here, that translates to pro-Turk and anti-Greek.

"Now you've got to deal with enemies, not friends, if you want to understand this. Are you with me so far? Good, okay. The Soviet guy will probably have to be anti-Greek because he's pro Arab. But on the ground here in Nick, and I don't mean in the UN or in Central Europe, who's the biggest enemy the Greeks have at the moment? The Brits and the Turks, right? Right. So who does the Russian guy find himself on the side of, pardon my preposition? The British.

"Assuming for a minute that the British guy, Hawkins, who I met yesterday afternoon by the way, and the UN guy, Kriesler (was that his name?), want to do business here, it's only logical that they should deal with our host and hostess at the good old Acropole. Look at this place! It's the crossroads of the world, and if it ain't, then the Acropole East down the street—the Chanticleer—is!

"It gets worse before it gets better. Kriesler has to support that Arab girl in the picture with our guys because she's the Turkish Lady, if we can believe Mikos. She hates the Greeks. She's not too fond of the Brits, though, but she swallows that because the guy she hates most, probably, is your good friend Mikos, the Yankee Soldier, who hates Hawkins. So unless I miss my bet and all that valuable education has been wasted, I would say that Miss Turkey and Hawkins and Kriesler and probably Mr. and Mrs. Acropole are all on the same side in the local ball game, and if you don't like the Greeks, then they're the 'good guys'. 'Bad guys' to the hundred thousand or so Greeks hanging around here with not much to do. That's the way Mikos sees it. With me, so far?

"Okay, now that's my guess on the local situation. But if you expand the range on your little radar here, you've got to look at who is paying Mr. Kreisler and Mr. Hawkins—the Soviets and the Brits, if Mikos is right. Now, both these guys are buddies and allies here in town, but up at the Big House where the paymaster sits, they are each expected to come up with something useful in the continuing saga of the Free World versus Godless Atheistic Communism. And here is where I don't like what I am hearing." He stopped for a moment to catch his thought.

"Did *you* know that Lew is sleeping with the Acropole lady?" Hunley asked.

"No, I didn't, but I don't have any problem with it. I think she's gorgeous and I guess we both feel the same way about Lew. Good for him."

"Well, let's suppose that they have an intimate relationship and in the course of this intimate relationship, one partner—the Lady—learns certain details about the life of the second partner—the Gentleman, in this case. What would she be able to do with these—shall we call them 'details'? Well if her friend Kriesler wanted to win some brownie points, he could certainly use access to these 'details' right? Right. And if Hawkins wanted to win some brownie points, he could do one of three things. One, he could claim to be monitoring the 'dialogue' so that the good guys would know what's going back and forth, since theoretically the 'details', being American, belong to him, being a Brit. NATO and all that, you know. Two, he could preempt and have the 'details' altered, mistaken, belated or just falsified. The problem with that is that Kreisler would get wise and the game would end.

"Or the three of them could get together, and considering the wide range of political, economic, ideological, and—yes—military intelligence that bubbles up from this place, they could control the spring and live happily ever after." Hunley stopped to get a reaction.

"What the hell do you mean?" Kerrigan asked, fascinated, but lost.

"Just this. Remember Mikos' exact words last night—this morning, actually. 'Everybody here is a spy, one kind or another'. I think we have a little private-enterprise intelligence factory here and I hate to say this, but I think Lew is some of the raw material." They sat for a moment and mulled it over.

"What you're saying is that they know when we fly and that information is sent on to the Russians up in the Pond."

"Possibly."

"Then how come we haven't been jumped until last night?"

"Maybe, Lew is on to them and he always makes sure they're not expecting us when we come. He fools the lady into giving them bum dope or maybe he charms her pants off, I don't know, but in any event they (a) never seem to know when we're coming and (b) we never get chased. Last night something went wrong."

Kerrigan felt better. He saw Hunley's point and it certainly made sense. They had never been bothered on any flight they had made until last night. Whatever Lew had been up to, it sure worked.

"So I guess Lew's relationship with the lady is a godsend for us, if there is such a thing, and a lot of guys owe their ass to him. Is that the way you see it?" Hunley had to admit that it could be added up that way, and everything Mikos had said led to that assumption.

"But what about the pictures?" Kerrigan asked, moving on. He still had problems with the whole thing. Why the hell had Mikos shown them off?

"Well," Hunley began. "Let's take them one by one. The first one was the one of the two of them swapping spit down there on the patio. If you're the pilot of a frigging big old black spy plane that flies into the Pond in the dark of night, I guess you shouldn't be smooching up the head of the local Spy Company." Kerrigan grinned at that one.

"Next, let's see, that was the one with the radioman Burdick taking—or was he giving—the money to the Greek guy. I thought about that long and hard and all that proves is that somebody who knows the Greek guy has a camera. Lyle Burdick can give money to anybody he damn well pleases, it's a free country."

"Is it?" Kerrigan asked. "Is it a free country? How would the Brits take to that if indeed, it was what's-his-name's deputy?"

"That's their problem." Hunley said. "I can't figure an angle on that. Surely, Mikos knows Ike is not bankrolling Grivas." But he had a nagging thought.

"The third picture was the group shot of them all, and if what I said here a minute ago is true, then that picture just documents the fact that they were all in the same room one time when somebody had a camera. The same with the one of the sailors and the Turkish girl. So they know her, so what? And the one of the beast getting fueled, I'll be damned if I can figure out what that's all about."

"Yeah, Bob, but don't they—all five of them together—make a case for American involvement with the local cat and dog fight, and aren't we the last ones in the world that should be having our pictures taken mixed up with the local Mob? Think about it. Suppose those five shots were used to illustrate an 'expose' of the US position and involvement in Cypriot affairs, and some lurid writer put a story together—just like the one you just told me—it wouldn't have to be proven or even true, for Christ's sake!"

Hunley was silent, thinking. Kerrigan certainly did have a point.

"You may be right," he said, slowly, thinking hard. Good God, worse, suppose there actually *was* a US spoon in the soup, suppose someone on the US side was really in touch with some of these birds and was…No way, José. No way. He dismissed it out of hand. Better, though…

"That may have been the tease for a blackmail shopping expedition. If what I'm thinking is right, Mikos and company are going to up the ante here and drag us Americans into the fray. And those pictures are going to be dynamite, if as you suggest, they see the light of day with the right set of words beneath them. Think about it. Our champeen Radioman Burdick is probably buying a rug or something in the picture, but in the caption he'll be giving money to Grivas forces to…what…buy gasoline for Molotov cocktails, or something."

Good grief, what did I say? Hunley thought, remembering the ride in the country in the dark. And now that *we* - Bob and I - "the American side" have seen them, how does that change things? What will we have to do about it? Oh shit…

When they finished breakfast and the conversation wound down to long, thoughtful stares and shakes of the head, they got up to leave the nook off the lobby. On the way out, they were surprised to see Lucore and Timmons coming in, principally because the two Senior Petty Officers never - and that was Never Ever - came to the Acropole. Their visit at this time of day suggested that something was either going or had gone dreadfully wrong with the airplane. Hunley was immediately concerned and he and Kerrigan went over to them immediately.

"Can we talk to you, Mr. Hunley? We've got a problem we need to talk about." Timmons was professional and business-like, frowning.

"Sure, Tim, "Hunley said immediately, and he and Kerrigan led them back to the library and tried to shut the big oak door, but it wouldn't budge. They pulled up chairs and sat at the uncleared table. Just then, one of the young waiters popped his head in the door and Hunley had him clear off the table and bring another pot of Nescafe and some more cups. The four of them made nervous small talk about the troubles outside, the difficulty sleeping and their anxiousness to get out of town, looking over shoulders and at shoes and feet until the kid came back with their coffee and then left them alone.

"What's up?" Kerrigan asked.

Timmons and Lucore both started to speak at the same time, and they stopped, smiled at each other—their first smile in a so-far grim day - and Timmons took them through their experience with Nikki at the Sylvan. Hunley was totally attentive, asking questions the probed the background of Nikki's relationship with them that neither of the officers had known.

"She said that she tells someone when we fly, who's in the crew, and she mentioned Mr. Elfers and someone she called the Jew man? Do you think she meant Mr. Gross?"

They both nodded.

"Then, she said she 'tells the UN person' and he also has Mikos working for him and she thinks he compares the two reports?"

"That's what she said," Lucore declared, earnestly. Hunley turned to Kerrigan and they looked at one another deeply for a second and then Hunley said, "No single-source unconfirmed stuff for this guy." He walked them back through the report once again.

"Tell me about her cousin."

"He's a mean looking son of a bitch," Timmons volunteered. "I saw him this morning getting on his bike, looked like he meant business. Maybe he'll find Mikos."

Then he pursed his lips and said "Don't you wish we were out of here and on the way home? I don't like this at all."

Lucore had to agree, but their dissimilar backgrounds came into play.

"I don't want to cut and run just yet. I'd like to even it out for Nikki. I guess we can't do that, can we."

Kerrigan looked at Hunley and said, "Tell them what we've been talking about." Hunley wished he had not brought it up, but there was not much he could do about it now. Almost reluctantly, he summarized the earlier conversation and as he got warmed to the subject, he was encouraged by the total concentration and attention of his listeners.

"We think that Mr. Elfers has been involved with the lady that runs this place and the Chanticleer—Nikki's boss—and that as a result, he's been able to keep the trips into the Pond as uneventful as they have been—until last night. We don't know what happened last night. We also think that Nikki's observation that the four of them 'split the money' is exactly right."

Kerrigan had to admit that Bob Hunley had hit the nail on the head, now that he heard the rest of the story from the two petty officers. His respect for the white-haired 'Hairpin' jumped.

Then, they described the set of photographs.

"We think the pictures, probably innocent all around, are going to be used to either put an anti-American story together to discredit us or to threaten us with publication if we don't do something. "Kerrigan continued.

"Your mention of the aviation gasoline in the Molotov cocktails tells us how the picture of the Esso truck fueling the Beast ties in. Several of you are in one of the shots with a nice looking, apparently Turkish or Arab woman in traditional jewelry. Could that be Nikki? I guess it is, based on what you've told us about her."

"It must be Nikki. We took that picture months ago, it was her birthday, but it never came out. Or, at least, we never saw it. Shit, that makes me mad! Remember, I had to fix the goddam camera!" They looked at each other a moment, anger welling up, burning, then crackling in each man's grimace. Blood in each pair of eyes.

Kerrigan continued, getting them back into the discussion.

"But what's the story on Burdick, the Radioman?"

Again, exchanged glances, charged now with a different emotion, the loyalty shipmates have for one of their own, good, bad or indifferent.

"Burdick is harmless. He's got a head and an ass that're too big for his hat and his britches and he gets them confused all the time, but he's a good radioman—the best, really—and he's the last one who wants to get mixed up with anything like this. His export import business couldn't handle it."

Now it was Lucore's turn to wish that the cat were still in the bag, but as long as Timmons had started it, he took up the thread and filled them in on the extra-curricular life of their First Class Radioman.

"So it's conceivable that the picture shows Burdick doing something Burdick would prefer not have widely publicized?"

"Yes sir."

"Just thinking out loud," Lucore began, but he hit the heads of several nails as he went on. "This seems to be a really hairy week here in Nick. I've been coming here for a couple of years, on and off, and this is as bad as—worse than—last Spring when EOKA started going after the Brits and the Turks, blowing things up. I was here in September when the Turks were going after the Greeks all through Turkey, and that was pretty tense too. But this is really bad now, and I'm wondering if coming here is more trouble than it's worth. I love Nick, but it seems to me with Adana up there opening up, we'd all be better off without all this shit going on all over us.

"If they're trying to get us out of here, why don't we just not come back, assuming that we can get the hell out of here tomorrow.

"If this place" and he looked around him cautiously, "is not secure and the Sylvan Solace is not secure and the Nicosia Officers Club—excuse me, but that's what we call the Chanticleer—is not secure, and our good buddy Nikki and our taxi buddy Mikos and Mr. Elfers' girlfriend and God knows who else—they're all playing grabass and our lives are on the line, what the hell?

"It seems to me that Mikos and his Greeks are up to something. Tim and I fueled the Beast last night and somebody had gotten to the tanker drains and drawn off a lot of gasoline before the truck got to us. We were the only 115/145 Aviation Gasoline load he delivered yesterday—I asked the guy—and I bet if you take a look at the gas your friend Hawkins is trying to find, it won't be straw colored like Esso Regular, but it will either be dirty brown because it will be green 130 grade and Purple 145 grade - probably some blue 110 - all mixed up, or it will all be all purple!"

"Sure," Hunley offered, "listen to the fire truck sirens. They're at it right now."

"Yeah, "Lucore agreed, "but if what you think is going on is true, then follow this one. They got the Institute, they hit the Post Office, they already got the radio station last May and the paratroopers and the Highlanders won't let them get close to the airfield, so what's a juicy target that they might be looking at?

"Call me for being the bad-ass kid from the Bronx, but wouldn't it be something if Mikos and his guys could get the UN guy and the Hawkins guy and Mr. and Mrs. Acropole all together at the Chanticleer and blow the place up? With Nikki there too? And her brother? Think about it."

They all laughed, but when the chuckles drained down and they thought about it, they all agreed that Lucore had a hell of an imagination.

* * *

Upstairs, Mort had gotten to bed at sunrise and had finally slept several hours, not before a seemingly endless recapitulation in his head, first of the flight and its outcome, then of its aftermath with Lew in the darkened bar downstairs. He was overjoyed at the work they had done in the aircraft. He was dazzled by their good luck in getting what they had gotten before the lightning, and preferred not to remember how close they had all come to disaster not once—over the Pond—but a second time—over the end of the runway. To his chagrin and frustration, he was at a total loss for advice that would help his buddy Lew out of his dilemma, and he lay for quite awhile, staring at the ceiling, smoking one cigarette after another, wondering what to do.

Suppose Winnie Barnet were here. What would he do? What would he say? Somehow, Mort knew the answer before he had even opened up the topic. Winnie knew. Didn't he.

Wagoner slept the sleep of the dead in the bed beside him, and Mort envied him until in his search for something to occupy his mind in the restless, noisy hours of the morning, he thought about Wagoner's trip and had to hand it to him—it had probably been three days since he had been to bed.

27

The *kaffe-klatch* broke up, finally, and Timmons and Lucore made the ten minute trip back to the Sylvan on foot, talking each other into and out of a dozen different strategies and tactics tailored to protect Mr. Elfers and the rest of the crew while avenging Nikki's family, punishing Mikos, ridding the world of Communism and British Imperialism, and putting an end to the Arab-Israeli confrontation.

At the hotel, they collected Lyle Burdick, Black and White and the five of them walked the twenty minutes to Paphos gate, dodging ambulances, police jeeps, Army Land Rovers, shoppers on bicycles, pushcarts, half-tracks, and even an ice cream truck. The checkpoint was bedlam at two o'clock in the afternoon, with long lines of vehicles lined up in either direction waiting to be waved through by the paratroopers who were in no hurry, and they had to get out of the way as an ambulance pulled around the line of cars and was waved through into town. The Sergeant Major saw them coming and made them stand to one side for a minute, but when he approached them he was cordial and in an apparently good mood.

"Morning, Sergeant Major," Timmons greeted him, smiling.

"Afternoon, actually Yank," he smiled, his waxed mustache precisely where and how it had been at five this morning."

"Got to sleep sometime," Timmons answered, good-naturedly, and they negotiated a motor-pool ride out to the airport with little difficulty. On the way, the blue-bereted Engineer corporal who drove them provided a rundown of the events of the day. While they had slept, there had been a fire-bombing at one of local open air markets in which several Greek civilians and a pair of English constables had been injured, fortunately not seriously; things were quiet in the Turkish parts of the city, and the unusually large mosque attendance had been quiet and orderly.

There was activity at the airfield, the military police and the constabulary joining forces with a Highlander platoon to search several of the Quartermaster storage areas, and the flurry of activity around this morning had everyone worried about the threat of sabotage, but nothing had come of it. Nonetheless, their IDs were carefully but courteously scrutinized at a new checkpoint set up where the airport approach road joined the main east-west highway from Nick, the Timmons noticed a number of cars and lorries sidelined at the sawhorses for searching.

Every aerodrome in the world has a fuel storage area adjacent to the runway, a "fuel farm" in the lingo, where fuels are stored before being dispensed to tank trucks and, eventually, by the trucks to the aircraft they service. It was usually deserted, save for the dispatcher and his driver cronies who played marathon card games with mysterious rules involving wagered pistachio nuts and paper clips.

They asked to be dropped off there, and while Timmons and Lucore made arrangements for a fuel truck amid an unusual level of seemingly disconnected activity, the others trundled out and walked out on the blacktop hardstand toward the aircraft. Beneath the "No Smoking Within 100 feet" sign in English, Greek and Turkish, today the fenced compound was full of bored-looking Tommys leaning against the pumps and filters, dying for a smoke, half-disappointed, half-relieved firemen at a false-alarm.

The weather had begun to cloud over and there was a threat of rain in the air, characteristic of this time of the year when the fronts marching through Europe bringing snow and rain stretched their way to the south and brought winter—less the snow—to the eastern Mediterranean. It would probably rain tonight, so Timmons planned to take on a departure load of fuel, turn-up the aircraft immediately after fuelling, and spend as much time as was needed to determine if they could make a Saturday noon departure for home.

They rode out in the cab of the tanker. White and Black helped gas the Beast, and it took longer than usual to fill the mains and auxiliaries since they were essentially empty tanks. Again, the tank drains were free of sediment and moisture, but this time neither Timmons nor Lucore registered any surprise. Before the fuel started pumping, Timmons had opened both cowls and checked the filters on the huge carburetors, each the size of a suitcase, and they checked each tank drain after fueling. Black filled his Zippo from the starboard auxiliary drain, taking care not to get any of the purple fuel on his trouser leg, since the stuff burned the skin if it got on the cloth and couldn't air out and dry.

They scrounged a power cart from the Line Shack, Black and White each manned a fire extinguisher and with a great deal of anticipation, hoping for the best, Timmons started first the Port, then the Starboard main engines. The smooth starts helped ease their concerns, and after warm-up and a magneto check with the four of them holding their ears against the full-throated roar of the big corncob engines, he started both jets and goosed them up to about 80% with no trouble and no hitches. Then he beckoned White to the cockpit, and Timmons put him in the left seat while he went back to the engine analyzer and checked the 28 pairs of plugs on each engine, primary and secondaries, until he was satisfied that there had been no apparent damage. When he was done, he went forward and had White shut down the engines.

Burdick was already into the bomb bay where he was rummaging through his section of the carryall. In a few minutes he was up the ladder on to the flight deck and he and Blackie were sitting like Oriental tailors with bits and pieces of black boxes spread all about them. Before long, Tim heard Burdick getting a VHF radio check on the ground control frequency and when, later, he heard one of the High Frequency sets crank up with its cooling fan motors humming, he crossed off the radios from his worry list.

Black and White had the main circuit breaker board open and in the daylight, Timmons got a look at the damage the strike had caused. The smell of burning insulation still hung near the board, but the damaged circuits had been on the very top row of bus bars and as they looked carefully at White's in-flight fix, Timmons was able to provide the extra pair of arms and hands the electrician needed to get everything back "right and tight".

By the time the sky darkened into twilight, they had policed up the interior of the Beast, locked the controls against the possibility of a gusty wind later in the evening, stowed the carryall and the manuals, off-loaded the trash and were ready for flight. The Auxiliary Power Unit was still connected and Burdick fired up the VHF transceiver on the Ground Control frequency and asked for transport for the crew. It was just beginning to drizzle.

It was dark when they got back to the Sylvan, raining, dinner aromas filling the lobby and the clink of silver and glassware coming through the open doors to the dining room as the staff—both of them—set up for the evening meal. They had already told Dimos that they would be eating in this evening. Timmons asked Dimos to let him use the lobby phone and he called the Acropole and got Mr. Kerrigan. Lucky. Sometimes it took hours to get a dial tone. He related briefly that the Beast had been checked out, everything seemed to be working well enough to get them home, the mains and auxiliaries were full and they would be ready for a 1300 Local departure. Kerrigan promised to get the word to the officers and told Timmons to count on the departure time.

Before he hung up, Kerrigan hesitated a minute and then said, "Tim? Any thoughts on what we talked about?"

"Yeah, well we've been talking about it, Lucore and me, and we decided that we'd tell the crew—mainly what they need to know to stay out of trouble. The Mickey guys don't have to know."

'Fine," Kerrigan said, and hung up.

Most of them were still weary from last night and if they hit the sack tonight, it might put their rhythms back on a daylight-wake schedule. As they started into the bar, Tim whispered to Lucore and instead of sitting at the bar, they headed toward a table at the far end of the room and herded the others with them.

"We need to talk about something," Timmons said.

When they had all sat down, Black and White had gone to the bar and brought over their usual—five Lowenbraus, on the tab.

"What's up?" Burdick asked.

"We've got a little problem," Timmons began, "and we may have to do something about it" - he glanced up at Dimos who was now behind the bar polishing glasses—"but keep your voices down and listen up."

* * *

Marta and Horst had cancelled their Friday night Chanticleer appearance, and dinner would be served to the few early birds who had prearranged reservations for the small, cozy dining room. It conveniently handled five tables of four, and tonight a table had been brought up from below for a party of six. The chef and a reduced kitchen staff were on duty, the electricity had been restored long enough for the icemaker behind the bar to have a half-filled coffer and the cocktail hour was in full swing. They even had phone service, a somewhat remarkable benefit after a night of turmoil. Over at the Acropole, Horst was getting ready to entertain the cocktail group, smaller than usual, inside tonight because of the threat of and then the reality of a December rain dampening a Friday night already affected by the curfew.

* * *

Earlier, Hunley and Kerrigan had sat together in silence after Timmons and Lucore had gone off, each wondering what to do next. It seemed appropriate that they put the various threads together into some kind of a pattern—the ride with Mikos, the business about Nikki, their concern about the photographs—so they decided to take it up the chain of command and talk it over with Lew. As soon as they had agreed on that course of action, they both began to tear the decision apart again and by mid-afternoon, they had gotten nowhere. They were both tired but restless, so they walked down across the river bed and through the residential neighborhood, past the Chanticleer, and down to the square where they stopped at the Victory and had a Coke, their preoccupation now almost palpable, but each drawing some comfort from the other's involvement.

When they got back to the hotel, without having mentioned it but in perfect agreement, they walked up the staircase to Lew's room and knocked. Kerrigan found it hard to believe that it was only twenty-four hours ago that he had knocked on the same door for the dippy weather briefing, but he felt himself wondering whether he would like to go back and restart the clock with yesterday's knock. There was no answer, and after a respectable minute of listening for sounds of arousal or sleep, they tried the doorknob. When it turned easily—it was unlocked—each looked into the other's face for suggestions and neither finding any, they looked in at the empty, fully-made bed, closed the door and split up, each to his chamber for more fitful napping.

They agreed to meet at six for dinner.

* * *

After Mort had left him at daybreak, Lew had sat alone in the early morning glare from the east, the Beefeaters almost gone, the ice long since gone, and he poured himself the last of the bottle with unsteady hand that barely got the liquid in the glass.

He was so tired.

His mouth was beginning to fuzz over—too many cigarettes, of course - and he was having trouble with his elbow on the edge of the bar. It kept wanting to slip and he kept putting it back but it kept wanting the slip and, oh, the hell with it. He gulped the last of the gin and got up, steadying himself on the bar, and checking that he was quite alone, he leaned on the bar as he moved step by step toward the staircase.

The world was not really spinning, just oscillating from side to side making navigation difficult, but he made it to the stairway, tripped once on the fourth step from the top, and although he really wanted with all his heart to stay in that position with his head on the landing and his knee buckled beneath him, he got up and kept going. Blindly, on instruments possibly, he made it to the end of the corridor and then to the end of the next and finally he was at the back of the building and the last thing he could recall was her door opening and then it was almost four o'clock in the afternoon and he was awake in her bed and he smelled her but he was alone.

28

In her own room, Nikki had had a terrible night, and after finally dozing from sheer exhaustion well after daybreak, she was frantic as she got ready for her what she needed to do.

Mehmet had left, on his bike, saying nothing, looking straight ahead, unwilling to be comforted or to answer her questions. She had taken the morning off, exhausted, sleepless for so long, and as she washed herself in the earthenware ewer in her apartment, she wished she could wash away the bitterness in her heart and the vengeance it cried for. She would shower tonight at the Chanticleer, where although she had no permanent place to sleep, there was a full bathroom beneath the dining room and the kitchen that she had to herself when she wanted it.

She dressed carefully, fashionably really, in a plaid skirt, the Pringle cashmere sweater Marta had bought her on her Christmas trip to Beirut last year, her legs bare and her head uncovered, silver clips holding back the long black hair glistening from today's hundred strokes. She let herself out and left the Sylvan Solace grounds the back way, circling around the block then off to her meeting.

Hawkins was on time and they spoke, cordially as always, but now with an edge to both their voices. Hawkins was bitterly disturbed by the news of her uncle and cousins. He had known about it, of course, and had already decided that Mikos had pissed in the whiskey once too often and that it was time. He put his hand over hers and tried to reassure her, but he knew that it would be a long time before the fire cooled.

She had time.

When Hawkins got up to leave, she stayed behind in the darkened church, all she could do to fight the temptation to burn the place down or desecrate it horribly. She hated the Christian Greeks so vehemently that when two small children roamed in with their nanny, looking about in total awe, she got up abruptly and left, her eyes brimming with tears. She regained herself almost immediately, and when she saw the car in the one-way side street off Varnava, behind the Archbishop's Palace, she hurried a bit until she came abreast of it, then opened the passenger side door and slid in from the narrow sidewalk.

At her right, Kreisler smiled briefly, put the Mercedes in gear, and they made their way very slowly in the traffic out to Stasinos and over to the Famagusta Gate. She poured out her story again to Kriesler, who, unlike Hawkins, had not heard it but who, like Hawkins, came almost immediately to the same conclusion.

He let her out at the gate and she caught one of the glorified panel trucks that passed for bus transportation that winter in Nicosia. When the bus let her off, she walked the six or so blocks up the gentle hill to the Chanticleer and opened things up. It was just past five, getting dark.

There were workmen hammering and nailing.

* * *

Forty five minutes later, Nikki greeted Phil, the assistant dishwasher, as he reported for work, a pleasant, harmless Greek veteran whom she genuinely liked while hating his country and all the other faceless Greeks who had brought her such repeated misery. He always wore the same costume, a frayed long-sleeved dress shirt made for a collar to be attached with a color button, but Phil never wore a collar. The shirt was always spotlessly clean, very shabby, mended here and there and not quite his size. His trousers were the full black cotton work pants the thousands of his Greek countrymen wore every day, and of course, Phil wore his every day because those were his only pants. He shaved on Saturdays, and today the gray bristle clearly needed mowing.

He had a paper sack with him today, and Nikki guessed he'd be bartering something for his beloved Players. He did not look well, and when she asked him how he was feeling, he answered non-committally and went into the scullery through the back door. He usually hung his apron on the door to the downstairs bath, and today as he grabbed it, he tried the knob and noted that the door was unlocked. As he passed the little cubbyhole used by Otto, the chef, he ducked in and picked up the black telephone receiver on the desk. After the usual click and a hiss, he heard what passed for a dial tone. He was pleased.

* * *

In the Old Town shed, the two bearded ambulance attendants had examined the thing carefully and although neither of them had ever seen a gurney before, they realized that it would work. It was a wheeled stretcher with folding adjustable legs, which allowed the contraption to be set at any desired height. A large knob on either side of the thing loosened the tension and they made sure it was as tight as it could be. Then they carefully put three of the jerry cans, tightly sealed to prevent the slightest leakage or odor, on the bed of the stretcher and draped a nondescript buff blanket over the whole rig. They practiced wheeling it and were soon able to assure themselves that they could maneuver it in. Then they took the cans off and one of them got on it. They had raised the bed about forty centimeters until now, without the cans, it was at the same level off the ground and they found that one of them could wheel it quite handily.

With two it would be no problem at all.

* * *

Earlier, when Marta had entered the office downstairs, Horst was there waiting for her, with his worried look vying for attention with his disgusted look.

"Your problem today, Sourpuss?" she said in German.

"Two problems. No three, really. Klaus and St. John both called this morning—the phone is working, by the way, so if you want to call the North Pole for Father Christmas, you better do it today because you never know when you'll have it working again."

"Very funny," she said, poking through he bills and papers on her desk. "What do they want, the two darlings."

"They want to have dinner with us tonight at the C, they'll pay, but I told them we have so much food and so few customers that they needn't fret about that. They wondered if we could have Nikki join us, and also your Yankee Whaler."

"What's up, Horst?" she said intently, shifting into her nearly unaccented American English, her mood suddenly changed. This sounded like something serious. She frowned, clearly indicating that she had no intention to involve Lew.

"I don't know, Love, but I told them I'd try to make it happen."

She thought it over a minute, her mind racing. She was furious at the both of them, as she tried to get out from under the pressure she was feeling from a source, long forgotten, now back in her life in a most disagreeable way. Damn! Something was wrong. They had agreed!

The bastards! They knew they were playing with fire, but they had agreed!

"Just this once!"

"What's the second thing?" she asked, provoked now, trying not to let it show.

"The goons who were supposed to come to put plywood where the window was after last night's little episode, cannot finish the job until later this afternoon or this evening. I pleaded with them—don't you know I have a business here, I can't have you working on the window when my customers are arriving for dinner, can you just hear it, how would you like to be having dinner with people hammering and sawing?"

"And they said…"

"Don't you know there's a curfew on?"

"What's the third thing?"

"The third thing is I don't know why they would invite Nikki. It's not her birthday or Attaturk's birthday or anything—it's what, December 16th—unless…more business, maybe? If that's what they're planning, I'd rather not have Nikki in on it. There's more dirty linen there that we don't need. As a counterpoint then, why *don't* you invite Lew to join us and see what happens?"

So they talked that one over a minute and as she reconsidered her earlier gut feeling, they both agreed that it really might be a good idea. If the intent was to talk "business," as Horst put it, and if the invitation to Nikki was their idea of intimidation by bringing in the fourth party to their complicated intrigues, Horst and Marta would trump their ace with Lew.

What a great play!

Marta scribbled the note, walked back up to her room and after assuring herself that the corpse in her bed had not quite expired, she poked the note in his boot and left as quietly as she had come in.

* * *

Lew stumbled out of bed, fully clothed except for his shoes, and made it to the bathroom before anything violent occurred. When he finished, he found his shoes and her note, inserted at attention in his left chukka boot. "Dinner at seven at the C."

He left with the note in his hand, found his own room and went in. It wasn't locked.

It got dark around five and it was getting there now.

29

The Chanticleer Restaurant and Cabaret sat on top of a small rise, in a grove of olive trees, with a less-than commanding view of the old city to the East but more of the residential district to the west, the mountains to the north purple and forbidding in the sunless winter twilight. The street, a "proper" street for Nick where so many streets were alleys or paths or narrow passages between buildings, was once an upper class venue, perhaps now fading to businesses and offices, but surely, one of the most pleasant parts of the city. Should the troubles end and the city grow, it would certainly expand outward in this direction. The building was clearly visible from the road, an eclectically "architected" old mansion built in the last century, the residence of poobah and civil servant and general in its heyday, fallen to ruin once, reconditioned and given a new lease on a life that had begin only a few years ago.

The sloping roof allowed water from the infrequent winter rains to drain down into gutters, and because of the peculiar geometry of the exterior and the irregular features of the site itself, a second bank of gutters, waist high, accumulated the run-off and conveyed it handily into the wash-water cistern. A sloped alley ran behind the property with a gate into a lower courtyard, normally kept open, much like the one at the Sylvan, and through this access, delivery trucks and employees came and went throughout the business day. A door to the scullery opened on this court. The new dishwashing machine, with its conveyor belt that fed wooden racks filled with dirty dishes through the washer and rinser, sat to the left in the spacious scullery immediately adjacent to the dumbwaiter to the kitchen above.

In front, where a large plate glass façade, its once most distinguishing feature, had looked out on a small car park and a smaller patio, a tarpaulin now hung, secured at the edges with hastily nailed furring strips, the whole rig doing a heroic job of keeping out the weather. A large welcoming oaken door, glass on top, with a bronze bas-relief sculpture of a crowing Chanticleer rooster crowned the entryway. Rimmed around the rest of the structure, each of the windows was well above anyone's height off the floor level and less than a half meter high. They provided light but not view, and the interior walls, tastefully but inexpensively decorated with local artifacts and works of art, set the tone of the place. Its second floor rooms had been redesigned away to make a domed dance floor, with bandstand and stage, and tables set around the center stage once accommodated patrons from all over the Middle East and Europe who found themselves out on the town in Nicosia.

The cabaret acts were less numerous now, but Saturdays were still good for a turnout and the bill for this week included the "twin" Dutch girl heartbreakers, a young British comedian, a knife thrower who doubled on alternate evenings as a hypnotist when his wife was too drunk to assume a steady target position, and the local favorites, Marta and Horst who might or might not appear, depending on press of business and better offers. Mixed-sex entertainment, in a setting where ladies and gentlemen could enjoy eating, drinking and entertaining one another in public were so popular with Western Europeans that it was difficult to realize that both the Greek and Turkish communities were offended by such displays.

To the Islamic Turks, such mingling was simply out of the question and to the traditional Greek, while their dancing and plate-smashing bouzouki revels tended to be far more raucous than anything that ever went on in the Chanticleer, there was simply no place for cabaret. If *enosis* ever happened, the Chanticleer would be out of business and if the Turks had their way, it would close tonight.

Between the nightly threats of violence, the curfew and the increasing cultural antipathy to it as fewer and fewer Western Europeans frequented Nicosia, even the most upbeat British "regulars" felt that their Chanticleer had little to crow about.

Lew had entered the place for the first time on the night he had met Horst and Marta, and it would be forever his and hers, in his mind, theirs forever—or, at least, always. He had vivid memories over vivid months—now years—of deeply personal immersion in Nicosia and in the Chanticleer and in Marta. Since much of his disposable time had been spent here, it was understandable that these memories were part of his impressions of the struggle, of EOKA and the turbulence and of the often-capricious violence that had marked the last few months.

Late one night on his June visit earlier this year, he had crouched beneath the grand piano in utter darkness with his arm around Marta, as Horst stood at the window in the foyer describing the roaming, marauding mob outside, neither of them willing to accept that the loss of electric power, the gunshots, the occasional explosions and the violence and confusion all about them signaled the beginning of an era in which lives were likely to come apart.

He remembered much—but not all—of his long conversation with Mort earlier this morning, and as he shaved and bathed and put on his only shirt and tie, his hands shook just a bit and he would have said that he felt better. If he had to characterize his mood in a single word, however, he was profoundly embarrassed by his own behavior over the last twelve hours, as if to wash away and atone for the justifiable pride he felt on the completion of the most successful and unquestionably one of the hairiest flights in his life.

He could not remember having spoken to Marta, but she had obviously put him to bed in her bed—where had she slept? Probably beside him.

On his way out, he noticed Hunley and Kerrigan sitting at the bar with Mort, and he stopped by to check in with them. He had been invited to dinner at the Chanticleer, he reported rolling his eyes, and intended to make the most of it. No mention of last night, this morning or this afternoon. Where had he disappeared to?

Kerrigan told Lew that he had talked with Timmons, that the Beast had been checked out and fuelled and that they were ready for tomorrow's 1300 departure, unless he had a problem with that. Wagoner was still asleep, but they'd be sure to wake him for the trip back. Everybody grinned. Lew displayed confident pleasure with Kerrigan and smoothly thanked them, but his insides were giving him a fit. He had neglected the aircraft, neglected the crew and instead, had gotten shit-faced at a time when he needed to be sharp, alert and dedicated. His Co-pilot and the nugget Navigator had simply filled in for him.

Now he was beyond embarrassment.

He was mortified, so he took his leave with a grin and a wave and went back out to the lobby. Horst was waiting for him, and they spoke casually for a moment before walking out into the light rain and trotting the few paces to Horst's boxy, red BMW.

* * *

Over at the Sylvan, Timmons and Lucore had just finished laying out the cards they had been dealt that afternoon.

Burdick was experiencing a reaction just short of apoplectic. In the beginning, he had reacted with coolness and disinterest, a little annoyed that his valuable recreational time should be taken up with business but curious, nonetheless. He was no boot sailor, and he realized the import of what was being said almost immediately. He also knew the local area and was both the most sensitive to its nuances and, of the five of them, the best informed on its politics. But when his own dealings the morning before unfolded—strictly off-limits to the rest of them, as far as he was concerned—his indignity turned to embarrassment and then, almost immediately, to anger, shame and fright.

He also realized that his only course of action at the moment was to join with the others in whatever damage limitation scheme they could invent.

30

London, England

Sunset on the meridian of Greenwich, and hence in London, did not officially occur until six on that Friday evening, December 16th, 1955. It had been getting dark since about five thirty.

In the days clustering around the winter solstice, there is a cold scrim that drifts in from the North Sea down the Channel and up the Thames. When the temperature and the humidity are just wrong enough, it coats the city with a pewter blanket that the splashes of color from the traffic lights and the scarlet busses and the glitzy billboards just beginning to appear a decade after the Blitz could never quite penetrate. It was gray-black everywhere, a dark cold kind of gray-black, so that by eighteen hundred on the official looking twenty-four hour clock in the Admiral's office, as the far more attractive brass replica ship's-clock struck four bells announcing the start of the second dog watch, it was quite dark.

On the Admiral's desk, a green-shaded brass Banker's lamp splashed its light over the rich leather topped desk that once supposedly belonged to John Adams. He had lived over in Number Nine Grosvenor Square when he was the Ambassador, so it was a nice thought, passed down. Probably looked the same then, except for the intercom to the side of the lamp.

Between the door and the desk, the five rich burgundy leather chairs had been set around the coffee table, removed from their place at the conference table in the corner. It was working meeting, and the Admiral was in his shirtsleeves, his old black cardigan keeping off the chill.

The room was drafty and had been since 1789, but it was a magnificent office. The others had their uniform jackets on, unbuttoned.

Stuart Sterling and Danny Arlen were assigned to the Commander in Chief, Eastern Atlantic and Mediterranean, the only two senior Naval Aviators on the Staff. Since the Admiral was an Aviator—it was a rotational assignment between communities—it just might have been the best professional assignment either of them had ever had.

Neither was immediately impressive for any memorable talent or obvious personal, intellectual or professional attribute - other than the fact that the rainbow of decorations on each of their dress blue uniform jackets contained a preponderance of red, white and blue. Uniforms were worn on the Staff almost never, but the invitation to the formal retirement luncheon earlier in the day had so specified, so they had piped four of their Royal Navy brethren over the side at Whitehall and come back to work at two thirty faintly redolent of Admiralty sherry.

Campaign ribbons, good conduct awards and commemorative medals "everyone" gets are multicolored affairs with a smattering of yellows, greens, even brown sometimes. The medal they gave you for getting shot at and hit was purple.

But the good stuff, the Navy Crosses and the Silver Stars and the Distinguished Flying Crosses—the heroism and valor awards, the red white and blue ones, always came first on the chest and stood out. Second and subsequent awards of the "good stuff" were worn as bright stars on the ribbon bars, and these two Commanders in their dress blues on this dreary Friday afternoon looked like the fourth of July in Kansas.

Sterling was the Air Operations Officer on a Staff in which Air Operations assets consisted, in their entirety, of the four blue-black Beasts regularly crouched a thousand miles away in North Africa. As such, Stu acted as the voice of their operators in the chamber of the gods, but they rarely bothered him and to his credit, he rarely bothered them. He was there for them when they needed help, and they tried to avoid needing help. A torpedo pilot in the Battle of the Coral Sea, he had helped sink a Japanese carrier and gone on to a number of impressive exploits through the rest of the War. His Navy Cross paid for the Japanese carrier, and the Silver Star came after a heroic afternoon in the air over Midway. The three Distinguished Flying Crosses rewarded perseverance, survival and longevity in the air war in the Pacific. Some of his equally distinguished contemporaries were carrier Captains now—Dave Welch in Wasp, Jimmy Flatley in Lake Champlain, Roy Johnson in the new Forrestal—and some, like Butch O'Hare, had never made it back. But without a war to fight and a throttle to push back and forth, Stu never bubbled up above the crowd, never made Captain, and in five years he'd be retired.

Danny Arlen's war record was as impressive as Stu's. He had had two F6Fs shot out from under him, but stayed the course through the early war into the Eastern Solomons and the Philippine Sea. Wounded twice, with multiple Distinguished Flying Crosses, he ended up, grounded, as a shipboard Staff Gunfire Liaison Officer preparing for the Iwo Jima invasion in January 1945. In February, when the assault began, he and a small group of Naval Officers assigned to the Fifth Marine Division so comported themselves that his Navy Cross was inevitable. He never flew again, however, and despite the discouraging glut of post World War II officers stagnating as Lieutenant Commanders in the immediate Post War years, Danny had distinguished himself in a second professional specialty—Intelligence.

Danny Arlen was the Staff Intelligence Officer, a comer, on his way up on a small, narrow stairway, and an officer of considerable talent. The wide range of European political winds and tides and currents washed over Danny's desk in the red brick Grosvenor Square headquarters. Many - including the Admiral

- considered his advice to the politico-military affairs wonks and to the schedulers and to the London Admiralty liaison types and to the Public Affairs weenies as the main battery of CINCNELM's firepower.

This had been a long session with the Admiral, as sessions with an extraordinarily busy executive go, ending now as the Chief of Staff and the British Admiralty Liaison Officer had left, their Fridays totally demolished when the message had been circulated after lunch.

Sixteen-oh-two-fifty-eight-zee had made quite a splash.

All had agreed that each word held momentous implications but what had it all meant? Stu read the "show stopper" again, possibly the eightieth time.

"BELIEVE ONE FLASHLIGHT LOST AS RESULT COLLISION WITH WATER FOLLOWING INTERCEPTION X ACFT DOWN MECHANICAL AT LEAST THIRTYSIX HOURS X UNODIR PLAN CNX 12-2 RETURN HOMEPLATE 17 DEC X UNABLE PROVIDE EXTENSIVE DEBRIEF THIS MSG DUE DETERIORATING LOCAL SECURITY SITUATION"

The Admiral had wasted no words indicating his concern. He hated to be surprised. He *was* the Navy and he wanted to know what the hell was going on. He was also more bark than bite. Everyone knew it. But Admiral Jack Cassady was a Naval Aviator, former skipper of the Saratoga, Carrier Division Commander, and more recently, Deputy Chief of Naval Operations for Aviation. These guys were his guys, and he knew it, felt it deeply.

"What do we know about what's going on out there? Burke called me this afternoon and apparently he found out about it late last night, but thank God he understands the distances involved. I didn't get the impression that it was a real shit-storm, not yet, but it looks like it's going to be *our* shit-storm when it comes.

"What does 'believe' mean? Did the damn thing go in or not? What will Washington want to know? What about the Brits? These are our guys and Christ only knows if they need help or hanging!"

"Well, Admiral," Danny had begun, "It's hard to tell from the message that they need either. They're following our Operation Order to the letter. They flew the mission and did what they were supposed to do and when they get home they'll tell us about it. That's the way the Op-Order has it working.

"Recall, if you will Sir, how we had our misgivings about this track when the tasking was issued, and you talked to Captain Barnet from Nebraska Avenue about it. But they landed safely in Nicosia sometime this morning, probably before sunrise. Their outgoing date-time group shows that. They'd been jumped, or at least intercepted by Flashlights. Shots fired? We don't know. Casualties? We don't know. Certainly they would have told us, told us if they had needed help even, and they didn't. That's a good sign. We do know they broke the airplane. How badly, we don't know.

"The operation was a success, and they probably—we hope - have wire recordings of the two radars they went after. Something must be going on in Cyprus to prevent them from contacting us with any additional details, or maybe, they figure it's no big deal and it can wait until they get back. Maybe under the circumstances, we're lucky we got what we did get from them! And speaking as the guy who ginned this whole thing up from the beginning and sent them crashing into harms way, I'm just awfully pleased and awfully proud of them."

He really hadn't "ginned the whole thing up" but he respected Winnie Barnet's habit of self-effacement and didn't want to make things more complicated than they had to be.

"I realize that, Dan, but I'm caught between the rock and the hard place here. I don't want to harass these guys. But I don't see how I can get the info we need unless I send Harding a personal message—but then I don't want to get Harding or the Brits involved in something that's none of their business. You and I met Harding last month at the first Baghdad Council meeting and I really like the guy, but this isn't his show. Then we have the damn Turks to worry about because sooner or later Ivan's going to bitch like hell and scare the shit out of the Turks! Any minute, the phone's going to ring and it will be the Pentagon or State or even the White House, for God's sake, and I don't know what's going on myself."

"Well, Admiral, the only thing we really have to worry about at this stage is the Press. The Soviets don't have a beef with us. Yet. If the message says what I think it says, the last thing in the world they'll want to announce is that one of their boys flew into the water at night chasing something in the dark. The Brits—technically—and here's where plausible deniability comes in—have nothing to do with it other than we used their airdrome in Cyprus. If the Soviets bitch to the Brits, Eden will go after Harding before he comes to us. That's the way he works. And Harding is one hell of a straight shooter, we all know that. And if what I just said is true, unless one of us here in this room talks to Fleet Street or one of the crew blabs to someone in Cyprus, that's it. As far as we know right now, there's nothing else that's gone on to stimulate anybody's interest, and everybody just has to lie low. I think that the fact that we have not heard anything else is a decidedly good sign, business as usual!"

The Admiral could see the point Stu was making, and to be fair and frank, what he was saying was the perfect answer to any inquiry he might get from the States, or from the Brits, for that matter. It was Standard Operating Procedure being followed to the letter.

But he was still intrigued, not by what he knew, but by what he still did not know.

"Stu, I would like you and Danny to get down there to Morocco and be there when they get in, when, Sunday? It's probably too late now for you to get to Malta before they leave Sunday morning without delaying them getting back, and this will give you time to get an R5D up from the Transport Squadron if there's not one already here. Use your discretion with the crew, impress upon them that this is all very routine and their normal habits of safeguarding of classified matter…you know what to say. Set up one of those teletype conferences over a secure circuit and let me know what you think.

"Then I would like you to decide whether it would make sense for the Pilot and the Evaluator to come up here and talk to me and if so, bring him up. Offer to bring the wives and kids up here if they want to come for the Christmas shopping, if you feel it appropriate, but the more I think about it, I guess Danny's right and this is all just business as usual.

"Danny, I want you to check with Nebraska Avenue, see what Winnie the Pooh has to say about all this. These guys are more his than mine, if the truth be known, and I want him cut in on this all the way. Readdress the 'Eyes Only' you sent them to him, too. He has the Washington contacts and he'll be able to give us all some good advice from the black part of the world. Ask him to comment, but tell him I don't want the message readdressed to anybody else until we know what happened. Let's see, it's almost six here so it's Friday lunchtime there. If he wants to, tell he can come over and talk to the two guys on Monday, if he can get away."

"I guess we should all be grateful that there's nothing more to it, that *they* didn't fly into the water or get their asses shot out from under them or have anything nasty happen to them when they got back to Cyprus! Let's go over to the Columbia for a drink."

In the anteroom, Chief Yeoman MacGregor was delighted to hear the muffled sounds of the meeting breaking up and checked the clock in wonder. He complained about playing Competitive Late-Staying with the Admiral, particularly on Friday evenings, but such was the nature of the job. He would deny to the death that he loved being part of things, in on all the scoop.

Just then, the secure phone rang one more time. Washington calling. Winnie the Pooh was checking in.

When the Admiral came out of the office fifteen minutes later and closed up shop, MacGregor was positive that the phone call had been a turning point in what had obviously been a difficult day for his Boss. There was the slight trace of a grin on his face and he looked five years younger.

Outside, Danny and Stu had compared notes. They met Lew Elfers together once, on an inspection trip the previous year. Lew and Stu had passed notes to one another about Operations matters, chiefly about the requirement, now that the Unit was a commissioned entity, that it act like every other commissioned entity and keep books, issue Instructions, document training, account for gasoline and oil, and blend in with the scenery. Stu secretly envied their nonchalance about all this but as the Enforcer, he had to hold their feet to the fire and he didn't make a pest of himself. Lew respected him for that.

Danny knew him from the occasional Operational Status Briefing Lew prepared and delivered whenever Danny had to come south, and Danny appreciated Lew's professionalism.

On the way over to Bayswater Road in the taxi, they agreed that they'd cut him all the slack he might need but so far, he was smelling like a rose.

Neither of them were strangers at the Columbia Club, but this was the first time they had been in the place in uniform and they were both somewhat edified at the reaction from the regulars. They were both privately pleased.

Kansas on the Fourth of July.

Neither would admit it.

31

But in the Chanticleer scullery as the Admiral's phone conversation ended in London, Phil Nicholaides had just turned on the main switch to power up the dishwasher when he slumped back on the conveyor belt housing, clutching his chest. The others immediately ran to his side and he asked them to help him to the bathroom. As they left the scullery past the cook's cubbyhole, Phil reached into his shirt pocket and drew out a scrap of paper with a phone number. The dishwasher banged away in the background.

"My nephew," he gasped, clearly in distress, handing them the paper. "Call my nephew, he will know what to do! Please. I am so sorry. I am so sorry." In the bathroom, he closed the door and they left him by himself for moment.

They reached the nephew immediately, and he said that he had been dreading the phone call, realizing that Uncle Phil was not well. He would send help right away. And he did.

In five minutes, an ambulance pulled into the courtyard and the two bearded attendants rushed into the bathroom through the scullery to check the patient. They immediately returned to the ambulance and wheeled in a stretcher cart covered with a long blanket. They wheeled it into the bathroom and the others crouched at the closed door while they attended to Phil. In a few moments, they had Phil on the stretcher, covered with the blanket, and wheeled him through the scullery, out the door and into the waiting ambulance. Then they were off, the siren wailing as they pulled into the alley and headed for the heart of town. The others were buzzing with the excitement and with genuine concern for their colleague. They closed the bathroom door, turned out the light and hung Phil's apron where it always hung, on the outside of the door.

* * *

"Got all your Christmas shopping done?"

At Nebraska Avenue, the wrappings from Jennifer's Roach Coach early lunch were going into the waste basket at about the same time Friday, when Winnie poked his head out the door and asked the innocent question. He had been on the secure phone, and she knew he had something up his sleeve.

"Shoot, I'm still working on Labor day!"

"Feel like a trip to England?"

"Yes, Sir, anytime. When?" she asked, humoring him. What was he up to?

"Get us a pair of Priority One seats on anything Government Air that will put us in London Sunday, and if that won't work, I'll spring for a TR for a couple of TWA rides if they're not all booked."

Here we go, she thought. Hang on!

TRs were the expensive way to go, government Transportation Requests, good as cash, redeemable for tickets to anywhere, anytime, payable out of Unit funds of which There Never Were Enough. She did not surprise easily with this man. She was surprised.

She went into his office and they had a brief discussion, informative enough for her to get on with the arrangements, not so informative as to shed bright light on anything that was going on. It had been that way all day, ever since she got into the office on the Friday after the Thursday they had both sweated. His mood was buoyant, he had greeted her with a smile and a thumbs up, and she knew everything had gone well during the night. She had not been called in, and she was able to piece together bits of the story from the phone calls she helped him place and the notes he passed from time to time asking for data points.

And so it came to pass that two VIP seats on Military Air Transport Service Flight 406S, a C-118 from Andrews Air Force Base outside of Washington to Mildenhall, were set aside for some Code-6 and his enlisted assistant, civilian clothes authorized, departure time Saturday morning at seven.

The next day, as they punched their way over the ocean helped along by the westerlies north of a big High pressure bubble in the central Atlantic, Winnie filled her in on the beginning, middle and anticipated outcome of the December Operational she had so diligently helped him craft since that day in October when the shit hit the fan. He left nothing out, relating—probably for the first time in his own words—the mechanics of his plot and the physics and biology that had made it work.

Strange, she thought. Captivated, mystified and totally awed as she was as he spelled out his intrigue, her immediate reaction was entirely personal. She thought of Dave, of what he had been through, of what he must have said and done to make this whole thing work. And she was so proud. So proud of him and of Winnie and of her small part in the bigger picture. The qualms, the uneasiness she had wrestled with about accepting a commission as a Security Group Limited Duty Officer, after the luncheon on Thursday, were gone. She wanted nothing more than to continue to be a part, a greater part, of this extraordinary competence.

"Did you know they call me 'Winnie the Pooh' over here in London?"

"Well, 'Tinker Bell' you're not, with all due respect," she said, after a moment, and she wiggled to get comfortable for a nap in the MATS seat purposely designed to prevent such useless foolishness.

* * *

Friday evening, Horst and Lew arrived at the Chanticleer and both were appalled at what greeted them.

On the small patio, three huge slabs of plywood had been placed to lean vertically against the outside wall. Several large planks, two-by-eights Lew would have guessed, were strewn here and there, with two-by-fours and smaller pieces of wood in a bundle on the patio. Workmen were positioning one of the slabs against the window opening, and their plan apparently was to secure the plywood over the canvas tarpaulin. Two small lorries were parked askew in the car park, and four workers tried to scurry back and forth and dodge the rain at the same time. Horst was visibly upset, and Lew heard him raise his voice several times during his conversation with the job foreman who seemed patient and accommodating, but firm in his position, whatever that was.

"God, what a mess! He says it will take them until nine o'clock to finish, and they'll be hammering and nailing all through dinner. He's not even the chap who's supposed to be here. I engaged our regular builder, the company that did the remodeling, to do this but this one says that the builder hired him to do the job because he's a specialist. A specialist! At nailing up plywood? I asked him if he could come back and do it in the morning and he said they wouldn't come back until Monday if they didn't finish tonight."

* * *

When Nikki had arrived earlier, her plan had been to take a shower at the Chanticleer and put on something more suitable for dinner, but she realized, when she got there, that all of her clothes were over at the Sylvan. So she rationalized about her costume, admiring the way the sweater set looked - and since she wasn't going to change and there was so much to catch up on after a half day off, she decided to skip the shower too. She had a pair of hose and a suspender belt in her desk, so in deference to the formality of the evening, at least she would not be bare legged.

God, where had Marta gone to? She needed her. She worked in the accounts office upstairs until the workmen arrived, then she went out to see what all the commotion was about and had, essentially, the same frustrating conversation with the foreman that Horst would have an hour later.

She was worried about Mehmet now, although she realized he was perfectly capable of taking care of himself, and would probably be up to the task of "taking care" of his parents' killers if he found them. She felt so guilty, so helpless, and yet, although it may have been "all her fault" as she told herself in her grief, she soon realized that she didn't care—she would have done everything she had done and was doing all over again.

Damn the Greeks!

When she heard the claxon of the departing ambulance, she hurried down to the basement area and found them all milling around, everyone talking at once. She asked them to be quiet and quizzed young Aram, not the senior, not the most intelligent, but the one with the best command of English.

She refused to speak Greek to anyone right now.

Poor Phil! She knew he looked bad when she had seen him come to work! Where did they take him?

Aram did not know.

What was the diagnosis?

Aram did not know.

What was his nephew's telephone number?

Aram did not know, Phil had taken the scrap of paper back.

She ducked her head into the bathroom and it was neat and tidy, the shower curtain hanging neatly in front of the stall. She thought she noticed an unfamiliar smell, but it might have been her imagination. She went back upstairs, wound up what she had been doing, and greeted Horst and Lew when they arrived.

Marta came alone shortly thereafter, and Nikki was amused at the behavior the two of them—Lew and Marta—as they carried on their polite banter and passed the time of day. Everyone knew Lew thought they were lovers and everyone who would be here tonight also knew a lot more than that.

She had never met Lew, and was quite interested in him, someone who had been described to her countless times. The American crews adored him and he was a hero to them, several times over. She was immediately attracted to him, jealously admitting that he and Marta were a smashing couple and, as they settled into a conversational exchange, she had to remark on what she noticed was a decided similarity in the way each addressed a subject and answered her polite social questions.

32

Loumides was dead.

Mikos was horrified to find him like that, garroted with something that must have been sharp and strong, piano wire perhaps, a favorite Turkish execution. They would pay. Grivas would be incensed, his relationship with Loumides intense now that almost daily infusions of cash were vital to the continuation of the struggle and the silent partner-bookkeeper a key channel for those infusions.

The shop itself seemed untouched, but he quickly opened the second drawer of the inlaid desk and reached up for the envelope. It was not there. Either the Turk had gotten it or Loumides had done something with it. Could he have sold the negatives to raise more cash for the effort? Who knew about the envelope? That goddam girl, what was her name, Lera? No, it couldn't have been her. She had taken the pictures and gotten them developed within an hour after she took them. They had only made one print, the enlarged one he had in the car. He shut the door quietly, peering out into the darkened street before he stepped out of the shadow of the doorway.

* * *

Mehment Incerogolou had one more stop to make, and he pedaled slowly, keeping up with the pack of riders hurrying home in the wet darkness. The few paved roads tended to be slippery, the rest had not yet turned to mud. A wet night. Most of the shops were open late, but the Greek civil servants and the office workers and the artisans began their trek to their homes between five and six and Mehmet had joined them.

Nikki had told him where to go, and he regretted that he had to go there. He had wanted to collect the envelope from the shop, but it had gone missing or had never been where it had been promised in the first place. At the foot of the alley, he got off the bike and walked it up the slight slope. He knocked on the door and she came into the circle of light. She wore an EOKA pin, crossed Greek flags.

"Are you Lera?" he asked in Greek.

"Yes," she answered in Turkish. "Are you cousin Mehment?"

"Your mother's cousin's son," he said.

"Wait" she said, leaving him in the doorway. She was back in a moment and she gave him the slim brown paper packet. He opened the flimsy clasp flap and inside, there were negatives, three regular "Brownie" size and two short 35mm strips. Their eyes locked for a moment and each read hatred and fear and loathing for what had been done to them and for what they had to do. He thanked her and left. One more errand tonight and he would go home and bury his family. He choked back the tears.

He was only twenty, but he was a man already.

33

Nikki did not have to worry about the dinner, but she checked the dining room anyway, and looked at the reservation book out of habit. There had been four parties scheduled tonight. Three of them had cancelled, partly because of the curfew and the weather, partly probably because the whole town knew that the place was torn up with repairs. She did not care, they didn't need the money, she rarely had a chance to have a nice evening even in "her own" club, and she was perfectly willing to keep the place empty tonight. She and Horst spoke briefly when he and Lew had arrived and she had gone to her office and called the Dutch girls in their hotel. The English comedian and the knife thrower were there with them, and they were overjoyed to hear than the club would be closed for cabaret and they had a free evening on the town.

"Some evening," the Englishman had said.

"Some town," the knife thrower replied.

She felt that she knew more about Lew than he knew about himself, and the experience of meeting him was more than she had bargained for. He was, first of all, larger than life, and she had heard over and over the respect and admiration the American fellows held for this handsome specimen. She loved Marta so dearly, and she suddenly felt a wave of panic sweep over her as she pictured the two of them together. She was a little annoyed at herself because of the depth of feeling she experienced looking at Lew.

She quickly joined Horst, Lew and Marta at the bar. She rarely consumed any alcohol—as a good Muslim, she not only had been raised to abhor it, but when she found that her upbringing on that score no longer mattered, she found she simply did not like it. The Americans over at the Sylvan were always after her to drink beer with them but she hated it and avoided it completely. Timmons had showed her how to mix a little gin with lemonade, however, and when she put ice in it and let it sit for a while, she found tasty and enjoyable. She slipped behind the bar and made one for herself, then served the others. She noticed that Lew was abstaining. Marta had her usual glass of Turkish white wine—the kind with the dead flies in the bottom of the bottle—and, of course, Horst had his beer. He pronounced it "biere."

Hawkins arrived in a Land Rover, and Nikki heard it drive off so she assumed he had sent the driver on his way. She hoped he made arrangements to be picked up later, but Hawkins always managed to take care of himself. He came in to the bar looking quite presentable for once, neatly dressed in a tie and blazer. He had a package with him, wrapped in black oilcloth, and he put it behind the bar and studiously ignored it for the time. He immediately complemented her on her appearance, and cordially pressed the hands of each of the others, showing his gentle, urbane side, full of meekness and boyish wonder. It was hard to realize that he had cut a kid's finger off yesterday.

In spite of their difficulties and the bizarre circumstances of their relationship, she looked on him for strength. She knew him as Hawkins and thought of him as Hawkins. He could never be St. John, although she knew that was his real name. Or at least as real as one might allow. She watched carefully as he was presented to Lew, whom Marta reminded him was "Commander Elfers, an American friend" and had to suppress a smile realizing what each knew of the other. They must have met before, of course.

"We're just us, so far tonight," Horst said by way of explanation to the others. We had clients for dinner but they've all cancelled save one party."

He then went into a detailed description of the plate glass repair, his sentences punctuated by the sound of hammering and the occasional worker's outburst of direction or instruction. They all finally managed to ignore the din, and enjoy each other.

Hawkins was telling an amusing story, something about an American tourist who was searching for the Five Fingers—the Pentadaktylos peak on the North shore—when the genial, white haired Kreisler arrived out of the night, beaming with conviviality, obviously glad to see Marta, gladder still to see Horst. They embraced him warmly and went immediately through the same charade with the American.

Lew remembered Klaus, of course—he liked him, really—and they both mentioned a brief earlier meeting. He had heard more about Klaus than he had about Marta's parents, brothers or sisters, and he deeply appreciated the bond between them. Klaus was, after all, responsible for her being here.

Nikki was poised behind the bar, not quite the barmaid, not quite the guest, but they all joined together for cocktails and eventually, Lew had her pour him a Beefeaters on ice with a twist of lemon, and he nursed it as they bantered back and forth in the bar.

Outside, the hammers were working and they could hear the occasional shouted comments of the workers. The rain had let up, they noticed, as they walked from the bar through the foyer to the dining room, the only window now above the massive oak door. Klaus and Hawkins were on their best behavior, Nikki noticed, and she thought that perhaps the evening might turn out to be halfway enjoyable after all.

She smiled warmly at Marta. Marta smiled back.

* * *

At seven forty five, Roger and Emma Wingfield pulled into the Chanticleer car park in their Humber, accompanied by their guest for the evening, Mrs. Wingfield's older maiden sister Philida, on holiday from her assignment as a Consular Officer in Her Majesty's Embassy in Teheran. Roger was a Queens

Counsel at home, serving on a twelve-month assignment with the Field Marshall's Staff, a specialist in the area of the status of forces and political-military affairs. He had been a Judge Advocate during the war, and he had served with Harding in the Far East and in Europe.

A trim, elegant man, he was well liked, competent and he loved his wife, but the main thorn in his side, the bane of his existence, was a sister-in-law whose protracted maiden status was wholly attributable to the fact that she had no concept whatever of when to shut up. She talked incessantly, and Roger counted the days until she would depart back to Persia or wherever it was she had come from.

In the darkened car-park, a clean-cut young man speaking impeccable English greeted them immediately, by name, before they had turned off the ignition. He held a clipboard and an electric torch, and offered the sincere apologies of the management. Pointing to the "damage corrective construction" in progress, the young man profusely begged forgiveness for the unexpected inconvenience, but they would be unable to accommodate any guests for dinner this evening, under the circumstances.

Instead, he continued politely, he offered his sincere hopes that they would "venture the short distance" over to the Acropole where they would be accommodated in fine style. It was, as they undoubtedly knew, under the same management and ownership. Regrettably, the Chanticleer would be closed until further notice.

In the Humber, they looked at one another with resignation, certainly not the most disagreeable social setback they could have imagined in the troubled city, and graciously made their way over to the hotel.

At the Acropole, ten minutes later, they were accommodated with warmth and ushered to a fine table in the well-appointed dining room. To Philida's great delight, they found themselves seated next to three absolutely smashing looking Americans, a tall gray haired chap, a shorter darker man and a really handsome young charmer.

When Phlida dropped her purse and it slipped out from beneath their table, the young man graciously retrieved it and presented it to her. She immediately took the occasion to begin an extensive conversation, explaining to the three that their plans for the evening had been so awfully disrupted, with the Chanticleer unexpectedly closed for the night, despite their reservation mind you, but the most awful damage to the building preventing any business whatever, but they had been diverted to the Acropole and wasn't it lovely here?

Kerrigan, the soul of aplomb, extricated himself from the conversation with the help of the Wingfields, but at the table, the three exchanged glances beneath furrowed brows.

What the hell was that all about?

What about Lew's dinner?

34

Over at the Chanticleer, the round table was attractively set in the center of the small dining room, another set off to one side for the Wingfields who had, inexplicably, not made an appearance. The overhead crystal electric lamps were lighted, and two twin candelabra bathed the table in the softness of candlelight nicely complementing the ceiling fixtures.

The hors d'oeuvres at the dinner table were splendid, tiny pieces of fig wrapped in slices of marinated lamb and then encrusted in dough and baked to a golden brown. The dipping sauce of mint and several other spices Lew did not readily recognize was the perfect compliment, and short glasses of very light Xynesteri wine, in the Cypriot tradition, were poured for all.

Back in the kitchen, Otto took off his apron and departed, leaving the evening's fare to his sous-chef, Andreas. The menu for the party of six had been pre-arranged, and Andreas was fully competent to put it together. When he had heard that the cabaret was cancelled for the night, Otto had arranged a rendezvous with the wife of the knife-thrower, and was anxious to get on with it.

As he left through the lower exit, he passed the idle dishwashing machine and realized that Aram would have very little to do. "Take the rest of the night off, Aram," he said. "You can do the dishes tomorrow. Tell Andreas to have the waiter put everything on the dumbwaiter."

Obediently, Aram left a few minutes later.

The workmen were still at it in the front.

* * *

Upstairs, the waiter cleared the small hors d'oeuvres plates and prepared for the soup course. Nikki was being charming, and she fondled Marta with her eyes as the older woman told them about Lew's first experience with Patsia, the Greek cream soup traditionally served with a lamb's eye in the center of the bowl. It was really a disgusting story, Lew believed, but he took the ribbing good-naturedly and managed to diplomatically steer the conversation to complement each of the attendees on the elegance of their appearance and their charm. Where did he learn that maneuver, Nikki wondered, delighted. To everyone's conversational delight, the soup was an elegant lemon chicken display, sprinkled with basil in honor of the season. The small talk continued, each conversant at his or her wittiest, most charming, each a model of urbanity.

Marta had selected the main course in Lew's honor. Each plate contained a small leg of baby lamb, carefully braised and dressed with rosemary and mint, accompanied by tiny potatoes on a bed of greens. It was Lew's favorite, and it sent him a message that he warmly returned each time their eyes met. Nikki caught the sparks—the others must have as well, she thought—just wait until they get in bed! Ugh.

Hawkins excused himself after the lamb course, and left the room. When he returned. He carried the black parcel he had parked behind the bar. He placed it beneath his chair, and rejoined the conversation.

As dinner neared closure and a round of delightful goat cheese with unleavened bread wafers was placed in the center of the table, coffee was poured—real coffee made from ground coffee. A uncorked bottle of port was placed by the cheese with a tray holding six glasses—not four for the men only nor five, omitting the "employee"—a political, social, cultural and ideological *gaffe extraordinaire* had the context been different, but in the event, it set the tone and set a strong statement of player equality.

Nikki was one of them.

The port was not touched.

Klaus looked about and was satisfied that they were alone. The serious conversation got underway. Lew had been expecting it.

"We had a fright," Klaus began kindly, almost jovially, looking Lew squarely in the eye. So this is how it begins, Lew thought, and decided to play for time.

"So did we," he smiled, meeting the gaze.

"Tell me about it," Klaus said.

"No, you first," Lew rejoindered, smiling all around the table. There was a little ice forming, he could tell, so he broke it.

"Were you all wondering how we would begin? I certainly was."

And he looked about at each of them in a most disarming way and the tension was broken and he could feel Marta's hand on his leg beneath the table.

"Well," Klaus began, accepting the challenge with a thin smile. After all, it was his party.

"As you know Commander, you and your colleagues have been coming here to Cyprus for the last two years and you have had an extraordinarily charmed life. You have flown in here every month—every *lunar* month - and you have parked your big black aircraft—you call it the 'Beast' I have heard—on the tarmac at our international airport. You and your twelve or thirteen mates then come to town, attempt to 'blend in with the scenery' as you put it once, I believe, and conduct your business covertly. Everybody in town knows when you come, why you come, where you go when you do go and when you leave. But I suppose you realize that.

"If all of us at this table have anything—anything at all—in common it is this. We all love the same person," and he turned to Marta with genuine affection and admiration. "Several of us have known her for over a decade, some not as long, but we all truly love her, and that fact must be central to what we say now.

"I need to begin by putting you squarely in the middle of our little picture for the moment. You are not normally there, but tonight, well, here we are. For some time now, all of us—except you and your immediate colleagues—have known that this trip to Nicosia is your last; that your flight last evening will be the last of your sorties in this part of the world to originate on Her majesty's soil; and, not to be overly dramatic, as a result, tonight is your last night here. We're here to say 'Bon Voyage'."

Lew, surprised, felt his stomach twist a little, and he vowed to maintain composure whatever happened. He tried desperately not to display the slightest emotion, thankful that he had had just the one drink and the one glass of wine. He looked at Marta and tried to keep that desperation out of his eyes. Hawkins took up the thread.

"You see, Commander, in a few days, January 1st to be exact, the existing agreement between Her Majesty's Government and your own concerning the use of RAF Nicosia has, by mutual consent, been modified to obtain now only in case of emergency, effectively ending your visits here unless you are on fire…or out of petrol."

He grinned innocently, but continued. "For your information, but don't divulge that you heard it here dear boy, you and your colleagues will be operating from that fine new facility to the northeast at Adana. The name of the exact spot in Turkish is, I believe Inçirlik."

Lew nodded to Klaus and Klaus continued.

"Now before we get to the heart of the matter, I want to put you into our local picture a little deeper than perhaps you would like to be. You come from a land of white hats and black hats, but the four of us, with the exception of our charming Nikki, have been working - I believe the idiom is 'both sides of the street'—for so long that ideology has long since left the picture. Think of this, for a moment—the five of us having dinner with you, talking about these things—it could only happen here on Cyprus.

"Let us discuss Nikki here for a moment. Nikki is the Secretary-Treasurer of the Acropole Corporation, a multinational enterprise that deals in good food, good wine, good accommodations and good information. Its principal officers are, naturally, Horst and Marta; its principal customers" with a bow to his right, "the two of us, Major Hawkins and myself.

"Of course there is no such Corporation, but if there were, it would have an unusual feature—the officers in the corporation and the customers would freely change roles from time to time and the customers would sell and the corporation would buy. But I am being obscure.

"Nikki is the coordinator for all Pan-Arab intelligence and militancy operations on Cyprus, an endeavor currently supported by the government of the Soviet Union, by the Arab league and surreptitiously, as far as the limited objectives in Cyprus are concerned, by Her Majesty's Government as well."

"Cyprus is a tinderbox," Hawkins continued, picking up the thread in earnest, pedantically, "and until we can withdraw with honor and expect to leave behind some semblance of a government in which our strategic interests will be regarded and fostered, we must support every effort to defeat the *enosis* movement and EOKA. I for my part have been entrusted with the counter-terrorism and counter-espionage function on the island, and as you may have heard, actively participate in the business when I can. Nikki, Klaus and I are allies, so to speak.

"Now to Marta. Marta and Horst, neither of whom has said a word for the last few minutes, are our trusted colleagues in every part of our respective enterprises. We go back a long time."

* * *

Downstairs, after Otto left, Aram puttered around for a minute or so, then left also. He let himself out but since Nikki, Marta and Horst were still on the premises, it never occurred to him to lock the door. As a matter of fact, he did not know how to lock the door, since he had never been entrusted with so high a degree of responsibility. He clicked out the lights on the basement level, however, before hopping on his bike and pedaling off. He had ten minutes to go before curfew, but that never seemed to bother Aram since he always rode the back streets home, usually well after midnight.

Upstairs, only the waiter Hassan and the sous-chef were at work in the kitchen helping each other tidy up before curfew. They lived together close by, and their relationship was such that any time they spent together was precious, no matter where it was.

At nine exactly, the last board was nailed in place and the workmen picked up and bundled into their lorry. They had been working these jobs all week and would be able to talk their way out of any curfew nonsense if they were caught, but tonight's unusual last order from the young man who must have been employed by the Chanticleer to supervise them, had them all befuddled and curious.

Why nail two two-by- eight beams across the main entrance door from the outside?

At nine-ten, as Hawkins was getting to Marta, a black '46 Dodge pulled around the corner. Its driver surveyed the surroundings, turned out the headlights and it drew slowly and silently into the car park beside Horst's Opel.

* * *

Over at the Acropole, Hunley, Kerrigan and Mort had finished dinner. While Kerrigan and Hunley had been reasonably close until they had been thrown together in Mikos' taxi the other morning, neither of them knew much about Mort. He was, after all, senior to both of them, a Department Head and the former Unit Commander of the group that had been amalgamated into the squadron when it had been commissioned in September. Here in Nick, however, having shared what was quickly becoming a legendary experience in everyone's mind, they felt a natural intimacy with him. Besides, he was their senior in the chain of command and they were bursting to unload their story as augmented by the Timmons-Lucore codex.

So they did.

Every minute of it, complete with smells, feelings, nuances, suspicions, dreads, and opinions, for what they were worth. To their surprise, Mort had some unburdening to do and by nine o'clock, the three of them had as complete a picture of the events of the last two years as recollections could make it, as complete a picture of the early morning lesson in geopolitics as the two of them could construct, and a fair and impartial telling of as much of the Nikki story as they knew.

As they sat in the lobby wondering what to do for the rest of the evening, Wagoner came downstairs bleary eyed but fresh and pink and after they had razzed him and used their considerable influence to get him something to eat—"a steak would be nice"- the night porter came over to where they were sitting.

The old man spoke little English, they knew, but Wagoner had no trouble figuring out that he wanted the others to come outside with him for a minute.

They eyed one another suspiciously and the three of them—Mort, Brian and Hunley walked slowly through the lobby out into the damp night air as the steak arrived at the bar from the kitchen and a place was being set there for Wagoner.

The rain had abated, a fine misty drizzle now, patchy clouds overhead.

The porter led them around to the side of the building where they confronted a young man, nineteen or twenty, on a bicycle, soaked to the skin, bright-eyed and agitated. He spoke fair enough English, but he looked pretty mean.

"I am Mehmet from Morphu, cousin of Nikki from the Sylvan Solace. I have just been with Timmons and…Lucore?…and they ask me to come here to find you. You stay here, please, they come here. They want to talk, to help Nikki. You stay, please? Maybe, fifteen minutes?"

They assured him that they would stay, and as he pedaled off in the night, they watched him until he disappeared around the corner to the southeast and then they went back inside, troubled, worried and keyed up. Wagoner was eating at the bar, and they came up to him and stood in a semi-circle around him while he ate. Mort did the talking and after about ten minutes, Wagoner was read into the problem.

The fifteen minutes dragged into twenty. It was twenty-five to ten when Mehmet came back into the lobby, dripping, obviously out of place and out of sorts. He spied Kerrigan and rushed over to him. "Chanticleer, "he said. "They say you come!"

He laid a wet hand on Brian Kerrigan's arm, Brian could feel the tension in the boy's body and the warmth of his heavy breathing, close to his face, smell his breath. From under his wet tent-like shirt, a cross between an anorak and a short Moroccan djalabah, Mehmet fished something out and handed it to him.

"For you," he said simply, and dashed out.

Brian had no need to open the slim paper packet. He sensed that the web Mikos had spun last night, trapping the two of them in a place they needn't be, was coming apart. Without a word, he handed the negatives to Hunley, whose expression spoke volumes—determination, chagrin and best of all, relief.

They roused Wagoner from the bar and they hurried out into the last drips of the drizzle, totally in the dark as to their mission, their purpose, their vulnerabilities and their intention. They did know, somehow, that Lew was in trouble.

On their way over to the cabaret, a couple of stars poked through the clouds.

* * *

"For the last two years," Klaus was saying," Marta has been of great value to us. She has diligently helped to provide us with information that we needed about your operations, and I think you will agree, your record of successful reconnaissance flights over—as you call it, the 'Pond'—has been remarkable. You have Marta to thank for that."

His manner was friendly, confidential without being conspirational, warm, pleasant, sincere.

Lew was devastated, in a fog. The nagging thought that he had put out of his spinning head this morning now came back to frighten him. He was not apprehensive, not worried, nor concerned, not agitated—but frightened! My God, My God, My God! There goes my heart…

Suppose,…*oh God, there's no way that could be true…*suppose Marta—or Horst, or Klaus or somebody, hell, maybe even Mikos—suppose somebody had been passing them actual, true, authentic track information. And suppose…*it can't be…*that the whole idea is not to jump or interdict or interfere with the flights but to <u>prevent</u> us from getting what we have come after!

Suppose that they have been spectacularly successful all these months, that they have prevented the acquisition of intelligence all these months and years, suppose the object of the game has been to tell the Flashlights when to turn OFF, not ON!

Here's what must have happened. They knew each time the Beast fired up to come check up on them. They would expect the visit and put away the silver and lock up the kiddies, and the Beast came and went and came back to Nick skunked! Some Dumbos, some minor stuff, but the crown jewels, the Kiterest and the Farmfish, the newest and most threatening air defense technology in the world was safe.

And it was safe because Lew Elfers was in love with Marta and they counted on Marta to let them know when to lock the store! Lew paled and his hand shook and he was weak with shock and disgust and disappointment and heartbreak. Marta, Marta, and he looked at her and she looked back at him and neither, for the first time in their relationship, could read the other's thoughts.

* * *

Tonu Kistagolu was a Turk. He had always hung out with the wrong crowd and had broken his mother's heart when he left the village of his birth on the north shore and gone to Nicosia, where at the age of seventeen, he had begun apprenticeship as an auto mechanic. He had so met and become an admirer of Mikos Constantanos, an American businessman, a taxi owner and entrepreneur. Mikos was fortunate to have a bright Turkish boy he could count on and tonight he was counting on him.

He need not to have worried. Tonu knew exactly what to do.

The rain had stopped. When he got out of the Dodge with Mikos, he slipped along the small street embankment and quickly entered the Chanticleer courtyard. He knew the layout like the back of his hand, memorized from his visit just a few hours ago. He counted on the back door to be open, and it was, although Phil had told him where to find the hidden key in case it was locked. So in he went, in the dark, the tiny flashlight cueing him to the bathroom door, into the bathroom, brushing aside the shower curtain, lifting easily the first of the five-gallon jerry cans he had stacked in the shower a few hours ago in his white coat when they had come to get their "patient".

Now out into the scullery, into the basement proper, a dank smelly place of exposed wooden beams anchored on the stone and concrete floor. The contents of the first can splashed easily on the north and east walls, and the second repeated the process on the south wall, then out into the scullery proper and up the short flight of stairs to the kitchen.

He grabbed a sack of flour from the larder Phil had pointed out, and quietly went outside to the cistern at the back of the building into which the sub-gutters on three sides emptied. He dammed up the trough with the flour sack, preventing any flow from the sloping sub-gutter into the cistern. Then he went back and got the other two cans. He had to put one down to let himself out, and he quickly moved around to the other side of the building where he poured the remaining ten gallons of purple liquid into the sub gutter system. The building was now ringed on three sides with a moat of high-octane aviation gasoline to a depth of three inches, floating on a trickle of rainwater.

* * *

"Marta wanted to give you a going away present, one that you would greatly appreciate, albeit that you would not know that it was her farewell gift to you. We discussed it and although it took a considerable amount of coaxing on her part, I think the outcome will assure you of our absolute lack of ideological animus. She asked us to deceive the Soviets intentionally, to tell them that you had divulged that your track was to the west, to the Bosphorus."

So he had, Lew admitted.

"It was your idea, actually," she said pleasantly to Hawkins, who bowed slightly in acknowledgement.

Marta and Hawkins/St. John/Billposter, at that moment, were announcing to each other that the double cross had worked, that their separate contracted undertakings on behalf of the shadowy Winnie Barnet were complete, that their contracts had been fulfilled, that he had gotten what he had paid for.

But he wasn't there to collect, and they were going to drink his root-beer.

"So we did," Klaus continued. "Being totally unexpected, you were awarded with the prize you had been seeking. But at great cost to others. Great cost! We had not expected that. In retrospect, we should have left well-enough alone."

"In order to settle the account, "Hawkins went on, "we have been forced to hedge our bet and violate our strict standards of conduct. Klaus was in great personal danger because of the unfortunate developments of the other night—by the way, the young pilot was rescued and is none the worse for wear, even if he is now in Turkish custody. Oh well, where was I? I took the liberty of obtaining this" and he reached beneath the table and took out the parcel he had brought in from the bar.

Lew began to feel his knees shake again, and almost dreaded what was coming next. It was a huge risk. Hawkins unwrapped the black outer wrapping to expose the taped envelope, perhaps three inches thick, that Lew and Mort had left in the Communications Center. Lew could see the faint impressions of the round flat cylinders inside the taped envelope. He was sick. Hawkins had obviously simply used his authority to remove it for "safekeeping" and here it was.

"I have, you see, free access to all the bins in the Communications Section."

"We have not opened it," he said to Nikki and the others, "but we are confident that it contains the track information and the recordings made last night. Is that not so, sir?" and his voice now had an edge to it.

"Yes," Lew said, his voice small. He looked at Nikki then, and at Marta and Horst, and he knew that the expression he was seeing on each face was one of coldness, of scores settled, of dues paid, of closure. He also noticed something else, noticed the look exchanged between Nikki and Marta and was struck dumb. At that moment, he smelled the gasoline for the first time. In the next instant, the electric overhead lights flickered and went out, and the building was in darkness except for the candles on the table.

Horst excused himself and went back toward the kitchen to see to the problem. In a moment, they heard his voice calling loudly for Andreas. There was no answer in the darkness.

Lew sat quietly in the candlelight, with almost excruciating awareness of the five pairs of eyes now totally focused on him as he sat, staring only at Marta. He almost expected her to tell him that she hoped he liked her present.

Then the flames erupted, exploded really, up the staircase, brilliant in the darkness, speeding now every which way, but at the table, there was no indication of the fury building beneath them.

35

They were three-quarters of the way to the Chanticleer when they caught up with the crew.

"What makes you think there's a problem," Brian asked Lucore when drew abreast and stopped a minute in the street to regroup.

"Something odd is definitely happening," he answered, and Burdick immediately broke in.

"They told me about the picture! That scum-bag Mikos is at the bottom of this and Mehmet said his car is parked outside the Chanticleer. We gotta get over there and get to the bottom of this, or…"

"That was a nice picture of you, "Hunley said dryly. "Were you buying or selling, we couldn't tell."

"Goddammit, "Burdick snapped, "Excuse me, Sir, but I was buying! I sure as hell don't have anything to sell these bastards, but I want to get a piece of Mikos right now, and if you all won't come with me, I'm on my way," and he turned and stamped off down the street. They all followed, soon joining him, and within a few minutes Kerrigan and Lucore, who were in front, held their arms up and stopped the procession. They could see the Chanticleer clearly, a half block away, and the empty car.

"He was right. There's the Dodge," Kerrigan said. Burdick started toward it.

"Show me where he had the pictures," he called quietly, with a great deal of vehemence, over his shoulder. Kerrigan looked at Hunley for guidance and Hunley nodded in the direction of the car, so Kerrigan followed Burdick. When the got to the car, Kerrigan looked around and saw no one. He very quietly opened the driver's side door, on the left, and pointed to the door handle. Burdick squatted down and began to fool with the handle, when Kerrigan noticed something else that surprised him.

Without saying a word, he reached behind Burdick's back and took the keys out of the ignition. Together, then, they twisted and turned the door panel until Burdick, greatly upset, stood and gave it a kick with all his might. The flap dropped down and they reached in. Burdick had the envelope in his hand, drew it out, and was reaching for the gun when they saw the first flames.

*   *   *

Mikos had told Tonu to go, to get out of the neighborhood, run!, go! partly because in the last minute he had lost his resolve to pin the event on Tonu the Turk, but mostly because he could not, try as he could, come up with a way to make it work. Beside, this was between Nikki and himself, and if he got her and he got the four spies at the same time, great! He regretted involving the American, but business was business.

The intensity of the flash inside and the speed with which it sped along the basement wall first fascinated, then frightened Mikos. His concern was accentuated by the unexpected heat from the blaze as it drew first from the natural draft up the stairway through the open door at the kitchen level, and then, off to the side, where the dumbwaiter hatch was left ajar.

For a moment, all he could think of was escaping from the blaze, but when he drew out into the courtyard, he got control of himself and headed for the gutter. He had been using wooden matches inside, struck against the box, and as he threw the first lighted match into the pooled and dammed gasoline, it sputtered in the liquid and went out.

Mikos had, up to this point, no experience whatever in the forced combustion of flammable liquid in an open air environment, and was unaware of the fact that in order for combustion to occur, a flammable fuel air mixture had to be present. There was fuel and there was air, but no flammable mixture. The second match simply went out in the liquid, like the first. The third did the trick. The air heated by the first two matches expanded and the surface tension of the gasoline relaxed in the warmer air to provide enough hydrocarbon molecules to form a sufficiently rich mixture.

Mikos Constantanous' last earthly recollection was one of consummate horror, as the resulting fuel-air explosion engulfed him instantly, preventing him from watching the speeding ring of fire as it sped around the building until it hit the cofferdam at the cistern, at which time it simply burned and burned and burned.

* * *

In the dining room, their first thought was to extinguish the fire, somehow. As a result, they wasted a couple of minutes looking things over, but without water or fire extinguishers, there was not much they could do. And it was spreading, from the west basement where they had first noted it, to the rest of the foundation, spreading quickly.

"Get them out of the building," Hunley yelled, and Wagoner and Black ran up to the front door and began pounding on it. They pounded for a moment, then noticed the two by eight beams nailed to the door and to the adjoining wall and jam. They were horrified, and began pulling at the planks before they realized that they had been secured with long gutter nails and were not coming off.

Inside, they were all up from the table now and Lew had dashed to Marta's side, holding his arm around her as to protect her from the as yet unseen danger they all sensed. Hawkins clutched the package, then handed it to Klaus who looked startled and surprised to have it in his hands, yet uncertain as to what he was going to do with it. Nikki ran to the front desk and frantically tried the telephone, but Mikos' wire-cutters had attended to the telephone wires when he had done the electric cable. She then ran toward the top of the stairs screaming for Horst, and emerged from the kitchen in a moment with a tiny red fire extinguisher, the pump kind that shoots a stream of liquid. She readied the instrument and looked for a direction in which to point it, when with a spectacular whoosh, the flames shot through the kitchen door and knocked her down. Hawkins ran to her side and he and Klaus bent over her, Klaus one-handed, cradling the package in his arm.

The heat was beginning to rise all about them, and Lew's immediate action was to rush Marta to the front door. He tried the door and when it would neither budge nor crack, he looked around at the windows and was horrified to note that they were all eight or so feet above the floor and almost impossible to crawl up to or through. He took a bar stool and stood on it, trying to open one, then gave up and threw an unlighted candlestick from the piano at the window. The glass shattered, but the opening now gave the encroaching flame and heat a clear passage through the building. Lew was disgusted with himself—he knew better. But with the relatively large dance floor off to the side, he also knew that they would have plenty of room to huddle and evade the flames until help arrived. Now the south and east foundation beams had held all they could under the intense heat and flame, and within moments, the dance floor, lacking foundation, looked like the hangar deck of a sinking aircraft carrier, listing, dimpled from the heat, smoldering and now bursting here and there into bright orange flame as the wooden underlayment caught fire.

Lew looked up for a possible avenue of escape, and saw immediately that the extensive remodeling that had eliminated the top floor of the building has created a warren of passageways that created the false, ornate ceiling. The flames were on the roof.

In the back of the building, Hassan and Andreas had been involved with one another in the semi-darkness of the main pantry, the outside wall of which through an unfortunate accident of architecture and hardware held the brackets and the pedestal and the regulator valves and the piping—as well as the two hundred-liter butane tanks - which provided the fuel for the kitchen stoves. Dire warnings to keep away open flames and strict prohibitions against smoking within fifty feet were stenciled in three languages on each of the two tanks. The sub-gutter ran within a foot of the closest tank. When it blew with a gigantic whoop, both young men were incinerated.

* * *

Outside, they were frantically trying everything they could think of to get into the building in any way possible, all thought of extinguishing the fire now beyond them.

"God," Blackie said, "if we only had wheels!"

Kerrigan heard him. "Why, "he asked excitedly, "what could we do?"

"I could bust a hole in that wall if I could get to it!" Blackie said. Kerrigan reached into his pocket and gave him the keys to the Dodge, pointing back to the embankment. "Try it!" he yelled. Blackie grabbed White and the two of them sped over to the Dodge, Burdick was sitting on the driver's side, his legs out the side, staring at the pictures in the dim light. They brushed him aside and got in. Burdick rescued the photos and tore them into tiny shreds.

The Dodge started right up and they pulled out of the parking space and tried to locate a spot that would give them a clear run at a section of the wall where it might give way. White had a better idea. The patio was easily accessible from where they were and from the patio, they would have a clear run at the plywood.

"The plywood, the plywood!" he shouted, and Blackie backed the car around and pointed it at the new plywood that had been erected that night. Neither of them knew that the plywood had been nailed over the canvas tarpaulin, but they would soon find that out.

Inside, bits and pieces of the ceiling began to fall, each small rockets of flame randomly dropping on their heads as they huddled on the dance floor. Hawkins drew Klaus over to one side and they stood up, in animated conversation, shouting over the crackle and hiss of the burning walls. Suddenly, Horst emerged screaming from the kitchen, his clothing on fire and as the two ran to intercept him, a massive ceiling beam gave way and fell in a shower of sparks and flames, knocking them to the floor and engulfing the there of them in dust and cinders and flame. They did not get up. Lew watched it happen, his arm shielding Marta's face from the flame. They had not said a word to each other since she had asked him to pass the cheese.

* * *

It was time to fetch the Major. Lance Corporal Gladney had been visiting with the blokes at the Paphos Gate, killing time until his pick up, and he looked at his watch one last time before getting in the Rover and starting it up. When the second propane tank exploded, Corporal Gladney wondered what it was, and began to worry because he did not like driving alone at night after curfew.

* * *

Blackie backed the car up as far as he could and then shifted to first gear. The Dodge had a fluid drive transmission, a post-war innovation for the American driver who loved being spoiled by gadgetry. The clutch could be used or not, depending on the driver's level of patience, expertise or both. When the car was placed in gear and the clutch engaged, however, there was no metal-to-metal direct mechanical contact between mover and transmission—just the fluid transmission doing its smoothest and gentlest to pamper the driver. It was, in a word, the best kind of car in which to learn to drive, the worst kind of car to try to ram through a wall. For when the automobile's forward progress was impeded by a barricade of any kind, the compliant transmission simply took up the strain and depending on the traction available, dampened the forward momentum.

The first time into the plywood, the quarter inch wall broke and splintered handsomely. Blackie backed up for another shot and the car ran forward, now having penetrated the plywood, into the canvas, which cradled it gently forcing the car to a smooth stop. Back again, large splinters clinging to the bumper, into the canvas. Back again. On the third assault, the furring strips began to give and after five crushing attempts, the engine now screaming from the abuse, the car broke the canvas free and rolled into the foyer of the Chanticleer. White jumped out and searched frantically. Nothing seemed like it should have, nothing resembled what he had anticipated, and nothing could be seen other than furiously burning timber, crashing ceiling material, and billows of smoke as the fire and the heat and the flames now sought the exit ripped through the street side wall.

Lew saw the canvass bow, and then billow as the last successful attempt catapulted the car into the building. He half dragged, half lifted Marta from behind the bar where they had been crouching after the horror of discovering Horst's body literally on fire, with Klaus and Hawkins lifeless beside him. The fumes were now overpowering. Smoke, burning furnishings, billowing soot and flames obstructed his forward visibility and the two of them half staggered forward toward the opening. He had to get to Hawkins, to the spot he had last seen Hawkins, to the black oilcloth packet, to the wire recordings and the intercept sheets and the fruits of the night's labors, but he had no idea where to turn. Then he saw it, clutched in Hawkins' arms, burning; saw it sizzle and pop and literally explode in a puff of what looked almost like steam. Suddenly, Marta left him and began back in the direction from which they had just come. He could see her, part of the room intensely alight with orange flame, other parts black with dense smoke. She had just reached Horst's body when a quarter of the ceiling gave way and with a horrible crashing roar, a portion of the outside roof crashed two stories to the floor below burying Marta beneath debris. Lew felt Blackie's hand on his belt and heard his shouts, but he knocked himself clear and ran toward Marta.

He was within fifteen feet of her when the rest of the roof collapsed, and the last he remembered was the scream in his throat as he tried desperately to reach her.

*   *   *

In the street, Gladney lost no time getting on the radiotelephone. The eight-foot whip antenna at the back of the Rover had been giving them trouble, and the Yanks had gathered around him desperate for any assistance they could summon. Gladney ran around to the rear of the Rover and started to fiddle with the antenna Lyle Burdick instantly noticed that the grounding strap had come loose from the dashboard installation, and he shoved the wire against the nearest part of the Rover's frame and grabbed the RT transceiver. Within seconds he had a good radio check with someone called Diamond Six and had relayed an urgent request for fire fighting equipment and ambulances at the Chanticleer.

White and Black had dragged Lew into what fresh air there was and he was sitting across the street on the patio embankment, dazed but alive and apparently not seriously hurt. When the ambulance arrived, the fire had largely subsided in the main part of the building—what was left of it—and the rear and sides were burning furiously. The attendants fussed over Lew but he made them follow him into the still remarkably hot rubble and they emerged after awhile carrying Marta as gently as they could. They laid her on a stretcher and Lew knelt on the muddy, ash-strewn ground and tried to comfort her. She opened her eyes once and looked at him for a long minute.

"Bon Voyage,…boomerang," she said with great effort and then he knew somehow that she was dead.

My God, My God, she can't be gone too, the wires, the intercepts the whole night's work, the reason why we're here, and now Marta. Boomerang. Something that always comes back.

How in the hell did she ever know about Boomerang?

36

They could all have hung around the smoldering ruin of the Chanticleer as long as they might have wanted, but they all smelled of smoke, Lew's clothing was almost completely burned off his body, and he was obviously dazed. The rest of them just wanted to get home. Gladney made two trips, and the crew found their beds in the Sylvan and their bottles of Keo; what looked like it could have devolved into a large hallway blast, turned out to be five very tired, very intimidated guys seeking comfort from one another and all of them trying to sleep through the nightmare memory.

At the Acropole, it was a different story. Gladney had dropped the officers off after he had delivered the crew, and when they walked into the lobby, a distinguished looking middle-aged English gentleman in a white shirt, no tie or collar, bedroom slippers and a cardigan sweater asked them to have the kindness to come with him to the little library, where, to their amazement, he had managed to free the door to allow it to close and provide privacy.

"My name is Roger Wingfield," he began, looking directly at each of the officers in turn. Kerrigan and Hunley recognized him as the dinner partner of the lady they had spoken to briefly at the next table at dinner, and he, in turn, seemed to know more about each of them than he needed to.

"We need to talk."

Lew seemed to recover and come out of his daze, self-conscious now about his appearance and the unmistakably foul odor in the room. Kerrigan excused himself, asking Wingfield's forbearance to make Lew more comfortable. They were about the same size and build, so he ducked upstairs to his own room and grabbed a pair of wash khaki trousers and a sweater which Lew gratefully slipped on, tossing his burned pants and shirt into the corner. They really smelled bad, and Hunley took them outside and got rid of them. While this was going on, Wingfield was completely silent, patiently waiting for them to rearrange themselves as if preparing for a formal speech from a dais. Mort and Dave Wagoner said nothing.

"I would like you to consider what I have to say to you tonight with the utmost seriousness. I understand that you have been through some very harrowing experiences, and I appreciate your discomfort, "looking at Lew.

"I shall ask you some questions, I'm afraid, and I shall write down your answers as well as your names and addresses. I am the principal legal advisor to the Field Marshall, and as such, I act as Her Majesty's senior judicial authority here on the island as long as martial law is observed, a fact that few people currently are aware of. There is no question of wrongdoing on anyone's part, at this moment, but the situation is quite confused, quite confused, and I'm afraid I shall need answers for the FM in the morning and I need your help.

"There has, as you know, been a tragic arson fire—oh yes, we're quite certain that an accelerant was used—at the Chanticleer. Odd thing, that, because my wife and I and her sister had reservations there tonight and when we arrived, we were shooed away. Lucky for us, what?

"There have been several bodies identified from fire this evening, of which you may be aware, most of them management, guests and employees of the Chanticleer." They looked at one another hesitantly, quizzically, wondering what was coming next.

Turning to Lew, whom he addressed directly now, he continued. "I would ask first if you recognize any of the names, and I ask you solely to confirm or deny whether any of these people were indeed at the establishment at the time of the tragic accident. As you may imagine, this is not the sort of thing I normally would involve myself in, but the circumstances tonight were somewhat extraordinary and the identities of the bodies need to be established.

"Major Edward Fitzgibbon Hawkins' body has been identified. Can any of you confirm his whereabouts tonight?" And he looked about perfunctorily, then back to Lew.

"I was a guest at the restaurant for a dinner party" Lew offered, "and I may be the only survivor. I can identify those that were there. Yes, Major Hawkins was with us, as was Mr. Kreisler, from the United Nations High Commission on Refugees, Mr. and Mrs. Lundy the owners of the Chanticleer and this hotel, their Secretary Treasurer" and he used the only term he could think of to describe her, "—a young I-would-guess Turkish woman whose first name was Nikki but whose last name I do not remember, and myself. There were at least two or three employees there at the time of the fire, and I don't know what happened to them."

"Had you ordered a taxi at any time during the evening?"

"A taxi? No sir, we had not."

"We found the remains of an American-made taxi virtually amidst the rubble of the building, and the badly charred body of its owner operator, a Mr. Mikos Constantanos outside the building."

"No sir, I have no knowledge of that." Hunley looked at Kerrigan, who ignored him and kept looking straight ahead.

"Can you think of any reason why the automobile would be, well, inside the remains of the building?

"No sir, I cannot."

"What would you say was the purpose of your meeting tonight?" he asked, shaking his head and shifting direction.

"My friends, Mr. and Mrs. Lundy, had a small dinner party to pay back some invitations they had received and they asked me to come to be the sixth person and partner the young lady."

"And did you know this young lady previously?"

"No sir, I did not"

"How do you account for the fact that of all the people in the building tonight, you were the only survivor?"

"I feel very fortunate that the other gentlemen who were members of my crew were in the neighborhood and helped me out of the building."

"Do you all realize that you all were in violation of the curfew laws this evening?" he asked, looking around at the others.

Hunley looked quickly at the others, and fixing his steely blue gaze on the British interrogator—whom he rather liked, actually - declared in an almost belligerent tone "It's a good thing we were, sir, or there would have been one fewer of us here."

They all agreed.

* * *

Wingfield was an experienced examiner, an excellent attorney, a fair judge, and, of all the people on Cyprus, probably the single best-informed person in every aspect of political and politico-military affairs in the region. He had a good idea how the American pilot happened to be on the scene of the demise of the top five individuals on his Watch List, including the single name on his counterespionage list, Edward/Emory St. John, the self-styled Major Hawkins. But he kept all that to himself and while he felt no compulsion to go back home and face a blistering cross examination from Phlida, he had no reason to further detain the Americans.

He was increasingly aware that he was not dressed for public exposure and besides, this was their last night on Cyprus.

Accordingly, he dismissed the others as politely as he could without letting them feel they were being dismissed, and he asked Lieutenant Commander Elfers to remain with him for a drink in the small library. Lew was expecting it, and having regained as much of whatever composure he still had available, he waited patiently while Wingfield went to the bar and fetched a whiskey neat for himself, a tumbler of Beefeaters with a sliver of ice for Lew, as he had asked.

"Commander," he began when they had settled in, "I deeply appreciate your cooperation tonight and I understand your reluctance to elaborate more fully on the events of the evening in the presence of your subordinate officers. Indeed, I am wholly without jurisdiction over any of your affairs, in accordance with our Status of Forces Agreement here on Cyprus, but let me tell you what I suspect went on at your dinner party and ask you for your comments when I have finished. You may be surprised at the, shall we say 'transparency', of some of your actions over the last several months."

"Perhaps you'd prefer me to tell you everything I know," Lew said quietly, looking him directly in the eye. "I would actually be more comfortable that way"

Wingfield gestured expansively, indicating that Lew had the floor. He was grateful, actually.

So he unburdened himself, this time semi-officially, this time soberly, this time with the advantage of having the bitter knowledge now of "how it would all end." It all *had* ended, ended in a heap of burned rubble with the strong odor of gasoline and burned roofing and searing flames and that crazy act of incredible devotion by Black and White and he was glad it was over. Glad to put it all in perspective finally, glad to be free of the addiction, ashamed and embarrassed by his puppy love infatuation, ready to reclaim the small tiny portion of his life that had been privately and secretly hers for so long.

And he had nothing to show for it except newly found wisdom. The wire recordings were gone, the track intercepts were gone, all traces of their spectacular success were burned and obliterated, exploded in the heat.

Why had they exploded, he wondered aloud to Wingfield. But they had.

Wingfield asked him one last question. "Did she say anything to you when you carried her out?"

"She said 'Boomerang'" Lew said. "How did she know that word?" Wingfield know what Boomerang meant. He now had closure.

"Does the word 'Billposter' mean anything to you?" Wingfield asked.

"Nothing," Lew replied, "nothing at all."

And then it was over.

The others were all at the bar when the two of them emerged, and Lew shook hands with his interrogator as he departed, and joined them, sitting in the same seat he had occupied when—a hundred years ago?—when he had unburdened himself to Mort.

* * *

It was well after midnight when Wingfield left the Acropole for the second time that evening, and instead of heading back to his elegant apartment in the new section that would become Homer Avenue, he drove the Humber with its official placard in place of a license tag back to Government House. Once inside, the Royal Marine sentry had the Cypriot policeman accompany him upstairs to his office and left him with a kettle on the electric ring. When he had gone, he took the bottle of Hennessey's Five Star from his desk drawer, always ready to deploy, depending on his strategy for the business at hand and his success in fulfilling it. He turned off the kettle and poured himself two fingers in one of the Waterford snifters he kept at the ready. He had some serious thinking to do, and some serious consulting with the Field Marshall in the morning, if he had his guess.

The secure telephone in the small cupboard beside the large oak desk rang with its almost eerie signal, one that he had difficulty getting used to since a scrambled call was such a seldom honor. He was, however, far from surprised, but uncertain as to the immediate cause of so high a seldom honor. At this hour, could the news have traveled? Surely not. Within a moment, the Foreign Office connection was completed and surprisingly clear, as it normally was in the late evening. London was two hours earlier but it was still unusual to receive a secure call at this time of night, even with the troubles.

Harrison was on the line. There was the usual fade and build as the sky waves jumped around and the scrambler did whatever the scrambler did, but all in all it was a good connection. He was used to using it, and remembered to key the handset as he spoke and release the key to listen.

"How did you know I'd be here" he asked when they settled down to business.

"I didn't *know*," he said with his characteristic sarcasm. He had been that way ever since they had met in the fourth form at Ilminster, and he wasn't going to change in his fifties. "I presumed that you were earning your money and you would be on the spot there, old chum. Now what can you tell me about it from your end? The PM is having an Eden fit, and wants answers."

"The PM? Why in the world would...what are we talking about, Jeffrey?"

"What do you think, old boy? The Soviet ambassador called him this afternoon and he has been with the Americans on and off all day—what a stinkpot this is! Eisenhower is said to have called personally, but I doubt it, and the Yanks are in terminal denial that anything happened at all! And of course, the Soviets won't let on what's bugging them but they keep after 'this incident! This incident!' and nobody knows what the hell they mean."

"You'll have to do better than that. I don't know what you're talking about."

"Righto. Here goes. This morning around eleven, the Soviet attaché came by—he's a decent sort and we work together some times. Seems an aircraft of unknown nationality barged into their airspace around Batumi last night...this morning, actually...and they sent two of their sexiest night fighters out to have a look at it. Well, the long and the short of it is that only one of them came back, and they are afraid, if I read them right, that the thing was in collision with the intruder. Well the Turks insist they have no aircraft missing and the RAFfies swear the same up and down. The Yanks, as I said, are in total denial and the Sovs are now in mortal fear that something will leak out to the press.

"Well we were talking it over at tea downstairs, and I remembered the Boomerang thing we were involved with out there in your garden patch, so I went back-channel to the Yank Navy people with whom we had made those arrangements. They expire, by the way, next fortnight and they'll not be renewing them. Anyway, the Yanks were very close lipped and I got the impression that they themselves don't know what actually happened, but they did know about it and insist that their Boomerang thing got back safe and sound."

"It did," Wingfield said. "I just talked to the pilot and the officers in the crew, not an hour ago, about something else actually." Jeffrey was pleasantly surprised. In his business, information was currency and inside, first-hand, fast-breaking information was solid gold. He had what he needed. The crew was, indeed, back safe and sound.

"May I ask what 'something else' means? Were they bad boys in your playhouse? Violated curfew? Loud after hours?"

"Nothing like that, Jeffrey. No, this was far more involved. We've had a very busy night of it, several deaths actually, rather important ones as a matter of fact, and I'm here trying to sort it out now. I have no knowledge of your 'incident' old boy, and if these Navy chaps here shot down one of the buggers, that's fine with me, but I don't have any knowledge of it. Yes, they did fly last night—everybody on the island knows it when they go off, you know, no way to keep it a secret. But they did get back this AM, had some trouble I understand, almost ran out of gas, got struck by lightning, no radios and all that…at least that's our story and it's the best we can do. I'm letting them go on their way tomorrow, bound for Halfar or Luqa I understand, you can catch them there if you need them, but I can't help you further."

"Well thanks anyway, Roger. My best to the Marshall. Is Philida still with you? Say hello for us, will you. Better you than us!." He and Philida had traveled in the same social circle after Cambridge. He couldn't stand her either.

He had a thought.

Remembering virtually everything Elfers had said to him an hour ago in the Acropole, Wingfield got up and went over to his file safe. It had a combination to release the time lock, and another to open the safe. Fortunately, he remembered each set of numbers and he fished for a minute before he pulled out the red striped folder marked "Boomerang" in neat India ink letters on the top. In the folder, each of the Top Secret messages pertaining to Boomerang had been filed with a disclosure sheet atop each one indicating who had seen it and when it had been seen.

Normally, Top Secret dispatch folders which covered "back burner" topics—war plans, force dispositions and the like - would have been locked away in Communications country, but anything with currency, anything with an operational or political flavor was normally routed to those with a "need to know" and returned to the cognizant office for safekeeping. He had, months ago, requested cognizance over Boomerang and the file, and here it was.

He wanted to see something, to confirm something that he had suspected all along, suspected when he had designated Hawkins as a counterespionage risk but that now was becoming self evident. He opened the folder and looked at the top item in the file, the operational directive for the flight they had flown on Thursday night. It was always originated by the odd sounding

"CINCNELM," hard to pronounce actually, meant Commander in Chief Naval Forces, Easter Atlantic and Mediterranean, a NATO hat, out of London. He knew them well. He had met Admiral Jack Cassady in Baghdad last month. Nice sort. Over his head, actually.

121745Z DEC 55

FM: CINCNELM

His eyes immediately went to the list of information addressees, the courtesy or ancillary recipients of the message, the ones who had to know what was going on but did not necessarily have to take any direct action on the message. It was as he had suspected.

INFO: OPNAV

ALUSNA ANKARA

RAF NICOSIA

COMFAIRMED

HQ MEF

HQ MEAF

He needed to consult his Signals publications to confirm that his memory had served him correctly in translating the arcane U.S. Navy abbreviations—acronyms, they called them. The first, "ALUSNA," as he recalled, was the American Legate and U S Naval Attaché in Ankara, the chaps who would be involved in arranging overflight clearances with the Turks. RAF Nick was always involved, since they counted on the boys in blue for their logistics, communications, maintenance, transportation and all the other transient support services they always needed. "COMFAIRMED," the Commander of the US Fleet Air assets in the Mediterranean was undoubtedly the aviation sub-command with military cognizance over the aircraft, located in Naples, if he recalled correctly. But they were not what he was interested in.

He confirmed in one glance, looking at the final two addresses, that the Middle East Air Force RAF command and the Middle East Force itself—his command, Harding's command, Major Hawkins command—was a principal information addressee. In Hawkins case, his job would have given him the presumption of "need to know" and he certainly would have had access to the Boomerang file. Sure enough, in his neat copperplate handwriting, Hawkins had signed to attest that he had seen each of the messages in the file, going back to 1953. The dates indicated that he had seen each message recently, the latest shortly after its delivery on Cyprus.

He sat quietly putting it all together, in his best methodical, prosecutorial, QC style, wondering whether the woman was the check on Hawkins' information to the other side, or whether his access was used to verify the woman's information. It made a difference, he supposed, but not much and when he was done, he drained the brandy from the snifter, locked up and went home. Emma and Philida were both asleep. It was still early enough for him to get some semblance of rest.

* * *

They all finally got some semblance of rest Friday night. But not immediately.

The crew in the Sylvan were subdued, grieving for Nikki, stunned that Mikos would have been near enough to have been caught in the fire, but jubilant and celebratory over their two heroes, who had gotten the car through the wall into the burning inferno. They had questions, of course, and nobody could figure out how Mr. Kerrigan had gotten Mikos' key. Burdick didn't say much about the fire and the excitement and nobody bugged him. White and Black were the stars of the show and Timmons and Lucore wisely let them bask in the glory.

At the Acropole, after Wingfield had left in his Humber, Lew, now pretty much up to normal speed, debriefed the others in a very rudimentary way, touching briefly, nonchalantly on the dinner, revealing nothing. He seemed subdued as well, either grief-stricken or somehow ashamed, hollow, but he managed to muster the strength to discuss the arrangements and logistics for the return trip. They assumed that the loss of Marta was foremost on his mind, unaware that he had come to grips so totally with information so devastating that he actually felt liberated in his unburdened state.

It was really the other thing that bothered him, the package, the envelope, the fruit of their labor. All gone.

Later, without their having noticed the pairing off, Kerrigan, Wagoner and Hunley realized that Lew and Mort had disappeared together into the library and shut the balky door again. Wagoner was quiet, the trace of something working at the corners of his eyes and mouth, but he said nothing. And after about five minutes alone together in the little library, when Lew emerged from their meeting, his backbone straight, his eyes steady and the trace of the same something on the edges of his lips. He looked ten years younger than he did when he had gone in there.

What was that all about? Kerrigan and Hunley wanted to know. Wagoner seemed to be in on it but he kept his own counsel.

So they went upstairs and Hunley helped Kerrigan burn the negatives in Brian's shower, checking each before the match took. Two of the three larger ones were images of people, the formal grouping and the crew with Nikki at the bar. The third seemed to be so good a likeness of the Beast that Kerrigan was tempted to keep is as a souvenir, but in the end, they burned it with the film strips showing Burdick's transgression and the pair of lovers on the roof.

They made an awful smell.

37

In the Wingfield apartment on the other side of Paphos, the telephone beside the bed rang at seven-thirty sharp. Roger Wingfield reached for it with one arm and struggled to get his glasses on his nose before he picked it up.

The maneuver didn't work, so he had to fumble through the first moments of the conversation, one hand picking through the few papers on the nightstand before he located them beneath the hastily written note to himself written at 2:30 that morning. He liked to talk on the phone with his glasses on. He could hear his wife and Philida chatting down the hall.

"Good morning, Sir," Dalyrmple said. "The Marshall would like a word with you this morning and I've penciled you in at 845 hours. Can you make it?"

"Yes, indeed. I've been expecting a session today. What kind of mood is he in?"

Sir John Harding was one of the most patient, professional and gracious military officers in the world, but having served with him in the Seventh Armoured "Desert Rats" and again, after he left hospital, in Italy in March of '44 through the end of the war, Roger knew that there were times that tried even the most patient of men's souls. He hoped this would not be one of them.

"I can't tell, sir, "Dalyrmlpe said, "but 8:45 it is."

Harding had started out as a Territorial Army Reservist before the First War, and had been called up and sent to the Middle East when his contemporaries were suffering through those horrifying days of endless trench warfare that even the most hardened Britons hesitated to recall now, forty years later. Almost forgotten as an active war front, the Middle East provided the Royal Army with some of its grandest opportunities for personal heroism and bravery. Harding had come home from Haifa as an acting Lieutenant Colonel, commanding a machine gun battalion of seasoned Tommys whose contribution to the British Middle East victory was legendary. He had lost his acting field grade rank almost immediately after the war, soldiering through the twenties and thirties until he was officially restored in 1938, by this time in India as a member of the colonial Army.

When World War II began, Britain relied on her seasoned combat officers and he went back to the Middle East with his Seventh Armored "Desert Rats," where unconventional warfare history was made under his steady command. Badly wounded in North Africa, he had sat out the war for a while but emerged as soon as he could walk again as Alexander's Chief of Staff in Italy.

After the war, he had succeeded Alexander as commander of the British forces in the Mediterranean, and was promoted to full General in 1949 as Commander of the British Far East Land Forces. He left the Orient in 1951 to command the British Army of the Rhine and when he was promoted to Field Marshal in 1953, he was at the top of the British military pinnacle as the Chief of the Imperial General Staff. He had postponed a well-deserved retirement earlier this year and accepted the post as Military governor and Commander in chief here in Nicosia.

He was fifty-nine years old, and had been a soldier forty-two years.

In Italy, Harding had relied on the young barrister assigned as one of his Judge Advocates to advise and implement the difficult task of setting up military governments in the civilian communities under British cognizance. Both were from Somerset originally, both graduates of Ilminster Grammar School, but in different decades. They had developed a relationship far more complex than the senior-junior officer bond characteristic of so many other wartime alliances that had transferred successfully to peacetime.

Harding relied heavily on Roger's clear head, common sense and uncommon forbearance; Roger was sometimes spellbound by the great leaps of intuition, imagination and foresight displayed by the older man, amply demonstrating the root of the tactical brilliance that had characterized the exploits of his Desert Rats. When the Field Marshall had been asked by Eden to take on the Cyprus job, with the strong concurrence of both the backbenchers and the Queen, the political machinery fired up to the task of allowing the promising Queen's Counsel, new to the silk, to accompany him to Cyprus.

Harding's strategy in Nicosia was, above all, designed to curtail the bloodshed and the violence that had swept the island since late spring. He had many critics, to be sure, but the principal thrust of his policy had been, to now, to forge an accommodation with the individual he considered the natural leader of the community, quite aside from Colonel Grivas. To this end he had been working hard to reason with His Excellency Archbishop Makarios III, and was at the lowest depth—or highest peak—of frustration with the petulant cleric on this particular Saturday in December.

Makarios had absolutely no intention of giving an inch. He and Grivas had put EOKA together personally when the cleric had come back from the States a year ago, and things had gone downhill since. Worse, the pompous bastard had absolutely no intention of even acknowledging the existence of the Turkish minority, further exacerbating relations with everybody. He kept talking about the Cypriot nation, as if there had ever been a single nation of the two distinct cultures and religions.

This morning, Roger prepared himself for the meeting intellectually as he made his way to Government House, but as he had allowed himself to skip even a cup of tea as he left the apartment, he was "a bit puckish" as he was waved into the large office and, therefore, relieved to see the tea pot in its cozy and the scones on the sideboard. He helped himself, unsuccessfully stifling a yawn, as Harding finished the dispatch he was reading, and greeted him as one greets a trusted accomplice in an involved intrigue.

"Short night eh?" the Field Marshall asked. He was dressed in tweeds, with a checked shirt and woolen tie, leather patches on the elbows of his jacket. Roger was in his Saturday business uniform, Gray's Inn blazer and flannels.

"Short night. Hated to see the Chanticleer go. We'd gone by for dinner and been sent away, you know, by one of their better-educated chaps. Spoke very well. I surmise that they were nailing the front door shut as we drove off. Pity."

"Now what's all this about the Russians loosing an aircraft in the Black Sea and trying to blame everybody but the Pope? I had a call from the PM last evening…"

"I got one from his Private Secretary around one this morning" Roger began. 'It's all part of the same story, actually, and while there's not much we can do about any of this at this stage, we've come out of it with surprisingly good fortune."

"I suppose Anthony was upset that I hadn't an answer for him so he had Jeffrey get to you later. Well, what have we?"

"The real story is what we no longer have, Field Marshall. I've spoken to you before about the couple who owned the Acropole and the Chanticleer. She was Czech, German papers actually, he German, both technically stateless, here as refugees then suddenly passported, all in order."

"I gather by your use of the past-tense that something has happened to them. I liked them both, met them several times."

"Yes, quite. They were involved in Berlin with St. John, who as you know went by 'Hawkins' here for some obscure reason of his own, and with the chap we knew as Kreisler, from the Refugee office across the square. They were also involved with the Hamouda woman known as Nikki who was the Arab League contact here."

"More past tense. How long is this list this morning?" He smiled thinly. He was not terribly saddened by the implied news.

"Two more—your favorite rug merchant Mr. Loumides, who you must realize, will be sadly missed by both the good Colonel Grivas and His Excellency, the Archbishop, plus his faithful courier, Mr. Mikos Constantanos, he of the black Dodge taxicab. And, oh yes, the black Dodge taxicab itself, burned to a crisp, *inside* the Chanticleer."

"Inside, what?"

"We'll straighten it out directly, but for the moment, we have what remains of the Dodge between the patio window and the piano bar of the Chanticleer and we haven't the foggiest notion of how it got there."

They both fell silent a moment.

"Quite a casualty list. I'd already heard about St. John from the Chief of Staff. Did you know that he had an active MI-5 channel that people were getting upset about because he was exceeding his charter? I know you didn't, sorry to seem spooky, but I just learned about it from our Colonel Spires this morning. Called himself Billposter. Now how does all that tie in with this airplane business, and the Black Sea, and their missing interceptor or whatever?"

Wingfield briefly covered the background factors that he felt were relevant.

He described the loose alliance of free-lance "data collectors" that had included the old Berlin hands, reluctant to describe them as intelligence agents. When Middle East HQ had moved from Cairo to Cyprus, these resident collectors had reaped a windfall, now that they were at the center of things.

He delicately touched on St. John's activities, reluctant to mention the withdrawal of a certain safeguarded package by Major Hawkins from the RAF Communications Centre as reported to his superiors by Flight Lieutenant Griffin. He would leave that for the moment.

"It seems that the American pilot, a Lieutenant Commander Elfers, was under the impression that he was having an affair with Mrs. Lundy, despite the fact that they were together only a few times over the period of their 'involvement.' He would apparently 'persuade' Mrs. Lundy to mislead the Russian side as to the intent of their operations, apparently believing that his subterfuge would lull the Russians into ignoring their penetration or near-penetration flights. So 'successful' were his efforts, in typical American self-deception, that he believed their safe flights into the Black Sea were wholly due to his paramour's false intelligence.

"Actually, the Soviets were trying desperately to *hide* their capability to intercept, not to show it off. Consequently, whenever the Americans would fly, the Soviets would simply sit on their hands and cackle, because their crown jewels or whatever were their electronic intelligence sweets were safe!"

"So, he was a master of misdirection," the Marshall said, sarcastically.

"Certainly. Every time they would fly, he would try to get her to pass false data northward, but in the event, her data just confirmed times and dates. Everybody knew when they were flying anyway, and the Soviets just sat around and laughed.

"Well, St. John knew all about the expiration of our agreement with the Americans and told Mrs. Lundy about it. Apparently, she had a turn of conscience or perhaps her hormones were acting up - but I think St. John or maybe even one of her old time US contacts that we don't know about - put her up to it, actually. So she persuaded Kriesler, who was her principal contact here, to purposely mislead the Soviets this one time. She knew this was to be their last flight from Nicosia, and she allegedly wanted to give the American some psychic reward for having duped him for so long, and then steal the reward back, if they possibly could manage it. So they hatched a plot, and probably told the Soviets that the Yanks had gone home.

"The plan was to let them get the data they were looking for and then steal it from them, hand it back if they could, destroy it if they couldn't, and claim a big reward from Up North. St. John was part of it, somehow, since he knew they would try to safeguard their wire recordings and charts with the Communications Centre, as they always did post-flight.

"So they flew their last flight from Nicosia, and had wonderful luck. The Soviets launched their interceptors, just as the Americans had both hoped and feared, and to their credit, they apparently captured the event on wire recordings, priceless intelligence prizes. Unfortunately, one of the interceptors probably flew itself into the water in the pursuit, but of course we can't be involved in that or even know about it. We'll continue to profess total ignorance.

"They returned to Nick sometime Friday morning, a bit of excitement in the return because they almost ran out of petrol on the way home and got hit by lightning, all sorts of adventures. But they got back. Now the rest of the plan had to be put in motion so Mrs. Marty invited them all to dinner.

"Well, by the time the thing played out, everybody knew what was going on. Mikos and his EOKA chaps were feeling hemmed in by the big four. Kriesler and St. John were both informing us on every move Grivas made, St. John because we were paying him to go after the Greeks, Kreisler because his people were in bed with the Arabs. They even picked up a casual, the Hamouda woman, who actually was employed at the Acropole and the Chanticleer and passed everything on to the Turks. The Greeks killed some of her relatives on Thursday, probably to send her a warning, and she informed both St. John and Kreisler Friday afternoon that she was out for blood. One of them—possibly both—invited her to the dinner party, but she may have been invited from the start. Under the circumstances, I wouldn't be surprised if some Yank agency had a piece of St. John, used him as a sleeper for this one time, but I can't prove it. Maybe he had a debt to pay, who knows?

"It seems that Mikos had been hoarding high-octane aviation gasoline that he and his chums were stealing from the RAFies, and he and Moumides hatched a plan to get rid of the—now five—of them. We knew earlier that they also had an elaborate misinformation plan for the press having to do with the Americans, and they were saving that for mischief. We've all the details but none of the reported photos that were to go with the story, and we have no idea what's become of them.

"Somehow, we think from the Americans, Mikos found out the five of them would be having dinner last night at the C, so Moumides pulled his strings and got a bogus carpenter crew out there in the early evening to work on the plywood replacement for the plate glass window Mikos had had smashed Thursday night. In the process, they managed to keep any business -

except for the principals and including Beatrice, Philida and myself—away while they physically nailed the exit doors shut. Meantime, I might add, somebody got to Moumides with piano wire and he was found in his shop this morning, dead about twelve hours.

"Just as the dinner party was getting to the port and cheese, St. John produces the packet of wire recordings and charts he had simply taken from the Centre, where he had free access. I wasn't going to tell you how he got the material because I wasn't certain, but the more I think of it, the more I believe it to be so. Now here's what I do not know and cannot determine. Was St. John going to give the packet to Kriesler, as he had promised, or was he going to give it to the American and blow the whistle on the others? Was he a blatant criminal or a heroic patriot?

"And the reason I will never know is because by this time, Mikos had gotten several jerry cans of his gasoline supplies into the building somehow during the day, and he and his chaps doused the foundations—it was wood, you know—and the sub-gutters that run around the place, and up it went in less time than you can even talk about it. The two employees who were working the dinner party were incinerated. The American managed to get himself out and he got Mrs. Marty out, but she was too far-gone to save. She apparently died in his arms. All very romantic. Except she and the Nikki woman were lovers, as well."

Harding turned his swivel chair toward the window overlooking the square, and thought for a moment.

"Do you think he'll ever know what was really going on? I would love to know what her final words were," he said slowly, thoughtfully.

Wingfield knew but let it pass.

"That's one of the mysteries. For another, we found what we think is what was left of Mikos Constantanos the rubble, but outside."

"Who killed Loumides?"

"Another mystery. Someone we now like, apparently."

"And the wire recording packet, the things that the American assumed he had risked his life for and the thing that the others had actually *given* their lives for - the *corpus dilecti*—all destroyed. What about that, Counselor?"

"That's the Americans' problem."

"That may be their problem at the moment, but think it through.

"Their precious secret parcel is entrusted for safekeeping to their friendly British allies. Whilst in 'safekeeping', it is physically stolen by a trusted Intelligence Officer and brought to a social dinner party with known enemy agents, where it meets with terminal misadventure and is destroyed. The mechanics of the compromise—lock substitution, hacksaw, misuse of authority, or whatever—will be beside the point from the American's position. Their precious jewels were entrusted to us and they're gone. Frankly, I'm appalled at the stupendous breach of all that is held sacred in the classified material control world—imagine handing something like that over without receipt!"

"It was not actually 'handed over', Sir," Wingfield pointed out. "The American chap was shown an unlocked lock-box in the office, and he put the material in it, locked it with his own lock and then departed. Access to it had to be by opening the lock, or from the Centre itself.

"It could only be accessed by authorized personnel…"

"Exactly," Harding said. "Exactly! And what did happen to it? One of our 'authorized personnel' walked into the Centre, walked off with it and it's gone. The box is undoubtedly still locked—from the outside!"

Wingfield and Harding knew immediately that they had neither seen nor heard the end of a sticky mess. Harding wanted to be as prepared as possible for whatever came next. He began to think out loud, and Wingfield followed along with him.

"I would say that in order of impact on what I am trying to do here on Cyprus, the deaths of the Europeans and of poor old St. John would rank first and foremost. Their deaths can only have a disruptive effect on our efforts here, but the bright side seems to be that until their replacements are found, vetted, trained and sent here, we can get along without the attention of our former Soviet allies."

"I don't think St. John is irreplaceable," Wingfield offered, "but he had a number of constituencies in Whitehall and thereabouts that will need attending to."

"Since we will never know whether he died a villain or a hero, do you see much point in investigating the issue?"

Wingfield was silent for a moment.

"We must look beyond our Cyprus problem, General," he began, using the lower rank form of address almost as a pet name, reminding Harding of their long association.

"The most significant thing that has happened is really the one that we both have both agreed that 'we know absolutely nothing about'. But we do, don't we. We know the Russians lost a very valuable fighter aircraft, or at least we think we know that, and we better believe that MEF will be drawn into that imbroglio once it hits our chums in Whitehall. Eden is talking cutesy with the two of them in the seat up there, now that Uncle Joe is gone. You know, Bulganin and the other one, the bald one—Khrushchev—are said to be thinking of coming to the UK in the Spring and the last thing Her Majesty's Government wants is a mess on its hands with those two. The PM is going to want answers, but we can't very well give him answers to something 'we know absolutely nothing about'," and he imitated the verbal emphasis his Chief had used a minute ago.

"But the more I think about it," he continued, "the more I become horrified at the implications the Americans are likely to draw from all this. Put yourself in their position. It may sound like a comedy of errors, but as soon as they turn the rug over on this classified material bollix, the whole thing—the fire, the deaths, the double and triple crosses…all these things are going to be part of some official record someplace and I would almost prefer to have problems with the Russians than with the Americans. The Russians don't pay any of our bills."

Harding considered this a moment.

"Why don't we put together an organized effort to find out as much as we can about this whole thing, find it out officially if we must, semi-officially if we can work with the Yanks on it, and get some of these answers down on paper so we can look at them and see how they sound when they all play together like an orchestra. We're going to have to do something with the Americans, so this is what I'm thinking about.

He paused, thoughtfully, thinking carefully, weighing each word, reciting as if for some legal record.

"We here at MEF have reason to believe that a British subject, a reasonably well placed Civil Servant in Her Majesty's Intelligence community—don't use MI5 unless we have to—who has died as the result of possible misadventure in a tragic arson fire here on Cyprus, had, before his untimely death, engaged in the unauthorized and possibly criminal removal of undisclosed classified material from the…blah, blah, blah…say whatever you like…and in order to establish 'line-of-duty' status, as opposed to 'misconduct' status, we are conducting an informal investigation.

"We are also vitally interested in 'damage limitation'—what did he know, what documents did he compromise, you know, that sort of thing. I'm just thinking out loud here, Roger. As part of our very preliminary findings, it appears that some of the unauthorized materials had been placed under lock by a transient American flight crew of the night of…blah, blah, blah. Now although we realize that no signature, custody receipt or formal responsibility for the material exists, we are concerned and of course regret what has happened. We would like to have a word with the American pilot, if possible, and would welcome the cooperation of…whoever he works for."

Wingfield thought about it for a moment. He nodded, slowly, deliberately.

"That contains the grain of a good approach, Sir, and would possibly work. We can promise 'extreme sensitivity' and because of the 'sources and methods' involved, we can classify the hell out of it. We can go the old boy route with Admiral Cassady in London—we both met him in Baghdad last month, if you will recall—and if we work fast, we might be able to wrap it all up before the New Year."

"Whatever we do," the Field Marshal said in a lower voice, now, "whatever we do, we - I - would like to distance ourselves from the airplane incident and avow no knowledge of anything that went on after the Yanks left Nick Thursday night. And for whatever it's worth—although I'm sure you're way ahead of me on this one—we have to take the most innocent, the most unconcerned, the most detached none-of-our-business or-interest posture with regard to the four—or was it five—fresh bodies in the Mortuary this Saturday morning.

"How would you and Emma enjoy a trip to London to do some Christmas shopping?"

Wingfield tented his fingers and stared off into the distance through the window, his gaze now on the terracotta rooftops and the hubris of the square below and the courageous, if not brazen, flutter of the Turkish flag atop the minaret off to the east. He turned then and looked straight into his Boss' eyes, the electricity of conspiracy flashing between them.

"What a wonderful suggestion, Excellency," the trace of a smile beginning, his eyes actually twinkling.

"Unfortunately, Emma's sister Philida is here on holiday from Teheran, so I would have to forego the remainder of my visit with her, but she and Emma can make do without me, I expect. Perhaps I could make some inquiries while I am there."

38

Later on that Saturday morning, the Beast crew all paid their bills and said their farewells. The mood at the Acropole was horrible, much tri-lingual wailing, ostentatious mourning everywhere, black drapes on the mirrors and on the doorpost.

Horrible.

On the way from the front desk to the taxi, Lew stopped and gave a last thoughtful glance back when he looked into the bar, past the piano, to the table by the window, but he soldiered on and what the others interpreted as his grief was private, controlled and seemed to be tempered by some kind of an inner peace. The others felt for Lew, now that they all knew about his relationship with Marta, but they were all glad to be getting on their way. Wagoner had to return to Morocco with the crew, rather than fight his way back to the US via TWA, although his supply of presentable clothing was virtually non-existent. He had Navy work to do. Things needed attention.

The three taxis—two from the Sylvan and one from the Acropole—happened to meet at the Paphos Gate and they traveled in convoy to the airfield.

Kerrigan knew Mort and Lew would be going to the Communications Centre to retrieve the package of wire recordings and track charts, but in the hubbub of activity attendant to their getting underway, he forgot to mention it to either of them. He assumed that they had been there already and taken care of it. But when could they have gone?

Whenever. It was not his problem.

Out at the aircraft, as they all put their flight suits on, Mort and Wagoner boosted themselves up into Lucore's galley and unfastened what they had taped to the underside of the galley table with the Ordnance tape. It came loose after a bit, and they checked it and looked at each other, then lowered themselves back to the pavement. Mort called Lew over and they had a word together, and could they actually have hugged one another?

A little later when Lucore went around asking everyone if they had taken any of the small Brit cans of tuna fish, somehow missing from his larder, Lew smiled but said nothing. Mort was also amused that White had not immediately discovered the loss of the Chapter of the manual containing the Jet Start Bus Circuit wiring diagram. Eventually, White remembered taking out the twenty or so loose-leaf pages from the manual the other night, but…well, they might be lying around someplace.

*   *   *

The flights back home were different from any they had ever experienced. The run to Malta was quiet, conversation subdued and monosyllabic. None of the sophisticated electronic machinery they had so confidently relied on Thursday evening was working. The open receivers, devastated by the literally explosive blast of direct current energy the lightning had delivered, were useless, torn apart inside. Switches were clicked and dials twirled and bulbs checked, but nothing the talented electronic wizards could do worked. Unused wire on the dead recorders were rewound tediously by hand, care taken to avoid the ruthless finger-slashing tendency of the coiled wire with tension-power off their burnt out motors. Nevertheless, they had their individual station logs, so the Mickey crew correlated and cross referenced Thursday night's signals with the intercept stations, times with frequencies, frequencies with bearings, and so, carefully, made the words that would go with the marvelous, priceless music they hoped had been captured on the wires.

True to his promise, Lew left the cockpit right after takeoff and with Hunley in the left seat and Brian riding co-pilot, the flight station looked once again like a training flight out over Palma. Black helped White search for the missing sheaf of wiring diagrams, for without them, further tampering with the circuit breaker panel would be out of the question. They were nowhere to be found.

Lew took Bryan's seat at the Navigation table and he and Wagoner got to know one another, leaving the navigation to the cockpit now that Lyle Burdick had fixed the birddog. Wagoner was totally impressed with Lew, knowing all that Mort had confided in him, unable to identify outward signs of the pain of his loss, in awe of the quiet competence and steady good nature that had returned as if summoned from the bottom of some depth of emotional reserve at which Wagoner could only marvel.

* * *

In Malta, the crew wasted no time after the Beast was fueled and the flight suits stowed in the carryall, and as they headed into Valetta, they agreed a night in the first class Phoenicia Hotel was what they all needed. They would pass up a trip to the Gut where the limey sailors chased down the ancient stone steps after the worst looking prostitutes in the world. Somehow, the adventure of the past few days had sobered them, and after anteing up more British pounds than their per-diem was going to handle, they booked a half dozen rooms in the stately old hotel and lived like Lords until they left the next day for home.

Lucore actually took a bath in a real tub, his first in 1955. It was, after all, December.

The officers went to their favorite old brownstone Hotel in Sliema, where the "hot and cold running chambermaids" made great sea-stories and tall tales, but where none such ever existed. They liked the Sliema waterfront, and they walked the gray and drizzly beach to their favorite City Gem restaurant down the promenade where they all ate Steak Bismark with a fried egg on the top, drank lots of stout and were all in bed by ten. Alone.

Hunley and Brian made Sunday morning's takeoff from the Luqa aerodrome, and they occupied the better part of a gray winter Mediterranean day boring holes in the sky toward the west, a "proper" flight plan on record. Procedurally correct voice reports were required as they entered and departed each Flight Information Region, and Navy one triple two zero seven blended in with the scenery. A normal navigational training flight from Malta to Morocco. Lew handled the navigation, with the radar available, the birddogs working, some imaginative dead reckoning occasionally required but all in all, successfully hitting checkpoints and making good time.

Between navigational fixes, Lew and Wagoner tried to nail together some kind of a comprehensive message that the unit would be required to transmit after they landed. It would be sent over secure landline or encrypted, and since it would be the first official detailed report of the Black Sea incident, it was imperative that it be as accurate as possible.

Lew had Brian's chart and logs before him, and referred to them continuously as he wrote. It was already several days later than it should be and that was, in itself, a cause for concern that would have to be addressed in the message. The local unrest and the ensuing difficulty with classified communications was mentioned obliquely, just enough to get them off the hook for "not writing home sooner" as Lew described it. Lew's first draft was comprehensive, and Wagoner was able to insert details of the intercepted radio transmissions that Lew had not known about. They passed the draft back to Mort and discussed it on the Evaluator's Intercom circuit.

Since the message would originate from the Unit and not from Lew or the mission aircraft, the Skipper would need to review it and add his own insights. He would be the "originator" of the message and he would need an extensive briefing to get up to speed. With some chagrin, Lew realized that very few people—a few crewmembers and the British lawyer - were the only ones who knew any of the details of the fire and its aftermath, and he wondered what, if any of that data, needed to be included in the post-mission message. For better or for worse, he decided that the two events need not be connected officially now—if ever.

Unlike the Saturday flight, on this leg conversation on the flight deck was intense, subdued perhaps, but each of the crew members forward of the wing spar reliving, then retelling his recollection of the night of fire and noise and ultimately, horror, as the bodies were pulled out on stretchers. They had, strangely, not mentioned any of this in Malta, even in the Phoenicia Bar before and after their dinner last night. The evening had held an artificiality to it, as if all had agreed that they would talk about anything but the events of the previous days. Somehow, the topic was so private, so special that their great need for these recollections to burst forth had to be held in check until they were in the Beast, in their element, in the shared intimacy of their "clubhouse" or den before they could look one another in the eye and let the conversational dams break loose.

The younger men—Black, White, even Brian—had never seen death at such close quarters, and the sight of the burned corpses would be with them forever. There were mysteries, small ones, that needed explanation and no amount of quiet flight deck conversation over paper cups of Lucore's coffee could succeed in putting the whole affair, with all its loose ends, together for the crew.

How was Nikki involved, what was she doing there?

How did the fire start in the first place? How did Mr. Kerrigan get the keys to the Dodge, and what was it doing there anyway?

Burdick was uncharacteristically silent in these proceedings, keeping his counsel, diminished from his usual dogmatic expansiveness, clearly a changed man.

When they passed abeam of the island of Majorca and headed for Gibraltar, Lew had Brian flick the Intercom Master switch to "All-Override" and he asked the crew to make sure everyone had a headset and could hear what he had to say. He had thought about this moment for several days, and his words were measured.

He reviewed, briefly, what they had accomplished and what had transpired on their flight. He commended the exceptional professionalism of the entire crew and thanked everyone for his performance. Finally, as a separate issue, he mentioned the fire in guarded terms, unwilling to make a specific connection with the operational performance the night before. He stressed the fact that there were a number of unknowns—factors that would probably never be known—and asked that the crew make no connection in their own mind or in any discussions that they might have with their shipmates.

Finally, asking their discretion in strictest confidence, he ventured the opinion that this had probably been their last sortie to Nicosia, and that the Cyprus phase of their lives—if there were such a thing—had ended.

When he unkeyed his microphone, he was strangely affected. He had come as close as he could ever recall to explicitly associating his professional life with the various torments and agonies of his personal life. Suddenly the dark, evil thing that he had caged so brutally since Thursday afternoon, when he had knocked on her door and told her what he wanted her to do, came free.

He could no longer ignore it.

He had been paid to honor a trust, and he had violated it.

He had taken the matter into his own hands, involved her in his rinky-dink scheme, ultimately been outfoxed, but in the process, he had betrayed the "special trust and confidence" placed in him by his country. And as reality came crashing down upon him, the enormity of his betrayal and the total criminality of his actions washed over him and he had to physically grasp the edge of the Navigation table to stem the shocky weakness creeping over him.

How would this play in front of a long green table?

"Yessir, I fixed it so we would have to go for months, maybe years, without getting anything useful up there. Whose idea? Why mine, sir, mine of course. I know what's best for everybody. Why didn't I report this to my superiors? They'd make me stop, and I didn't want to stop, I liked being with this lady, and besides, she always smelled nice! But we only got the really good stuff because of what I did, what I told the lady to say, I was in control!

Grasping at straws.

You were, were you? Is that why the lady died?

Each of the others was absorbed with his own thoughts, some feeling relief, some incipient nostalgia, as each mile of the gray-blue winter Mediterranean passed underneath, distancing them from the odor of cook fires and gasoline and burning tires in the early morning, from the NAAFI and from Ledra Street and the Chanticleer that was no more, from the sound of the belled geep and the muezzin on the minaret spire, from all that was.

Incredible as it had been, they all seemed to already have known. It was over. Nicosia was over.

They would not be going back.

And when they landed, the Skipper and the Exec and the Duty Officer and all the wives and all the kids and most of the squadron had turned out late on a pewter Sunday afternoon in December, the week before Christmas, to welcome them home.

It was a tradition.

There were even a couple of strangers in the crowd.

39

It was a stroke of luck, a stroke of genius and a good show all 'round.

On Cyprus, Squadron Leader Price, Saturday's Middle East Air Force Command Duty Officer, was eager to please and resourceful enough to do it well. As Coordinating Area Logistics Commander, the Middle East (Royal) Air Force—MEAF - processed all the Air Transport Command traffic in and out of the Eastern Mediterranean, and Price knew exactly what to do when Field Marshall Harding's office called at noon and asked for VIP Transport to London "soonest".

By four PM, a hastily packed Wingfield was well on his way aboard a 211 Squadron Viscount en route to Brindisi. They picked up an hour with the time change westward, and at Brindisi, they joined with one of the only Comets still flying after the disastrous accidents that had grounded the commercial jet fleet that year. The RAF had quietly modified their own six airframes and kept them in service, and it was one of the six, hastily dispatched from Blackbushe, that picked Roger up at the quaint line shack/terminal at Brindisi. It had him at his old club in the City well before midnight, with a fine single malt, and good thoughts about the RAF Transport Command.

He was used to late hours, short sleeps and frequent interruptions in his earlier incarnation in the field, but he marveled at the fact that he felt as good as he did on Sunday morning. He had spent Friday night with the Americans at the Acropole and then on the blower in his office sorting things out. A short kip, then work all Saturday morning, quick pack, say bye to Emma—and Philida, thankfully - five hours total in the air (the new 'jet' was marvelous! - his first jet flight). He breakfasted at the Club, old Pennyworthy had passed on, a new maitre d' in his place. He toyed with the idea of Church at St. Paul's but thought better of it when he considered his agenda.

He had explored as many permutations of the situation as he could, based on what the American pilot had told him. He assumed that the account he had gotten was correct, and he trusted the American, Elfers, instinctively.

But suppose they had not gotten what they had gone after.

Suppose they had, either by misfeasance or default or just plain carelessness, gone through the flight and had recorded nothing at all! What a wonderful way to escape a superior's wrath. The more he thought of it, the more convinced he became that he was on to something. He recalled the old British Music Hall comedy routine about the teacher, the dog and the pupil who could not produce his homework.

Well, why not?"I'm sorry, Mum, but Archibald ate my paper."

But somehow, Elfers did not seem to be the type to pull something like that. He had been so brutally honest, so self accusatory in telling about his relationship with the Czech woman.

Of course, a ploy.

Maybe a ploy.

Maybe not.

When he called Downing Street and explained who he was and why he was calling, the Duty Officer wasted no time in connecting him with Jeffrey Harrison at home. Jeffrey was expecting the call. The tone was all business now, no more old school joking. The PM had discussed his warrant with Harding on the secure phone last evening, and Harrison had been instructed to set up a meeting with Admiral Cassady this afternoon, Sunday.

If Mr. Wingfield would have the kindness to call at the Admiral's residence for luncheon at one this afternoon, the Admiral and Mrs. Cassady would be pleased to make his acquaintance.

"I know him already," Roger said.

"He knows you, too, but that's the way this briefing sheet reads. Have a lovely lunch."

He did. The Cassadys were lovely people and he and the Admiral closeted themselves in the walnut study of the lovely old Georgian House and had a lovely chat. Lovely.

He was amazed, then secretly delighted, to learn how little the Admiral seemed to know about the late events in Cyprus, about the incident in the Black sea, about the fire and about Lieutenant Commander Lewis Elfers, United States Navy. Apparently, his people would be debriefing the crew this afternoon on their return from Malta, the first news of the events.

The phone from the Admiral's Quarters to the Headquarters was a secure line.

Cassady saw no reason to allude to the, now, several, transatlantic phone calls he had enjoyed since the flap started with that message Friday morning. Here it was Sunday at one and in the past twenty four hours, he had spoken in person with the Chief of Naval Operations, the Director of Naval Intelligence, the Chief of Information, the State people in Washington and Moscow and the troops down in Morocco. He would like to have had another chat with the Naval Security Group guy—must be a genius, what a piece of work those guys are!!—but he was on a Military Air Transport Service flight and wasn't due in until later.

And because Wingfield was the kind of a person he was, he began by telling the Admiral, literally, all he knew about the situation and the sources that provided this background, within reason. His sources for the more intimate details of the Cypriot Enosis infrastructure were nobody's business, least of all an American Admiral on his twilight tour. The Admiral, in turn, was as unaffected as a village tobacconist, and they got on famously. He did not, however, get where he was by being naïve, stupid or without guile.

At three-thirty, Wingfield left, with an appointment at 20 Grosvenor Square on the morrow at three, but without the slightest indication of how much the Admiral really knew. About anything.

By four, the Admiral had made up his mind on a course of action and had called his Headquarters, from whence a Secret Priority message had been dispatched to Morocco and had been received and passed to the Eyes Only recipients, Commanders Sterling and Arlen who had arrived there this morning.

In the message, Cassady recapped the Cyprus situation in vague terms, indicating a series of unknowns—based on the latest Wingfield worst-case scenario—and stressing to his two representatives now in Morocco that (a) it was imperative that proof be obtained that the parcel checked in to the Communications Center actually contained sensitive and highly classified material and (b) that it was equally imperative that some documentation be identified to substantiate the interception incident alluded to in the message they had all memorized over the weekend.

If, as Wingfield seemed to want to believe, (a) were true, then it would be difficult, if not impossible, that (b) would exist, given the fate of the parcel. Cassady, a square-shooter by birth, wanted a square-shooter's finale to the incident, and he knew this was the way to get it.

He also directed that the three of them - his two Commanders and the pilot - report to him at the Headquarters not later than 1400Z, two tomorrow afternoon, London time, use of squadron operational assets authorized.

Fly one of those big bastards up here if you have to, but get here.

* * *

In Port Lyautey, Morocco, on Sunday afternoon, Ginny was—at least not yet—feeling well, so Harry Fitzgerald, their next-door neighbor in the Quonsets and his wife, Judy, took the Elfers kids down the hill to the hangar to meet the aircraft when it arrived around sunset. The kids were in the Maintenance Office stringing paper clips and shooting at one another with staplers, while the grown-ups attended to their business and Judy chatted with the other wives.

Lew did the paperwork for Harry, listing the mechanical discrepancies, the "squawks on the bird," signing a yellow sheet for each separate flight so that the engine time and the pilot and crew time could be properly entered into the record. Ginny's condition was not serious, Judy insisted, just a cold, and Harry had given Lew that oblique look they both understood meant that Ginny was in the bag again…or still. With all that had happened and the devastating insight into his own problem that he had had an hour ago, Lew almost hated the thought of going up the hill and taking something else on.

He finished the paperwork and briefed Harry on the fuel starvation experience and the lightning strike and the jury-rigging they had to do to get the jets going. The Chief Electrician had already been buttonholed by Black and White and they were poring over the diagrams in the Erection and Maintenance Manual, trying to replicate their experience for the Chief. They still had not found the missing pages from their own copy of the manual. The other crewmembers were drifting in and out, and the hangar was dotted with little groups of people, at the center of each a flight-suited crewman just off the airplane spinning what sailors everywhere love to hear—a real sea story.

When Lew was done with his paperwork, he went upstairs to the Skipper's office where Mort was being introduced to Stu Sterling and Danny Arlen who had arrived from London in the earlier part of the afternoon. The Chief Yeoman was collecting copies of orders and endorsements. Everyone was in civilian clothes except Lew and Mort, still in flight gear. The Skipper closed his door and asked the Chief to make sure nobody disturbed them, and they all went in and sat on the big easy chairs and on the sofa around the coffee table. It was all very informal, very relaxed, very nonchalant, but everybody was on edge and two conversations started at once, then stopped, with apologetic grins.

"Lew," the Skipper began, "before we get too involved in this, we have to go up to London tomorrow morning, all of us. We'll take 209 and burn jets all the way, if we have to, leave here around seven. Clearances are expedited. Now, what the hell happened?"

"When?" Lew asked, smiling. "Which 'happening' do you want first?"

"Well," the Skipper began, "you were scrubbed on Wednesday, we know, and you flew Thursday night instead. We got your message from Nick direct, and we also got it readdressed from the Staff—I guess you did that, Stu," and Stu nodded.

"Yeah, Lew," Stu said. "We weren't sure RAF Nicosia could find Electronic Countermeasures Squadron Two in their copy of the NATO Communications Guide—you know how the Brits are out there, don't you. We knew you were following the Operation Order to the letter and appreciated it, but we wanted to be sure everyone here knew as much as we did, even if it was going to cause concern."

"What caused the concern?" Lew asked.

There was a second of silence, a missed beat in the conversation. Mort and the Skipper exchanged glances.

"Two things. We were curious about the condition of the aircraft—you said it was broken and we didn't know how badly or if we were going to have to send you another engine or what. Then when we waited around and never got a follow up, we didn't know whether it was a really bum airplane or really bum communications." Of course they would, be, Lew thought. We should have downplayed that or not mentioned it, now that it was all over. Their job would have been to get us back in the air if we were really broken badly. What a goof! Here we thought that the intercept and the fire were the big deal!

Lew answered as best he could.

"We weren't too sure when we wrote that message what the condition of the Beast was. We were sweating the local situation and the spill-out from what happened up North, to be frank. We had fuel exhaustion on all four engines and had performed one of those midnight operations on the electrical system after a bad lightning strike, so we didn't know what to expect. We knew we could fly it if we could get it started and in all the excitement the following night, we should have let you know, but when the thing started up normally on Friday afternoon, we figured we had it knocked and we could get home. What else caused the concern?"

"Well, the local situation and your inability to communicate with us had us worried as well."

"Us too," Lew said. "But it all worked out, finally." The less said the better.

"Beside that," Lew insisted.

It was Danny's turn. "Look, you guys, I just want you all to know that Mort has briefed me on what must be on those wire spools and I've got to say—as the guy who wrote the two messages that put you into this thing—that this has been an absolutely outstanding accomplishment. When we got the requirement tasking from the Naval Security Group, we had our qualms about pulling it off—in fact, we were going to ask them to back off - but the Admiral got a call from the boss of the Group himself and apparently there was a lot of national attention on this thing. Anyway, the Admiral told us to congratulate you on that score, and I think he wants to talk to you personally, Lew. We've spent a lot of Staff hours on you this past weekend and there's a lot you'll all be interested in. Turns out, for example, that this was the last Cyprus run. We'll be running you out of Inçirlik up by Adana from now on."

Suppose, Lew thought, *I said yeah, so I heard, and they said who did you hear it from and I told them.*

Instead, he murmured a quick "Is that so?" and raised his eyebrows and looked appropriately interested in the "news."

Danny purposely omitted the point that determining the actual—not the imputed—content of the wire reels was a top agenda item, but it was difficult to see a way to get that done before they went back to London...principally because he also purposely neglected to discuss—or even mention to the others—that he had quietly taken custody of the wire reels and the logs and provided Mort with an official hand receipt to establish chain-of-custody. The Admiral had insisted.

Lew didn't say anything more, although the Skipper reacted positively.

Then Lew asked, his eyes laughing, mocking them, 'Doesn't anyone want to hear about the damn Flashlight? I thought that's what this huddle was all about."

The others looked at one another apprehensively.

"God Damn it!," the Skipper exploded. He was a mercurial guy, florid of face when excited, and the veins were standing out on his forehead now. "Of course we want to hear about it, Lew! Let's get to it, come on, come on" and he slammed his hand down on his desk.

"Yes. Of course," Danny said. "The Admiral wants to hear about it too. The Brits want to. The Turks want to. The State Department and the Pentagon and the goddam President would want to if they knew about it but nobody has said a word about it officially. It is as if the incident never happened, but we'll want to get a complete minute-by-minute account. The only indication we have that anything like that occurred is that one sentence in your message from Cyprus. So right now, the Flashlight is a non-problem. And that's not what this huddle is all about."

Oh, oh.

"Then tell me," Lew said. "What the hell's going on?"

The Skipper was beside himself. Lew gave him a claming sign, and looked Danny in the eye.

"Well," Danny began. "Seems like we've got one of those damn security breech things on our hands."

Oh oh.

Lew was confused, uncomfortable, ashamed and just about devastated. In the course of the next thirty minutes, he managed to keep his calm, answer—or evade effectively—each of the questions that would require an explicitly incriminating answer.

He and Mort did, with the assistance of Wagoner who was called in to help in the details, provide sufficiently compelling and corroborated narratives of the flight and the interception to completely persuade the two Staff members of the genuineness of their report. Mort was able to produce the handwritten flight logs of the radar intercepts, and Wagoner's notes contained times, frequencies, transmission summaries and comments that were entirely persuasive. Nobody mentioned the wires.

They agreed that Wagoner would accompany them to London and as the two Commanders left the flight line area for the Officers Club, they both began to realize that despite what they both felt in their gut, neither (a) nor (b) had been nailed down. There was no proof whatever of what was in the package left at the Centre. If the wire spools and the logs were in that package, how did it survive a fire that killed a half dozen people and end up now, on Sunday afternoon, in Danny's brief case? If something else, what?

Was Lew lying, and was everyone else in on it? The wires held the key to what had started out as an unexplained detail, but the more they thought about it…well, there was one way to find out. Tomorrow in London. Showtime. Danny patted the round bulges through the thick leather case and felt a little chill.

The Admiral was way ahead of them. But then, that's what he got paid for.

And Winnie Barnet was way ahead of the Admiral, if the truth were known, and his Military Air Transport Service flight was landing at Mildenhall right about now.

As the others milled around after the meeting, Lew quietly asked Mort about the wires. Surely they could put them on a playback machine in the shop and…

And then he learned that it was all out of his hands.

He was devastated.

40

Monday, the flight up to London was actually exciting for the two Commanders who had never been in a Beast before and never seen a hybrid jet-piston aircraft perform such tricks.

They leveled off at twelve thousand feet just south of Larache, on the border between Spanish and what last month was French Morocco, and cruised at an indicated airspeed of 285 knots, giving them a true airspeed around 325 and a ground speed fast enough to get them into the London Control Zone with plenty of time to spare. The Skipper flew—he had insisted on coming along. The enlisted crew newly home from Nicosia had the day off.

Once chocked, the five officers piled out of the Beast and quickly pulled off whatever pieces of flight gear they had put on over their blues, and piled into the Staff sedan that had come to Blackbushe to fetch them. They were in the office by one.

Grosvenor Square was laid out by Sir Richard Grosvenor in the eighteenth century and its buildings had been the homes of the elite for three centuries. John Adams, the first American Ambassador, lived at Number 9 and Americans of importance had clustered around the Embassy building at Number One since the thirties. CINCNELM was headquartered in Number 20, a red brick Neo-Georgian affair that looked like a block of upper-middle-class flats on the west side of the square. Outside, the American Flag, Cassady's personal four-star Admiral's flag and a plaque noting the building's use in 1942 by Eisenhower marked it as American territory. The postman knew it as 7 North Audley Street, where the second entrance had been lately added around the corner.

As they pulled up in front of the building, their driver pointed out the other buildings around the square and took pains, as he probably always did with all newcomers with American accents, to note that the American lease on the property prohibits occupants from hanging clothes or other washing out the windows to dry and keeping "any living fowls" on the premises and would they be kind enough to comply with these restrictions.

It got a laugh.

Once up on the second floor, Mort, Wagoner and Danny Arlen disappeared into a secure work area at the end of the passageway, and Stu brought the Skipper and Lew in to meet with the Chief of Staff. He had purposely been left out of the weekend merrymaking, and he felt both relieved and honored not to have to mess with them. The visit was cordial and perfunctory, a courtesy really, and as Stu showed them around the building, the clock ticked out to two.

In the work room, Arlen felt like a fifth wheel as the tension—or was it the relief from tension—crackled through the air as the other four went through the motions each felt most appropriate to mask strong urges to hug and embrace one another. Winnie Barnet grabbed Mort's hand, Jennifer not so overcome as to be indiscreet in her pleasure at seeing Wagoner, but almost so, in her not-quite-appropriate First Class Petty Officer hug of a Lieutenant.

After all, she had started him on his way last Tuesday! Wagoner was visibly surprised, pleasantly beyond words, but that's another story.

Surprisingly, most of the communications between the three Nebraska Avenue Security Group types in that charged few minutes was wordless, each now understanding how masterfully the game had been played, two of them in awe of the Coach, the Coach proud and edified by his players.

Arlen didn't get any of this. He wasn't supposed to.

Promptly at two, they all presented themselves in the anteroom and MacGregor showed them into the Admiral's office. The aviators sensed the presence of a fellow aviator almost immediately, and before long, Arlen, Mort, Wagoner and a fourth person Lew would have been surprised to learn was a female enlisted Communications Technician in civilian clothes wheeled in a cart with a trio of black boxes resembling radio receivers. Lew recognized them as mates of the wire recorders at the Pluto station in the Beast. They were hooked up to a pair of amplifiers and two speakers, and a cathode ray oscilloscope.

As they were positioning the cart, the door opened again and another man in civilian clothes entered, warmly greeted by the Admiral and by Mort, deferentially by Wagoner. For a moment, Lew couldn't place him, and then, suddenly, he saw behind the civilian clothes and through the thicket and brambles of his own troubles and as their eyes locked, Lew was transported back in time, face to face once again with Winnie Barnet. He could not shake the feeling Winnie's eyes were almost literally devouring him, that the last of the protective windings around the place where Lewis Chambers Elfers really lived were being painfully ripped away, but that somehow, some way, it was going to be all right. It was the damndest feeling.

Cassady introduced the Commander of the Naval Security Group, and they all moved toward the polished walnut Conference table in the office as he called for them to take seats. As he pulled back his chair, Lew glanced once more at Barnet, unable to shake the unbearable feeling that the man was reading his thoughts.

Before the Admiral sat down, he went over to his desk and flipped one of the switches on the inter communications box on his desk. He spoke into the box.

"Chief, please hold all calls and don't let anybody in for the next half hour or so."

"Aye, aye, Admiral," MacGregor responded.

Cassady sat at the east end of the polished conference table, between the waist-high windows overlooking the Square, still in December gray. In the corner, on a quad stand, stood the flags of the United States, the United States Navy, Great Britain and his personal flag with the four white stars on a plain field of blue. Thin sunlight backlit the Admiral, but as they were sitting down he nodded to Arlen who reached over and switched on the overhead light, a plain white-globe affair that spoiled the solemnity of the setting but lighted the room effectively. On an easel to the Admiral's right, Stu had taped a large-area Aviation Planning Chart, showing the Eastern Mediterranean, Turkey, the Black Sea and the territory to the east as far as Pakistan. The crew had planned the flight two weeks ago on a copy of the same Chart.

The Admiral knew how to conduct a meeting.

"Gents," he began, then graciously "I mean *Lady* and Gents," and he smiled, breaking the ice. Jennifer was flattered. Lew wondered who she was, but noticed that Wagoner obviously knew her and she knew him. Well.

"We've got a very complicated situation here. We haven't got a lot of time to take care of things—in an hour the British government guy will be here—and we have got to get as any facts out on this table as we possibly can before he comes. He was at the Quarters Sunday for lunch and he told me the whole story—as you told it to him, I might add—about the business at the, what was it, 'Chanticleer', in Cyprus Friday night."

He was addressing Lew directly.

"I must admit that he got my attention with the tale of your relationship with the Czech lady—that was pretty dumb—but he seemed to feel that you had done whatever it was you did with a secondary objective of keeping your troops from getting shot at."

Except for Mort and Wagoner, and probably Winnie, none of the others had a full grasp of what the Admiral was talking about, but the enormity of the situation and its expanded scope got their attention. He took about five minutes to sketch elements of the whole story to the others, and Lew admired the superb job he did. Jennifer was astounded at the accuracy of her own hunches.

"Now, the Brits lost their man in the fire, and they will do anything to keep his memory clean and their skirts out of the mud. Anything. He was probably a scoundrel, but there's no way of knowing—he could have been doing everybody a favor, or thought he was doing everybody a favor, in which case, he is not quite so awful. Maybe even a hero."

Jennifer, for some reason, caught Mort's eye at that precise moment and a look passed between them. They both glanced obliquely at Winnie, who simply ignored them.

"They—the Brits - are hinting," he went on, "that you made up the story about the interception by the Flashlights and engineered the theft and destruction of the parcel to cover your ass. That you had come back empty-handed and were afraid of the repercussions."

Again he looked at Lew.

Lew was horrified. He had never even dreamed of that interpretation. He instinctively started to speak, to protest, and the Admiral held up his hand.

"I have a 'pro' bias here, but it seems to me that if there was an interception and if there was a valuable collection event in the Black Sea Thursday night and if we do have evidence of it, then any imputation that you were deceiving anybody…let me put that another way…that you were covering an unsuccessful mission by faking results and then 'loosing' them…goes away.

"So," he said, turning to face the cart. "This is the moment of truth. Let's hear the music!"

Lew's heart was in his mouth. Suppose that there *had* been a wire malfunction, suppose that the electrical disaster in the Beast *had* filled the wire reels with artifacts, effectively blanking everything out, suppose…the wire was blank! Nobody had ever really heard the recordings. My God!

Show time.

One amplifier speaker on the signals recorder, the other on the radio and internal communication tracks, the two synchronized against a common time signal generated within the system.

Mort and Wagoner got up and fiddled with dials until a blast of high pitch, ear-shattering squealing filled the room and they adjusted the volume and the squealing subsided into a steady clicking. That would have both the audio and the video trace of the intercepted signals, the eerie green oscilloscope now glowing with dancing pulses chasing one another across its face.

Lew's heart sank.

"Search radar," Mort said quietly, whispering, facing the others, describing the clicking filling the room. They all watched the green trace on the smallish round dial. There wasn't anything else going on. The tension was unbearable. Almost immediately, the second speaker came alive with a burst of unintelligible speech.

Lew relaxed.

"Routine chatter on their Ground Control frequency" Wagoner said, matter-of-factly.

And so it went. The Ground Control frequency became more active, Wagoner translated the taxi request, the runway, weather and altimeter settings and the other speaker began to reflect a subtle, then obvious change in noise pattern as the operators switched to the closer-in radars and the more discriminating air search equipment. Mort kept up a running commentary. Everyone was fascinated.

Time sped by, and in what seemed like an instant, they had switched to the tower frequency, then to the air-to-air tactical frequency, then Wagoner toggled in the aircraft interphone dialogue and piggy-backed it on the second reel. The memory of the night became alive, the reports from Mickey, the air heavy with suspense.

"Pilot, Tail, here one comes, I can see him way off against a cloud heading for us."

"No fire, no fire!" Lew yelling into the mike.

"No fire, aye!" Lucore responding.

Simultaneously, the accompanying hideous howl as the pitch and the repetition rate of the clicks became squeals and then screams and then shrieks in the paneled office on a Monday afternoon in London, England, as everyone in the room heard and saw, for the first time the West, recordings of the airborne Fire-Control Kilo Band Kiterest and Foxtrot Band Farmfish radars.

Jennifer had months and years of signal intelligence experience, and her hands were shaking and her mouth was dry.

Winnie sat as if in a trance, smiling idiotically, had anyone noticed.

Mort turned the gear off and looked at the group.

"Gentlemen, that's what you sent us out there to get and that's what we've brought you."

Lew was almost—not quite, but almost—overwhelmed with relief. Half of his dragon had been slain. He thought fleetingly of Marta.

The Admiral was visibly impressed by what he heard and seen, not that he had a technician's appreciation for the pitches and clicks and screams out of the amplifier and the jiggling lines on the scope, but by the professionalism and, goddamit, heroism, of these guys. He said so.

"But what in the hell was in that package?" he asked Lew.

"Cans of tuna fish," Lew answered, quietly," and some wiring diagrams."

And then he told them how it had gotten there.

And why.

And then, he thought, there weren't any secrets any longer.

Mort, remembering the last minute phone call from Winnie, kept his own counsel, just as he had managed to keep his own fish, the real fish, inside the boat.

The real "why".

41

The Admiral kept Wingfield waiting almost a quarter hour, convinced that he had the whole story, or at least as much of the whole story as anybody else had, including Wingfield. More, actually, since he had heard the recordings, seen the traces and knew why the package had exploded in the heat of the Chanticleer fire.

Lew had been forthcoming, embarrassingly so, and if Winnie Barnet and Danny Arlen had been quietly upset with some of his revelations about the security issues on Cyprus, they kept it to themselves. The Admiral had thanked them all and reassured them that he would handle the rest of the details.

On his part, Wingfield was convinced that he had a political solution to a difficult situation in his grasp. And so he did.

He assumed that the material that had been destroyed was, indeed, the packet of wire recordings and the data that went with the packet. He had no reason in the world to assume otherwise.

He knew St. John had stolen it, but was still unclear on the old rogue's motives. If the Americans were to assert that classified material - valuable, critical, classified material - left in custody in a simple lock-box had somehow subsequently been removed and accidentally destroyed in a civilian setting, they would be forced to divulge the nature of the material and, hence, indicate their involvement in snooping into, if not actually penetrating Soviet airspace.

The Soviet intelligence apparatus would of course learn the details in short order, regardless of the ingenuity and intricacy of the cover-up, and consider their precious radars compromised. The role of the American pilot would be made known, considering the tenaciousness of Fleet Street, furthering the embarrassment factor for the Yanks, and US-UK relations might become strained at the junctures. Even without press coverage, the Yanks had an embarrassment on their hands, one of their own caught wandering down the wrong path.

If, on the other hand, the Americans were to quietly acquiesce, give up their claim, however valid it might be, and accept the fact that their precious classified packet had indeed been carelessly stowed, then filched as the end game in a process their own pilot had initiated, it would be seen as a diplomatic victory for Wingfield and would greatly benefit the Cyprus effort.

It was unfortunate that the poor Elfers would be taking it on the bum for all this, but he certainly had it coming. He rather liked the Yank, though, and regretted doing it to him. He knew all that the crew had gone though to get their precious wire reels, but there would be other opportunities.

But not from Cyprus.

The meeting was cordial, but there was no doubt in either mind that two slick operators were having a go at it.

"Well, Counselor," Cassady began, consulting his typed notes. "I think I've gotten to the bottom of your problem. Speaking now in my capacity, whatever it is, in all this, the 'American side', I guess, makes no representation that any classified material or devices were mishandled by anyone associated with Her Majesty's Government."

Wingfield showed no emotion. A seasoned Queen's Counsel, a difficult case, a favorable verdict. No emotion. Just a little tug at the corners of the mouth.

"The material that went missing in Cyprus last, when was it, Friday some time, was personal in nature, of trivial value, and subsequently replaced. I have no intention of saying any more about the issue, but since I understand you have heard the sordid story from our Lieutenant Commander Elfers' lips, you can appreciate the…shall we say, chagrin and embarrassment that underlies our desire to drop the matter here."

He thought Wingfield looked tired. He must be exhausted after all this, and he'll probably want to get back home tonight.

He also looked greatly relieved.

Score one for Britain.

"Secondly, we have concluded that in view of the totality of the circumstances, there is no plausible reason to suspect duplicity on the part of the American crew. The packet was turned over to your people, but our investigation indicates that if you pursue this matter further, you will find that there was no representation whatever of its content nor of classification. It was simply a 'left parcel', as your English expression goes, as in a train station, without markings, and no receipt was asked for or tendered. So, as to any suspicion that you may have had as to the motives of the American crew, I believe we have a non-issue that you probably will want to put to rest in your mind. There was no intent, nor was there any reason, to dissimulate or deceive anyone. Between us, I believe that avenue is closed. It never should have been opened. It was unworthy of you, but I understand what you were after.

"Now, as to the supposed incident involving the Soviet aircraft and the unfortunate accident that has been rumored to have taken place that evening: we have no information that we can add to the skimpy details that have been made known unofficially. We have received no official word from the Soviets, and I understand that the only basis for interest in this line of investigation is the interpretation of some remarks by their Air Attaché on Friday. For the record, our subsequent investigation indicates that one of our aircraft on a training mission over international waters was in the *general geographic area* rumored—and I would stress that word because we have had no official dialogue on the matter - *rumored* to be the site of a possible single aircraft mishap, but the crew was regrettably unable to provide any corroborating details upon debrief.

"Finally, we are obviously unable to affirm or deny any indication at this time that any information of an intelligence nature was gathered by the crew of the aircraft that flew last Thursday night. This is in accordance with our longstanding agreements on this issue, which, as you know, are a matter of official record. I might point out, that the interests of both of our Governments require the greatest amount of delicacy on your part in dealing with the intelligence aspect of any operations conducted by us with your concurrence and clearance, from British soil.

"Now," he said, looking up. "The connection between these three statements is yours to make, of course. Notice, I've been reading. The wording is important, and the wording shall so appear in the Memorandum For the Record, the *aide memoire,* that I'll be delighted to provide to you and to our record. It will, of course, be of appropriate classification and I'll forward it to you through channels dictated by that classification.

"The fact that there is no reason to believe that your Mr. St. John was in any way connected with improper handling of any United States governmental material puts us out of your loop and effectively means that there is no reason, based on our interests, for us to involve ourselves in his actions or explore his culpability, nor, need you continue to inform us on this matter.

"Our statement regarding the whereabouts of our aircraft, similarly, means that there is no reason for us to issue any further statement regarding denial of involvement in the aforementioned accident. Accordingly, I guess, no further comment on that issue is appropriate. And the least said about Mr. Elfers the better."

Slick. Some lies, perhaps, here and there, but slick lies, skillfully worded.

They shook hands and Wingfield left for his Club.

He liked the world as it looked from his perspective when he got there.

As far as the world knows, St. John's activities were his own personal business, and his successor can continue in whatever footsteps he pleases. St. John died in the line of duty. Rest his soul. The Americans are embarrassed and without the electronic intelligence they craved so badly, and they can continue to chase after it from Turkey. They will crucify that pilot, blame the loss of their package on him, but they're out of my hair. Nobody has anything to offer that indicates any knowledge of an aircraft accident on the night of December 15th. The Russians have nothing to bitch about.

Harding will be relieved.

He sat in his favorite leather chair, relaxing, ready to confront the only piece of the puzzle that had bedeviled him since he had so eloquently explained things to the Field Marshal on Saturday.

Hawkins had access to the actual flight plans before any of the previous flights had taken off. He had read each message in the file when it had been received.

Assuming he was in contact with Krisler, there was no need for the Marty woman to be involved at all. All she must have been needed for was to confirm that she had been asked to "decoy" a flight.

With the actual track in hand, confirmed by the fact that the Yank had asked her to lie about it, there was never any doubt on the Soviet side as to when they came calling. They made sure they did not "illuminate" the target, and their precious gems were safe. It was a double safety arrangement, had been for years.

On Thursday night, both "safeties" failed. Why?

"Hormones," he had suggested on Saturday, knowing well that Marta Marty nee Czrodny was well beyond the age or the constitution for hormonal susceptibility. No, something, someone else.

"Suppose, "he began, to himself. "Suppose…" It couldn't be.

Couldn't it?

The Americans.

Of course.

It had to be.

Someone had gotten to both Hawkins and the woman, someone with a greater claim to them than Krisler's money, someone had persuaded them that this last Boomerang thing had to be a success from the American viewpoint, and so it had been.

What the nameless, faceless Americans had not anticipated, however, had proven them not as clever as they thought.

Hawkins had plucked their defeat from the jaws of victory, and the precious wire recordings were burned to a crisp.

He and the woman had kept up their part of the bargain, and they had double crossed the double crosser.

If only the Yanks had anticipated Hawkins' larceny.

42

Lew went with Stu to the Operations Office after the show-and-tell with the Admiral broke up, just before three. Years of practice in handling and compelling and denying his emotions gave him the ability to focus on the conversation now, a conversation about altitudes and flap-limiting speeds and gear-down low-altitude maneuverability over water at night, lightning strikes, fuel starvation.

It was "pilot talk, "fascinating to Stu, and it caused Lew to concentrate on something other than the empty pit in the center of his gut, black and dark, about to swallow him.

The Admiral had told Lew to stand by for a "short discussion" and when Chief MacGregor appeared at Stu's door, he knew the summons had arrived.

When he entered the office, the Admiral was ushering Captain Barnet out. They shook hands warmly in passing, each keeping to the script, and the Admiral motioned Lew to sit in the chair that had been drawn up next to what he assumed was the Admiral's chair behind the desk.

Cassady returned to this chair in a moment, and Lew sat facing him as he slewed the easy chair around to face his visitor. The desk was clear, completely free of any traces of bureaucracy, save for a desk pen set, a coffee cup inscribed "Operation High Jump—South Pole" and the intercommunications box Lew had seen him use earlier. One of the amber lights flicked on as they sat. He had a file folder open before him. The wheeled cart was gone and everything left behind from the earlier meeting had disappeared except the easel with the chart of the area. Lew was glad to see a familiar object.

Cassady looked him square in the eye for a moment, and Lew did his best to return his gaze. Something passed between them.

"What the hell am I going to do with you?" the Admiral began.

"Here you carry on an affair with a known hostile for a couple of years and you justify it by saying that it helped to save the lives of the crews. I'm convinced that's what you thought, but all you were really doing was fooling yourself and compromising your own position."

Lew thought quietly for a moment, searching for the right response.

"I know, Sir. I have had a long time to think about it since the fire."

The Admiral seemed to consider what he had said, the he looked down at the file in front of him and back at Lew.

"Then you fly that bird of yours off into the darkest night of the year, in thunderstorms, evade hostile interceptors and put one in the drink without firing a shot, take a lightning hit, run out of gas on short final and bring back the electronic intelligence coup of the year. A Great job!"

He smiled then, almost proudly.

"But…then…you stupidly leave what you believe to be the fruit of all your labors in a rinky-dink box with the padlock off your gym locker or something, and when it turns up in the middle of a five-alarm fire, you unsuccessfully risk your ass to get it back! Thank God for old Mort Gross and his Jewish premonition. I'm sorry about whatever emotional loss you may have felt about your girlfriend, but you do have a wife and kiddies and I feel for them, under the circumstances.

"What the hell are you, a hero? A dupe? An idiot? You're not a failure, by any means, but I don't think you consider yourself a roaring success, either."

There it was, Lew thought, as stark a statement of his own introspective conclusions as he would ever hear, from a stranger. Bad enough a stranger. But a four-star stranger?

Then a glimmer of light began to glow in his dark mood, and Lew felt himself stiffen, felt his own feeling of self worth slowly, almost imperceptibly, grow.

"Well, I thought I was doing the right thing with the parcel in the Comm Shack, Admiral. We'd done it that way for two years because the difficulty in obtaining secure stowage for anything on Cyprus was always a challenge, particularly at four in the morning. I also thought I was doing the right thing with Marta, and it turned out that by her doing what I asked her to do, we got the stuff we heard earlier. Coincidence?"

The Admiral almost scowled, but then he looked down a second and when he raised his eyes toward Lew again, they were gentler.

"They say that something called 'coincidence' is the luck of the battlefield. So what you're saying is that you're not an idiot—and I believe you—and you were not a dupe and the way things turned out was the luck of the battlefield. That coincidence was at work? Something like that?"

"I never thought about coincidence, but maybe there was some of it, yes Sir."

"Let me tell you about coincidence. I come from a little town in south central Indiana, Spencer it's called, down in Owen County. Just about as far away from the sea or the ocean as you can get and still be in the USA.

"Well, in August 1943, there was a change-of-command on the Carrier Saratoga out in the Pacific. The Captain was a guy named Hank Mullinix, and he came from - guess where - a little town in Indiana called Spencer. And guess who relieved Hank Mullinix as the Commanding Officer of USS Saratoga?

"I did. The only time in history two guys from a little town in nowhere were principals at the same change of command. Now at the time, the paper in Spencer made over something they called 'coincidence', so I've had a dozen years now to think about what that word means. And I'm not going to tell you what I've come up with and I'm not going to tell you any of the details about how that all happened, but I want you to think about it and try to apply it to your own situation. I have no idea where it will get you. But events and their timing are funny sometimes, and neither Hank nor I would have been there had it not been for prior decisions, random events, Kismet, the Hand of God—whatever—that probably had nothing to do with either of us directly."

The Admiral checked his watch, as if he wanted to continue at great length, but was out of time. Lew was on the point of begging him to continue, to shed some light on what he was saying because he felt that here, almost in his grasp, was the hint of a thought that could lead him back to his self-respect and his honor and the confidence others thought he possessed innately.

Jack Cassady rose, and Lew got up with him, out of respect now, admiration.

"Here's what I'm going to do here. I'm going to forget about the business with the lady.

"If anybody asks, and I don't think they will, I'm going to stick with the version of the package story I fed to the British, that it was a personal parcel of no value, subsequently replaced.

"I'm going to write to your Skipper and have a nice letter put into your record that may get you promoted some day. If we have to go to war again, I want to be around lucky guys like you.

"And then I want to shake your hand."

And he did.

*   *   *

As he left the office, Lew was surprised to see Captain Barnet sitting in MacGregor's chair behind the desk in the anteroom, and the woman who been with them during the audio session seemed to be briefing him about flight times and transportation arrangements. Winnie introduced him to Jennifer as an "associate" of his, and they were joined in a minute by David Wagoner. David warmly thanked Lew for his "experiences" over the last few days, and they shook hands as two recent strangers, now comrades in arms.

Lew gathered that David would be going back on a commercial flight with Captain Barnet and the attractive Eurasian woman, and he wished them all well. He could not help the strange sense of—what?—alienation, perhaps, certainly mystery, as he began to sense that the three of them were all connected together in some way that had involved him, conspirators maybe, in something he did not quite understand.

They passed a moment of pleasantries before Lew hurried off to round up the other squadron people for what promised to be an evening of unspeakably joyous celebration in some unimaginably restrained setting that only the Brits could provide on short notice, but it was a festive time in London, a week before Christmas, and they would make the most of it.

Winnie Barnet watched him leave down the hall, and turned inquisitively to Jennifer and David. The look that passed between them was wholly theirs, difficult to describe.

She flipped the button down and the amber light went off on the box by the phones, but they both continued to stare at the intercom for a moment, until they looked back at one another and realized it was over.

They turned, then, and walked unannounced onto the Admiral's office, while David took MacGregor's chair and looked over his airline ticket.

The Admiral was behind the desk, eyebrows raised in question, as he reached for the toggle switch under the amber light on his intercom box.

"Did you get all that?" he asked Winnie.

"Got it all. Masterful job, Admiral. Was all that true about Mullinix?"

"Sure," he said, a twinkle in his eye. "Think he bought all that crap about coincidence?"

"Think he had a choice?" Winnie asked, as fleeting images of Marta and St. John and Krisler flashed through his mind.

"You, sir," the Admiral said slowly, "are a master."

Epilogue

And so, with the last of the sessions in London, the Boomerangs were over.

They changed the name to Parsifal after the first of the year, which did nothing for anybody, and elevated it officially to Code Word status, just adding to the paper work. After a couple of dry runs to check the place out, they began flights from Turkey in March 1956. They never went back to Nick.

It wasn't the same in Inçirlik, although Adana had its charms. Caviar and white wine were cheap, haircuts cost a dime, but the toilets in town were something else again. There was a real base there, finally, but they slept in tents and then trailers for the first year until it got organized.

Petty Officer Burdick found a good supplier of rugs, and with the Turkish exchange rate advantage, everybody bought gold rings. Black and White now have Turkish in their repertoire and Timmons carries two quill shafts everywhere he flies.

Bob Hunley figured that one day when he had to go back and finish that dissertation on the Law of the Air, he'd be able to write from first-hand experience. But what was he going to write?

Lew's okay. He and Ginny seem to have come together more, recently, and they seem to be in it for the long run. She's not drinking, but that's just today. Check again tomorrow.

And Brian still has his ideal. Shirley still envies Lew.

Admiral Cassady thought about putting them all in for medals but after a chat with Barnet, decided that there were enough skeletons in the closet to warrant, instead, a nice, classified letter to the Skipper commending them all. Classified heroes. There were a lot of them, and more coming, he thought. Besides, he always thought there was more satisfaction in keeping a secret than in sharing one. The following May, when he turned sixty, he retired. Folks around Spencer, Indiana, would see him now and then, until he moved south.

Captain Winnie Barnet had a smile on his face all through the January Quarterly. The bills had finally been posted, and he had, after all, just bought a new farm. He had a right to gloat, and he did.

Jennifer was commissioned Ensign, US Navy, in February 1957 and shortly thereafter became Mrs. David Wagoner. They both retired in 1972 and became expatriates—the good kind—in Denmark. They write Travel Books.

Wingfield never could figure out why the packet of wire reels had exploded in the fire.

Afterword

Most of this story is set on the island of Cyprus in 1955, in a far different time and place.

Fifty years of headlines have shaped the world since those tense and tentative days, and the changes that have occurred on Cyprus have been every bit as cataclysmic as those affecting the broader global community, but far less well known.

By 1955, the British had left Egypt in consolidating their interests in the region, and moved their military headquarters to Nicosia, the ancient capital of the Crown Colony island of Cyprus. Nasser was becoming a political force to be reckoned with the Middle East, and the ancient Greek-Turkish enmity on Cyprus was beginning to play out against the broader global political bi-polarization. Cyprus seethed with agitation for change.

The Greek majority actively sought *enosis,* or union with Greece, the Turkish minority bitterly opposed it, and so began the "troubles".

As the British further consolidated their political responsibilities, the Greek Cypriot Archbishop Makarios became president of a "free and independent "Cyprus in a political solution that pleased no one. After a decade and a half of "freedom and independence" - perceived by many to pertain only to the Greek-speaking majority - Turkey invaded Cyprus to right what it considered the deplorable situation of the Turkish Cypriots.

The current division of the island along the "Green Line" still separating the two communities is the result. The Green Line runs through Nicosia—now called Lefkosia—and the northern part of the city and of the country itself is under Turkish mandate today. *Enosis* never happened, although now, a half century later, progress toward political pluralism has a fair chance to supplant the enforced apartness of the two cultures.

Readers of fact-based fiction are sometimes confused between the facts and the fictions. Patrick O'Brian's Aubrey novels of the Royal Navy in the Napoleonic War are replete with historical characters who are made to speak and act and influence the story, and to a lesser, far less classic extent, so is this one.

To set the record straight, the incidents forming the core of this story are completely imaginary, yet the places and times in which the story "happens" are, in some cases, accurately described. Some liberties have been taken with the geography of downtown Nicosia, which may annoy or confound seasoned travelers to the old city, and some of the peripheral events—the burning of the British Institute, for example—occurred a few months earlier. Grosvenor Square is, of course, Grosvenor Square and Number 20 is there for all to inspect. CINCNELM, alas, became CINCUSNAVEUR—Commander in Chief, U. S. Naval Forces, Europe.

Field Marshall Harding was a historical figure and his background, as presented here, is a matter of record. So were Admirals "Thirty-One-Knot" Burke and Jack Cassady. Admiral Cassady did grow up in Spencer, Indiana, and did indeed relieve Hank Mullinix, also from Spencer, in USS Saratoga, in August 1943. His two aviator Commanders, Sterling and Arlen, are fictional. Field Marshall Harding's career is accurately described, but of course, Wingfield's parallel career is imaginary. Jimmy Flatley, Roy Johnson, Butch O'Hare and Harold Lorenzen really existed, great figures from that period.

Some Code Words and Nicknames are historically correct—"Mickey" and Pluto," for example; "Boomerang," "Billposter" and the use of the pet name "Beast" are not. Care has been taken to accurately describe the strengths and weaknesses of the "Beast," but the aircraft itself no longer exists and the author has had to rely on memory in making engineering sense of a great number of his recollections. That the "Beast" strongly resembles one of the eight or nine P4M-1Q aircraft once operated by the Navy in obscure parts of the world is just one of those coincidences that writers of fiction always disclaim.

A few—but not many - liberties with time and place have been taken in the telling of this tale, for it is—in every respect—a "tale". Except for the village of Aga Episcopu (which is a composite, even in name, of a Greek and Turkish village), actual locations are the backdrops, and effort has been made to describe them accurately. The Acropole Hotel is no more, closed as a result of the 1974 invasion, and the property has been converted to a private English high school. The Chanticleer and other such places that offered cabaret for both sexes to enjoy no longer exist on Cyprus. Some places still have live Greek music and some kind of dance shows, but they are mainly for Greek dancing instead of any kind of performance. For the record, the Acropole and the Chanticleer were never commonly owned, and the relationship between the two establishments in the book is entirely fictional. The end of the Chanticleer came with a whimper, not with the fictionalized bang described, and it handsomely survived the troubles of 1955.

Finally, except as noted above, all the protagonists are fictional characters. Any resemblance in name, description, action or personality is completely coincidental.

The pressures and tensions and satisfactions experienced by real persons who were placed in similar situations are, however, largely as described.

Glossary

Air Almanac. The publication of the United States Hydrographic Office listing the minute to minute astronomical data on selected heavenly bodies required to perform in-flight celestial navigation.

Aldis lamp. A bright, focused lamp with changeable colored lenses that can be easily and accurately pointed as a signaling device.

Auxiliary Power Unit. APU's can be mobile power carts, full sized power supply vehicles or in-aircraft mounted auxiliary generators and air conditioners. They are used to supply power to aircraft for starting and for ground operations when the engines are not in use.

Axial Flow. Said of jet engines and their components if air passes through the engine on a straight path parallel to the fore and aft axis of the engine. The YAK-25 "Flashlight" had axial engines. They tend to be long and skinny.

Bird Dog. A radio compass. It points to the radio station the operator has tuned in.

Bren Gun Carrier. A light armored vehicle to carry infantry across ground denied by small-arms fire and, specifically, the Bren light machine gun and its team.

Catalina. The venerable PBY seaplane used by the Navy for sea based patrol operation throughout World war II.

Centrifugal Flow. Said of jet engines and their components if air passes around the axis of the engine on a plane perpendicular to the axis. The Beast's J-33 jet engines had centrifugal compressors. They were big and round.

Civil Air Ministry. The British Civil Air Ministry operated the civilian aviation activities out of RAF Nicosia and shared facilities with the RAF. It operated the civilian terminal and handled air cargo and passengers into and out of Nicosia in close liaison with the military.

Corncob Engine. The Beast's R-4360-24WA reciprocating engines had 28 cylinders in four banks of seven. Smaller engines were thinner (fewer banks) and the size of the 4360 gave it its nickname. Each engine developed 3500 horsepower, about one HP per pound of weight.

Dighenis Akritas. The code name for Colonel Grivas, the EOKA leader, derived from the name of the Greek hero who defended Cyprus from the Saracens.

Dzeus fittings. A kind of screw attachment that holds covers and cowlings tight to their frames but are easy to loosen with a simple turn.

E6B Plotter. A small (pocket size) plotter used to plot true and magnetic courses (headings) required to make good a desired track over the ground, based on forecast wind direction and velocity entries.

Enosis. The union of Cyprus with Greece, sought by the Greek (Christian) community on Cyprus and bitterly opposed by the Turkish (Moslem) community.

En-route Supplement. A publication listing every aeronautical facility within a geographical area with detailed information on frequencies, runways, administrative requirements and other data of interest to pilots and navigators.

EOKA. In Greek, Ethnikí Orgánosis Kipriakoú Agónos, the guerilla organization advocating Cypriot union with Greece.

Fingerprint (radar). The frequency, pulse width, pulse repetition frequency, antenna rotation rate and beam shape of an intercepted radar signal. Every radar model has unique fingerprints, which, when known, assist opponent forces in developing countermeasures and evasion techniques.

Fire Bottle. A CO_2 fire extinguisher. It is usually manned by an outside observer during engine start on large reciprocating engines.

Fiscal Year. In 1955, the US government's Fiscal year began on October 1st. All funding authorized and appropriated by Congress came on-stream on that date, but the claimants for "out-year" funds had a 36 to 40 month cycle to develop legislative requests that would lead to more funds.

Flux Gate Compass. A refined magnetic compass. The Earth's magnetic field produces small electric phase-shifts, which are converted to a voltage and read on a dial indicating compass heading.

G2. Military Intelligence. On Cyprus during the troubles, G2 handled all prisoner interrogations.

HO-214. A Hydrographic Office publication giving the altitudes of selected stars at selected positions and times to assist the celestial navigator.

ICS. The Internal Communications System or intercom within the aircraft. In the Beast, switches at each station controlled connections between stations, but four of the stations had an extra switch to connect to the radios for transmission. In radio silence, these switches had to be carefully monitored to insure no inadvertent transmissions were made.

IFR (Instrument Flight Rules). Ground controllers assume responsibility for flight monitoring and altitude assignment. Pilot need not have sufficient visibility to avoid other aircraft.

J-33. The Manufacturer's (Allison) designation for the two jet engines in the nacelles of the Beast underneath the piston driven propeller engines. They had a centrifugal compressor with an axial turbine and weighed 1800 pounds.

Latitude by Polaris. Polaris, the "North Star" sits in the sky over the north pole. A measurement of the height of Polaris above the celestial horizon provides the observer with his own latitude, which is a measure of the observer's angular distance from the equator.

Martin Mariner. The Navy's first-line sea-based patrol aircraft ("Splash boat) (officially the PBM series) in the forties. It was replaced in the fifties by the P5M Marlin aircraft, a larger and more capable sea-based aircraft.

Mickey. The term used to refer to the electronic interception, analysis and recording devices and operations in the Beast aircraft, to the area aft of the wing spar in which these devices were located, and to the operators of these devices collectively.

Middle East Force. The British major command of all forces in the eastern Mediterranean and Asia Minor. Middle East Air Force and Royal Army, Middle East, were component commands.

Military Payment Certificate. Currency issued by the Armed Forces after World War II for use by military personnel stationed in overseas areas where black marketeering in "green" US currency could become a problem. MPCs were only redeemable on base and were altered periodically to prevent black marketeering in MPCs themselves.

Milk Wagon. A boxy utility vehicle, similar to those used to deliver milk from house to house in the fifties, used at airports throughout the world to deliver crews and supplies to and from transient aircraft.

Monitorable bus. An electric power distribution point (a "bus') which has been designed to "monitor" the electric load and disconnect certain items in a prearranged sequence in order to insure that power is available for more essential items. In the Beast, jet starts caused several less essential items to turn off until the start had been completed.

NAAFI. As explained in the text, the British equivalent of the Navy Exchange

Naval Security Group. The former name for the Naval Security Group Command, which was established formally as a Command in 1968. Prior to that time, the Group was a staff adjunct to the Office of the Chief of Naval Operations, sometimes referred to simply as "Nebraska Avenue."

P2V-5F. An advanced version of the venerable Neptune anti-submarine aircraft, the standard Navy land-based patrol aircraft. It had two R-3350 reciprocating engines and two J-34 under-wing jets. It was replaced by the P2V-7 and both were redesignated in the sixties, the—5F to the SP-2E and the—7 to the SP-2H.

Petty Officer. Navy non-commissioned officers are called "petty officers" and they are designated by their occupational specialty and pay grade. Jennifer was a Communications Technician (her specialty) Second Class (her pay grade) when the story begins.

Phonetic Alphabet. To avoid confusion when saying letters in voice transmissions, the military developed the system of giving each letter a word-name, so that A was always said as "Able", B was "Baker" and so forth. In 1955 as the US and NATO military forces worked more closely together, it was apparent that the US phonetic alphabet presented pronunciation difficulties for non-English speakers. To correct the situation, a new alphabet was promulgated and is in use today. A is "Alfa", B is "Bravo" etc.

Plane Captain. In the US Navy, the Plane Captain was the enlisted person primarily entrusted with the material readiness and mechanical condition of an operating aircraft. In single engine activities or squadrons, the Plane Captain was the ground crew member who fueled and did line (basic) maintenance on his or her assigned aircraft. In multi-engine units, the Plane Captain was the Crew Chief and Flight Engineer, and the aircraft always flew with a Plane Captain on board. In some current multi-engine units, the term has been phased out in favor of the term Flight Engineer.

Plane Commander. In 1955, the Pilot in Command of the aircraft was known as the Plane Commander and was, technically at least, also the "mission commander". Later, as non-pilot specialists became more numerous in various aviation activities, it was not uncommon for the pilot of the aircraft to be responsive to a Mission Commander who was not a pilot, but a specialist in the tactics required by the particular mission. In this story, Lew Elfers is the Plane Commander and Mission Commander, but Mort Gross is, in effect, the mission commander.

Pluto. The term used to refer to the station in the Beast aircraft equipped with voice radio interception and recording devices, and to the operator of those devices, usually a foreign language specialist. Derived from the name of the Disney canine companion to Mickey Mouse.

Purple Code. The Japanese counterpart to the German Enigma code that was successfully broken by US cryptographers during World War II. It encoded the alphabet-like Kata Kana syllabary, and required a Japanese language specialist to interpret it into plain text before translation.

R4360-24WA. The manufacturer's (Pratt and Whitney) designation for the Beast's two propeller engines. The R signified it was a reciprocating engine. They displaced 4360 cubic inches, and in their 24th model, had both water injection (W) and a single stage supercharger (A).

Radar Order of Battle. A catalogue of all potential enemy electronic facilities in a region of military interest with their characteristics and capabilities.

Radio Compass. A "bird dog". It points to the radio station the operator has tuned in.

Roach Coach. A mobile canteen.

Sapper. A Royal Army military engineer. In Cyprus in 1955, the Royal Army Engineers ran the motor pools and wore characteristic blue berets. The term is derived from the medieval specialty of the engineers by that name that borrowed under fortifications and front lines to place explosives.

Six-by-six - A twin rear-wheel military truck, standard in most armies during and after World War II. US version is the M35A2 and subsequent models.

TBM—A single engine carrier based torpedo aircraft used in World War II for anti-shipping operations. It had an aft machine gun ball turret.

Tenner. A ten-shilling note, half a Pound Sterling, worth about $1.30 in 1955. Sometimes "tanner".

"Two pipper". A Royal Army lieutenant, whose rank insignia is two "pips" or small devices on a diamond shaped tab. A subaltern wears one, a captain three. (A "pip" is a grape seed.)

Visual Flight Rules (VFR). The Pilot is responsible for avoiding other aircraft under strict requirements for sufficient ceiling and visibility to enable visual avoidance of other aircraft and obstruction. Control from the ground not required. Also refers to weather conditions clear enough to enable VFR flight.

WAVES. The World War II acronym for Women Appointed for Volunteer Emergency Service in the Navy.

WWV. The National Bureau of Standards (now NIST) radio time signal.

About the Author

John McIntyre flew surveillance flights throughout Europe and the Middle East during the Cold War.

Printed in the United States
66502LVS00004B/15

9 781410 798763